GALACTIC WF

Pro Wrestling in Space

J.A. Cooke

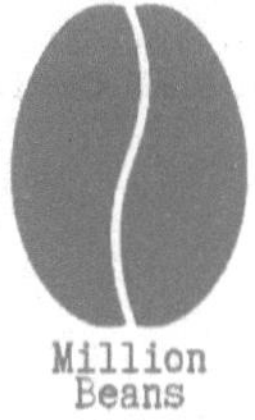

Million Beans

For more information, or to book an event, visit :
http://www.millionbeans.co.uk

ISBN (Paperback) – 978-1-7384355-0-0
ISBN (ebook) – 978-1-7384355-1-7

First Edition: Published November 2023 by Million Beans.

For Stacey and the boys.

*And for the wrestlers, past and present,
who've inspired so many.*

WEEK ONE

GOOD EVENING, LADIES AND GENTLEMEN, AND THANK YOU FOR INVITING THE GALACTIC WRESTLING FEDERATION INTO YOUR HOMES. I'M GENE KELLY, JOINED HERE AT RINGSIDE BY MY BROADCAST PARTNER, LORD FARQUAD, AND BOY HAVE WE GOT A HECK'VE A SHOW LINED UP.

THAT'S RIGHT, GENE! WE'VE GOT FEMALE ACTION COMING UP, AS MAD DONNA TAKES ON DIRTY DIANA. WE'LL ALSO SEE THE TAG TEAM TITLES PUT ON THE LINE, AS THE CYBORGS DEFEND AGAINST THE GHOSTBUSTERS. AND THAT'S NOT ALL!

IT SURE AIN'T, FARQUAD, AS THE SECOND ROUND IN OUR TOURNAMENT TO CROWN A NEW NUMBER ONE CONTENDER FOR THE GALACTIC HEAVYWEIGHT

CHAMPIONSHIP CONCLUDES. WHEN WE GO OFF THE AIR TONIGHT, THE COMPETITION WILL HAVE WHITTLED DOWN TO A FIELD OF EIGHT.

I JUST HOPE THAT FATBOY SLIME CAN KNOCK OFF HIP HARRISON IN TONIGHT'S MAIN EVENT. CAN YOU IMAGINE IF HARRISON BECAME NUMBER ONE CONTENDER?

IT BEARS NOT THINKING ABOUT, FARQUAD. BUT EVEN IF HARRISON WERE TO GO THE DISTANCE AND WIN THE TOURNAMENT, HE HAS LITTLE HOPE OF EVER BECOMING THE GALACTIC HEAVYWEIGHT CHAMPION — HELL, I'M NOT SURE IF ANYONE IN THE TOURNAMENT HAS WHAT IT TAKES TO DEFEAT OUR CHAMPION. HE'S BEEN UNSTOPPABLE SINCE WINNING THE TITLE TWO CYCLES AGO.

THE WINNER OF OUR TOURNAMENT WILL HAVE THE PRIVILEGE OF CHALLENGING FOR THE GALACTIC WF'S TOP PRIZE AT OUR NEXT PAY-PER-VIEW EXTRAVAGANZA, BATTLESTAR GALACTICA. BATTLING FOR THE BELT IS WHAT EVERY KID IN SIANARD GROWS UP DREAMING OF, BUT EVER SINCE JUDAS BECAME THE CHAMP, THAT DREAM HAS BECOME A NIGHTMARE. I THINK HE'LL TAKE THAT CHAMPIONSHIP TO THE GRAVE, GENE! THEY'LL HAVE TO PRISE THE BELT FROM HIS COLD, DEAD HANDS.

BATTLESTAR GALACTICA IS JUST FOUR MOON ORBITS AWAY AND YOU DON'T WANT TO MISS IT. TICKETS ARE SOLD OUT, BUT YOU CAN STILL BE A PART OF THE ACTION BY ORDERING ON PAY-PER-VIEW.

AND SPEAKING OF OUR CHAMPION, BLONDIE IS PLAYING OVER THE P.A. SYSTEM HERE AT THE ROCK ARENA. *ONE WAY OR ANOTHER* — THAT CAN MEAN ONLY ONE THING. HE'S HERE!

IT'S JUDAS! LISTEN TO THIS PLACE — THE CROWD IS GOING WILD!

AND HE'S GOT A MICROPHONE. OUR CHAMPION HAS SOMETHING TO SAY. LET'S HEAR IT, FOLKS.

***

'The powers that be at Galactic WF headquarters are doing everything in their capacity to find me a suitable challenger. I saw some excellent competition in last week's tournament matches with some of the best competitors that the galaxy has to offer. And tonight, you — the fans in attendance and the millions watching at home — will have the chance to witness more up-and-coming talent put on what I'm sure will be quite a show, as the second round concludes.

'Those who survive the night will have their mettle tested as the tournament speeds up on the road to Battlestar Galactica. There will be no more resting periods as all quarter-final matches will take place on next week's show, followed by the semi-finals a week after that. The two remaining gladiators will square off in

the tournament final, three weeks from tonight. And, after several moon orbits of gruelling battle, the winner of the tournament, the last man standing, will go head-to-head with me at Battlestar Galactica — the Galactic WF's biggest show of the cycle.

'I may be undefeated in competition here in the Galactic Wrestling Federation and, as the longest reigning champion in history, some of you might think it's a sure thing that I demolish whichever chump outlasts the rest of the field in the tournament finals, but I assure you all that I am not taking this lightly. Whoever comes out victorious will have proven to us all that they are not to be underestimated, or overlooked, even for the Heavyweight Champion of the Galaxy.

'However, as much of a fight as the tournament winner will put up, I promise you this: that I, the master of the mat, the wrecking ball of the ring, the destroyer, Judas, will find a way to win. One way... or another.

'To prove just how seriously I'm taking this threat to my championship, I'll be competing in a warm-up match right now. I hope you all enjoy this preview of what's in store for my challenger at Battlestar Galactica. Send out this evening's victim!'

***

FOLKS, IF YOU WERE STILL ON THE FENCE IN DECIDING WHETHER TO ORDER BATTLESTAR GALACTICA ON PAY-PER-VIEW, JUDAS MUST SURELY HAVE CONVINCED YOU IT'S WORTH THE INVESTMENT. THE TOURNAMENT WINNER COULD PRESENT THE MASTER OF THE MAT'S

BIGGEST CHALLENGE YET BUT THE CHAMP PROMISES TO CLAIM VICTORY, ONE WAY OR ANOTHER. LADIES AND GENTLEMEN, YOU WILL NOT WANT TO MISS IT!

ONE WAY OR ANOTHER — MAN, I WISH I HAD COME UP WITH A CATCHPHRASE LIKE THAT BACK IN MY WRESTLING DAYS, GENE. THE CROWD JUST LOVES TO SAY IT ALONG WITH JUDAS. THEY EAT IT UP AND SO DO I!

HE'S A CROWD-PLEASER ALRIGHT. AND LOOK HERE: JUDAS'S OPPONENT HAS JUST CLIMBED INTO THE RING.

HIM? HE'S A TWIG COMPARED TO THE DESTROYER! HE'S GOING TO BE DEMOLISHED, GENE. WHAT IS THIS GUY THINKING?

HE'S THINKING THIS IS HIS OPPORTUNITY TO STEP INTO A GALACTIC WF RING. THIS IS HIS CHANCE TO SHOW THE GALAXY WHAT HE'S GOT, ON THE BIGGEST STAGE POSSIBLE. THE SPOTLIGHT'S ON HIM, MILLIONS ARE WATCHING THROUGHOUT SIANARD, AND HE GETS TO SHARE THE RING WITH THE GALACTIC HEAVYWEIGHT CHAMPION. WHAT AN HONOUR!

WHAT AN HONOUR? WHAT AN IDIOT! JUDAS IS GOING TO KILL THIS CHUMP. HE DIDN'T EVEN PREPARE ANY ENTRANCE MUSIC, SO I DOUBT HE'S PREPARED TO BATTLE THE BEST WRESTLER IN ALL OF SIANARD.

WELL, FARQUAD, I GUESS WE'RE ABOUT TO FIND OUT. BOTH COMPETITORS ARE IN THE RING AND THE REFEREE IS ABOUT TO RING THE BELL.

OH MAN, I DON'T THINK I CAN WATCH. BUT I CAN'T LOOK AWAY EITHER.

THE BELL SOUNDS AND HERE WE GO AND—

OH MY BRADSHAW! HE KILLED HIM!

THIS KID — I THINK HIS NAME WAS ANAKIN — IS DOWN AND HASN'T MOVED. JUDAS PRODS THE LIFELESS BODY WITH HIS FOOT, TURNING THE KID OVER SO THAT HIS SHOULDERS ARE ON THE MAT.

AN UNORTHODOX COVER THERE FROM JUDAS.

A LITTLE DISRESPECTFUL, PERHAPS, JUDAS PINS THE KID WITH JUST THE TIP OF HIS TOE. THE REFEREE COUNTS — ONE, TWO, AND THREE. IT'S OVER. ONE MOVE — ONE DESTROYER KICK — IS ALL IT TOOK.

YOU CAN CALL IT DISRESPECTFUL, GENE, BUT THIS CROWD LOVES IT. IF THIS PLACE HAD A ROOF, IT WOULD HAVE BLOWN COMPLETELY OFF.

YOU'RE NOT WRONG, PARTNER. AND FOR THOSE OF YOU AT HOME WHO BLINKED AND MISSED IT, LET'S TAKE A LOOK AT A SLOW-MOTION REPLAY OF HOW THIS WENT DOWN.

SLOW IT DOWN ALL YOU WANT. IT STILL WON'T TAKE VERY LONG.

THE MOMENT THE REFEREE SIGNALLED FOR OUR TIMEKEEPER TO RING THE BELL, JUDAS LEAPT INTO THE AIR, LAUNCHING HIMSELF AT THIS KID, ANAKIN.

REMEMBER THAT NAME, BECAUSE I DOUBT WE'RE GOING TO BE SEEING ANAKIN AGAIN. HE STILL HASN'T MOVED.

WHILE AIRBOURNE, JUDAS FLICKED HIS RIGHT LEG UP TOWARDS ANAKIN'S HEAD. ANAKIN, SHOWING SIGNS OF INEXPERIENCE, DIDN'T HAVE HIS EYES ON HIS OPPONENT. HE WAS WATCHING THE REFEREE INSTEAD. THEREFORE, JUDAS'S BOOT CONNECTED WITH THE SIDE OF ANAKIN'S HEAD — AND WITH SUCH FORCE THAT HIS NECK BENT NINETY DEGREES.

A ROOKIE MISTAKE IF EVER I SAW ONE. AND I'VE NEVER SEEN SOMEONE'S HEAD TURNED DOWN LIKE THAT.

I THINK IT'S SAFE TO SAY HIS NECK BROKE UPON IMPACT. THE KID STILL HASN'T MOVED AN INCH SINCE HE COLLAPSED IN A HEAP ON THE CANVAS.

HE MIGHT BE DEAD, GENE.

WELL, AS THEY SAY: THIS AIN'T BALLET. WE'LL KEEP YOU INFORMED OF ANY FURTHER DEVELOPMENTS IN THIS SITUATION THROUGHOUT THE EVENING.

I HOPE THE TOURNAMENT COMPETITORS WERE PAYING ATTENTION. THAT'S WHAT THE WINNER'S UP

AGAINST AT BATTLESTAR GALACTICA. THAT DESTROYER KICK IS GNARLY.

***

His work complete, the heavyweight champ made his way up the entrance ramp and passed through the curtain beneath the gigantic screen — referred to as the jumbotron — at the back of the stage. As he arrived in the dimly lit backstage area, the championship belt, oversized and gleaming gold, draped over his enormous royal blue right shoulder, he was met with an irate-as-usual boss. Everything was bigger and badder in the Galactic Wrestling Federation — from title belts and jumbo screens to temper tantrums behind the scenes.

'For the love of Bradshaw, Judas! Did you have to go so hard on that kid?' Mr Montgomery, the owner and chairman of the Galactic WF, sat in his director's seat, headset on, facing a series of monitors.

'You won't be complaining when the viewing figures come in,' said Judas. 'Besides, I think I did a good job out there in selling the pay-per-view. You should thank me.'

'You know I'm always grateful for everything that you do for the Galactic WF. For all that you do for *me*. For all that you sacrifice.

'I'll add that you walked a fine line extremely well in your promo tonight. There's not a shred of doubt in my mind that you're going to destroy whichever challenger steps up at Battlestar Galactica, but you were also able to sow a single seed of doubt in the minds of our audience. Those who were thinking of skipping the

8

pay-per-view, figuring it would be another foregone conclusion, are out there, right now, wondering what they're going to miss if they don't order the show. You showed them what you can do to an amateur, but when you're up against the cream of the crop, the winner of our tournament, it'll be a whole different story.'

'I'm gonna hit the showers.' Judas threw a salute toward his boss and disappeared down the dark corridor to find his private dressing room. The other wrestlers all shared a communal space.

Mr Montgomery grabbed a passing stagehand by the arm. 'Would you just look at that,' the chairman of the board said, gesturing towards the hallway Judas had just wandered down. 'That man doesn't realise just how much he's given to us all. If it wasn't for him, our champion, you wouldn't be in a job. And he's going to keep us all in employment for a long, long time. I hope you're grateful. Are you grateful?'

'Yessir.' The stagehand was careful not to stutter, no matter how nervous he was. It was a bad idea to show any signs of weakness around the boss.

'What's your name, son?'

'Patrick, Sir.'

'Patrick, eh? Well, Patrick, you keep working hard around here and you'll go far. The universe is the limit for the Galactic Wrestling Federation.

'Now, I need you to find out what's happening with that kid whose head Judas just kicked sideways. Make sure he's not dead or anything. And double check he signed the waiver. Last thing we need's another lawsuit. It's bad enough the sponsors get a little tetchy anytime someone's crippled on one of our shows.'

'Yessir.'

'That's the spirit.' Mr Montgomery loosened his grip on Patrick and gave him a hard pat on the back, sending him on his way.

***

IT'S ALMOST MAIN EVENT TIME, GENE!

IT CERTAINLY IS. THIS CROWD IS ELECTRIC AND WHO CAN BLAME THEM? WE STARTED THE NIGHT WITH THE HEAVYWEIGHT CHAMPION, JUDAS, LIVE AND IN LIVING COLOUR, GIVING US A PREVIEW OF HIS SKILLS AS HE DAMN NEAR DECAPITATED A YOUNG ROOKIE BY THE NAME OF ANAKIN.

AND FOR THOSE OF YOU WONDERING, WE'VE HAD WORD THAT ANAKIN IS BEING ATTENDED TO AT A NEARBY MEDICAL FACILITY AND HIS CONDITION IS STABLE. I JUST WOULDN'T EXPECT TO SEE HIM RETURNING TO THE RING ANY TIME SOON.

HERE'S HOPING THE KID MAKES A SPEEDY RECOVERY. IT TAKES SOME SERIOUS GUTS TO GO TOE-TO-TOE WITH THE CHAMP.

BUT THE ACTION DIDN'T END THERE, AS WE SAW THE GHOSTBUSTERS CAPTURE THE TAG TEAM TITLES, DEFEATING THE CYBORGS IN A HULLUVA CONTEST.

AND DON'T FORGET, WE HAD FEMALES IN ACTION TOO. DIRTY DIANA'S MOVED UP THE RANKINGS TO BECOME THE NUMBER ONE CONTENDER TO THE FEMALE CHAMPIONSHIP AFTER A DECISIVE VICTORY OVER MAD DONNA. AND WHAT AN OUTFIT SHE WAS WEARING!

OH, WOULD YOU STOP? REGARDLESS OF HER GARMENTS, DIANA NEEDS TO KEEP FIGHTING AND KEEP WINNING IF SHE WANTS TO SECURE A TITLE MATCH AT BATTLESTAR GALACTICA. DON'T FORGET TO CONTACT YOUR PAY-PER-VIEW PROVIDER NOW; WHOEVER ULTIMATELY CHALLENGES SASHA STRATOSPHERE FOR THE GALACTIC WF FEMALE CHAMPIONSHIP, YOU JUST KNOW THE CHAMP'S GOING TO PUT ON A CLINIC. YOU DON'T WANT TO MISS IT!

SPEAKING OF BATTLESTAR GALACTICA, THE TOURNAMENT TO FIND A CHALLENGER FOR JUDAS HAS CONTINUED THROUGHOUT THE EVENING, STARTING WITH BART SPIKE OVERCOMING PARKER JONES TO MOVE INTO THE NEXT ROUND.

THEN, IN OUR SECOND TOURNAMENT MATCH OF THE NIGHT, BECKS TRAPPED CART-MAN IN A VICIOUS ANKLE LOCK. WITH NOWHERE TO GO, CART-MAN HAD NO CHOICE BUT TO TAP OUT BEFORE HIS ANKLE BROKE. BECKS GOES THROUGH TO FACE BART SPIKE IN THE

QUARTER FINALS. WE'LL HAVE THAT MATCH FOR YOU ONE WEEK FROM TONIGHT.

AND, JUST BEFORE THE LAST COMMERCIAL BREAK, X-STATIC CAUGHT PRINCE PETE OFF GUARD FOR JUST A MOMENT, WHICH WAS LONG ENOUGH TO ROLL HIM UP FOR A QUICK THREE-COUNT. AS A RESULT, X-STATIC WILL MEET THE WINNER OF TONIGHT'S MAIN EVENT NEXT WEEK.

SPEAKING OF TONIGHT'S MAIN EVENT, LET'S GET TO IT. IT'S FATBOY SLIME VERSUS HIP HARRISON.

FATBOY'S ALREADY MADE HIS WAY TO THE RING AND HERE COMES HIP HARRISON. JUST LOOK AT THIS GUY, GENE — TALK ABOUT PRETENTIOUS.

HE'S CERTAINLY NOT A SHOWMAN IN THE TRADITIONAL SENSE THAT WE'RE USED TO SEEING HERE IN THE GALACTIC WRESTLING FEDERATION. BUT HE'S A SKILLED WRESTLER, WHOSE WIN-LOSS RECORD EARNED HIM A SPOT IN THE TOURNAMENT.

YEAH, WELL I DON'T LIKE HIM AND NEITHER DOES THIS CROWD. LISTEN TO THEM, THEY'RE BOOING HIM OUT OF THE BUILDING.

HE'S NOT EXACTLY ENDEARED HIMSELF TO OUR AUDIENCE. CASE IN POINT: HE'S WALKING TO THE RING WITH NO SHOWBOATING, NO CROWD INTERACTION.

IT'S LIKE HE DOESN'T EVEN WANT TO BE HERE. AND WE DON'T WANT HIM HERE EITHER.

THERE'S A CHANCE WE NEVER SEE HARRISON AGAIN ONCE FATBOY'S FINISHED WITH HIM. THIS IS, WITHOUT A DOUBT, HIP HARRISON'S TOUGHEST CHALLENGE YET. SLIME OUTWEIGHS HARRISON THREE TIMES OVER. NOT TO MENTION THE FACT THAT FATBOY'S EXTREMELY WIDE BODY IS IMPOSSIBLE FOR GRAPPLERS WITH EVEN THE LONGEST OF REACHES TO WRAP THEIR ARMS AROUND. THAT RULES OUT SEVERAL MOVES FOR HARRISON, INCLUDING YOUR BASIC SUPLEX AND BODY SLAM.

WHAT YOU'RE SAYING IS THAT HARRISON, THE BEARDED BERK, IS AT A HANDICAP IN THIS MATCH? BECAUSE SLIME CAN HIT HARRISON WITH EVERY MOVE IN HIS ARSENAL.

WHETHER OR NOT WE LIKE HIM, ONE THING I WILL SAY ABOUT HIP HARRISON, THE BEARDED BRUTE AS HE LIKES TO CALL HIMSELF, IS THAT HE TAKES HIS COMPETITION SERIOUSLY. HE'S NOT TAKEN HIS EYES OFF OF FATBOY SLIME SINCE HE MADE HIS WAY THROUGH THE CURTAIN. HE'S TRANSFIXED, FARQUAD! HARRISON'S AT A PHYSICAL DISADVANTAGE HERE, BUT FATBOY WOULD DO WELL NOT TO UNDERESTIMATE THE BEARDED BRUTE'S RING SMARTS.

HE'S AN IDIOT, GENE. I HOPE FATBOY SQUASHES HIM.

YOU MAY GET YOUR WISH ANY MOMENT NOW. THE REFEREE CALLS FOR THE BELL, AND WE'RE UNDER WAY.

NEITHER MAN'S MAKING A MOVE.

FATBOY'S LAUGHING. I GUESS HE DOESN'T SEE HIP AS MUCH OF A THREAT.

NOR SHOULD HE.

THE BEARDED BRUTE'S EYES REMAIN FIXED ON THE MASSIVE FRAME OF FATBOY SLIME. HIP LOOKS SO… CALM.

HE KNOWS HE'S A DEAD MAN. SLIME'S SO BIG, HE HAS HIS OWN GRAVITATIONAL PULL!

FATBOY SLIME TAKES A STEP TOWARDS HIP HARRISON, BUT THE BEARDED BRUTE REMAINS STILL. SLIME CONTINUES TO MOVE ACROSS THE RING, PICKING UP THE PACE, AND HERE COMES THAT THUNDEROUS RIGHT HOOK HE'S KNOWN FOR AND— NO!

HIP… HE… WHERE'D HE GO?

I'VE NEVER SEEN SUCH SPEED. HE REMAINED AS STILL AS A STATUE UNTIL THE VERY LAST MOMENT, DUCKING WHEN FATBOY'S BALLED-UP FIST WAS MERE MILLIMETRES FROM HIS CHEEK.

SLIME STUMBLES FORWARD, CARRIED BY THE MOMENTUM OF HIS OWN MISSED STRIKE.

HIP HARRISON'S RUNNING AWAY TO THE FAR CORNER OF THE RING. HE'S SCARED, GENE.

DON'T SPEAK TOO SOON, FARQUAD. HIP JUMPS, HIS FOOT LANDING ON THE MIDDLE TURNBUCKLE, AND HE SPRINGBOARDS BACK, CHARGING ACROSS THE RING TOWARDS SLIME, WHO'S STILL STUMBLING ABOUT, FACING THE OTHER WAY.

TURN AROUND, FATBOY!

THE BEARDED BRUTE LEAPS INTO THE AIR, AND THRUSTS HIS LEGS OUT IN FRONT OF HIM. HE SAILS THROUGH THE AIR LIKE A TORPEDO, FEET FIRST. HE DEFINITELY HAS THE SPEED ADVANTAGE OVER HIS OPPONENT, WHO'S STILL FACING THE WRONG WAY, HOLDING ON TO THE TURNBUCKLE TO STEADY HIMSELF AFTER HE MISSED THAT PUNCH A MOMENT AGO.

WATCH OUT!

HARRISON CONNECTS WITH A HELLUVA DROPKICK, LANDING IT WITH GREAT AIM, RIGHT IN THE CENTRE OF SLIME'S BACK. FATBOY FLIES FORWARD, FACE FIRST. HE NARROWLY AVOIDS COLLIDING WITH THE TURNBUCKLES, HIS HEAD SLIDING BETWEEN THE MIDDLE AND TOP ROPES.

OH! BUT HIS HEAD HIT THAT UNFORGIVING CORNER POST INSTEAD! HE MIGHT BE UNCONSCIOUS.

THAT'S RIGHT, LADIES AND GENTLEMEN, FATBOY SLIME'S CRANIUM JUST COLLIDED WITH THAT COLD, HARD, STEEL POST. NOT ONLY THAT, BUT HE NOW APPEARS TO BE STUCK BETWEEN THE ROPES.

THIS IS TERRIBLE! HE'S WEDGED IN! SOMEBODY NEEDS TO DO SOMETHING.

THE REFEREE ATTEMPTS TO PULL SLIME FREE BUT HE'S NOT BUDGING.

I THINK I JUST SAW A LITTLE MOVEMENT. COME ON, REF — GET HIM OUT OF THERE.

BUT WHAT'S THIS? HIP HARRISON'S ON THE MOVE AGAIN. HE'S GOING TO HIT THAT TORPEDO DROPKICK AGAIN, FARQUAD.

SOMEBODY STOP HIM!

THERE'S NOTHING ANYONE CAN DO AS HIP TAKES FLIGHT ONCE MORE. THE REFEREE DIVES OUT OF THE WAY, AND THE SOLES OF HIP HARRISON'S FEET CONNECT WITH THE GARGANTUAN REAR END OF FATBOY SLIME.

I DON'T THINK HARRISON HAS A 'SOUL', GENE. LET ALONE ONE ON EACH FOOT.

FATBOY'S HEAD BOUNCES OFF THE RING POST YET AGAIN, AND I THINK HE'S… YES, HE'S FREE. HIP HARRISON'S TORPEDO DROPKICK HAD ENOUGH FORCE BEHIND IT TO PUSH THE HUGE MASS THAT IS FATBOY SLIME'S CARCUS THE REST OF THE WAY THROUGH THE ROPES. HIS COLOSSAL FRAME FALLS TO THE EDGE OF THE RING, THE RING APRON AS WE CALL IT. HE ROLLS A LITTLE, AND DROPS TO THE CONCRETE FLOOR BELOW, LANDING WITH A SPLAT.

COME ON, SLIME. GET UP!

HE'S ONLY GOT UNTIL THE REFEREE'S COUNT OF TEN TO CLIMB BACK INTO THE RING, OTHERWISE HE'LL LOSE VIA COUNTOUT AND HIP HARRISON WILL BE AWARDED THE VICTORY.

OH NO! THIS IS TERRIBLE, GENE. THAT HIP HARRISON'S NOTHING BUT A COWARD. HE DIDN'T WANT TO FIGHT FACE-TO-FACE, SO HE ATTACKED POOR OLD FATBOY FROM BEHIND. NOW HE'S TRYING TO TAKE A CHEAP WIN.

THE REFEREE'S COUNT IS ALREADY UP TO FIVE AS FATBOY SLIME STIRS. THE REFEREE, JUDGE DREAD, PAUSES HIS COUNT MOMENTARILY TO TELL HIP HARRISON TO GET BACK AND ALLOW SLIME SOME SPACE TO GET INTO THE RING, IF HE'S ABLE TO DO SO.

HIP'S NERVOUS. HE CAN SEE FATBOY GETTING UP AND HE KNOWS HE'S ANGERED THE BEAST.

WE'RE UP TO SEVEN AND SLIME'S GOT A HAND ON THE EDGE OF THE RING.

IT'S GOING TO BE A CLOSE CALL!

EIGHT… HE'S STANDING UPRIGHT.

NINE… AND HE ROLLS IN BENEATH THE BOTTOM ROPE JUST AS THE REFEREE WAS ABOUT TO COUNT TEN.

PHEW!

JUDGE DREAD ONCE AGAIN INSTRUCTS HIP HARRISON TO BACK OFF AND ALLOW FATBOY A CHANCE TO GET TO HIS FEET.

GOOD — WE WANT A FAIR FIGHT HERE.

I CAN'T SAY I'VE SEEN MANY REFEREES BE SO STRICT IN RECENT CYCLES, BUT IT'S GOOD TO SEE. WE'LL HOPEFULLY GET A GOOD, CLEAN FIGHT.

FATBOY'S UP. LOOK AT HIM! HE'S HUGE! AND HE'S GOING TO CRUSH THAT BEARDED IDIOT, HIP HARRISON!

I CERTAINLY WOULDN'T WANT TO BE STANDING ACROSS THE RING FROM AN ANGRY FATBOY SLIME. THE REFEREE STEPS ASIDE AND HERE WE GO AGAIN.

SLIME WASTES NO TIME NOW. HE'S NOT LAUGHING ANYMORE. HE CHARGES AT HIP HARRISON LIKE A LOCOMOTIVE. BUT HIP MOVES OUT OF THE WAY ONCE AGAIN. FATBOY'S WISE TO IT THIS TIME AND STOPS HIMSELF BY REACHING OUT FOR THE TOP ROPES. HE STEADIES HIMSELF IN THE CORNER OF THE RING BUT HE'S GOT HIS BACK TO THE BEARDED BRUTE, WHO RUNS IN BEHIND HIM, DROPS DOWN, GRABS THOSE ENORMOUS LEGS, AND PULLS SLIME OVER BACKWARDS, ROLLING HIM UP AND PINNING HIS SHOULDERS TO THE MAT. THE REFEREE GETS INTO POSITION, COUNTS: ONE, TWO, THR— NO! SLIME KICKS OUT BEFORE THE REFEREE'S HAND HITS THE MAT FOR A THIRD AND FINAL TIME.

THAT WAS TOO CLOSE! CAN YOU IMAGINE IF HIP HARRISON WON WITH A FLUKE PIN LIKE THAT? HE'LL DO ANYTHING TO GAIN A CHEAP VICTORY, GENE!

A WIN'S A WIN, FARQUAD. ISN'T THAT WHAT YOU USED TO SAY? AND LOOK HERE! HIP HARRISON, SENT SPRAWLING ACROSS THE RING WHEN SLIME KICKED OUT OF THAT PIN ATTEMPT, SCRAMBLES BACK UP AND OVER TO SLIME, WHO'S ONLY JUST PULLING HIMSELF UP TO A VERTICAL BASE. SAY WHAT YOU WILL, BUT HIP IS DISPLAYING A MORE AGGRESSIVE SIDE. HE RUNS IN AND CONNECTS WITH A KNEE TO SLIME'S JAW. HE GRABS THE LEFT ARM OF SLIME WITH BOTH HANDS AND HE'S PULLING HIM BACK DOWN TOWARDS THE CANVAS. HARRISON'S USING HIS ENTIRE BODY WEIGHT TO GET FATBOY SLIME TO THE MAT AND — OH MY BRADSHAW! FATBOY'S DOWN TO ONE KNEE.

NO WAY!

HIP HARRISON CONTINUES TO WRENCH THE ARM. HE WON'T LET UP.

SURELY THE REFEREE SHOULD STEP IN? HIP HARRISON'S GOING TO RIP FATBOY'S ARM OUT OF ITS SOCKET.

FATBOY COLLAPSES ENTIRELY! HE'S LYING FACE DOWN IN THE RING AND WAILS IN AGONY AS HARRISON WRAPS HIS LEGS AROUND SLIME'S ARM. THIS ALLOWS

THE BEARDED BRUTE TO LET GO WITH HIS HANDS AND POSITION HIS ARMS AROUND SLIME'S FACE. HE LACES HIS FINGERS TOGETHER OVER FATBOY'S NOSE AND YANKS BACK.

THIS IS TERRIBLE. THAT BRUTISH MANIAC'S GOING TO TEAR FATBOY IN HALF IF WE DON'T STOP THIS.

YOU COULD BE RIGHT, FARQUAD. BUT IT'S UP TO FATBOY TO DO SOMETHING. SLIME'S ARM IS TRAPPED AT AN UNNATURAL ANGLE BY HARRISON'S LEGS, WHILE THE PRESSURE HIP'S APPLYING TO SLIME'S HEAD AND NECK MUST BE EXCRUCIATING. THIS IS A PICTURE-PERFECT EXAMPLE OF A CROSSFACE THAT HARRISON HAS DUBBED THE BRUTE LOCK.

SLIME'S GIVEN UP TRYING TO SWAT HARRISON AWAY WITH HIS FREE HAND. HE CAN'T REACH AROUND. BUT HE'S HAVING BETTER LUCK IN HIS ATTEMPT TO DRAG HIMSELF — AND HARRISON — TOWARDS THE ROPES. HE'S TRYING FOR A ROPE BREAK.

IF FATBOY SLIME REACHES THE ROPES, HIP WILL HAVE UNTIL THE REFEREE'S COUNT OF FIVE TO LET GO OF THE HOLD.

HE'S HALFWAY THERE! HE'S...

HIP HARRISON WRENCHES BACK ON THE HEAD AND NECK OF FATBOY UNLIKE ANYTHING I'VE EVER SEEN. HE'S GOING TO BREAK HIS DAMN NECK IN HALF!

YOU HAVE A SHORT MEMORY, GENE. WE SAW THAT KID ANAKIN'S NECK BENT AT A SIMILAR ANGLE EARLIER TONIGHT. I DON'T THINK FATBOY CAN GO ON. HE'S GOT NOWHERE TO GO. NO WAY OUT!

FATBOY'S FREE ARM IS IN THE AIR. HE'S FORMS A FIST AS HE DOES WHAT HE CAN TO MANAGE THE PAIN. HIP PULLS BACK EVEN HARDER AND SLIME TAPS OUT TO THE BRUTE LOCK! IT'S OVER!

NO!

YES! HIP HARRISON'S THROUGH TO THE QUARTER FINALS.

I CAN'T BELIEVE MY EYES. THE REFEREE'S RAISING HIS HAND IN VICTORY. EVEN HIP DOESN'T LOOK HAPPY ABOUT IT.

HIS EXPRESSION HASN'T CHANGED SINCE HE MADE HIS WAY INTO THE ARENA. HIP HARRISON LOOKS FOCUSED.

THAT'S A POLITE WAY TO PUT IT. WHAT'S HE DOING NOW?

HE'S DEMANDING A MICROPHONE FROM ONE OF OUR STAGEHANDS. WE'RE ABOUT TO HEAR HIP HARRISON SPEAK.

DO YOU HAVE ANY EARMUFFS I CAN BORROW?

I MAY NOT BE A FAN, BUT I'M INTRIGUED TO HEAR WHAT THIS INTENSE VERSION OF HIP HARRISON HAS TO SAY. HE LOOKS ANGRY.

***

'Two down, three to go.

'It's safe to say somebody doesn't want me to get through this tournament. Just look at the brackets — from the moment they were revealed, I could see what they'd done. In the first round, I had to overcome The Great Goliath. Turns out he wasn't so great after all, but it still took everything I had to take him down. Then, this week, they had me matched up against that massive waste of space, Fatboy Slime, and you all just saw what happened there. I'm exhausted though. And if none of these giants can beat me, I think that's the idea: to tire me out, ready for my next opponent. Maybe cause me an injury along the way as a bonus. Who knows?

'As we found out tonight, my next opponent is X-Static. Not the biggest horse in the race, but probably the most aggressive. Definitely the most violent. He pulled out what looked like a fluke win this evening, but make no mistake, next week, his instructions will be to take me out. Expect the chainsaws and electrified barbed wire to come out in that one.

'And this is my point. The brackets are incredibly lopsided. The toughest competition is concentrated on the righthand side — no offense to anyone on the left half of the bracket — and it's been put together in a way that I, in theory, shouldn't stand a chance in hell. No matter who else wins their matches, I'm going to come up

against the biggest, the baddest, and the sickest that the Galactic Wrestling Federation can throw at me. When the finals are all said and done, Judas is going to come face to face with a battle-worn contender. And they're doing everything they can to make sure it's not me. They fear me.

'I'm not just talking about Judas — the sadistic psychopath we call a champion. No, he's just a part of the problem. A symptom. Or a by-product.

'My main problem is with you, Mr Montgomery.

'Didn't expect me to call you out, did ya'? Nobody dares mention your name, but you know what? I'm not afraid to tell the world what you're all about. For those of you who don't know, Mr Montgomery is the owner of the Galactic WF. Some of you may have heard his name before but, even then, you still likely know little about him — and that's by design.

'Mr Montgomery makes every key decision around here and has a bigger influence on what goes on in the Galactic WF than wins and losses do. But it's not just the Galactic WF that he holds influence over. What you all need to know is that Mr Montgomery is also a member of—

***

SORRY, FOLKS. WE APPEAR TO BE EXPERIENCING TECHNICAL DIFFICULTIES. THE MICROPHONE THAT HIP HARRISON WAS USING SEEMS TO HAVE CUT OUT.

IT'S NO LOSS. HE WAS TALKING GIBBERISH.

I'LL AGREE WITH YOU THERE, PARTNER. HE WASN'T MAKING A WHOLE LOTTA SENSE.

THANK BRADSHAW FOR TECHNICAL DIFFICULTIES. THAT BROKEN MIC'S SPARED US ANY MORE OF THAT CRAP.

AND WE'RE OUT OF TIME, ANYWAY. THANK YOU ONCE AGAIN FOR JOINING US THIS EVENING FOR ANOTHER NIGHT OF ACTION THAT ONLY THE GALACTIC WRESTLING FEDERATION CAN DELIVER. GOODNIGHT, EVERYBODY!

***

Backstage, while Hip Harrison was delivering his post-match monologue, all hell broke loose.

'What's that Hip Harrison doing?' Mr Montgomery asked nobody in particular, staring intently at his monitor.

'He's asking for a mic. He must want to speak,' Patrick nervously replied. Nobody else had answered the boss, so the stagehand thought it wise to respond before the silence stretched too long. Mr Montgomery was known for losing his cool.

'Costa, this is Montgomery.' The Galactic WF chairman now spoke into his headset's microphone, his voice transmitted to the headsets of all production crew members. Costa Fortune was the ring announcer. 'Give him a mic. I'm curious to see what this guy has to say.'

'I didn't think you liked him, Sir,' Patrick whispered.

'Hip Harrison? I can't *stand* him! He's everything that's wrong with his generation. You can tell his sort just by looking at that scruffy beard of his. Nevertheless, he's through to the next round of the tournament and might sell a few fans on tuning in. Plus, we're live and, like we always say, you never know what's going to happen in the Galactic WF. We're unscripted and uncut. This is what we're all about! Besides, what's the worst that could happen?'

Mr Montgomery watched intently, grinning, while Hip Harrison spoke about the tournament.

'See, this is what I'm talking about. All he's doing is whining and complaining. *Poor me, this is unfair, blah, blah, blah.* He's making a fool of himself on galaxy-wide television. How pathetic.'

Hip Harrison was right about almost everything he said, including the fact that Mr Montgomery was not expecting The Bearded Brute to say his name.

'What did he just say?' Mr Montgomery sprang to his feet. His chair fell backwards. 'You! What's your name? Peter! Did you hear that?'

Patrick, who thought he was building a good rapport with the boss, now wished he wasn't standing so close. 'Y-yes, Sir,' he said. 'He s-said that h-he's… he's…'

'Just spit it out!' The irony was that plenty of saliva accompanied those words. Patrick was indeed standing too close.

'He said he's calling you out.'

'Do something. NOW! STOP THIS!' Mr Montgomery threw his headset down on the desk.

Patrick didn't need to be told twice. Not when the boss started yelling.

'Yessir.' He turned and ran for the production gallery. Mr Montgomery oversaw everything in running his show, although he preferred to sit beside the curtain to the arena instead of being locked away in the production gallery. He claimed it was so that he could remain approachable to his wrestlers, while also keeping his finger on the pulse of what his paying audience reacted to.

'DAMNIT!' Mr Montgomery swiped his monitor, knocking it off the table along with the headset he'd forgotten about — the headset through which he could have spoken directly to the director in the production gallery. 'What are you all looking at?'

Everyone in the vicinity — other members of the crew, a couple of wrestlers, and a company executive — all stood, staring, frozen.

'Gah!' Mr Montgomery picked up his chair and threw it towards the small crowd, which disbanded immediately. Sovereign Noble, the Galactic WF commissioner, was the only person to remain. Even if he had the luxury of running away from his boss like all the underlings, he used a cane to get around and, as a result, wasn't too quick on his feet these days.

'You need to do something about this,' Mr Montgomery snarled.

Sovereign nodded. He knew well enough that there was no use in trying to speak in a situation like this.

The backstage monitor may have broken as it dropped to the floor, but Hip Harrison's voice could still be heard, echoing over the arena's P.A. system.

But it's not just the Galactic WF that he holds influence over. What you all need to know is that Mr Montgomery is also a member of—

'No!' Mr Montgomery cried. But then there was silence. 'What happened?'

'It would seem that young Patrick must have pulled the plug on Harrison's mic from the production room,' said Sovereign. 'And just in the nick of time.'

'That was too close,' said Mr Montgomery. 'Something needs to be done about this.'

'I'll have Hip Harrison removed from the tournament, Sir. In fact, he'll be removed from the roster.'

'No. That won't work. If we fire him now, after what he just said, you know there'll be a portion of our fanbase, perhaps small, but certainly vocal, who'll start asking questions. Not to mention the media. We can't just make him disappear — it'll add fuel to his claims. And besides, if we keep him here, we can ensure we remain in control of the narrative and destroy him in the process. He will regret the day he ever dared to utter my name in the public sphere. We're going to break him!'

Sovereign Noble nodded. 'Very good, Sir.'

Previously...

A long time ago in a galaxy far, far away… there was a blue and green planet, named Earth by its occupants. Following the ancient calendars of the human race that once roamed it, the year would now have been 3,127AD. All that remains in Earth's place, however, is a charred husk.

Although the planet is fossilised, the people who inhabited it turned to space dust, a ripple effect ensures its presence is still felt across the universe. The ripple is formed from broadcast transmissions that pass through much of space harmlessly enough. That was until approximately 60 Earth years ago when the first signals reached the Sianard Galaxy, a small cluster of five planets that orbit one another while travelling together around the Wavain Star. Technically, this group of planets is a solar system, but those in charge of naming such things preferred how 'galaxy' rolled off the tongue as they dissected one of Earth's more prominent languages. Their setup is unique within the known universe, as each of the five planets — Chase, Neja, Las Esferana, Kingdom, and Stateside — is bound by the gravitational pull of the other four. As a result, it would appear to distant observers that the small group of globes are caught in a continuous dance, weaving in and out of each other as they complete a cycle around Wavain.

Smaller rocks orbit Wavain alongside the planets. While none of these naturally possess the atmosphere required to house life, the largest of these has been built upon, complete with manufactured breathable gases. Known simply as The Rock, this glorified meteoroid with a pumped-in atmosphere serves as a central entertainment hub for Sianard, with shopping malls, multiplex theatres, bowling alleys, restaurants, and its crown jewel: The Rock Arena.

Each of the five planets hosts its own life forms. The dominant creatures on all five planets are, in fact, humanoid, both pertaining to their physical attributes (standing on two legs, opposable thumbs) and level of sentience — they can all think, communicate, dream, desire, love, hate, laugh, and reason. While the five humanoid races possess many similarities, there are enough subtle differences in their genetic make-ups to have caused tensions over the millennia. Those hailing from the planets of Kingdom, Stateside, and Chase all have blue flesh, while those from Las Esferana are of a red complexion, and residents of Neja have a grey pigmentation. Kingsmen are typically shorter than their blue contemporaries, the Statesmen and Chasers, but the Chasers are hairier, and Statesmen have skin as smooth as silk. There are just enough differences for certain members of each race to be bigoted of mind and mouth.

When the first of Earth's radio broadcasts reached Sianard, almost everyone, no matter which planet they were living on, or the colour of their skin, was a mechanic or a farmer. They were all engineers, in a manner of speaking, which was how many had the technology already in place to receive Earth's signals.

There was no formal language beyond names and a few key phrases. Most communication was handled — quite literally — by a crude form of sign language. It was all anyone had needed in Sianard.

And then, the airwaves had arrived, first bringing audio that was interpreted by a few bright minds. Sianardians were quick to learn Earth's languages, which rapidly spread across the galaxy. Many pondered what life was like in this strange, far-away place — a question that was soon answered when the pictures came in. These moving images could be displayed on a screen, accompanied by sound, to depict life on Earth.

There was politics, comedy, music, nature, destruction and construction, sporting competition, a thirst for knowledge, and an unconscious desire to dumb down. And violence. There was a *lot* of violence. Sometimes it was a work of fiction: choreographed for maximum effect in action movies or cheesy as hell in a soap opera. More often than not, it was real. News bulletins highlighting senseless wars and crimes; documentaries examining the vicious nature of humanity.

And then there was professional wrestling, which some Sianardians had initially pondered might be an elaborate work of fiction, given the high drama and preposterous situations the competitors often found themselves embroiled in. After some debate, though, it was determined that professional wrestling was, in fact, real.

***

'A charred what?'

'Husk. Like an empty shell.'

'That's all that's left of it? What happened?'

'We're still examining a few theories, but the prevailing one is that the Earthlings slowly but surely burned their planet to a crisp.'

'I don't understand. Why would they do that?'

'We believe it was unintentional. That the Earthlings didn't know what they were doing — at first, anyway. Our readings tell us that the process started slow and that there will have been more than enough warning signs for them to change their ways and save their planet. I guess, ultimately, they decided not to.'

'Wait a minute — you're saying they chose to, what, go extinct?'

'It's not so simple, but I guess you could say that. And, if we keep mimicking the Earthlings' way of life, we'll be heading for the same fate: the end of all five of Sianard's planets.'

'What do you mean? What caused it?'

'They were reckless. As the Earthlings became more advanced as a species — developing methods for mass manufacturing, draining the planet of fossil fuels only to burn them, and re-filling the land with mountainous volumes of waste — they found it difficult to change their ways, to revert to methods of doing things that were friendlier for their environment. We've learned that, through sheer recklessness, the Earthlings put a hole in their planet's ozone layer, which serves as a shield against much ultraviolet radiation.

'Via transmissions we retrieved, we discovered the humans figured out what they had done. What they continued to do. Yet, they made little-to-no effort to stop. Their planet heated at a rapid rate — ice caps melting, oceans rising. Some areas close to the equator became uninhabitable, causing a major migration of both humanity and wildlife. There was a mass extinction reported around this time, too, as thousands of species could not survive while the humans overdeveloped land, displacing natural ecosystems and throwing the environment out of balance. But this still wasn't enough to convince those in power to take major action.'

'How come I've not heard anything about this? Shouldn't this be common knowledge?'

'Well, that's just it. You've stumbled upon the reason I'm now out of the SSC.'

'What? You're… what happened?'

'I started asking too many questions that didn't align with The Council's vision. So, they discredited and dismissed me.'

'Can't you blow the whistle?'

'I tried, but several falsehoods now attached to my name mean that nobody will take me seriously. That's why I need your help.'

***

That conversation took place several cycles ago. Hunluka, better known across the galaxy by his ring name, Hip Harrison, had just started his career in the wacky world of professional wrestling. Half Statesman on his mother's side, half Chaser from his father, Harrison was tall, blue and hairy. For wrestling — both as a courtesy to his opponents (who wants a face-full of armpit hair?) and for aesthetics (wrestlers not only want to show off their chiselled abs, but a lack of body hair ensures nothing gets caught and tangled when in a grapple) — he shaved himself all over, except for his thick head of hair and the long, wiry beard that earned him the nickname, *The Bearded Brute*.

Harrison's mother, Saldari, died when he was the equivalent of nine years old. Her death came out of nowhere. She simply dropped dead one morning. His father, Franklo, distraught and displaced, having moved to Stateside when he'd married Saldari, moved himself and his son back to Chase, where he resumed his previous life as a farmer and mechanic.

While Franklo had found some comfort in a familiar life, the future Hip Harrison, whose life had already been torn apart from the loss of his mother, found himself in a strange new world, completely unrecognisable from everything he knew. Although much of Sianard had evolved, adopting more of an Earth-like culture, Chase was an old-school state. Much of the population continued to farm for a living and dabble in engineering in their downtime. Forget tractors and trucks — there were all manner of vehicles bounding up and down the fields on Chase. The inventiveness and innovation were through the proverbial roof.

Out of sorts, the bereaved Hunluka had eaten little of his evening meal one cold night, and asked to excuse himself to his sleeping quarters. Franklo was a master with his hands and had a great engineering mind, but hadn't the faintest clue of how to ease his son's grief. He silently nodded in response to Hunluka's request without looking up from his meal. Upon entering his room, Hunluka switched on his mother's television, which he'd brought with him from Stateside. His father, who was never one to sit and watch other folk on a screen when there was always plenty to do, was going to throw 'the tube' away before the boy had salvaged it.

Crashing onto the bed and grabbing the remote control, Hunluka channel surfed across a wave of nineties sitcoms, seventies cop shows, and millennial drama. He wasn't in the mood for any of it: laughter, cheese, or anything down and heavy. Just as he was about to give up the channel hopping, figuring sleep would at least provide the escape he sought, an explosion on the screen caught Hunluka's attention. His finger hovered above the remote's standby button. It wasn't the type of explosion you'd see in the background as Starsky and Hutch drove their Ford Gran Torino away from some warehouse at high speed. This was a wild, yet well-choreographed, display of colourful pyrotechnics. As the noise from the fireworks died down, he heard the roars of thumping rock music and a raucous crowd.

What is going on? Hunluka's jaw was hanging low. He'd never seen anything like this. And then: the moment that cemented this as a life-changing moment. As the music rose to a crescendo and the smoke from the pyro cleared, there, on the stage, stood the most impressive figure Hunluka had ever laid eyes upon.

Luscious locks of golden hair draped over muscular red shoulders. Bulging biceps so thick that they each donned a headband from which neon tassels dangled. An oversized gold belt wrapped around the creature's waist.

'Ladies and gentlemen,' came a voice from off-camera, 'please welcome *your* GALACTIC HEAVYWEIGHT CHAMPION! From the hidden depths of Las Esferana, this is BRUUUUUTUS MAAAAXIMUUUUSSSS!'

At the sound of his name, Brutus Maximus flexed every visible muscle in his body, which appeared to trigger another round of pyrotechnics. By this point, the young Hunluka was sitting up in his bed, completely hooked by the spectacle. The proceeding match, which saw Maximus defeat his arch-rival, Sid 'Stretch' Armstrong in an absolute nail-biter, cemented Hunluka's initial thought that professional wresting might be the coolest thing he'd ever seen. The icing on the cake came after the match, when Brutus grabbed a microphone to deliver his iconic catchphrase: 'Another opponent mauled, por que Las Esferans es Feral!'

When the show was over and Hunluka hit standby on the remote, he lay in bed dreaming of becoming the Galactic Heavyweight Champion and plotting how to achieve such a goal. That night, for the first time since the untimely death of his mother, the future Hip Harrison had a smile on his face.

***

'What are you doing?' a perplexed Franklo asked his son the next morning.

The boy was hugging a chopped section of tree trunk to his chest, kneeling and standing, kneeling and standing.

'Hun?'

Hunluka dropped the trunk and exhaled deeply. 'Just working out.'

'Are you feeling okay?'

'Best I've been since we moved here,' said Hunluka.

'Huh. Well, be careful not to put your back out. I'll be in the shedhouse, tinkering with the motor.' Franklo withheld his smile until he turned away from his son. He wasn't sure what had sparked it, but Hunluka appeared jovial for the first time since Saldari had passed away, and Franklo was terrified of jinxing it.

***

Being the new kid at school can be tough. But when you're the new kid from a different planet who has a dead mum and never smiles, the other kids avoid you like you have the plague. Hunluka's first few weeks at school on Chase were a lonely affair. That was until one day, when another boy — tall, skinny, bespeckled, generally awkward — sat down next to him at lunch.

'What are you eating?'

Hunluka finished his mouthful slowly, pondering whether to answer. So far, each time a fellow student had struck up a conversation with him, it had been a trap. No matter how he replied, they'd find a way to make a joke of it and set the other kids off laughing. These ribs didn't even make sense most of the time, but it was the sentiment that stung.

However, considering his new lunch mate's physical appearance — little in the way of muscle mass; and was that a sprinkling of freckles or acne on his face? — Hunluka chose to play along.

Never judge a book by its cover, Hunluka's father always told him. But in this case, there was surely no way this kid was leading him on. *What a pencil-neck geek*, Hunluka thought, and not in a mean-spirited way, but out of relief that he might finally make a friend.

'Shackleberry jam sandwich,' he replied.

'Sounds good,' said the other boy. 'Well, I'm not sure about good, but something different at least.'

'It's tastes alright. But it's a good source of protein.'

'Keeping note of what you put into your body, eh?'

'I'm watching what I eat. I'm in training, so I've got to take in enough calories each day to build muscle mass, being careful not to store too much fat or ingest too much sugar. Or too little of each.'

'What are you training for? If you don't mind me asking.'

If Hunluka was walking into a trap, it would snap shut on the answer to this question. He inhaled. 'I want to become a professional wrestler when I grow up. But for that to happen, I've got to look the part. I know it sounds stupid.'

No laughter followed. No wise cracks. 'It doesn't sound stupid to me,' said the other boy. 'I think it's great to have an aspiration. Something to work towards. Have you tried out for the school wrestling team yet?'

It was something Hunluka had briefly considered, even watching a practice session from the bleachers. From what he saw, the wrestling they were doing wasn't the same as what he watched on TV. Besides, the team probably wouldn't accept an outcast like him. So why bother?

'Nah.'

'Fair enough. From the little I've seen of both the amateur wrestling here at school and the professional stuff on TV, the amateur sport would give you a foundation of skills to build upon, I would think.'

'I'll give it some thought. So, what's your deal?'

'I'm not one for sports and can't play any musical instruments. But I'm good at and interested in science. Therefore, I have no friends here.' The boy raised both arms to shoulder-height, gesturing to the cafeteria full of students around them.

'What? Why not?'

'Because I'm a geek. A nerd. A dweeb. Whatever word they're currently using to sum up someone who's into the actual classes here at school. Science is my passion.'

'Could be worse.'

'How so?'

'You could have no friends *and* a dead mum.'

'Ouch. Sorry.'

Hunluka laughed. 'It's not your fault. I miss her so much, but I'm coming to terms with it, I guess. So, what's your name?'

'They call me Nemo.'

'Who's they?'

'Well, no one. But I've always thought it would sound cooler than my actual name: Nemandika.'

'I like it. Good to meet you, Nemo.' Hunkula extended a hand, which Nemo shook.

'So, what do I call you?'

'I'm Hun— no, you know what?'

'What?'

'I want a cool new name, too. Call me Hip. Hip… Harrison.' Hunluka had seen an *Indiana Jones* movie on TV the night before.

'Nice to meet you too, Hip.'

Hip and Nemo were as close as any tag team from that day on.

Best Friends 4 Life!

While Hunluka had been the awkward new kid in school, the newly christened Hip was a completely different person. At Nemo's insistence, he tried out for the wrestling team and not only discovered that he had an aptitude for the sport but, because of his natural talent, pinning the school's second-ranked heavyweight during his tryout, the team accepted him. The coach welcomed Hip with open arms — literally — wrapping those burly pythons around the boy, trapping him in a bear hug.

'You're going to be our next champion,' Coach Cosatto beamed.

And he was. Hip put his all into training, supported by his coach, team, and his friend, Nemo, who could often be spotted in the bleachers during practice, half-watching while studying with a book in hand. Nemo may have been a self-proclaimed geek, but showing support for Hip, as well as the rest of the team, made him their unofficial mascot. Before long, they would also invite Nemo to attend wrestling tournaments, to assist where he could by supplying beverages and snacks. Nemo became *one of the boys*, as did Hip. Popular by proxy.

***

Nemo joined Hip to watch wrestling almost every week on television. They both cheered on Brutus Maximus as he defended his championship. Together, they jumped up and shouted at the television monitor when that dastardly opportunist, Cliff Hardcastle, shoved Maximus into the referee, causing the match official to stumble into the turnbuckle. While the referee's gaze was temporarily averted, Hardcastle scored a low blow — totally illegal and an instant disqualification if the referee had seen it — and rolled Maximus up, pinning the champ's shoulders to the mat. The referee turned around just in time to see the pin and count *one… two…*

'Kick out! Kick out!' the boys screamed at the screen.

…three.

'NO!'

'What are you boys yelling about up there?' Franklo called up the stairs.

'Brutus Maximus just lost the championship, Dad. He was robbed!'

'Oh dear,' Franklo shouted back, not quite matching the emotion in his son's voice. 'I'll be out in the shedhouse if you need me, working on my motor.'

Hip rolled his eyes. For as long as he could remember, his father had always been working on that damn motor and never seemed to get around to finishing it. Hip had no idea whether it was intended for some sort of vehicle or what, and Franklo sure wasn't spilling the beans.

On the television, Cliff Hardcastle pushed the fallen Brutus Maximus out of the ring and snatched a microphone from the ring announcer. 'Haha! You see that? You all wrote me off. Brutus Maximus took me lightly, but look at me now!'

Hip and Nemo joined in with the booing from the televised arena audience.

'Remember, kids,' Harcastle continued. 'Anything is possible. Just don't be afraid to *go low* if you have to.' The new champion winked at the camera. 'Brutus fell off a cliff and the Hardcastle era has begun.'

'I can't believe it,' said Hip, echoing the commentators as the broadcast ended. 'I'll never let that happen to me when I'm in the ring. And I damn sure wouldn't sink so low. Pathetic!'

Although Nemo became a fan of wrestling — both the school's amateur and the television's professional varieties — he wasn't a hardcore fan like Hip. Science was still his thing.

Hip reciprocated his friend's support of his wrestling endeavours by assisting with experiments in Nemo's parents' shedhouse, which, for all intents and purposes, served as Nemo's lab. The family's craft remained exposed to the elements out on their landing strip.

Hip also quizzed his friend from the science books Nemo borrowed from the school library. Nemo not only wanted to ace every school test, he wanted to be a walking, talking scientific encyclopaedia.

'That could be your hook if you ever entered the wrestling biz,' Hip told Nemo during one such study section. 'It's not all about your skills as a fighter. You also need a character trait to draw attention over the rest of the pack, something memorable that will stick in the minds of the audience. You could be "Nemo the Encyclopaedia". I can see it now: you'd dress up as a giant book and your signature move could be the Brain Buster.'

A side effect was that Hip also gained a good understanding of science. So much so that he was in the top five of his class. Not that he retained anywhere near the knowledge that Nemo did.

Likewise, Nemo discovered one lunchtime, when the school bully, Damien Dementor, tried to steal his lunch, that he had picked up one or two moves from watching so much wrestling. Damien pinned Nemo against a wall by the collar, holding his spare fist in the air with the threat being that said fist would collide with Nemo's face if the geek didn't comply.

Nemo surprised himself when he replied: 'Give it your best shot, numbskull!'

As Damien threw a punch, Nemo launched both his legs into the air, catching the bully in the stomach, while gravity also pulled him out of the path of the oncoming fist. Nemo pulled himself back up, but Dementor had already recovered and was charging towards him. Nemo sidestepped, causing Damien to crash into the wall. Dropping to a knee, Nemo heeded the advice of Cliff Hardcastle, throwing his arm between Dementor's knees and swinging upward as fast as he could. The bully crumpled while Nemo picked up his lunchbox and continued on his way to the cafeteria.

When school was out, not just for summer but once and for all, Nemo departed for the galaxy's greatest scientific college: The Discovery Realm in Kingdom.

As for Hip Harrison, he too packed his bags, departing instead for Las Esferana to attend the Brutus Maximus Wrestling Academy. He was a two-time planetary champion in the amateur stuff, but he was looking to go pro, and what better teacher could there be than the former Heavyweight Champion of the Galaxy?

***

The lives of Hip and Nemo almost reflected each other in the intervening cycles. Not on the surface, as Nemo's time was largely spent in classrooms, lecture halls, laboratories, and libraries, while Hip could mostly be found in the gym or sparring in the ring. But, beyond that, both were working hard, dedicating every waking hour to honing their respective crafts.

Nemo's research papers impressed his professors so much that they soon began finding their way to several notable and high-profile scientists and organisations across the galaxy. By the time Nemo graduated, with honours, he had his pick of institutes and organisations from all corners of Sianard, all of which had been courting him for at least a cycle and a half.

Meanwhile, Hip Harrison discovered early in his time at the Brutus Maximus Wrestling Academy that, just because his name was above the door, it didn't mean that the former Galactic Champ actually taught any classes. Brutus owned the school, had funded its existence, but it was the former Galactic Tag Team Champions, Los Diabolicos — Diego y Doro — who ran it day-to-day.

The first few moon orbits were tough. So tough, in fact, that more than half of the class quit during the first ten practice sessions, which mostly involved learning to fall safely (taking a bump, as the professionals called it) and running the ropes. Running the ropes meant sprinting from one side of the ring to the other, turning to rebound off the ropes at the other end, resulting in a slingshot effect that sent you running back the other way with increased momentum. After running back and forth a few times, Harrison and his classmates would reach high speeds, and the aim was to dodge one another, as the coaches set two trainees running simultaneously on different paths — left-to-right and up-and-down.

Aside from the potential to collide with a fellow combatant during these drills, running the ropes might not sound too bad. But those ropes aren't made of elastic and they're certainly not soft or suitable for sensitive skin. They bite into the flesh, cutting deep until the epidermis hardens up to it. Hip watched as several bloody and scabbed backs exited the building, never to be seen again.

His back may have been sore, every muscle might have ached, but nothing was going to deter Hip Harrison from living out his dream. You only live once — as he well knew thanks to his mother's sudden death — so you might as well give it your all. Besides, he'd put himself through worse training regimes on the farm, running up the hill with a tree trunk hoisted over his shoulders.

Six survivors remained when Los Diabolicos announced to the class that they would learn some new skills at last. Grappling, striking, and high flying were all in play. They also confirmed a suspicion Hip had held for a while: 'We know the start of this programme has been tough, and that's by design. We just needed to separate the wheat from the obsolete. To know who *really* wanted to do this. Who had enough passion!' From that day on, Diego y Doro's teaching style became less drill sergeant and more nurturing.

Everyone in the class might have displayed enough passion, but some took to the art of pro wrestling better than others. It was painfully obvious that three of the remaining students weren't cut out for it. The other two had a lot of potential, learning the ropes (and how to jump off them) at a decent pace.

One student was the clear standout. Hip Harrison took to pro wrestling like he was born to do it and went on quite the undefeated streak in sparring against his classmates. He even pinned Diego during one session, causing everyone in the gym to pop. During the next practice session, Los Diabolicos asked Hip to stay at the end of class.

'Do you have any idea why you are here?' Doro said, once the other students had left.

Hip knew how well he was progressing and wondered whether he was about to be booked for his first professional match. Instead of saying that, he played it humble, shaking his head.

'Well,' said Diego, 'Is no secret that you are top of the class. And we have chosen you for a big opportunity.'

I'm going to be booked on a show. I'm graduating.

Doro continued: 'You're moving on from the school. But you will still be learning.'

Diego switched off the lights, plunging the gym into darkness. Familiar music filled the room and, when the chorus hit, the lights came back on to reveal Brutus Maximus standing in the middle of the ring, striking his signature pose — left foot forward, left fist raised, right hand pointing up to the heavens. The former

Galactic Champ may have been wearing sweatpants and a plain black t-shirt, but he could still pull off quite an entrance.

Hip was speechless. *What's going on?*

'Hola, Señor Harrison. Is great to meet you at last. I've heard many good things about your training. Diego y Doro tell me you show great potential.'

'I… it's… a pleasure to meet you, Sir.' Hip struggled for words. His idol was right there, talking to *him*.

'I'm going to cut right to the chase,' Brutus said, climbing through the ropes and hopping down to the floor. 'I've been searching, for many years, for someone to pass the torch to, so to speak. I've been looking for someone that I can train personally, one-to-one, so that they might become as great as I once was. But I needed a good quality clay to mould. Los Diabolicos tell me you are the best clay we will ever see.'

'Uh, thank you,' said Hip, trying hard to keep his excitement bottled up.

'What I want to know,' said Brutus, 'is would you like to be my apprentice?'

If the moment hadn't been so surreal, Hip Harrison would have answered yes in a heartbeat. Instead, he stood there, dumbfounded, until Doro nudged his shoulder.

'Yes, please,' he said at last.

'Good, then pack your bags. We'll be touring Las Esferana and Neja, where you'll wrestle on small shows each evening and receive feedback from me along the way. We'll train together every day.'

'Okay.' Hip Harrison thought that, surely, he must be dreaming.

***

The following cycles were a blur for both Hip and Nemo. Hip toured some of the more colourful — as well as some of the darker — corners of the galaxy, with the legend that was Brutus Maximus serving as his invisible hand. Brutus mentored Hip in every aspect of professional wrestling, inside and out of the ring, but remained hidden from view come showtime.

'Is true that my accompanying you to ringside could help get you noticed,' he once told Hip. 'But I fear that being associated with me could also hinder your career. The fans, the promotors, the other wrestlers, all of them would unfairly compare you at this early stage of your development to me in my prime, when I had years of experience under my belt. That belt, by the way, was the Galactic Heavyweight Championship.'

Brutus winked and nudged Hip's shoulder. He relished in reminding his apprentice of his past accolades. 'They will also claim that any opportunity you rightfully earn was handed to you unfairly because of our relationship.

'Besides, I'm not in this for my own personal fame and glory. I've got enough of that. I'm doing this for the love of the sport and because I truly believe you could be the next big thing.'

***

A galaxy away, Nemo, seen as a prodigy in the scientific community, took a research role with the Sianard Scientific Council's (SSC for short) Earth and Space Exploration Unit (ESEU). Those strange transmissions that had first arrived in Sianard not even one-hundred cycles ago had reshaped the galaxy's entire way of life, distilling new languages and cultures, while almost obliterating the old ways. Sianardians spent much of their free time watching television content from Earth, as well as new content from across the five planets of Sianard. In fact, when it came to professional wrestling, while one network aired American Wrestling from Earth every Starsun Eve, another channel broadcast Sianard's own Galactic Wrestling Federation at the same time.

The idea of Earth fascinated Nemo. This faraway, almost mythical place that had unknowingly influenced so much of life in Sianard. The ESEU at the SSC was a fairly young organisation. Its purpose was to determine Earth's location and how long transmissions take to reach Sianard, as well as what life is like on Earth today. The end game was to make contact with the Earthlings.

However, when Nemo had been working at the ESEU for almost a full cycle, that dream had been dashed. Everything the small team did was confidential and Nemo was bound by the SSC to not discuss any of his work with external parties without authorisation. Disclosing anything about what the ESEU had found not only invited the wrath of the SSC but also that of the Galactic Council of Sianard (GCS), the governing body of the Galactic

Empire. The SSC is, of course, funded by the GCS and must therefore tow the approved narrative.

What the general population of the five planets remained unaware of was that Earth had been located when one senior physicist on Nemo's team identified the direction from which the transmissions were arriving, determined the rate at which they distorted and, therefore, how far they had travelled. The ESEU team had developed a drone that could reach Earth's estimated coordinates and send live images back.

Goblets clinked in celebration as the first images arrived. The festivities were, however, a little premature as, when the excitement died down and the photography was examined, it revealed that Earth was no longer. The planet, which exuded life in many forms through its broadcasts, was a burnt crust.

'Scorched Earth!' exclaimed Nemo's boss, Dr Bret Barker DSC, upon seeing the images.

'Scorched is the wrong word,' Nemo replied. 'Scorched would mean it's dried, damaged, which it could well have been a thousand cycles ago. But this… this is burnt. Carbonised. A more apt description would be to call it a "charred husk". It's like some celestial being cooked it on a barbeque.'

Work immediately turned to finding out just what in the blue hell happened to the once-blue planet. Without access to a time machine to go back and look, Nemo and the rest of the ESEU team hatched a plan to retrieve some of the later incoming broadcasts from Earth. They built another drone — this one with a satellite receiver instead of a camera — and dispatched it in the direction of Earth. It collected transmissions as it went, sending them directly back to the ESEU lab.

'It's like seeing into the future,' one of Nemo's colleagues, a Kingsman who went by the name Nightwing, said excitedly when the first broadcasts started coming in. 'We could find out who wins the next World Cup or Superbowl and win us a wager.'

'I guess we built a time machine after all,' Nemo replied.

As the drone travelled deeper into space, the team sifted through as much of the content coming in as they could, with a focus on news reels and nature documentaries.

It quickly became apparent that Earth was in trouble. The natural balance of the planet was tipping out of kilter. The documentaries explained the science: that Earth was heating at an accelerated rate due to the rapid advancement of human civilisation. Greenhouse gases — mostly carbon emissions — were destroying the ozone layer, which maintained the planet's habitable climate. The major cause by far was the burning of fossil fuels for powering the long list of conveniences the humans had created for themselves. Transportation, mass farming, central heating. The Earthlings made efforts to find new methods of energy production, but their implementation was ultimately too slow. The news reels revealed those in power to be too often dragging their heels in inciting change. Life had become too easy for too many. Change, even for the greater good, was hard work.

The documentaries eventually stopped. So did the sport and the fiction — the dramas, the sitcoms. A continuous stream of breaking news was all that remained as the planet broke apart. Mass migrations saw climate refugees escape the severe heat of their homes nearest the equator, travelling either north or south, essentially splitting the planet in two. Middle Earth, as it became known, was a no-go zone, littered with the cooked corpses of those who didn't leave in time. What land remained in the still-hospitable areas shrank fast as Middle Earth widened, while sea levels also rose.

News coverage mainly comprised the growth of the hot zone, the estimated number of human deaths over the previous twenty-four-hour period, and the growing unrest from a large population occupying ever smaller areas of land. Humans ultimately die out because of the pursuing heat, lack of food and resources, and each other. Desperate times and all that.

And then the drone reached the end of the transmissions. The final news reel was from the land mass once known as Norway. It detailed a war waged between two surviving clans over what they suspected to be the last remaining herd of reindeer.

And, finally, Earth stopped broadcasting. Fade to black.

'We cannot leak this,' said Hawk King, one of the top-ranking professors in all of Sianard and head of the SSC. It was rare that he appeared at the lab; this was only the second time that Nemo had seen the man in person.

'But, Sir,' said Nightwing, 'so much of Sianard's current culture models itself after that of Earth. If we don't warn the GCS — and the public at large — we might see the five planets go down the same path of destruction.'

Hawk King inhaled deeply. 'No. All that would accomplish is widespread panic. A population in panic is a dangerous thing. We would see riots, increasing crime rates, anarchy. We keep this to ourselves. Anyone found to be spreading such gossip will find themselves exiled immediately and discredited. Do I make myself clear?'

'But what about when the transmissions we brought back are eventually broadcast across the galaxy?' Nemo asked.

'Yeah, and even if we don't make it public, we at least need to inform the GCS,' added Nightwing. 'The council will want to act or to at least determine the potential damage we're doing to our galaxy.'

'Maybe I wasn't clear enough.' Hawk King sighed, not from exhaustion but from irritation. 'None of you are to utter a word of this beyond these walls. What's not to understand?

'As for the GCS, don't worry about them. I know the council rather well and will be discrete in disclosing such sensitive information.'

The ESEU team nodded its collective understanding. 'Good,' said Hawk King. 'Now, onto other business, unrelated I assure you: the Sianard Scientific Council has undergone an audit by the Galactic Council of Sianard. The GCS has, I'm told, made the difficult decision to divert some of the SSC's funding elsewhere. Given the ESEU's work has culminated in somewhat of a conclusion recently, I'm afraid to say that they have slashed your budget.

'You two.' Hawk King pointed at Nemo and Nightwing. 'As the most junior members of the team, it pains me to say that you are surplus to requirements. A case of last in, first out, harsh as it may seem. But you're both young and spritely. I'm sure you'll land on your feet. Just remember: not a word of Earth's fate outside these walls. With so few of you knowing the truth, we can easily discover the source of any leak and, should such a task prove too difficult, we will simply discredit everyone in this room, banishing you all from the scientific community. Not to worry though, as I hear the mines in Neja are always in need of additional labour.'

***

Nemo wasn't concerned about his future career prospects so much as he was worried about the future of the entire galaxy. The more he looked around him, the more terrified he became of the parallels he saw between the five planets of Sianard and the former Earth. He approached Nightwing about going to the GCS with their findings — SSC be damned!

'Yeah, sure,' Nightwing said in response, but his body language said something entirely different. When Nemo called upon his former colleague, someone he considered a friend, just a few days later, he received no answer. He left several messages, but Nightwing never responded.

Realising that Nightwing was perhaps not the friend he'd thought (*maybe he was just worried about his own scientific career*), Nemo acted alone in blowing the whistle. He was going to go straight to the main chamber of the Galactic Council and confront anyone and everyone that would listen. He still had his SSC credentials and would bring those to back up his story.

Nemo travelled to Stateside without telling a soul. Discretion was key to ensuring the SSC didn't catch wind of his plan.

He located the GCS headquarters via pages on SIN — the Sianard Information Network — that he should no longer have had access to. Not that he would remind the powers at the SSC of that fact.

The Galactic Council was incredibly secretive and, while politics had been a performance — almost entertainment, not dissimilar from professional wrestling — on Earth, those calling the shots in Sianard remained anonymous. They would certainly not risk putting their power up for grabs in a public vote. As Nemo had discovered during his research on Earth, the political landscape had clearly been censored when broadcasts were shown on Sianardian televisions.

Even on the private pages of the GCS SIN-site, there was no mention of who the Galactic Council actually comprised. Yet, it still shocked Nemo to find just how much classified information he had access to as a lowly SSC researcher — a *former* lowly SSC researcher, at that. What he found was the schedule for councillors — including when they broke for lunch. With this information to hand, Nemo's plan was simple: he would try his luck in getting into the building with his old SSC pass, walk the corridors with a perceived sense of purpose (*exude confidence and nobody will question whether you belong*) and track down the council chambers, cornering its members as they recessed.

Nemo was a bundle of nerves in the days leading up to what he thought of as *the mission*. He'd seen the *James Bond* films from Earth, as well as the first twelve *Mission Impossible* movies. He knew the key to stealth was to look as if you belonged. The *Bond* franchise was still running, in fact, only with Sianardian actors, all from Kingdom, taking up the mantle of *007*.

Still, the thought of potential danger — and the unknown — caused Nemo to become a nervous wreck. Overthinking the situation, imagining every conceivable way things could go wrong, it was enough to drive anyone slightly mad. But Nemo had been here before. When interviewing for his position in the ESEU (never mind the fact they'd approached him; he was still worried he would mess it up), when studying for final exams at The Discovery Realm, and every now and again during high school when he would panic at the thought of getting into a fight with a bully.

Yet, while nerves could consume Nemo before an event, he was always alright on the night. He charmed in his interview for the ESEU research gig, aced his final exams at college, and, of course, when he was physically confronted by the school bully, Damien Dementor, Nemo came out on top. As much as Nemo worried, when crunch time arrived and he no longer had time to overthink, he was as cool and calm as they came.

One benefit of overthinking a situation was the meticulous planning and preparation it incited. Nemo knew the floor plans of the GCS HQ by heart as he entered the building. He could summon an on-demand image of the map in his head. Hip Harrison once asked Nemo, when the pair were studying for a final exam at high school, whether the latter had a photographic memory. The way Nemo's mind worked wasn't far off — although he always compared his process of recollection more to opening a book in a library than projecting images.

Nemo flashed his SSC pass at the disinterested security guard at reception and gained access without a second glance. Past the first hurdle, Nemo exhaled slowly. He was relieved to have made it into the building, but also anxious about being one step closer to confrontation. He pushed that thought away and focused instead on each step of the mission.

As Nemo made his way through the corridors of the GCS, it was like he was playing a videogame, constantly checking his imaginary map to know where to go and where to hide. There was less action, though. There were no villains to dodge or take out. In fact, it was almost mundane. At one point, a council office employee came around the corner and, while Nemo was certain he would question him as to why he was there, the staff member simply muttered a hello as he passed by.

Nemo had planned to hide in the lavatories nearest to the main council chamber to listen for the sounds of councillors breaking for recess. He'd even made a note of where he could access air vents, as well as staircases and exits in case he needed to make a quick getaway. But none of that was necessary. Instead, he saw a bench right beside the door to the main chamber and, as there was nobody else around, he took a seat and pondered how active his imagination had been. He was almost disappointed that this was all going so smoothly.

After a short while, he heard a ruckus from behind the doors and, moments later, they burst open. Nemo jumped to his feet as a barrage of cloaked figures wandered out.

'Excuse me,' he said, brushing the arm of the first gentleman to emerge from the chamber. The councillor looked at Nemo as if he were something nasty on the bottom of his shoe before continuing down the corridor.

Next out was a female councillor, who looked to be from Las Esferana.

'Excuse me, Madam,' said Nemo, side-stepping in her way.

'I'm very busy. This had better be good,' the councillor said.

'I'm from the SSC and need to speak with someone on the council urgently about a potential imminent threat to all life on Sianard.'

The councillor raised an eyebrow. 'If you're making this up…' she said without finishing the thought. 'Look, come with me. Those on the council that you'd want to speak to are still in the chamber.' She turned, scooting past others that were exiting the chamber and shuffled back through the doors.

Stunned by how easy this was, it took Nemo a couple of seconds to get moving.

The chamber was an oval-shaped room, dim like a theatre in the round, with rows of soft bench seating laced around the speaker's area in the centre.

As Nemo emerged inside the chamber, he saw three figures in the middle of the room. They appeared to be deep in conversation.

'Excuse me, gentlemen,' said the councillor who had ushered Nemo inside. 'This man claims to be from the SSC and would like an audience to discuss some impending doom to the galaxy. I have a craft to catch, so I'll leave you to it.'

As the councillor left, Nemo nervously raised a hand. 'Hello,' he muttered.

The figures remained still, their conversation dead. The mission now didn't feel so easy.

Nemo took a few hesitant steps towards the cloaked trio. Did one of them seem familiar? Something about their mannerisms.

'I'm, um, from the SSC and I have serious concerns to raise regarding the future of our environment. The GCS needs to take action. If I could just have a moment of your time?'

Nemo's eyes remained fixed on the figure he thought he might know, although he couldn't quite place them. He would have to wait, as one of the others spoke first.

'You're from the SSC, you say?' Nemo recognised this voice. Did he know two of these three council members? 'That's funny, because I seem to recall firing you.' The figure turned to face Nemo, lowering his hood.

'Hawk King?' Nemo gasped. 'I don't understand.'

'And I don't understand what you think you're doing here when I made it perfectly clear that what you found — or rather, what you *thought* you discovered — was not to be discussed any further,' said the head of the SSC. 'But we had a feeling you'd be making an appearance here sooner or later. Isn't that right, Nightwing?'

The figure whose mannerisms had seemed familiar to Nemo removed his own hood to reveal himself as Nemo's former colleague.

'Nightwing? So, this is why you ghosted me. How could you?'

'I get why you're upset,' said Nightwing, 'but you've got to look at the bigger picture. There's more at stake here.'

'More at stake?' Nemo was astounded. 'What could pose higher stakes than the end of the galaxy?'

Nightwing opened his mouth to respond, but the third figure placed a hand on his shoulder. The still-hooded figure chuckled.

'From what I gather, they considered you one of the brightest stars this side of the universe,' said the third man. 'But despite all the education you've undertaken, it seems they failed to teach you one important fact: it's money that makes the galaxy swirl. We're talking extremely high stakes here. Higher than you could ever grasp. Your friend Nightwing here gets it.'

The figure paused, removed his hand from Nightwing's shoulder, then lowered his hood. Nemo hadn't recognised the voice, but he knew the face. He'd seen it in magazines and online — in publications and on sites shown to him by his old friend, Hip Harrison. The face smiling back at him was that of Mr Montgomery, owner of the Galactic Wrestling Federation.

WEEK TWO

WELCOME BACK, LADIES, GENTLEMEN AND ALL OTHER LIFE FORMS! BEFORE THE COMMERCIAL BREAK, CHUNKASAURUS DEFEATED HAN DUAL TO ADVANCE IN OUR TOURNAMENT TO DETERMINE THE NEXT NUMBER ONE CONTENDER FOR THE GALACTIC HEAVYWEIGHT TITLE, CURRENTLY HELD BY OUR CHAMPION, JUDAS.

AND COMING UP NEXT, GENE, WE'VE GOT X-STATIC TAKING ON THAT IDIOT HIP HARRISON.

CAN THE ELECTRIFYING PSYCHOPATH, X-STATIC, ELIMINATE HIP HARRISON FROM THE TOURNAMENT?

HERE'S HOPING X-STATIC ELIMINATES HARRISON FROM THE GALACTIC WRESTLING FEDERATION ENTIRELY AFTER THAT STUNT HE PULLED, HIJACKING THE SHOW, LAST WEEK.

MY BROADCAST PARTNER IS REFERRING TO WHEN THE BEARDED BRUTE WENT OFF ON SOMEWHAT OF A RANT AFTER HIS LAST MATCH.

HE'S A BABBLING BUFFOON, GENE! SPEWING SOME SORT OF CONSPIRACY THEORY CRAP.

SPEAK OF THE DEVIL: HIP HARRISON IS MAKING HIS WAY TO THE RING.

OH, IS THAT HIM? HE CAN'T EVEN GET DECENT, RECOGNISABLE ENTRANCE MUSIC. EL GENERICO ROCK FOR AN EL GENERICO DOUCHEBAG.

YOU REALLY CAN'T STAND THE GUY ONE BIT, CAN YA'? AND HERE COMES HIS OPPONENT, X-STATIC.

X-STATIC'S PUMPED UP. HE KNOWS THE STAKES ARE EVEN HIGHER IN THIS ONE. NOT ONLY DOES DEFEATING HIP HARRISON MEAN HE WOULD ADVANCE IN THE TOURNAMENT, BUT IT WOULD CERTAINLY RESULT IN THE GALACTIC WF BRASS LOOKING FAVOURABLY UPON HIM FOR TAKING OUT HIP TRASHINGTON. THINK ABOUT WHAT A VICTORY HERE WILL DO FOR HIS CAREER.

BOTH COMBATANTS STARE EACH OTHER DOWN, JUST WAITING FOR THAT BELL TO RING AND THE MATCH TO BEGIN. HARRISON LOOKS MORE AMPED UP THAN USUAL. BUT THEN, HE HAS SOMETHING TO PROVE AFTER LAST WEEK'S SHENANIGANS. PERHAPS HE KNOWS HE

MADE AN ERROR IN JUDGEMENT AND IS SEEKING REDEMPTION HERE, TONIGHT.

COME ON ALREADY. WHY ISN'T THE REFEREE STARTING THE MATCH?

YOU MAY BE ABOUT TO GET AN ANSWER. HERE COMES SOVEREIGN NOBLE, CANE AND ALL. I WONDER WHY THE COMMISSIONER OF THE GALACTIC WF HAS TAKEN SUCH A KEEN INTEREST IN THIS PARTICULAR MID-TOURNAMENT MATCH.

NOBLE'S A SMART GUY. MAYBE HE'S DISQUALIFYING TRASHINGTON FOR LAST WEEK'S ANTICS.

***

Sovereign Noble spoke into a microphone from the entrance stage: 'I apologise for the minor interruption before we kick off this eagerly anticipated contest. But I need to inform the referee, as well as the competitors, about a last-minute change to the rules of this match. To spice things up a bit, this main event will no longer be a traditional one-on-one wrestling match.'

X-Static licked his lips, grinning like a Cheshire Splorg. Harrison, meanwhile, glared at the Galactic WF commissioner. A change to the match with no prior warning could only mean one thing: the fix was in.

'To add a little excitement,' Noble continued, 'this following contest will now be an exploding barbed wire death match!'

The crowd erupted.

'You've got to be kidding!' said Hip Harrison. But, with no microphone to hand, his protest fell on deaf ears.

'I'll have no complaining from you, Sunshine,' Noble continued, gesturing towards Harrison. 'After all, it was during your little speech last week that this idea came about. Now, as soon as the crew finishes setting up those contraptions, ring the bloody bell!'

***

HAHA! HIP HARRISON DOES *NOT* LOOK HAPPY.

I CAN'T SAY I BLAME HIM, GIVEN THAT OUR PRODUCTION CREW ARE UNWINDING SEVERAL REELS OF BARBED WIRE AROUND THE RING ROPES AS WE SPEAK.

AND LOOK: THEY'RE HOOKING THE BARBED WIRE UP TO SOME SORT OF DEVICE. SOVEREIGN NOBLE DID SAY 'EXPLODING' BARBED WIRE, DIDN'T HE?

I BELIEVE SO, PARTNER.

WOO-HOO! THAT DOOFUS, HIP TRASHINGTON, IS GONNA FRY!

THAT PSYCHOPATH X-STATIC IS SALIVATING. DROOL IS DRIPPING FROM HIS CHIN AS HIS EYES REMAIN LOCKED ON HIP HARRISON. HE'S SICK!

WELL, GENE, I MIGHT NOT HAVE BEEN A FAN OF X-STATIC AND HIS BRAND OF EXTREMELY CRAPPY WRESTLING BEFORE — AND I STILL CAN'T STAND SO-CALLED 'HARDCORE WRESTLING' — BUT THIS TYPE

OF MATCH STRONGLY FAVOURS A WIN FOR THE ELECTRIFYING PSYCHOPATH, AND DESTRUCTION FOR THE BEARDED BUTTHEAD, AND— WHOA!

THAT EXPLOSION, LADIES AND GENTLEMEN, APPEARS TO SIGNIFY THAT OUR PRODUCTION CREW HAS DONE ITS JOB. THE BARBED WIRE SURROUNDS THE RING AND, AS PER THE TEST JUST CARRIED OUT, SHOULD ANYTHING — OR ANYONE — COLLIDE WITH IT, THERE WILL BE AN EXPLOSION AT THE POINT OF CONTACT.

HIP HARRISON SURVEYS HIS SURROUNDINGS AS X-STATIC CONTINUES TO STARE AT HIM. THE REFEREE RECEIVES THE FINAL NOD FROM OUR PRODUCTION TEAM THAT EVERYTHING IS SET AND CALLS FOR THE TIMEKEEPER TO RING THE BELL. THIS CONTEST IS OFFICIALLY UNDER WAY.

X-STATIC PACES BACK AND FORTH LIKE A CAGED ANIMAL WHO'S JUST BEEN SET FREE. HE'S A PREDATOR ABOUT TO FEAST. TRASHINGTON IS THE PREY!

CALM YOURSELF, FARQUAD. WE'VE GOT A JOB TO DO.

HARRISON'S GAZE LOCKS ONTO HIS OPPONENT. HE SEEMS RELATIVELY CALM GIVEN THE CIRCUMSTANCES. ODDS ARE HIGH THAT ONE OF THESE TWO ATHLETES — IF NOT BOTH — WILL END THE NIGHT AT A NEARBY MEDICAL FACILITY.

X-STATIC POUNCES! HERE WE GO!

THE ELECTRIFYING PSYCHOPATH CHARGES TOWARDS HIS OPPONENT. I'M NOT SURE THIS IS THE WISEST OF MOVES IN THIS ENVIRONMENT BUT, THEN AGAIN, I'M NOT A PROFESSIONAL WRESTLER. I'M JUST A COMMENTATOR, FOLKS.

OH NO!

HARRISON SIDESTEPS AND X-STATIC STUMBLES TO A HALT MERE INCHES FROM THE EXPLOSIVE BARBED WIRE.

THAT WAS TOO CLOSE.

YOU'VE GOTTA BELIEVE THAT THE MOMENT ONE OF THESE TWO COMPETITORS HITS THE EXPLODING BARBED WIRE, THIS MATCH WILL BE OVER.

X-STATIC HASN'T MOVED. HE'S FROZEN IN PLACE, EYES WIDE OPEN. I THINK HIS LIFE JUST FLASHED BEFORE HIS EYES.

HERE COMES HARRISON, CAUTIOUSLY APPROACHING THE ELECTRIFYING PSYCHOPATH FROM BEHIND. THE BEARDED BRUTE LOCKS HIS ARMS AROUND X-STATIC'S WAIST AND WRENCHES HIM OFF HIS FEET. X-STATIC IS KICKING BUT HARRISON IS TOO STRONG AND LAUNCHES THE PSYCHO OVER HIS HEAD. X-STATIC CRASHES TO THE MAT, BOUNCES BACK UP AND STAGGERS BACKWARD ACROSS THE RING.

LOOK OUT!

SWINGING HIS ARMS AROUND IN CIRCLES, STEADYING HIMSELF WITH NOTHING TO GRASP BUT THE AIR AROUND HIM, X-STATIC ONCE AGAIN STOPS JUST A SPLORG'S WHISKER AWAY FROM THAT DEMONIC BARBED WIRE.

HARRISON ISN'T WAITING AROUND. HE'S SNEAKING UP BEHIND X-STATIC AGAIN. TURN AROUND!

HIP HARRISON THROWS HIS RIGHT LEG INTO THE AIR. HE'S GOING TO KICK THE ELECTRIFYING PSYCHOPATH INTO THE UNFORGIVING RAZOR WIRE!

BUT X-STATIC SCOUTS IT AT THE LAST MOMENT, TURNING AND DUCKING OUT OF THE WAY. HARRISON IMMEDIATELY PLANTS HIS LEG TO AVOID COLLIDING WITH THE EXPLODING BARBED WIRE-COVERED ROPES.

LOOKS LIKE TRASHINGTON TWEAKED HIS KNEE ON THAT LANDING. TO SEE THAT LOOK OF PAIN AND DISCOMFORT ON THAT IDIOT'S FACE MAKES ME FEEL ALL WARM AND FUZZY INSIDE.

HE'LL BE IN A LOT MORE PAIN AND DISCOMFORT IF THAT BARBED WIRE TEARS INTO HIS FLESH WHILE EXPLOSIONS ERUPT ALL AROUND HIM.

X-STATIC IS BACK UP. HE'S OVER TO HARRISON IN A FLASH AND TAKES HOLD OF HIP'S HIPS. HE'S NOT WASTING ANY TIME.

THE SEVERITY OF THE SITUATION HAS SUNK IN FOR THE ELECTRIFYING PSYCHOPATH. HE REALISES HE NEEDS TO END THIS MATCH AS SOON AS POSSIBLE TO HAVE THE BEST ODDS OF MAKING IT OUT IN ONE PIECE.

X-STATIC HAS THAT WAIST LOCK ON TIGHT AND HARRISON'S STRUGGLING AGAINST IT. HE'S GOT TO BE CAREFUL NOT TO INADVERTENTLY KNOCK THOSE ROPES — THEY BOTH DO.

HARRISON'S PUSHING BACK, STEP BY STEP, AND NOW THEY'RE BOTH IN THE CENTRE OF THE RING.

X-STATIC STILL HAS HARRISON AROUND THE WAIST AND— SNAP DRAGON SUPLEX! THE ELECTRIFYING PSYCHOPATH ARCHED BACK WITH SUCH SPEED, SUCH FORCE, THAT HIP HARRISON FLEW BACKWARDS OVER X-STATIC'S HEAD AND LANDED ON THE BACK OF HIS OWN CRANIUM. HIP'S DOWN AND X-STATIC IS IN CONTROL.

IT WAS A THING OF BEAUTY, GENE. I DIDN'T THINK THAT STREET FIGHTING MANIAC POSSESSED SUCH SKILL. TRASHINGTON LIKELY THOUGHT HE COULD WRESTLE CIRCLES AROUND HIS OPPONENT TONIGHT. HE MUST BE AS SURPRISED AS ANY OF US.

TONIGHT HAS BEEN FULL OF SURPRISES AND IT'S NOT OVER YET.

HIP HARRISON IS CRADLING HIS HEAD WHILE TRYING TO FIND A WAY BACK UP TO HIS FEET. HE CAN'T

USE THE ROPES FOR LEVERAGE AS HE NORMALLY MIGHT.

X-STATIC IS READY AND WAITING FOR TRASHINGTON TO GET UP. HE'S CLEARLY GOT SOMETHING BIG IN MIND.

I DON'T THINK I'VE EVER SEEN X-STATIC THIS FOCUSED. HIS EYES BURN WITH A BRIGHT INTENSITY WE'VE NEVER SEEN BEFORE FROM THE LUNATIC.

HIP'S BACK UP BUT THAT GNARLY SUPLEX SEEMS TO HAVE KNOCKED HIM SILLY.

AND HE TURNS AROUND RIGHT INTO THE CLUTCHES OF X-STATIC ONCE AGAIN. THE PSYCHOPATH HOISTS HARRISON UP ONTO HIS SHOULDERS IN A REVERSE FIREMAN'S CARRY. THE BEARDED BRUTE APPEARS DAZED AS HE LIFTS HIS HEAD TO SEE WHERE X-STATIC IS TAKING HIM.

X-STATIC IS BACKING UP. YOU DON'T THINK HE'S GOING TO… NO WAY. HE'S GOING TO THROW HARRISON LIKE A JAVELIN, FACE FIRST INTO THE EXPLODING BARBED WIRE. THIS IS GOING TO BE GREAT!

WE ADVISE ANYONE WATCHING WITH CHILDREN TO SEE THAT THEY LEAVE THE ROOM NOW, AS I THINK WE'RE ABOUT TO WITNESS A GRUESOME END TO THIS MATCH.

I SAY LET THE KIDS SEE. IT'LL MAKE FOR A GOOD LESSON THAT THIS IS WHAT HAPPENS TO MORONS WHO STEP OUT OF LINE.

IN THE NAME OF BRADSHAW, DON'T DO IT. THE MATCH DOESN'T NEED TO END THIS WAY. JUST SLAM HIM DOWN AND PIN HIM!

WHERE'S THE FUN IN THAT? OH — HERE WE GO!

X-STATIC CHARGES, FULL STEAM AHEAD, WITH HIP HARRISON DRAPED OVER HIS SHOULDERS. HE'S GONNA THROW HIM AND— NO! HIP HARRISON SLIPS FREE, SLIDING BACKWARDS, LANDING ON HIS FEET BEHIND X-STATIC.

THAT ELECTRIFYING IDIOT HAS TOO MUCH MOMENTUM WITH THE DEAD WEIGHT OF HARRISON NO LONGER WEIGHING HIM DOWN.

YOU'RE RIGHT. X-STATIC TRIES DESPERATELY TO SLOW HIMSELF DOWN, HORROR ETCHED ACROSS HIS FACE. BUT HARRISON GIVES HIM A BOOST. A SMALL SHOVE IS ALL IT TAKES AND X-STATIC COLLIDES WITH THE RAZOR-SHARP BARBED WIRE, FACE FIRST AND—

HE'S GOT TO BE DEAD!

HOLY SMOKES, WHAT AN EXPLOSION. ARE THEY ALRIGHT?

HOLY SMOKES IS RIGHT. I CAN'T SEE A THING THROUGH ALL THAT SMOG.

THE MEDICAL TEAM ARE ON HAND, LADIES AND GENTLEMEN. SHOULD ANY OF OUR COMPETITORS NEED URGENT CARE, THEY'LL PROVIDE IT AS SOON AS THEY CAN GET INSIDE THE RING.

SOMEONE NEEDS TO REMOVE THAT EXPLOSIVE BARBED WIRE FIRST. IS THE REFEREE EVEN STILL ALIVE?

THE SMOKE IS CLEARING AND JUDGE DREAD IS STILL STANDING, AS IS HIP HARRISON.

SON OF A POODWINK!

HOWEVER, X-STATIC IS IN EXTREMELY BAD SHAPE. THIS IS NOT A SIGHT FOR THOSE OF A WEAK DISPOSITION.

HE'S TWISTED AND TANGLED IN THE ROPES LIKE A PRETZEL. SOMEBODY HELP HIM!

I'M BEING INFORMED THROUGH MY HEADSET THAT THE PRODUCTION TEAM HAVE DEACTIVATED THE REMAINING EXPLOSIVES TO ALLOW JUDGE DREAD TO FREE X-STATIC FROM THE ROPES, IN ORDER FOR THE MATCH TO CONTINUE AND A CONCLUSION TO BE REACHED IN THIS HIGHLY UNORTHODOX CONTEST.

THERE'S NO WAY X-STATIC CAN CONTINUE. JUST LOOK AT HIM — THE BARBED WIRE IS TEARING HIS FLESH TO SHREDS LIKE PULLED HOG ON A BARBECUE. THERE'S BLOOD EVERYWHERE AND HIS HAIR IS STANDING ON END FOLLOWING THAT

EXPLOSION. IT'S LIKE SOMETHING OUT OF A CARTOON… OR A HORROR MOVIE… OR BOTH.

THIS DOES NOT LOOK GOOD AT ALL. AS THE REFEREE CAREFULLY ATTEMPTS TO REMOVE X-STATIC FROM THE GRIPS OF THAT SADISTIC BARBED WIRE, HE CAN'T HELP BUT CAUSE FURTHER INJURY TO THE COMPETITOR. SOME OF THOSE CUTS LOOK DEEP AND THEY'RE OPENING EVEN WIDER.

IF THERE'S A SAVING GRACE, IT'S THAT X-STATIC HAS NO CLUE WHAT'S GOING ON.

HE HASN'T MOVED OF HIS OWN FREE WILL SINCE THE EXPLOSION.

HIP HARRISON IS STANDING ACROSS THE RING, APPEARING SOMEWHAT CONCERNED FOR THE WELLBEING OF HIS FALLEN OPPONENT BUT, EQUALLY, COULD BE IN SHOCK. THAT COULD HAVE BEEN HIM.

SHOULD HAVE BEEN. I BET HE WAS PLAYING POSSUM UP ON X-STATIC'S SHOULDERS. WHAT A DIRTY TACTIC.

WE CAN'T SAY FOR SURE, BUT LET'S NOT FORGET THAT X-STATIC WAS MORE THAN HAPPY TO THROW HARRISON INTO THAT… THAT DANGERZONE.

THE REFEREE HAS FINALLY BROKEN X-STATIC FREE FROM THE BARBED WIRE.

X-STATIC CRUMPLES TO THE MAT. HE'S OUT. THE REFEREE CHECKS ON HIM AND IT APPEARS THIS MATCH

IS OVER. JUDGE DREAD SIGNALS TO THE TIMEKEEPER—BUT WAIT! HIP HARRISON GRABS THE REFEREE'S ARM. WHAT'S HE DOING?

I DON'T LIKE THE LOOK OF THIS. DOESN'T HE REALISE HE WAS ABOUT TO BE AWARDED THE VICTORY VIA REFEREE STOPPAGE? IS THAT NOT ENOUGH?

APPARENTLY NOT. THE BEARDED BRUTE'S TELLING THE REFEREE TO KEEP THE MATCH GOING. HE DRAGS THE CARCASS OF HIS OPPONENT INTO THE CENTRE OF THE RING, LAYS THE ELECTRIFIED — OR SHOULD THAT BE *EXPLODED* — PSYCHOPATH OUT, FLAT ON HIS BACK, AND— TALK ABOUT SENDING A MESSAGE. THIS HAS TO BE DIRECTED TOWARDS OUR COMMISSIONER, SOVEREIGN NOBLE, AND THE CHAMPION, JUDAS, AS WELL AS EVERY OTHER COMPETITOR IN THIS TOURNAMENT.

HIP HARRISON STANDS OVER THE TOASTED REMAINS OF X-STATIC AND PLACES A SINGLE TOE ON HIS OPPONENT'S CHEST. THE REFEREE HASTILY DROPS TO THE MAT, SLAPS HIS HAND TO THE CANVAS — ONE, TWO, THREE. MERCIFULLY, THE MATCH IS OVER.

SON OF A POODWINK!

HIP HARRISON IS ONE STEP CLOSER TO BECOMING THE NUMBER ONE CONTENDER TO THE GALACTIC HEAVYWEIGHT CHAMPIONSHIP.

SPEAKING OF THE GALACTIC HEAVYWEIGHT CHAMPIONSHIP, THERE IT IS, AROUND THE WAIST OF OUR CHAMPION. IT'S JUDAS.

THE CROWD, WHICH HAD FALLEN INTO STUNNED SILENCE FOLLOWING THE SHOCKING CONCLUSION TO THAT MATCH, HAS ERUPTED AT THE SIGHT OF THE HEAVYWEIGHT CHAMPION. JUDAS IS STANDING AT THE TOP OF THE ENTRANCE RAMP AND HE'S... SMILING.

THAT'S NOT A SMILE, THAT'S A SMIRK.

ONE HAS TO WONDER WHETHER JUDAS VIEWS HIP HARRISON AS SOME SORT OF THREAT.

OH, PLEASE.

WHY ELSE WOULD HE BE OUT HERE? HE HASN'T PUBLICLY ACKNOWLEDGED ANY OF THE OTHER TOURNAMENT PARTICIPANTS LIKE THIS. PERHAPS JUDAS BELIEVES HIP HARRISON COULD WELL BE HIS NEXT CHALLENGER.

IF THAT IDIOT, TRASHINGTON — WHO SHOULD BE CHARGED FOR ATTEMPTED MURDER AFTER WHAT HE JUST DID TO X-STATIC — MAKES IT TO THE FINALS OF THE TOURNAMENT AND SOMEHOW WINS, AT LEAST JUDAS WILL TAKE HIM OUT. ONE WAY OR ANOTHER, AS THE CHAMP SAYS.

ATTEMPTED MURDER? YOU KNOW HOW IT GOES IN THE GALACTIC WF. THE GUYS AND GIRLS THAT STEP INTO THE SQUARED CIRCLE UNDERSTAND WHAT

THEY'RE SIGNING UP FOR. ANYTHING GOES WITHIN THE CONFINES OF A MATCH.

NOW, WOULD YOU LOOK AT THIS: HIP HARRISON'S EYES ARE LOCKED ON THE EYES OF THE CHAMPION AS OUR PRODUCTION CREW WORKS TO CLEAR THE BARBED WIRE TO ALLOW MEDICAL PERSONNEL TO ATTEND TO X-STATIC. THE CROWD IS GOING WILD; NOT A SINGLE PERSON IN THIS ARENA IS IN THEIR SEAT. THIS IS ELECTRIC!

WHAT'S HARRISON TRYING TO SAY? HE'S MOUTHING SOMETHING AT JUDAS. WHY DOESN'T HE GRAB A MIC?

HE'S IN THE ZONE, FARQUAD. THIS IS A MOMENT BETWEEN CHAMPION AND POTENTIAL CHALLENGER. HARRISON APPEARS TO BE TELLING JUDAS TO GET READY, BECAUSE HE'S COMING FOR HIM AND THE GALACTIC WF CHAMPIONSHIP.

IT LOOKS LIKE TRASHINGTON'S SAYING SOMETHING ELSE. CAN WE GET A CAMERA MIC NEAR HIM AND— OH NO, I'M MISTAKEN. HE'S JUST REPEATING HIMSELF LIKE THE BLITHERING IDIOT HE IS.

YES, WELL, WITH NOTHING ELSE TO ADD AND WITH OUR ALLOTTED TIME ON THE NETWORK ABOUT TO EXPIRE, ALLOW ME TO THANK YOU ALL ONCE AGAIN FOR WELCOMING US INTO YOUR HOMES. WE'LL SEE YOU

ALL, SAME TIME, NEXT WEEK AS THIS UNPREDICTABLE AND EXHILARATING TOURNAMENT CONTINUES. GOOD NIGHT!

***

Hip Harrison knew better than to ask for a microphone. There was no chance in hell that those running the show would risk giving him a voice in front of a live and televised audience. Not after last time. Instead, he shouted. Not only would a small section of fans seated in the front few rows possibly hear what he was saying, but there was always the chance of some eagle-eyed viewers at home being able to read his lips. It was only a matter of time before someone pieced together what he said and posted it across SIN, on wrestling fan forums, message boards and in comments sections.

Harrison later discovered that one of his biggest detractors — and company stooge — Lord Farquad, had inadvertently drawn attention to what he, Harrison, was trying to say before quickly backtracking. The commentators, along with everyone else at ringside, as well as the referee inside the ring itself, all wore headsets and ear pieces that allowed Mr Montgomery and his team of directors and producers to communicate with them during the live broadcast. It didn't take a genius to figure out why Farquad suddenly lost interest in what Hip Harrison was saying.

As soon as Farquad claimed he was mistaken, it was immediately apparent to the savvier fans — those who not only watched the shows, but would spend countless hours following the ins and outs of the Galactic Wrestling Federation online — that whatever Hip Harrison was trying to say was worth listening to. Especially since they'd cut his mic off at the mention of the Federation's reclusive owner a week earlier. Hip Harrison was clearly trying to uncover some dirt on Mr Montgomery, and the Galactic WF was doing what it could to give the impression that there was nothing to see here.

In the weeks to follow, Hip Harrison's crowd support grew.

***

When the broadcast ended, and the house lights rose, Costa Fortune wished the audience a safe journey home. Hip Harrison exited the ring and walked up the ramp towards the entrance stage. Judas had left the moment the show was off the air — he was probably already in his craft, flying home to his luxury villa on Las Esferana. As The Bearded Brute made his way behind the curtain, he spotted Sovereign Noble in discussion with one of the medical personnel who had attended to X-Static.

'Is he okay?' Harrison asked.

The medical professional looked up and, after a moment spent processing who was asking the question, he nodded. 'It looked worse than it was.'

'Good,' said Harrison. He turned to Sovereign Noble. 'What were you thinking?'

Noble raised a hand and opened his mouth to speak.

'Don't answer,' Harrison added. 'I know what's going on around here. I'm just disappointed in you. Given your background, your experience in that ring. You were one of the greats — now look at you.'

A speechless Sovereign Noble could only look on, leaning heavier than usual on his cane, as Hip Harrison walked away, shaking his head.

Previously...

Back in his day, Sovereign Noble had been one of the most ruthless, aggressive and technically gifted wrestlers to come out of Kingdom. Noble never had an impressive physique, wasn't overly strong, and never once attempted anything flashy, like jumping from the top rope. But he was resilient and, as soon as the bell rang to start a match, it was as if a switch had flipped inside his head. Gone would be the polite gentleman who had entered the ring as Sovereign tapped into his sadistic side. As soon as the match was over, should the referee raise his hand in victory, Noble would offer to shake hands with his opponent and bow to the audience.

Not that Noble's opponents often reciprocated the handshake. Too frequently they would find their fingers disfigured at the hands of the Sadistic Sovereign, which emerged between the bells. One of his favourite moves was to grasp his opponent's fore and middle fingers, bending and contorting them in ways that were torturous. It was usually at the point that the fingers broke, or the tendons tore, that his opponents accepted defeat and tapped out.

As skilled as Sovereign was at bending his opponents' various body parts, he wasn't shy about bending the rules when the referee's view was obstructed either, jabbing his fellow competitors with a thumb to the eye, or biting their hands to escape a hold. While these nefarious tactics had earned him the nickname of The Crafty Kingsman and helped him to win hundreds of matches, not to mention the Interplanetary Championship twice, they also led to his ultimate demise.

It was in a match against Judas — a promising up-and-comer at the time. Noble was the Interplanetary Champion and opening the show with an exhibition match against the rookie. However, the contest became a little more competitive than Noble had expected, so the grizzled Kingsman attempted a tried-and-tested sequence that had seen him to victory dozens of times before: he waited for the referee to move behind his opponent, then charged. Judas ducked, but that was okay, because The Crafty Kingsman wasn't aiming for Judas. Instead, he knocked the referee down, making it appear as if he had collided with the referee accidentally, as intentionally attacking a match official resulted in an instant disqualification. In the few moments it took the referee to regain his bearings, Sovereign would spin round, drop to his knees, and hit his opponent with a low blow (another instant disqualification, if the referee saw it). But Judas was ready for him, catching Noble's hand on the way up. Sovereign Noble suddenly found himself in a vulnerable position, on his knees with his larger opponent towering over him. Noble tried to stand, but Judas maintained wrist control, twisting slightly to prevent Sovereign from being able to get to his feet.

The Crafty Kingsman attempted to hit Judas with his other hand, but Judas simply deflected the shot by kicking Noble's arm away, which wrenched on both arm sockets. Sovereign knew he was in trouble and tapped into another side of his personality — a side that died that very night — by flashing a cheeky Kingsman smile up at Judas as if to say, 'Just kidding.'

Judas smiled back. Only, there was no cheekiness in that smile. No warmth.

'Please,' Noble said just before Judas's knee connected with his jaw, knocking him out.

Perhaps Judas would have gone straight for the pin. Maybe the referee would have awarded Judas the victory via KO. But the referee hadn't recovered from being knocked down by Noble; Noble had come in hot and the referee's head had hit the turnbuckle with some force on the way down and whipped back, causing another blow to the head as he hit the canvas. He too was out for the count, as the saying goes.

Judas was livid, his short temper boiling over at the audacity of Sovereign Noble's attempt to cheat the undefeated rookie into a loss. As the match was still ongoing, anything that Judas did to Noble was exempt from galactic law. Not only did Sovereign Noble need to pay, but he would serve as a warning to anyone else on the roster who thought they could swindle a cheap victory over The Master of the Mat.

The future Galactic Heavyweight Champion climbed between the top and middle ropes, dropped to the floor, brushed the ring apron aside and reached underneath, pulling out a folding chair.

Why was such an item under the ring? These chairs, made from a solid, steel-like substance, were used by all members of the crew at ringside, including the timekeeper, ring announcer, and referees between bouts. Spares were kept below the ring so that they were easily accessible if needed. Other objects stashed beneath the canvas included tables and ladders, which were used by the production team when setting up and tearing down the arena before and after shows, a variety of electrical equipment and wiring, toolboxes filled with everything from hammers to screwdrivers and saws, and health and safety equipment, including medical kits and fire extinguishers. Lifting the ring apron was like entering a toy store for those with sadistic minds.

Besides the tools of the trade left behind by the production crew, wrestlers sometimes stashed objects of their own under there, such as baseball bats and sledgehammers, for use during their matches later in the evening. The only time the use of weapons was deemed to go too far was when Slack Jaws, considered by many to be the most psychopathic wrestler in Sianardian history, pulled out a stick of dynamite and a lighter. While competitors sign away their right to press charges against their opponents or the federation between bells, the Galactic WF would have been in hot water should an entire arena of spectators and crew members have been blown to smithereens. Thankfully, security officers and fire marshals were quick on the scene, extinguishing the fuse and dragging Slack Jaws away, never to be seen again.

Chair in hand, Judas slid back into the ring and surveyed the scene. Sovereign Noble remained unconscious. The referee was still struggling to regain his bearings, which meant he wasn't paying attention as Judas strode across the canvas towards his downed opponent with a weapon in hand.

Approaching Sovereign, Judas unfolded the steel chair, lifted Noble's left leg, and threaded it through the gap between the chair back and seat before lowering it back down to the mat. The Destroyer then made his way to the nearest turnbuckle and climbed, positioning himself on the second rope. Judas took no pleasure in this — or so he told himself. There was no honour in hurting a fellow wrestler when they were defenceless. But cheaters never prospered and examples needed to be made.

Sovereign Noble's eyes were closed. His breathing was shallow. Confident that Noble would not be moving anytime soon, Judas set the upturned chair leg in his sights. Noble's leg lay still, his ankle wrapped between the unforgiving steel-like substance.

Like a bear caught in a trap.

Target acquired, Judas smiled. And jumped.

His foot connected with the end of the chair leg, forcing it down towards the mat. An ankle was shattered, a career was ended. Sovereign Noble regained consciousness in an instant, an explosion of pain going off like a mushroom cloud from his ankle and up his entire leg. The chair, folded flat with Judas standing on its leg, offered no mercy. It was down to the bone and cartilage to give way.

Hearing the screams of the Kingsman and the disturbed murmurs from the crowd, the referee regained his bearings. As the ref had seen nothing untoward with his own eyes, the match continued. Judas could have pinned Sovereign Noble, or even allowed his opponent to give up, but where was the fun in that?

Instead, Judas snatched the chair from Sovereign's leg and slung it beneath the bottom rope. It crashed to the floor below.

'What were you doing with that?' yelled the agitated referee, while Sovereign Noble writhed in agony at his feet.

'You can't prove anything,' said Judas. 'Now, pay attention while I end this match.'

With that, The Wrecking Ball of the Ring grabbed the foot attached to Noble's smashed ankle and twisted, hard. Sovereign Noble rolled immediately onto his front, his body following his foot as Judas continued to rotate it. His scream rose in pitch until it was almost silent. Judas wrenched Noble's leg back; there was no longer an escape for The Crafty Kingsman as The Destroyer continued to twist what remained of his ankle.

The ankle lock was applied for all of two seconds. Noble tapped immediately. Nobody could hear him scream.

The referee called for the bell, declaring Judas the victor. The timekeeper dutifully rang the bell. Judas held on for a further few seconds, as if he was so completely caught up in the fight that he hadn't realised it was over. In truth, he relished the pain he was inflicting. However, all good things must come to an end and he eventually let go of the ankle.

Medical staff wheeled Sovereign Noble out on a stretcher that night. The Crafty Kingsman was no more. His in-ring days were over, but Mr Montgomery had a new role in mind for Mr Noble. The Galactic WF was lacking a public-facing authority figure. Someone who was visibly involved in making the matches and reprimanding the wrestlers where needed. Noble's ankle may be permanently damaged, but his toughness is never in doubt — even now as he hobbles around with a cane for assistance rather than follow the advice of doctors by inhabiting a wheelchair. Plus, Sovereign Noble was one of the best to ever cut a promo. His microphone skills included a sharp tongue to match his wit — perfect for a commissioner who would need to keep the audience entertained while making matches.

WEEK THREE

'What have you two got in store for that Harrison twerp tonight?' Judas had just arrived at The Rock in time for another weekly episode of the Galactic Wrestling Federation. He didn't share the dressing rooms provided for other wrestlers on the roster. As soon as he had won the championship two cycles ago, Judas demanded his own space, away from the peons. He had also stipulated a weekly audience with both the Galactic WF commissioner, Sovereign Noble, and the federation's owner, Mr Montgomery. Judas knew his own worth, as did they. The Destroyer was an attraction, and attractions brought in the bucks.

'As a matter of fact, we were just discussing that particular thorn in our side,' said Mr Montgomery. 'Our commissioner here believes he has a solution. Isn't that right, Noble?'

Sovereign Noble nodded, nervously. 'Harrison's opponent this evening is Big Bale. As you know, they don't come much tougher than Bale.'

Judas grunted.

'Present company excepted, of course.' Noble continued. 'The odds are against Harrison winning the match, anyway. But, to play it safe, I'll be making another surprise appearance before the match starts. We have already given Bale the heads up as to the change in stipulation, giving him time to strategise.'

'Good, good,' said Judas, stroking his square jaw. 'Because we can't risk that bearded bastard getting any further in this tournament. He's already made it through to the semi-finals. If he wins tonight, there's a fifty percent chance he's my next challenger. I can't have that.'

'And neither can I,' said Mr Montgomery. 'The Galactic WF cannot allow that degenerate to catch even a sniff of that Galactic Heavyweight Championship. He gets a hold of that and I'm done. *We're* done.'

'What exactly does he have on you, anyway?' asked Judas.

'Nothing that concerns you and nothing that I can't handle. Besides, my main concern is with you. If you should lose the championship, where does that leave us? You're undefeated, Judas, in case you'd forgotten. People pay to see you. You're the reason we make a killing at the box office every week and why we have the highest ratings on television. If you lose a match, let alone the championship, you lose your aura with it. No aura, no allure; we'll see fans abandon us the second your winning streak ends, you mark my words.'

'Well, I guess it's in all of our best interests to ensure Hip Harrison goes down.'

'Why do you see him as so much of a threat?' Sovereign Noble asked, forgetting himself momentarily. 'Do you think he's actually good enough to beat you?'

Judas was quick, especially considering his size. He was arguably faster than some of the high-flying cruiserweights on the roster. That speed caught Sovereign Noble completely off-guard. In less than the blink of an eye, the Galactic WF commissioner found himself pinned up against the wall, struggling for breath as the Heavyweight Champion held tightly onto his collar, twisting.

'You'd better watch what you say, Commish,' said Judas, his voice barely a whisper. 'You know I can beat anyone you put in front of me. Hell, you know first-hand what I can do if someone tries to pull one over on me. How is the leg, by the way?'

'It's fine,' Noble squealed due to his restricted airwaves.

'There's just something I don't trust about that Harrison guy. I'd much rather mow down another giant, like Big Bale.'

Deep down, Judas was afraid of stepping in the ring with Hip Harrison. The Bearded Brute may not be the biggest dog in the yard, the quickest, the most athletic, or even the most technically gifted wrestler. But Judas had been watching Harrison climb the ranks. He had a quiet confidence about him that made Judas nervous. Hip Harrison was smart and extremely ring aware, as they said, knowing exactly when to side step an opponent and where to lure them. And, if need be, The Bearded Brute could battle back against the best of them, which made Judas most nervous of all. Like any bully, Judas was terrified at the prospect of someone actually fighting back.

'Let him go, for Bradshaw's sake,' Mr Montgomery said.

Judas held onto Sovereign Noble's shirt for a moment longer before dropping it.

The commissioner fell to the floor and reached for his cane, the handle of which resembled a golden skull with a crown wrapped around its cranium.

'Your plan had better work.'

***

WE'VE WITNESSED ANOTHER SPECTACULAR EVENING OF ACTION AND IT'S NOT OVER YET. IT'S MAIN EVENT TIME, FOLKS.

HARDLY A CASE OF SAVING THE BEST FOR LAST WITH TRASHINGTON.

WHAT MY PARTNER IS REFERRING TO, LADIES AND GENTLEMEN AND EVERYONE ELSE, IS THAT HIP HARRISON CONTINUES HIS JOURNEY ACROSS THE FIELD OF COMPETITORS FILLING OUR TOURNAMENT TO CROWN A NEW NUMBER ONE CONTENDER TO THE GALACTIC HEAVYWEIGHT CHAMPIONSHIP.

AND IT'S THE SEMI-FINALS. IF TRASHINGTON WINS TONIGHT, THERE'S ONLY ONE MORE MATCH BETWEEN HIM AND A SHOT AT JUDAS IN THE MAIN

EVENT OF THE BIGGEST SHOW OF THE CYCLE: BATTLESTAR GALACTICA.

EARLIER THIS EVENING, WE SAW SNIPER SKY DEFEAT CHUNKASAURUS IN OUR FIRST SEMI-FINAL CONTEST. SKY WILL FACE THE WINNER OF OUR NEXT MATCH, BEWEEN HIP HARRISON AND BIG BALE, NEXT WEEK.

IS THAT THE SOUND OF GENERIC STOCK MUSIC I HEAR? THAT MUST MEAN TRASHINGTON IS ABOUT TO GRACE US WITH HIS UNWANTED PRESENCE. THE GUY'S NOT ONLY AN ANNOYING, CONSPIRACY PEDDLING NUTJOB, BUT HE'S ALSO TOO CHEAP TO PAY OUT FOR DECENT ENTRANCE MUSIC.

I AGREE, TO AN EXTENT, THAT ENTRANCE MUSIC IS PART OF A WRESTLER'S OVERALL PRESENTATION. MUSIC AND THEATRICS CAN GET COMPETITORS NOTICED, HELP THEM STAND OUT FROM THE REST OF THE PACK, AND CAN EVEN BE USED TO INTIMIDATE AN OPPONENT.

DON'T I KNOW IT. MY MUSIC PLAYED A BIG PART IN SIGNIFYING MY ARRIVAL, BACK IN THE DAY. MY GRAND ENTRANCE ALWAYS GAVE ME A MENTAL EDGE OVER MY OPPONENTS. TRASHINGTON'S NOT GOING TO BE GETTING IN ANYONE'S HEAD.

HE SEEMS TO LIVE RENT-FREE IN YOURS, BUT THAT'S ANOTHER STORY.

WHAT WAS THAT?

HARRISON IS IN THE RING. HE'S READY TO FIGHT AND HERE COMES HIS OPPONENT AND FELLOW SEMI-FINALIST. HERE COMES BIG BALE!

BALE IS GOING TO TEAR HIP IN HALF. YOU LOOK BACK AT THE OPPONENTS TRASHINGTON HAS COME UP AGAINST IN THIS TOURNAMENT SO FAR AND BALE COMBINES THE STRENGTHS OF ALL THREE. THE HEIGHT AND LEVERAGE OF THE GREAT GOLIATH, THE GIRTH, SPEED AND POWER OF FATBOY SLIME, AND THE UNHINGED DISPOSITION OF X-STATIC.

BALE ENTERS THE RING AND THE SIZE DIFFERENCE IS CLEAR, LADIES AND GENTLEMEN. HIP HARRISON IS GIVING UP A HELLUVA'N ADVANTAGE IN TERMS OF WEIGHT, HEIGHT AND REACH.

HARRISON IS A BIG GUY IN HIS OWN RIGHT. JUST LOOK AT THE REFEREE FOR COMPARISON — AN AVERAGE-SIZED GENTLEMAN LOOKS MINISCULE COMPARED TO THE BEARDED BRUTE, BUT MICROSCOPIC IN THE SHADOW OF BIG BALE.

IT'S GO TIME! SQUASH HIM, BALE!

WAIT A MINUTE. WHAT'S THAT?

I KNOW THAT MUSIC… IT'S…

THE GALACTIC WRESTLING FEDERATION COMMISSIONER IS MAKING HIS PRESENCE FELT YET

AGAIN. SURELY, WE'RE NOT ABOUT TO SEE MORE EXPLODING BARBED WIRE.

I DON'T CARE WHAT IT IS. ANYTHING TO TAKE OUT THE TRASH. OH, GENE, I'VE JUST HAD AN IDEA! WHAT ABOUT A 'TAKE OUT THE TRASH' MATCH? THE WINNER IS THE FIRST TO INCAPACITATE THEIR OPPONENT TO WHERE THEY CAN DUMP THEM IN THE BACK OF A GARBAGE TRUCK AND DRIVE THEM OUT OF THE ROCK ARENA. WHAT DO YOU THINK?

I THINK I'M GLAD YOU'RE NOT THE ONE MAKING THE MATCHES AROUND HERE.

***

'My apologies, once again, for interrupting just as a much-anticipated main event is about to get under way,' said Sovereign Noble, leaning with one hand on his cane at the top of the entrance ramp. 'But last week's impromptu added stipulation received some rather positive feedback from our audience. In fact, television ratings jumped through the roof and our advertisers were *ecstatic* — if you'll pardon the pun.

'So, with that in mind, who'd like to see something different, again, tonight? Who wants a little extra *table* dressing?'

The crowd filled the arena with noise.

'Good,' Sovereign Noble continued. 'Because this semi-final contest is now a tables match! The only way to win is to put your opponent through a table.'

The crowd cheered even louder. In the ring, Hip Harrison's gaze remained locked on the commissioner. Sovereign Noble had truly stacked the decks against him.

Big Bale, meanwhile, was grinning from ear to ear.

'Referee,' said Sovereign Noble, 'you know what to do.'

***

ARE YOU KIDDING ME? FOR THE SECOND WEEK IN A ROW, WE'VE SEEN THE STIPULATIONS OF A MATCH CHANGED JUST MOMENTS BEFORE THE BELL RINGS. WHAT IN THE BLUE HELL IS GOING ON AROUND HERE, FARQUAD?

I DON'T KNOW WHY YOU'VE GOT SUCH A BEE IN YOUR BONNET, GENE. I THINK THIS IS FANTASTIC. WE'RE GOING TO SEE TRASHINGTON SLAMMED SO HARD THAT HE GOES THROUGH A SOLID WOODEN TABLE. HE MIGHT NEVER GET BACK UP FROM THAT. BALE'S BEEN KNOWN TO CHOKESLAM OPPONENTS WITH SO MUCH FORCE THAT THEY'VE MADE A CRATER IN THE RING. THIS IS GOING TO BE GREAT!

SOMETHING SEEMS A LITTLE OFF ABOUT ALL OF THIS. MAYBE IT'S JUST THE JOURNALIST IN ME.

IF YOU ENJOY COLLECTING A PAYCHECK, YOU MIGHT WANNA STOP QUESTIONING EVERY DECISION MADE AROUND HERE AND CALL THE ACTION.

WELL, WE'RE CERTAINLY IN FOR AN ACTION-PACKED END TO WHAT HAS BEEN AN EXCITING NIGHT.

THE REFEREE IS KEEPING BIG BALE AND HIP HARRISON IN THEIR CORNERS WHILE OUR PRODUCTION CREW STOCKS THE RINGSIDE AREA WITH TABLES. I'M TOLD THAT THERE WILL BE NO DISQUALIFICATIONS AND NO COUNTOUTS IN THIS MATCH. THE COMPETITORS CAN HIT EACH OTHER WITH WHATEVER THEY WOULD LIKE AND CAN BATTLE ANYWHERE IN THE ARENA AND BEYOND.

YOU MEAN TO SAY THE FIGHT COULD SPILL OUTSIDE THE BUILDING?

POTENTIALLY. AND ANY TABLE THEY ENCOUNTER IS FAIR GAME. A TABLE MUST BREAK TO END THE MATCH.

I CAN'T WAIT TO SEE TRASHINGTON'S BODY CRASH THROUGH A TABLE BUT, GENE, THERE'S JUST ONE THING MAKING ME SLIGHTLY NERVOUS.

WHAT'S THAT, PARTNER?

WE'RE SITTING AT A TABLE. THE COMMENTARY DESK IS EXEMPT, RIGHT?

A TABLE'S A TABLE. IF HARRISON AND BALE BRAWL TOWARDS US HERE ON THE STAGE—

LET'S HOPE IT DOESN'T COME TO THAT. I THINK THIS THING IS ABOUT TO GET UNDER WAY.

THE REFEREE GIVES FINAL INSTRUCTIONS TO BOTH WRESTLERS AND CALLS FOR THE TIMEKEEPER TO RING THE BELL.

HERE WE GO!

HIP HARRISON COMES OUT OF THE GATE HOT. HE KNOWS HE'S GOT A MOUNTAIN TO CLIMB, BOTH FIGURATIVELY AND PERHAPS LITERALLY, AGAINST BIG BALE. HE CHARGES ACROSS THE RING, JUMPS, THROWING HIS ARMS INTO THE AIR, HE…

GETS CAUGHT. HA!

THE STRENGTH AND POWER OF BIG BALE IS UNBELIEVABLE. HE JUST CAUGHT HIP HARRISON LIKE THE BEARDED BRUTE WAS NOTHING MORE THAN A FOOTBALL.

HARRISON'S STRUGGLING. HE CAN'T WRIGGLE FREE FROM THE GRIP OF BALE. THIS IS FANTASTIC!

HOW COULD ANYONE POSSIBLY ESCAPE THAT GRIP? BALE TAKES A STROLL ACROSS THE RING WITH HARRISON HELD IN HIS ARMS LIKE A BABY.

THERE'S A TABLE SET UP JUST OUTSIDE THE RING. YOU DON'T THINK…

I THINK BIG BALE HAS GOT SOME BAD INTENTIONS, PARTNER. HE HOISTS HARRISON UP ABOVE HIS HEAD IN ANOTHER SHOW OF UNREAL STRENGTH.

BALE'S GOING TO TOSS TRASHINGTON OVER THE TOP ROPE. HE'S BUILDING UP SPEED—

AND HE LAUNCHES HARRISON INTO THE AIR LIKE A RAGDOLL. THAT'S GOT TO BE A TWELVE-FOOT DROP TO THE OUTSIDE OF THE RING AND—

OH NO!

—A SICKENING THUD ACCOMPANIES A GNARLY LANDING AS HIP HARRISON'S RIBS COLLIDE WITH THE SOLID WOODEN TABLE. SPINE ON THE PINE, INDEED. BUT HE'S NOT OUT OF THE RACE JUST YET AS THE TABLE DIDN'T BREAK.

IF THERE'D BEEN EVEN A CRACK IN THAT TABLE, WE'D BE SPARED FROM SEEING ANY MORE OF THAT BEARDED BUM. IT WOULD HAVE BEEN THE BEST OUTCOME FOR TRASHINGTON, TOO, AS ALL THAT AWAITS HIM NOW IS A FURTHER BIG BALE BEATDOWN.

YOU MAY BE RIGHT THERE, FARQUAD. HIP HARRISON IS HURT AFTER THAT NASTY FALL ONTO THE TABLE. HE'S CLUTCHING HIS MID-SECTION AS HE CRAWLS TOWARDS THE RING APRON.

JUST CRAWL AWAY, YOU IDIOT!

I DON'T THINK IT'S IN HARRISON'S NATURE TO GIVE UP. HE'S COME THIS FAR IN THE TOURNAMENT AND HE'S NOT OUT YET.

AT LEAST WE'RE IN FOR SOME GOOD ENTERTAINMENT IF THAT IDIOT THINKS HE CAN FIGHT BACK.

BALE APPEARS TO SHARE THAT SENTIMENT. THAT GRIN HASN'T LEFT HIS FACE AND HE'S NOT WAITING AROUND. HE MAKES HIS WAY ACROSS THE RING, LEANS

THROUGH BETWEEN THE MIDDLE AND TOP ROPES, AND REACHES FOR HIS DOWNED OPPONENT.

WHAT'S HARRISON DOING? ALL I CAN SEE IS HIS LEGS. HIS UPPER BODY HAS DISAPPEARED BEHIND THE RING APRON. IS HE TRYING TO HIDE BENEATH THE RING? HOW PATHETIC!

SOMETIMES YOU'VE GOTTA CREATE SOME SEPARATION BETWEEN YOU AND YOUR OPPONENT. FIND SOME SPACE TO CATCH YOUR BREATH AND RECOVER.

THAT MAY BE SO, BUT IT WON'T WORK HERE. BALE HAS TRASHINGTON BY THE SEAT OF HIS PANTS. HE'S LIFTING THE BEARDED MUPPET OFF THE FLOOR WITH ONE ARM. I'M NOT SURE WHY I CONTINUE TO BE AMAZED BY THE FEATS OF STRENGTH DISPLAYED BY BIG BALE. IT'S LIKE HE'S GOT SUPERPOWERS.

HARRISON FINDS HIMSELF PULLED OUT FROM UNDER THE RING AND… WHAT'S THAT IN HIS HAND?

WATCH OUT, BALE!

TOO LATE! HARRISON APPARENTLY FOUND A FIRE EXTINGUISHER BENEATH THE RING IN CASE OF EMERGENCIES. THIS BEING AN EMERGENCY OF SORTS FOR THE BEARDED BRUTE, HE SPRAYS NITROGEN AND CARBON DIOXIDE DIRECTLY INTO THE FACE OF BIG BALE.

BALE STAGGERS BACK INTO THE RING, CLUTCHING HIS EYES. HE MAY BE BLIND. THIS IS TERRIBLE!

AS BALE SCRAMBLES FOR SOMETHING, THE RING ROPES PERHAPS, TO REGAIN HIS BEARINGS, HIP HARRISON SLIDES BACK INTO THE RING, FIRE EXTINGUISHER STILL IN HAND.

SOMEBODY NEEDS TO DO SOMETHING BEFORE— HARRISON'S CLOBBERING BIG BALE IN THE HEAD WITH THAT FIRE EXTINGUISHER. HOW MUCH DO THOSE THINGS WEIGH?

THEY WEIGH ENOUGH TO KNOCK BIG BALE DOWN. THE SOUND OF THAT CANISTER COLLIDING WITH BALE'S HEAD WAS SICKENING. THE BIG FELLA NOW FINDS HIMSELF IN A POSITION HE'S NOT ACCUSTOMED TO: DOWN ON THE MAT.

HARRISON WAS ABOUT TO GO FOR THE COVER.

A WRESTLER'S INSTINCT KICKING IN. HIS OPPONENT IS DOWN AND, IN A TRADITIONAL MATCH, HE WOULD LIKELY SCORE A PINFALL VICTORY. UNFORTUNATELY FOR HARRISON, THIS ISN'T A TRADITIONAL WRESTLING CONTEST.

THANK BRADSHAW FOR THAT. AND WHAT'S BETTER IS, THERE'S NO WAY TRASHINGTON CAN LIFT THE BIG GUY UP TO PUT HIM THROUGH A TABLE.

YOU'RE RIGHT, FARQUAD. BALE'S JUST TOO BIG AND HE'S NOTHING MORE THAN DEAD WEIGHT. EVEN IF HARRISON WAS STRONG ENOUGH TO LIFT THAT AMOUNT OF SHEER MASS, BALE'S BODY IS SO ENORMOUS THAT I DOUBT HE COULD GET ENOUGH OF A GRIP.

I THINK HIP'S JUST COME TO THE SAME CONCLUSION. HE'S NOT EVEN ATTEMPTING TO LIFT THE BIG GUY. INSTEAD, HE'S LEAVING THE RING. I GUESS THIS MEANS BALE WINS VIA FORFEIT.

NOT SO FAST. HARRISON IS COLLAPSING THAT TABLE AT RINGSIDE — THE ONE BALE THREW HIM AT LIKE A LAWN DART A MINUTE OR TWO AGO — AND SLIDING IT INTO THE RING.

HE'S DRAGS IT OVER TO THE CORNER OF THE RING AND PROPS IT UP AGAINST THE TURNBUCKLE.

IF HE CAN SOMEHOW SEND BALE RUNNING INTO THAT CORNER, WITH AN IRISH WHIP PERHAPS, THEN ONE WOULD ASSUME THE BIG MAN GOES THROUGH THE TABLE AND HARRISON WOULD BE DECLARED THE WINNER.

NOT IF BALE SENDS TRASHINGTON THROUGH IT FIRST. WHILE THE BEARDED IDIOT'S BEEN SETTING UP THAT TABLE IN THE CORNER, THE BIG GUY'S COMMANDEERED A BOTTLE OF WATER FROM A MEMBER OF THE RINGSIDE CREW TO RINSE THOSE

NASTY CHEMICALS FROM HIS EYES. HE CAN SEE AGAIN.

HIP HARRISON TURNS TO FIND BIG BALE STARING — *GLARING* — AT HIM FROM ACROSS THE RING.

HE LOOKS LIKE A DEER CAUGHT IN THE HEADLIGHTS OF AN ONCOMING CRAFT. BALE CHARGES ACROSS THE RING LIKE A RUNAWAY FREIGHT TRAIN!

BUT HARRISON SIDESTEPS AND BALE CRASHES THROUGH THE TABLE AT TREMENDOUS SPEED!

HOW FAST DO YOU THINK BALE WAS TRAVELLING? I KNOW HE'S A BIG FELLA, BUT THE TABLE'S COMPLETELY OBLITERATED.

LOOKING AT THE INSTANT REPLAY, IT APPEARS THE TABLE IMPLODED.

DOES THIS MEAN TRASHINGTON'S WON? IS HE THROUGH TO THE TOURNAMENT FINAL?

I WOULD THINK SO, ONLY THE BELL HASN'T RUNG. THE REFEREE LOOKS TO BE CLARIFYING SOMETHING WITH OUR RING ANNOUNCER, COSTA FORTUNE.

*****

Big Bale's enormous frame lay prone like a beached whale on a bed of not sand, but broken wood. If Harrison hadn't moved out of the way, he would have likely broken several bones — a couple ribs from the initial impact of the freight train that was Bale's body connecting with his own, and several more, including arms and legs, once Bale's momentum forced him through the table and crushed him against the turnbuckles behind it. It could well have been the end of Hip Harrison's career.

However, Harrison knew when Big Bale was coming at him. The Bearded Brute had studied enough of the giant's matches to know that whenever Bale was knocked down, his impulse upon rising from the mat was to charge at his opponent with little or no thought behind his actions. Hip had been playing possum and timed it right, so when he dodged out of the way, it left no time for Big Bale to slow down.

Harrison couldn't hear what was being said between referee Judge Dread and ring announcer Costa Fortune, but knew it couldn't be good news. If the match was truly over, the ref would have raised his arm already. Something was up.

When Judge Dread finally finished talking, Costa Fortune made the following announcement:

'Ladies and gentlemen, the referee has informed me that in order for this match to end, a competitor must *put* his opponent through a table via an offensive manoeuvre. As Big Bale ran through the table himself, with no physical involvement from Hip Harrison, this match will continue.'

Harrison took a moment to collect himself, prodded Bale's lifeless body with his toe, shook his head, and exited the ring.

***

WHERE'S HE GOING? IS HE FINALLY FORFEITING?

I'M NOT SURE, FARQUAD. IT LOOKED AS IF HARRISON WEIGHED UP BIG BALE, SO TO SPEAK, AND DECIDED HE HAD NO CHANCE IN HELL OF SHIFTING THE GIANT. HOW IN SIANARD DO YOU LIFT A COLOSSUS LIKE BALE AND SLAM THEM THROUGH A TABLE?

THERE'LL BE NO MORE GOADING BALE INTO PUTTING HIMSELF THROUGH A TABLE. THE REFEREE SAW PAST THAT CHEAP TACTIC. BESIDES, BALE'S STILL NOT MOVED SINCE HIS TERRIBLE CRASH. IF TRASHINGTON CAN'T FORCE BALE THROUGH A TABLE, HE REALLY HAS NO CHOICE BUT TO GIVE UP AND TAKE A LOSS.

I'M BEING INFORMED THAT THERE WILL BE NO STOPPAGES IN THIS MATCH BECAUSE OF A WRESTLER'S INABILITY TO CONTINUE. ONE COMPETITOR FORCIBLY PUTTING THE OTHER THROUGH A TABLE TRULY IS THE ONLY WAY THIS CONTEST CAN END. HOW CAN HARRISON ACCOMPLISH THAT?

HE CAN'T. TRASHINGTON HAS GONE BACKSTAGE. HE'S PROBABLY TELLING THOSE IN CHARGE THAT HE'S FORFEITING THE MATCH AS I SPEAK. THAT MEANS BIG BALE IS THROUGH TO THE FINAL WHERE HE'LL FACE SNIPER SKY NEXT WEEK TO DETERMINE THE NEXT NUMBER ONE CONTEN... WHAT'S THAT NOISE?

THERE'S SOME SORT OF COMMOTION BACKSTAGE. IT SOUNDS LIKE THINGS ARE BEING KNOCKED OVER OR THROWN ABOUT.

IS THAT IDIOT TRASHINGTON THROWING A TANTRUM BACK THERE? CAN WE GET A CAMERA ON THE SCENE? I NEED TO SEE THIS, GENE.

ONE OF OUR CAMERA OPERATORS IS RUNNING UP THE ENTRANCE RAMP TO GIVE US EYES ON WHAT'S GOING ON BEHIND THE CURTAIN AND— WHAT THE HELL IS THAT!?

THAT POOR CAMERA OP! HARRISON ALMOST RAN HIM OVER. HE COULD HAVE KILLED HIM, GENE!

I DON'T BELIEVE IT — HIP HARRISON'S DRIVING A FORKLIFT! EVERYONE IN THIS ARENA IS ON THEIR FEET.

WHAT IN A CELL DOES HE THINK HE'S DOING? HE'S COMMITTING GRAND THEFT AUTO. HE'S…

…DRIVING DOWN THE RAMP, STRAIGHT TOWARDS THE RING.

LOOK OUT! HE'S GOING TO… HE'S CRASHED INTO THE RING.

THE IMPACT OF THAT FORKLIFT CRAFT COLLIDING WITH THE RING IS COMPARABLE TO BIG BALE'S OWN COLLISION WITH THE TABLE AND TURNBUCKLE. IT BUDGES THE RING BY A FOOT OR MORE AND SENDS THE REFEREE FLYING THREE FEET INTO THE

AIR AT LEAST. JUDGE DREAD BOUNCES OFF THE ROPES AND TRIES TO FIND HIS BALANCE.

DID YOU NOTICE THE FORCE OF THE CRASH DIDN'T EVEN NUDGE BIG BALE AN INCH?

NOW THAT YOU MENTION IT, I THINK I SEE WHAT HIP HARRISON'S UP TO. THERE ARE NO RULES, ASIDE FROM SENDING YOUR OPPONENT THROUGH A TABLE. THE BEARDED BRUTE MAY NOT BE ABLE TO LIFT THE GIANT BALE WITH HIS BARE HANDS, BUT A FORKLIFT SHOULD DO THE TRICK!

I'VE SEEN NOTHING LIKE THIS BEFORE! SURELY THIS IS BREAKING SOME SORT OF RULE OR REGULATION.

ANYTHING GOES IN THIS TYPE OF MATCH. WHAT HARRISON DOES HERE IS ONLY LIMITED BY HIS IMAGINATION.

HE'S LOWERING THE FORKS BUT THE ROPES ARE IN THE WAY. SOMETHING'S GOTTA GIVE.

NOTHING'S GIVING SO FAR. THE PRONGS CONTINUE THEIR DESCENT, PUSHING THE ROPES DOWN LIKE THEY'RE NOTHING MORE THAN AN ELASTIC BAND.

THE PRESSURE HAS FORCED THE FORKLIFT'S FRONT WHEELS AN INCH OR TWO OFF THE GROUND BUT, ASIDE FROM THAT, YOU'RE RIGHT. IF ONLY THOSE ROPES WERE STRONG ENOUGH TO TIP TRASHINGTON OVER BACKWARDS.

THE FORKS MAKE CONTACT WITH THE CANVAS AND SINK LOWER STILL, BECOMING EMBEDDED WITHIN THE THIN, FOAM LAYER THAT COVERS THE SOLID PINE, WHICH MAKES UP THE RING'S FLOOR. THE FORKS — WHICH I'M TOLD CAN ALSO BE CALLED BLADES — THRUST FORWARD AND SLOWLY APPROACH THE LIFELESS BODY OF BIG BALE.

THOSE THINGS, THOSE… BLADES — IS THAT WHAT YOU CALLED THEM? — THEY LOOK AS IF THEY COULD TEAR RIGHT THROUGH FLESH.

HARRISON SLIDES THE PRONGS BETWEEN THE RING MAT AND BALE'S OVERSIZED FRAME, AND THE ONE ON THE LEFT HAS CAUGHT A FOLD OF THE BIG MAN'S TISSUE. BUT THERE'S NO GIVE FOR FLESH AGAINST A DAMNED MACHINE!

IS THAT FLESH OR BUTTER? YOU'D THINK THE LATTER GIVEN HOW EFFORTLESSLY THAT BLADE JUST SLICED THROUGH IT.

THE WOUND APPEARS TO BE OF THE SURFACE VARIETY, THANK BRADSHAW. BOTH BLADES ARE NOW BENEATH THE BEHEMOTH AND HIP HARRISON SWITCHES GEARS. THIS CAPACITY CROWD AT THE ROCK ARENA IS ON ITS FEET. YET, THERE'S LITTLE NOISE. I DON'T THINK OUR AUDIENCE CAN QUITE BELIEVE WHAT THEY'RE WITNESSING, AND NEITHER CAN I!

I CAN'T BELIEVE NOBODY'S DOING ANYTHING TO STOP THIS AND… WHAT'S HAPPENING NOW?

THE FORKS RAISE BIG BALE FROM THE MAT. THE GASP FROM THE CROWD ECHOES THE SOUND OF THE FORKLIFT'S HYDRAULICS.

THIS IS TOTAL RECKLESSNESS. TRASHINGTON IS LIFTING BIG BALE UP FURTHER AND FURTHER. BALE'S GOTTA BE TWENTY OR THIRTY FEET ABOVE THE GROUND ALREADY. IF HE FELL, THERE'D BE AN EARTHQUAKE. NOT TO MENTION, THE BIG GUY WOULD BE NOTHING MORE THAN A PUDDLE — OR MAYBE AN OCEAN — AFTER GOING SPLAT.

HARRISON REVERSES AWAY FROM THE RING. HE NEEDS TO GET TO A TABLE.

LOOK OUT BELOW! THAT BEARDED JABRONI'S SPINNING THE FORKLIFT TRUCK AROUND. BALE'S SWINGING AROUND UP THERE ABOVE THE HEADS OF OUR PAYING AUDIENCE. HE COULD KILL SOMEBODY.

THAT WAS A HIGH-RISK MOVE BUT HARRISON PULLED OFF THE TURN IN ONE. WHAT A MANOEUVRE!

WHERE'S HE GOING NOW?

HARRISON DRIVES BACK UP THE ENTRANCE RAMP. THE FORKLIFT STRUGGLES TO CLIMB BENEATH THE HUGE WEIGHT OF BIG BALE.

THAT'S A SLOW CRAWL FOR SURE. BUT WHERE IS HE TAKING BALE. THERE ARE NO TABLES ON THE STAGE... EXCEPT... OH NO!

YOU GOT THERE A SECOND AHEAD OF ME, FARQUAD. THE FORKLIFT REACHES THE STAGE AND HARRISON STEERS RIGHT. HE'S COMING TOWARDS US AND OUR COMMENTARY DESK.

WE'D BETTER GET OUT OF DODGE BEFORE A GIANT FALLS FROM THE SKY RIGHT INTO OUR LAPS.

...

...

APOLOGIES FOR THE MOMENT'S RADIO SILENCE, LADIES AND GENTLEMEN. IF YOU'VE JUST TUNED IN, WE HAVE QUITE A SCENE DEVELOPING HERE AT THE ROCK ARENA, AS HIP HARRISON HAS SCOOPED UP THE UNCONSCIOUS BIG BALE USING A FORKLIFT CRAFT AND HAS DRIVEN IT OVER TO OUR COMMENTARY DESK AT THE EDGE OF THE ENTRANCE STAGE.

LORD FARQUAD AND I HAVE EVACUATED THE AREA AND OUR WONDERFUL PRODUCTION TEAM HAS BEEN QUICK TO EQUIP US WITH BACK-UP HEADSETS SO THAT WE CAN CONTINUE TO COMMUNICATE WITH THOSE OF YOU WATCHING FROM HOME.

TRASHINGTON HASN'T THOUGHT THIS PLAN THROUGH. HE'S STILL GOT TO PUT BIG BALE

THROUGH THAT TABLE. HE CAN'T SHIFT THE BIG FELLA OFF THOSE BLADES.

HARRISON'S POSITIONED BALE ABOVE THE ANNOUNCE DESK AND IS TRYING EVERY SWITCH AND KNOB INSIDE THE CAB. HE MUST BE LOOKING FOR A WAY TO TIP THE BLADES SO THAT BALE FALLS THROUGH THE FURNITURE AND ENDS THIS MATCH. HOWEVER, IT APPEARS THAT FUNCTIONALITY IS NOT AVAILABLE.

HA! THERE'S NO WAY HE CAN PUSH BALE OFF THOSE PRONGS *MANUALLY*. WHEN IS HE GOING TO REALISE THAT ALL HE CAN DO IS FORFEIT?

I DON'T KNOW ABOUT THAT, BUT HE SEEMS TO HAVE REACHED ANOTHER REALISATION — THAT HE NEEDS TO CHANGE TACTICS. HE LOWERS THE BLADES, AND BALE, ONTO THE TABLE.

HE'S ASKING THE REFEREE SOMETHING.

PROBABLY CHECKING THAT WHATEVER HE HAS IN MIND CONSTITUTES A VICTORY GIVEN HOW BALE'S RUN THROUGH A TABLE EARLIER DIDN'T COUNT, DESPITE THE FACT HE IS STILL UNCONSCIOUS FROM IT ALMOST FIVE MINUTES LATER.

SHUT UP, I'M TRYING TO HEAR WHAT THEY'RE SAYING.

YOU CAN FILL US IN THEN, FARQUAD.

OKAY. WHAT TRASHINGTON ASKED WAS WHETHER THE REFEREE COULD AWARD HIM THE WIN IF HE WERE TO CONTINUE TO LOWER THE FORKS UNTIL THEY BROKE THE TABLE, GIVEN THAT BALE'S LYING ON TOP OF THEM. DREAD POINTED OUT THAT, TECHNICALLY, THE FORKS WOULD BE GOING THROUGH THE TABLE — NOT BALE — SO IT WOULDN'T END THE MATCH.

TRASHINGTON'S NOW TUGGING ON THE REF'S HEARTSTRINGS, SAYING THAT BALE NEEDS MEDICAL ATTENTION AND THAT HE DOESN'T WANT TO HURT THE BIG MAN ANYMORE IF HE DOESN'T NEED TO. HE'S ASKING IF THERE'S ANOTHER WAY THE MATCH COULD END WITH HARRISON ADVANCING TO THE TOURNAMENT FINAL. BUT THE REFEREE IS SHAKING HIS HEAD, AS YOU CAN ALL SEE.

IT'S INTERESTING THAT HARRISON WANTS TO PROTECT HIS OPPONENT'S HEALTH AND WELLBEING. YOU DON'T SEE TOO MUCH OF THAT HERE IN THE GALACTIC WRESTLING FEDERATION.

SEEMS LIKE A COP-OUT TO ME. HE KNOWS HE CAN'T WIN THIS MATCH AND... WHAT'S HE DOING NOW?

HARRISON RETRACTS THE FORKLIFT'S BLADES OUT FROM UNDERNEATH BIG BALE, WHO NOW LIES

PRONE ON OUR COMMENTARY DESK. HARRISON, MEANWHILE, CLIMBS UP TO THE ROOF OF THE CAB.

HE'S NOT GONNA JUMP, IS HE?

HE IS! HIP HARRISON LEAPS FROM WHAT MUST BE TWELVE FEET IN THE AIR AND… HE RICOCHETS OFF THE MASSIVE GUT OF BIG BALE.

THE TABLE DIDN'T EVEN BEND. LET ALONE BREAK.

AS EVERYBODY HAS JUST DISCOVERED, OUR COMMENTARY DESK ISN'T A REGULAR TABLE. IT'S SPECIALLY REINFORCED TO WITHSTAND A METEOR SHOWER TO ENSURE THAT, NO MATTER WHAT, THE SHOW CAN GO ON.

TRASHINGTON'S STANDING UP AND HE CAN'T QUITE BELIEVE THAT DIDN'T END THE MATCH.

ON THE PLUS SIDE, BALE'S STILL LYING PRONE ON THE TABLE. AT LEAST HARRISON HASN'T GOT TO START FROM SCRATCH. BUT HOW IS HE GOING TO CAUSE BIG BALE TO BREAK THROUGH THAT SURFACE TOP?

WHOSE SIDE ARE YOU ON?

I'M NOT ON ANY SIDE, FARQUAD. I'M AN IMPARTIAL ANNOUNCER, JUST AS YOU'RE MEANT TO BE.

WHATEVER. YOUR HERO HIP TRASHINGTON IS CLIMBING BACK INTO THE CAB OF THAT FORKLIFT. HE'S GOT TO FIND ANOTHER TABLE TO BREAK BALE THROUGH.

HE HAS SOMETHING ELSE IN MIND! THE RETRACTED BLADES RISE ONCE AGAIN, HIGH INTO THE AIR. WHAT IN BRADSHAW'S NAME IS HARRISON THINKING?

THOSE PRONGS ARE EVEN HIGHER THAN THEY WERE BEFORE.

THEY'VE GOT TO BE THIRTY-FIVE FEET IN THE AIR. THEY'VE REACHED THE HIGHEST POINT THEY CAN GO TO. HARRISON EXITS THE CAB AND CLIMBS ONTO THE ROOF. HE LOOKS UP AND AROUND, SURVEYING THE SCENE. THE CROWD CHEERS.

WHY ARE THEY CHEERING HIM? DON'T ENCOURAGE THIS IDIOT.

HARRISON SHRUGS AND BEGINS HIS ASCENT. HE CLIMBS… AND CLIMBS… AND HE REACHES THE BLADES AT A DIZZYING HEIGHT — PERHAPS FORTY FEET IN THE AIR — AND THIS CROWD HAS COME UNGLUED.

HE'S SUICIDAL! HOMICIDAL TOO. THIS CROWD IS BLOODTHIRSTY!

THE BEARDED BRUTE SHUFFLES TO THE TIPS OF THOSE BLADES. HE LOOKS UNCERTAIN AS HE PEERS DOWN.

I BET HE'S HAVING SECOND THOUGHTS. HE MUST BE — WHAT? — FORTY-FIVE OR MAYBE EVEN FIFTY FEET IN THE AIR. HE'LL HURT HIMSELF AS WELL AS HIS OPPONENT.

WELL, HE'S UP THERE NOW. ALL HE NEEDS TO DO TO FINISH THIS MATCH IS—

LOOK OUT!

FOR THE LOVE OF MANKIND! HIP HARRISON JUMPS FROM THE TOP OF THE FORKLIFT! HE SAILS THROUGH THE AIR, PICKING UP SPEED AND—

OUR TABLE'S SHATTERED INTO A MILLION PIECES! WHAT ABOUT BIG BALE? SOMEONE NEEDS TO CHECK ON HIM.

THE REFEREE CALLS FOR THE TIMEKEEPER TO RING THE BELL AND THIS ONE IS, MERCIFULLY, OVER. BIG BALE HAS CRASHED THROUGH NOT ONE BUT TWO TABLES.

THE FIRST IS STILL LYING IN SMITHEREENS INSIDE THE RING, BUT OUR COMMENTARY TABLE IS EVEN WORSE FOR WEAR BENEATH THAT MOUNTAIN OF SIANARDIANITY. GOOD GRIEF.

NEITHER MAN HAS MOVED AS WE TAKE A LOOK AT THE SLOW-MOTION REPLAY. THE IMPACT WAS SO SUDDEN THAT BIG BALE WAS RESTING ON THAT TABLE ONE MOMENT — THE NEXT, THE TABLE WAS NO MORE.

AS WE CAN SEE FROM THE REPLAY, HIP HARRISON EXECUTED A SWAN-LIKE SENTON BOMB. CHECK OUT HOW HE ARCHES HIS BACK AND THRUSTS HIS ARMS BEHIND HIM, KEEPING THEM STRAIGHT THE ENTIRE TIME, PULLING HIS SHOULDERS TOWARDS EACH OTHER.

THIS CAUSES HIS BODY TO FLIP, HEAD OVER HEELS, AND A LITTLE FURTHER, JUST BEFORE HIS OUTSTRETCHED SHOULDER BLADES LAND ON BALE. A PERFECT TWO-SEVENTY ROTATION.

I'VE GOTTA GIVE HIM CREDIT. TRASHINGTON COULDN'T HAVE PERFORMED THAT MOVE ANY BETTER THAN HE DID. BY SOMERSAULTING AS HE DID, THE BEARDED BUM GAINED MOMENTUM AS HE FELL, INCREASING IN VELOCITY BEFORE CRASH-LANDING ON BALE. HE HIT WITH MUCH MORE FORCE THAN HE WOULD HAVE DONE IF HE'D SIMPLY JUMPED. FOR PROOF OF JUST HOW HARD TRASHINGTON'S BODY COLLIDED WITH BALE'S, JUST CHECK OUT THE WAY THE BIG GUY'S BELLY RIPPLES IN SLOW MOTION AS THEY BOTH GO THROUGH OUR ANNOUNCE DESK.

WHAT A TURNOUT FOR THE BOOKS, FOLKS. MY BROADCAST COLLEAGUE IS PAYING HIP HARRISON A COMPLIMENT. ANY FARMERS WATCHING HAD BETTER CHECK OUTSIDE TO MAKE SURE THEIR PIG CATTLE AIN'T FLYING AWAY.

AS A FORMER COMPETITOR, I CAN APPRECIATE A WELL-EXECUTED MANOEUVRE. I STILL THINK THE GUY'S NOTHING BUT TRASH AND HOPE HE DIES IN A CRAFT ACCIDENT.

THAT'S THE FARQUAD WE ALL KNOW. LOVE HIM OR HATE HIM, I DON'T THINK HE CARES.

I REALLY DON'T. NOT UNLESS YOU'RE SIGNING MY PAYCHECKS.

BACK TO THE LIVE ACTION HERE ON THE ROCK: MEDICAL PERSONNEL ARE CURRENTLY TENDING TO BOTH WRESTLERS. THEY'RE TRYING TO FIGURE OUT THE BEST WAY TO GET BIG BALE UP ON A STRETCHER.

COME ON, GUYS! THE FORKLIFT IS RIGHT THERE.

TEN FEET OR SO TO THE RIGHT OF BALE, WHERE HIP HARRISON WOUND UP AFTER BOUNCING OFF BALE'S BELLY LIKE A TRAMPOLINE, WE HAVE SOME MOVEMENT.

PLEASE, SAY IT AIN'T SO. I HOPED HE'D BE HURT SO BAD THAT HE COULDN'T MAKE IT TO THE TOURNAMENT FINAL NEXT WEEK.

HIP HARRISON IS A SURVIVOR.

LIKE A COCKROACH.

THE TRAINERS HELP HIM TO HIS FEET AND THE BEARDED BRUTE IS SPEAKING TO THEM. HE'S CONSCIOUS AND REASSURES THEM HE CAN STAND ON HIS OWN TWO FEET. THEY LET HIM GO AND HE RAISES HIS ARMS IN CELEBRATION OF WHAT WAS A TRULY MAGNIFICENT VICTORY. A HARD-FOUGHT BATTLE THAT WILL GO DOWN IN THE HISTORY BOOKS. THAT SPECTACULAR JUMP FROM THE TOP OF THE FORKLIFT WILL SURELY BE INCLUDED IN HIGHLIGHT REELS UNTIL

THE END OF TIME — AND BY BRADSHAW, HE'S STILL STANDING, TRIUMPHANT.

WHO'S THAT RUNNING IN FROM BEHIND? IT'S—

FOR THE LOVE OF BRADSHAW, IT'S SNIPER SKY. HIP HARRISON'S OPPONENT IN THE TOURNAMENT FINAL NEXT WEEK TAKES THE BEARDED BRUTE DOWN WITH A HELLACIOUS CUTTER OUT OF NOWHERE!

HA! IF TRASHINGTON WASN'T IN BAD ENOUGH SHAPE GOING INTO NEXT WEEK'S FINAL, HE'LL BE IN AGONY NOW. HE JUST LANDED ON HIS UPPER BACK AS HE CRASH-LANDED ON BALE FROM SIXTY FEET UP, AND NOW THE CUTTER — ALSO KNOWN AS AN RKO IN SOME CIRCLES — FROM SNIPER SKY.

SNIPER SKY CLAIMS HIS OPPONENTS NEVER SEE IT COMING AND HIP HARRISON SURE AS HELL DIDN'T.

TRASHINGTON ONLY KNEW HIS FELLOW TOURNAMENT FINALIST WAS THERE WHEN SNIPER CAME FLYING PAST, WRAPPING THOSE LONG ARMS AROUND HIS NECK AND PULLING HIM FACE-FIRST TO THE GROUND.

IT ONLY TAKES A SECOND FOR SKY TO HIT THAT MOVE. IF THE WAY HE PULLS ON THE NECK ISN'T GNARLY ENOUGH, HIS OPPONENT'S FACE HITS THE GROUND WITH THE FULL FORCE OF SNIPER'S BODY WEIGHT.

IT GIVES ME GREAT PLEASURE TO SAY THAT HIP HARRISON IS OUT COLD. HE MAY HAVE MADE IT TO THE TOURNAMENT FINAL, BUT THERE'S NO WAY HE'S GETTING PAST SNIPER SKY.

SKY RAISES *HIS* HANDS IN THE AIR AS THIS CROWD SHOWERS HIM IN, WELL, SOME OF THEM ARE BOOING. PERHAPS HARRISON IS DEVELOPING A SWELL OF SUPPORT FROM A PORTION OF OUR FANBASE.

STUPID IDIOTS.

ON THAT NOTE, WE'RE JUST ABOUT OUT OF TIME. THANKS FOR JOINING US, LADIES AND GENTLEMEN, AND FOR ALLOWING THE GALACTIC WF INTO YOUR HOMES. NO MATTER WHAT MY BROADCAST COLLEAGUE SAYS, KNOW THAT WE APPRECIATE AND RESPECT YOU ALL.

YEAH, YEAH — HANG ON A SECOND. WHO'S THAT CHECKING ON TRASHINGTON? IS THAT IVY JANE? WHAT'S SHE DOING HERE?

I DON'T KNOW. WHOEVER IT IS HAS THEIR BACK TOWARD US, BUT WE'RE ALL OUT OF TI—

Previously...

Ivy Jane stood out from the rest of the females on the Galactic WF roster. She often wondered why in the hell they'd hired her. Sure, she had placed in the top five of *Sianard Wrestling Illustrated*'s 100 Best Female Wrestlers of the Cycle as a rookie and topped the list during her second cycle in the sport. And sure, Ivy was the youngest wrestler of any gender to win a title belt on her home planet when she was crowned Nejan Female Champion at just seventeen cycles of age for Neja Championship Wrestling. But ever since signing with the Galactic WF, which came with an initial jolt of fanfare given the reputation and name she'd built for herself on the independent wrestling circuit, she'd found herself trapped in a constant struggle. The big leagues presented tougher battles than Ivy had ever imagined.

That's not to say Ivy Jane had a tougher time inside the squared circle. In fact, the in-ring competition was a doddle, particularly compared to some of the wily, grizzled veterans that toiled away on the indie scene. The Galactic WF hired most of the females on its roster because of their aesthetics. If you looked good in skimpy clothing and were athletic enough to roll around on the mat during matches that many backstage within the company — not to mention troll-like fans on SIN message boards — referred to as 'bathroom breaks', you were handed a contract and taught the basics to get by with. As for women who'd grown up wanting to be wrestlers, just like their male heroes, you worked for a hotdog and a handshake on the indies, and would never be taken seriously enough by the fans to make any actual money.

Ivy became the exception to the rule. At nineteen, with a trio of championship belts clinging to her waist and draped over her shoulders, she didn't want to do anything else with her life but wrestle. However, when she looked around the dressing room of whichever show she was on that weekend, she also realised that she didn't want to waste her talent in front of small crowds that comprised maybe a couple of hundred people, going out there and leaving her all in the ring in exchange for a pretzel and, perhaps, if the show was sold out, twenty bucks. Not only was the payment piss-poor or, in most cases, non-existent, but she would need to get a 'proper job' to pay the bills and support her 'weekend hobby'; at least, that's what the older women frequently told her.

What made the situation all the more frustrating for the young Ivy Jane was that the Galactic WF would frequently sign male wrestlers that she had been on shows with enough times to know they weren't as good as her. They'd been called up because this was just another a male-dominated industry. And they'd sure as hell have a better position on the card than any of their female counterparts, with better pay to boot! Skill, talent and work ethic didn't come into it.

With her bright, red hair and pale grey Nejan complexion, it wasn't as if the powers that be at the Galactic Wrestling Federation were knocking down her door to come in and work the 'bathroom breaks' anyway. Not without peroxiding her locks and enhancing her chest. Rather than follow the trail laid by those before her, Ivy Jane forged her own path.

***

She needed to do something bold and brash. Something that had never been done before. Something a little controversial that might send a few shockwaves towards the Galactic WF bigwigs. Ivy's plan came to her the moment a male wrestler by the name of Jazzy G came bursting into the locker-room one weekend at an indie show on Chase, bragging about how he had just been signed by the Galactic Wrestling Federation because they had 'finally recognised talent'.

As far as Ivy Jane was concerned, Jazzy wasn't even talented enough to lick her boots clean, let alone compete on the biggest stage the sport had to offer.

That night, Jazzy G competed in the main event and picked up an easy win over a young trainee. The Chase Wrestling Corporation — a small, bush-league federation with a name that sounded more impressive than its shows ever were — booked the match to go on last because its owner wanted to entice a few last-minute attendees through the doors by promoting the chance to see a future Galactic WF superstar.

As Jazzy celebrated to end the night's festivities, Ivy Jane took her chance. She approached the sound technician backstage and threatened him into playing her entrance music. It took little effort; a raised fist was enough to do the trick.

As the music changed from 50 Cent to something so full of screams and shouts that it was unintelligible through the tiny venue's tinny P.A. system, Jazzy G stopped dead in his tracks. His triumphant smile flattened, then dropped completely. When he saw Ivy Jane step through the curtain, his smile returned at the thought that this chick, while not as hot as some of the tail he'd encounter in the Galactic WF, was more than adequate to see him to a good time on his last night performing in hick towns.

'What are you grinning about?' Ivy Jane had a microphone in her hand. As she climbed into the ring, Jazzy G noted the pissed-off expression on her face. She'd look hotter if she smiled, he thought. And a blue tan wouldn't hurt either.

'I hear you're jetting off to The Rock,' Ivy continued, 'and I wanted you to know that I think it's bullshit.'

The crowd, which had gone from cheering Jazzy's easy victory to standing in confused silence, cheered once again at the use of profanity.

As the noise abated, Ivy continued: 'We all know you got the call because of your size and what those in the mainstream might call "good looks". I feel I should clarify that you're not my type, just to make sure your head doesn't grow too big. Not rough enough around the edges — a tad boring, you could say. And not only that, but you're a talentless hack. You have less skill in your entire clumsy frame than I have in my little toe.'

Jazzy G nervously glanced from side to side and shrugged at the crowd. 'What are you getting at?' he asked Ivy Jane as he turned to face her again.

'What I'm getting at is that I'm better than you and, deep down, you know it. What I'm getting at is that I'm the most decorated athlete on the independent wrestling scene and your future employer hasn't shown me any interest, yet they'll employ a worthless meathead like you. What I'm getting at is that I want to prove my worth by whooping your ass right here, right now!'

The crowd, a hundred-strong or thereabouts, cheered once more.

'Hey, Ref! Get back out here,' Ivy Jane called. 'We have a bonus match tonight. Unless soon-to-be galactic superstar, Jazzy G, doesn't think he's good enough to take me on.'

Jazzy smirked. He snatched the microphone from Ivy's hand. 'You think you can embarrass me? Is that it? Jealous are you, babe?

Well, I don't think I can beat you; I *know* I can beat you. It normally goes against my moral code to hit a woman, but I think you've earned the right by running your big mouth. Come on, Ref! You heard the little girl. Get back out here!'

Ivy Jane's frame was perhaps half the volume of the muscle-bound Jazzy G. But what she lacked comparatively in size, she could more than make up for in skill. There was a reason she had won so many championships and accolades early in her career. From her very first training session, Ivy Jane had grasped two things that some wrestlers could go their entire lives without understanding: ring psychology and ring awareness. She knew that, when faced with a bigger opponent, the key was to use her speed against them, as well as their own momentum when the chance presented itself, and how to use their surroundings to her advantage.

When the bell rang and Jazzy G charged towards her, attempting to take Ivy Jane's head off with a vicious clothesline, Ivy ducked just enough to feel Jazzy's rock-solid arm brush against the hairs on her head. She turned quickly to see Jazzy hit the ropes sternum-first, which caused him to stumble backward, towards her. While Ivy had no chance of ever dead lifting Jazzy to deliver a suplex, she now found herself in a position to deliver one of the German variety, using his own backward momentum. In the split second that Jazzy backpedalled three paces, Ivy Jane wrapped her arms around his midsection as far as they would reach (he was too thick for her hands to meet in the middle) and arched her back down toward the mat, pulling the surprised Jazzy G with her. It worked a treat; Jazzy's momentum allowed Ivy to throw him over her head as she landed on the canvas, the back of *his* head crashing to the mat half a second later.

The crowd roared at the sight of a 120-pound female delivering a snap suplex to a 300-pound beast.

Dazed, Jazzy G stumbled back up to his feet. As he regained his bearings, he turned to find Ivy Jane on the top rope a moment before she flew towards him with her legs outstretched. Her thighs landed on Jazzy's shoulders and, in one smooth motion, she wrapped her ankles behind his neck and once again threw herself backwards, down towards the mat, pulling Jazzy with her. Only, this time, she didn't land on the mat but swung below Jazzy's legs, dragging him head-over-heels. As Jazzy landed on his back, Ivy Jane held onto his calf muscles with all her might; together, they resembled a ball of flesh and spandex, and she had his shoulders pinned to the mat. Jazzy tried everything he could to wriggle free, rolling from side to side and attempting to split his legs to break Ivy's grip on them. But it was to no avail as the referee slid into position to gain a clear view of Jazzy's shoulders pinned to the mat, and counted one-two-three.

Ivy Jane released the hold the moment she heard the bell ring and jumped up, arms pumping in pure jubilation. She'd been confident that she could defeat Jazzy G, but couldn't believe it had only taken two moves to get the job done. The tiny crowd could well have filled a hundred-thousand-seat stadium with the amount of sound they generated. They were going banana! For a moment, Ivy could sense, almost feel, Jazzy G's eyes boring into the back of her head. Anticipating a post-match attack, she spun round, guard up. However, the downtrodden Jazzy only shook his head and slunk out of the ring. This had been his night of celebration and some small hick girl had stolen it from him.

Fan-shot footage of the match between Ivy Jane and Jazzy G went viral on SIN message boards. Within days, Jazzy G had seen his Galactic WF contract revoked, although Ivy Jane still heard nothing from the powers that be.

***

While Ivy Jane still received radio silence from what many on the independent circuit called 'The Fed,' her star shone brighter than ever thanks to her viral victory. Every small-time promoter in Sianard wanted the woman that SIN comments sections had crowned 'The Man Eater' on their show — the nickname was marketing gold. She received offers for immediate championship matches with her choice of male or female title to contend for. Any show she agreed to work was an instant sellout. Although her impromptu match with Jazzy G was a shot fired towards the Galactic Wrestling Federation, Ivy Jane had inadvertently sparked a boom in business for indie wrestling.

She made the most of her increased demand, working every conceivable date to make as much money as possible (it turned out promoters had bucks to pay after all — no more wrestling for free popcorn, a small soda and *the exposure*), but kept her eyes on the prize. If The Man Eater caught wind of The Fed signing another indie wrestler, she would book herself on his final independent show to repeat the challenge she made to Jazzy G. The crowds at these small shows, often comprising the most die-hard of wrestling fans, caught on, booing the Galactic WF's new signee and cheering Ivy Jane as the defender of the small leagues.

The first few new Galactic WF recruits arrogantly accepted the challenge. Sure, she'd beaten that loser, Jazzy G, and a couple of other pencil-neck geeks, but this time she was up against the real deal — a future Galactic Heavyweight Champion. Only, time and time again, Ivy Jane brought their egos back down to size — and their shoulders to the mat. She beat Marko Polo with a quick roll-up cover; outsmarted "Switchknife" Blake Silver, defeating him via countout in what became a race back to the ring; and caught Chips McCoy in an armlock, forcing him to the canvas and wrenching back in a move she'd adopted from one of Earth's great female champions, the Dis-Arm-Her — a name that certainly added insult to injury of men with fragile sensibilities. He, of course, tapped out.

McCoy and Polo lost their Galactic WF contracts as a result, while Switchknife had his deal with The Fed renegotiated to include further training and less money because of his potentially avoidable loss.

Ivy Jane would have been lying if she said she wasn't nervous before going out to face the largest of the Galactic WF signees she challenged. Bain The Pain was an absolute monster among men, and it came as a surprise to just about everyone that he had passed The Fed's mandatory drug testing before getting hired —

especially to those who had the displeasure of sharing a locker-room with Bain as he injected his ass with some sort of glowing, green substance that certainly wasn't natural.

As Ivy entered the ring to challenge Bain, the big beef head waved her off, exited the ring, and walked away. Bain would apparently not risk jeopardising his dreams of fame and fortune in a match with a girl. Ivy saw this as her greatest victory yet — she was clearly getting somewhere after all if the big men were now scared, or at least hesitant, to face her. If she was a conspiracy theorist, she may also have wondered whether his soon-to-be bosses had instructed Bain to walk away from her challenge. Perhaps she was on The Fed's radar after all. And she enjoyed a good conspiracy theory.

Every male wrestler she then confronted turned tail and left the ring. Usually without saying a word. As Ivy Jane led the crowds in chants of 'Coward' and 'Scaredy Rat,' they would quietly walk to their dressing rooms. It was almost symbolic, the way they disappeared behind the curtain — or so Ivy thought — as they'd never be seen on an independent wrestling show again and, often, would have undergone some 'rebranding' before popping up on television screens several cycles later. Not only were they walking away from Ivy Jane and the challenge she presented, but they were also walking away from life as they knew it.

While she was still very much a hot commodity — easily the most popular wrestler and biggest draw on the independent scene — Ivy Jane saw her offers dry up like an RKO out of nowhere.

Promoters stopped calling, and she had to pick up the telephonator to call *them* for the first time in a while. When she wasn't put through to a voicemail machine, she was promptly told by bookers, who'd been bending over backwards to get her on their cards just weeks earlier, that they were too busy to speak and that they'd call her back. But they never did. Something was up.

The conspiracy theorist in Ivy Jane came to the forefront of her mind once again and accurately filled in the blanks. The Galactic WF had pressured all the small, independent promoters around the galaxy to stop booking her, to prevent further embarrassment of their prospects. The only shows she could get on were those that didn't feature The Fed's newly signed talent as they finished up their previously contracted dates, or even those who were on the Galactic WF's radar as an up-and-comer. Ivy Jane had been relegated to the smallest of shows, featuring rosters of trainees and rookies, where the pay was nothing more than the hotdogs and handshakes she'd outgrown.

Ivy Jane loved the business, despite its many flaws. Not willing to allow the Galactic WF to blackball her, she hatched a new plan. It was simple, really. She'd do just as she'd done before. The difference now was that she would have to fund herself for a while and risk arrest.

***

When a promoter next informed Ivy Jane that they would not be booking her for their show — a card featuring rumoured Galactic WF signee Bad News Booger — Ivy Jane bought herself a ticket.

She even paid the extra two bucks to secure a seat in the front row. For the first time, she was thankful that while the Galactic WF could command hundreds of bucks for a seat in the nosebleed sections of The Rock, independent wrestling could barely charge ten bucks for a ringside seat. As a wrestler, of course, she wished The Fed didn't have such a headlock applied to the sport so that everyone could get an even shake of the paying customers.

Still, she had made it inside, and it didn't break the bank. Playing the role of a fan, Ivy wore a replica mask of her favourite Las Esferan luchador, Gran Machismo, while also covering her body art with a baggy sweater. She couldn't risk anyone recognising her before Booger was in the ring as she didn't doubt she would be swiftly escorted from the gymnasium — although, if that happened, she was prepared to create a scene that would surely be captured on tape and go viral. Doing so would at least answer the question a good deal of indie wresting fans had been posting on SIN message boards, asking where Ivy Jane had been lately. The prevailing rumour was that she must be pregnant. Why else would a female stop wrestling?

Nobody questioned the lone luchador sitting in the front row. More than half of the wrestlers on the card had shared a locker-room with Ivy over the cycles and none of them seemed to recognise her. Some even interacted with her, the mask inviting its fair share of attention. She was careful to only respond with physical gestures so as not to risk being identified by her notoriously raspy voice.

Ivy Jane spent the entire show perched on the edge of her seat. Not because of the high-octane action she was witnessing up close, but because she was anxious about what she was about to do. The show was relatively short, clocking in at just over two hours. But to Ivy, it felt as long as Battlestar Galactica 32, which held the record for the Galactic WF's longest ever event at a whopping six hours and fifty-one minutes. Therefore, when Bad News Booger finally entered the ring for his main event showcase against some unheard-of rookie, Ivy leapt from her seat, hopped over the barricade, and slid into the ring before the match had even started. She couldn't stomach the wait any longer — not while Booger picked up an easy win and showboated in front of the crowd.

Booger's face betrayed his tough-guy demeanour when the masked fan entered the ring. A look of alarm flashed across it. There was no security at a small-time show like this. He would have to deal with the intruder himself while the promoter rallied the other wrestlers backstage to go out and help. But as Ivy Jane removed her mask, revealing her long, red hair, Bad News visibly relaxed. This was no threat. It was *just* a girl. Was she after an autograph? Maybe she wanted something more — a taste of the Booger, perhaps?

After a few seconds of grinning like a splorg in heat, Bad News Booger finally realised who the redhead standing across the ring was. Not some ring rat groupie looking for a night of action away from the ring. Ivy Jane was looking for action, but it wouldn't come at Booger's pleasure.

'What are you doing here?' Booger yelled. The audience had already come unglued, screaming louder than they had for anyone else all night.

'You know why I'm here,' said Ivy. 'Are you going to accept my challenge of your own free will or are you just another sell-out coward?'

Sell-out Cow-ard! Sell-out Cow-ard! Wrestling crowds are always quick to pick up a new catchy chant.

'I have nothing to prove to you,' said Booger. 'I'm not giving you the attention. I'm not giving you a match. I'm not giving you nothing.'

'Aw, that's a shame. I guess I'll just have to beat it out of you then.'

Ivy Jane's dropkick landed on Booger's chest before he had time to flinch. Bad News staggered backwards into the ropes and Ivy Jane, who had sprung back up to her feet as soon as she landed from the dropkick, charged and met him there with a thunderous clothesline that sent Booger flailing over the top rope and to the floor. To his credit, Bad News Booger landed on his feet, although there wasn't much stick to the landing. Embarrassed, he threw an arm towards the ring while turning away, waving off Ivy and her challenge before making a swift exit.

The crowd sang a chorus of *Na Na Hey Hey Kiss Him Goodbye,* following which they filled the room with chants of *I-vy! I-vy! I-vy!*

'It appears you're still owed a main event,' Ivy cried.

The crowd responded accordingly.

'Then, how about Booger's scheduled opponent come out here and face me instead?'

Several seconds ticked by until a nervous trainee shuffled through the curtain. It looked as if someone had forcibly pushed him from the other side.

As the kid nervously climbed into the ring, Ivy asked: 'What is your name?'

'M-M-Maxamilian, M-M-Mam,' he stuttered.

'Well, M-M-M-Max, let's make you famous.' Ivy grabbed his hand, flung him forwards and pulled him back, catching him with a ripcord clothesline. The move resembled a ballroom dance before Ivy's arm almost decapitated the poor boy.
The referee on standby called for the bell to be rung as Ivy landed the move, and he called for it to be rung again just three seconds later.

'What do you think you're doing?' the promoter screamed when Ivy Jane had the audacity to walk backstage after hijacking the show. He was a short, stout chap who went by the name of Gentleman Jack. Ivy had worked for him before, in exchange for a medium nachos and small soda.

'What do I think I'm doing?' Ivy yelled back at him. 'Did you see all those cameras pointed at me out there? Did you hear the reaction that none of the other wrestlers received tonight? I'll tell you what I'm doing: I'm making sure your next show sells out at the mere possibility I might show my face. You're welcome, Jacky Boy!'

Bad News Booger was nowhere to be seen. He wasn't anywhere to be seen on Galactic WF television either… unlike Ivy Jane.

***

Ivy's unsanctioned match against Maxamilian renewed the buzz surrounding her on SIN forums and wrestling news sites. Online commentators ferociously debated whether the stunt was genuine or planned. Some argued that Gentleman Jack must have paid Ivy Jane to make the surprise appearance at the end of the show, planting her in the crowd to add to the drama. Pro wrestling may be a competitive sport in Sianard but promoters weren't above adding a sprinkle of showmanship. Other message board marks even claimed it was 'obvious' that Ivy Jane had signed with the Galactic WF and that this was an intricate marketing ploy to build up her name value before she finally arrived in the big leagues.

'Just wait until she shows up in the front row at The Rock,' one commenter by the screen name of 1-2-3 Kid posted on the *Wrestling With My Thoughts* forum. 'The crowd will go completely nuts. They know what they're doing. They'll have an instant star and top contender on their hands in the female division.'

Audiences at wrestling shows across the galaxy began chanting Ivy's name from the moment they entered the venue until the ring announcer bid them a safe journey home.

I-vy Jane! I-vy Jane! I-vy Jane!

It was relentless but didn't initially affect the Galactic WF's universe. The fans at smaller, independent shows were more likely to be die-hard aficionados who were knowledgeable of SIN speculation and rumour, whereas crowds at The Rock, although including those same die-hards, were diluted by casual fans — the mainstream audience, who watched the shows on TV then forgot all about the world of wrestling until it reappeared on their screens a week later — and families attending for a fun night out with the kids.

So it was that, over several weeks, small pockets of the crowd started chants of *I-vy Jane!* during Galactic WF broadcasts. And as with any movement that gains momentum organically, whether in politics or music or pro wrestling, those chants grew louder and louder at an incredible rate, and there was no stopping them once the ball got rolling.

Each week, more and more fans caught on to the chants. Casual viewers either educated themselves on who Ivy Jane was or joined in with the cheers just because everyone else was doing it. Soon enough, the entire arena was chanting for Ivy Jane at Galactic WF shows. Viewers could hear the cries clearly through their televisions as the live audiences verbally highjacked the show to support a wrestler who wasn't even there. Herd mentality at its finest.

The Ivy Jane chants became the cool thing for Galactic WF crowds to do. A mild form of rebellion amidst the escapism. It pissed Mr Montgomery off, royally.

While this was going on, Ivy Jane maintained radio silence. There was an Earth saying about how absence makes the heart grow fonder and, in Ivy's case, remaining out of the spotlight was only making her star shine brighter, with crowds everywhere clamouring to see her. She once again had small-time promoters keeping her telephonator off the hook, but she ignored them and their generous offers. There was only one call The Man Eater would answer and, after months of crowds chanting her name, she finally received it.

'Hello, this is Sovereign Noble, commissioner of the Galactic Wrestling Federation,' the Kingsman on the other end of the line proclaimed. 'May I ask, is this Ivy Jane with whom I am speaking?'

***

It took several cycles longer than it should have, given her talent, but the Galactic Wrestling Federation finally signed Ivy Jane to a contract. Even though she would appear on television regularly, performing in front of much larger audiences than she had been used to, the pay was barely more than she had made in her best cycles as an independent wrestler. Still, the figure listed on her contract was a guaranteed minimum, and there was plenty of opportunity to earn more in merchandise sales, not to mention that the bigger stars were paid extra for special appearances and other media projects. Ivy didn't hold out much hope as far as the extra earning potential was concerned, since she didn't possess the supermodel looks of the 'top' female talent, as well as the female division's poor placement on the card. But Ivy Jane *was* confident in her abilities and knew she'd be running roughshod through the division in no time. Ivy Jane believed that by becoming a champion, she might alter the perception of female wrestlers in the Galactic WF.

The Fed's management had other ideas.

At first, Ivy Jane didn't question the fact that she was only matched up against freshly signed former models who possessed very limited in-ring training. They were greener than grass and The Man Eater picked up a series of easy wins. Ivy appreciated that, as a new signee herself, she had to start at the bottom of the totem pole, so to speak. Nothing she had done prior to her first appearance on Galactic WF television counted here. Ivy simply needed to work her way to the top, which was fine with her.

However, those greener-than-grass yet extremely attractive women started getting booked in matches versus top contenders, while Ivy Jane remained at the bottom of the pile, only ever matched up against even newer recruits. In fact, most of her bouts were dark contests — untelevised matches that only the live audience sees before the cameras roll — in which she faced women not even signed to The Fed yet, but who had 'the right look'. Nobody told Ivy to her face, but she quickly worked out that she had been assigned the role of gatekeeper to the female division, taking part in try-out matches for her opponents. Although Ivy Jane was victorious in every single one of these contests, management would deem whether the inexperienced prospect was 'tough enough' to withstand a career in the ring. If so, said prospect's own prospects would immediately be better than Ivy Jane's own, as the former Man Eater was rarely featured on television and never given a real shot to prove herself as a top contender.

The Galactic WF had hired Ivy Jane — one of the best wrestlers in the entire galaxy — to bury her career.

Still, Ivy remained confident in her abilities and even made a few friends. In the female locker-room, she soon discovered that although the vast majority of those in the division had never even watched a wrestling match prior to their Galactic WF try-out, most had gained a strong appreciation for the athleticism, discipline and pageantry of it all. Ivy Jane found that the former models and cheerleaders sitting atop the division had developed into some fierce fighters, providing adage to the old saying that looks can be deceiving. The Galactic WF Female Champion, Sasha Stratosphere, was every bit as good as anyone Ivy Jane had come up against on the independent scene. Stratosphere may have been handed an opportunity based on her looks, but there was no denying the work she'd put in to become the best wrestler she could be. Sasha was dedicated to the craft in a way that many lifelong fans getting into the business simply weren't. It was one thing to *want* to be a wrestler, but it was another to put in the work to actually *be* a wrestler.

'It's a shame they don't treat you as seriously as they should,' Ivy said to Sasha one night in the female locker-room. Sasha had just defended her championship against some flavour of the month who wasn't even fit to lace up her boots, let alone wrestler for the title.

'Who? The fans or the office?' Sasha replied.

'Both.'

Sasha smiled and gripped her championship belt tightly. 'I just hope, if I keep putting in the work, that one day they will view me as credible and, by extension, view the entire female division as legit. We've got some badass poodwinks in this locker-room and don't you think for one moment that I don't know who you are, Ms Man Eater. I've seen what you're capable of and, if I get my way, you and I will meet in that ring one day with this—' Sasha patted the faceplate of her title belt '—on the line. I could certainly do with the challenge.'

From that moment on, Ivy and Sasha nodded to each other whenever they met backstage, respect flowing both ways. They each kept racking up the wins, remaining undefeated, although many of Ivy's did not appear on record.

Another relationship that Ivy Jane forged backstage was with someone she'd encountered a few times on the indies, yet never spoken to. After twisting some wide-eyed doe into a pretzel and racking up another win, Ivy Jane made her way towards to the female locker-room with her head down. The producers were always quick to speak to her opponents after a match, but never bothered checking on Ivy. On this evening, she overheard them offering yet another contract to a pretty young thing who couldn't last five minutes in the ring. Both literally and figuratively.

Ivy marched sullenly through the backstage area when a gruff voice from behind said, 'Hey, keep your chin up! Don't let them break you.'

Ivy turned around to see Hip Harrison leaning against the wall. She hadn't noticed him as she'd skulked past. 'What if I'm already broken?' she asked.

'Well, if that's the case — which I doubt — then don't let them see it.'

'Why do you doubt it?'

'Because you're Ivy Jane. The Man Eater! From what I've seen, you don't break easy.'

'Maybe not. But it feels like I may not belong here. Perhaps I'd be better off going back to where I came from.'

'Sure, if that's what you want. But you worked your ass off to get here and have proven yourself more than reliable in doing what *they* want from you. I wouldn't step away from the grind now if I were you. I have a feeling that things are about to get good around here.'

Hip Harrison hadn't intended for that last sentence to serve as a pickup line. Yet, following months of post-match conversations and pep-talks, a budding romance emerged from the foundation of friendship that was laid. It was not only Ivy leaning on Hip for support either, as The Bearded Brute confided in her what he knew about Mr Montgomery, as well as his anxieties in chasing the Galactic WF Heavyweight Championship and exposing The Fed's chairman to the citizens of Sianard.

Hip Harrison and Ivy Jane became each other's rocks, although they kept their relationship secret. This was Harrison's idea, as he feared the repercussions Ivy Jane might face should someone as powerful as Mr Montgomery discover her link to the proverbial thorn in his side. The best-case scenario would see her out of a job. But Ivy didn't care about that. She only played along in keeping the extent of their relationship under wraps because it made Hip feel better.

What didn't make Hip feel better was getting knocked out with a cutter from behind on the steel grating of the entrance stage. Having witnessed Harrison's head crashing into the unforgiving stage floor from behind the curtain, there was not a chance in hell that Ivy Jane was going to keep her distance. She didn't hesitate in running to The Bearded Brute's side.

Who cared if anyone saw? So what if it was all on camera? What were they going to do? Fire her? Let them! At least then, she could return to wrestling formidable opponents and winning championships.

What The Man Eater didn't count on was that Mr Montgomery saw firing somebody as too easy. If the vindictive chairman held a grudge against you, he would toy with you first, before chewing you up and spitting you back out.

WEEK FOUR

'I'm booked tonight.'

'Who's the newb this time? Will I have seen her on a billboard?'

'No, I mean I'm *booked*. As in, I'm on the actual card. I'm going to be on TV.'

'That's great news.' Hip Harrison was cautiously pleased for Ivy Jane. It really was great that she was back where she belonged — in front of the biggest audience possible against a proper opponent. But the office's reasons for pushing Ivy into a more prominent position on the card made him anxious.

Following last week's show, two things of note had happened. Hip spent a couple of nights in hospital, undergoing a series of tests to make sure his head was in the right place (his brain to be more specific) following the cutter he'd fallen victim to at the hands of Sniper Sky on the entrance stage. Meanwhile, Ivy Jane had discovered renewed fan support as a result of her impromptu appearance at the end of the broadcast. SIN message boards were abuzz at the sudden re-emergence of The Man Eater and speculation was running wild as to why she had come to the aid of The Bearded Brute.

Hip knew that if the Galactic WF kept Ivy off the televised show, the chants of 'I-vy Jane!' would ring relentlessly throughout the arena once again, interrupting the scheduled programming. The best-case scenario for The Fed was for Ivy to have developed a little ring rust, having whittled away her talents against inexperienced cheerleaders, resulting in a series of losses against active members of the female roster until it was deemed safe to pull her from the show again. There was also likely some form of repercussion in Ivy's near future for having publicly aligned herself with The Bearded Brute. Harrison knew from personal experience that, once Mr Montgomery had a reason to dislike you, he would not cut you from the team. Instead, you'd find yourself backed into a corner every week.

Still, Hip was fighting back well enough, and no-one puts Ivy in a corner. So, for now, he was happy for her.

'So, who are you up against tonight?'

'Judge Judith.'

'She's quite the striker.'

'I know, but I'll be ready to block. She won't know what's hit her. Anyway, are *you* sure you're ready for Sniper Sky? I am worried after what he did to you last week, not to mention the toll the last few weeks have taken. I mean, you jumped off a forklift from — what? — sixty feet in the air. Your body must be screaming for a rest.'

'I'd be lying if I said I wasn't feeling sore. But I can't rest now. There's just one more match between me and a championship bout with Judas. It's everything I've been working towards and my one shot at exposing Mr Montgomery for what he is and what he's hiding. Besides, when I win tonight, I'll have a few weeks to recover before the pay-per-view.'

'*When* you win? Someone's confident.' Ivy kissed Hip on the cheek. 'But you know, there's no way they're going to let you rest up before a match with Judas.'

***

WELCOME BACK, LADIES AND GENTLEMEN, AND IF YOU'RE ONLY JUST JOINING US, YOU'VE PICKED A HELLUVA TIME AS WE'RE JUST MOMENTS AWAY FROM OUR MAIN EVENT, WHICH CARRIES EXTREMELY HIGH STAKES AHEAD OF THE UPCOMING BATTLESTAR GALACTICA PAY-PER-VIEW.

THAT'S RIGHT, GENE. THE WINNER OF OUR MAIN EVENT TONIGHT, PITTING SNIPER SKY AGAINST THAT PARTY POOPER, HIP TRASHINGTON, WILL BE NAMED THE NEW NUMBER ONE CONTENDER AND GO ON TO FACE JUDAS AT BATTLESTAR GALACTICA WITH THE GALACTIC WF HEAVYWEIGHT

CHAMPIONSHIP ON THE LINE IN WHAT IS SURE TO BE THE MOST ANTICIPATED MATCH OF THE YEAR.

THE CLASH BETWEEN SKY AND HARRISON GETS UNDER WAY IN MERE MOMENTS, SO STICK WITH US. IF YOU HAVE ONLY JUST JOINED US, YOU'VE MISSED AN INCREDIBLE NIGHT OF ACTION, INCLUDING THE RETURN OF IVY JANE, WHO HASN'T LOST A STEP SINCE WE LAST SAW HER ALMOST A FULL CYCLE AGO, AS SHE DEFEATED JUDGE JUDITH WITH A BEAUTIFUL NECKBREAKER/HEADLOCK COMBO.

I'LL GIVE JANE HER DUE. SHE WRESTLED A GREAT MATCH. BUT THERE'S JUST SOMETHING I DON'T LIKE ABOUT HER. PROBABLY SOMETHING TO DO WITH GETTING TOO CLOSE TO THE TRASH AT THE END OF LAST WEEK'S SHOW. LEAVES A FUNNY TASTE IN THE MOUTH.

HERE WE GO, FOLKS! WE'RE BEING TREATED TO THE SOULFUL VOICE OF SEAL, AS FLY LIKE AN EAGLE PLAYS THROUGH THE P.A. SYSTEM HERE AT THE ROCK ARENA, SIGNIFYING THE ARRIVAL OF SNIPER SKY.

I'VE ALWAYS LIKED SNIPER SKY, AND HIS EXCELLENT TASTE IN ENTRANCE MUSIC CERTAINLY HELPS HIS CAUSE. I ALSO LOVED WHAT HE DID TO HIP TRASHINGTON LAST WEEK AND HOPE WE SEE MORE OF THE SAME RIGHT NOW.

SKY APPEARS CONFIDENT AS HE CLIMBS THE TURNBUCKLE TO POSE FOR THE CROWD. HE BASKS IN A WAVE OF FLASH PHOTOGRAPHY AS IF HE HASN'T A CARE IN THE GALAXY.

I SHOULDN'T THINK HE'S GOT TOO MUCH TO WORRY ABOUT, GIVEN HALF THE BATTLE HAS ALREADY BEEN WON. IF HIP HARRISON ISN'T STILL RECOVERING FROM A HEAD INJURY FOLLOWING THAT CUTTER, HE'S AT LEAST GOT TO BE AT A MENTAL DISADVANTAGE GOING INTO THIS MATCH. HE KNOWS SNIPER SKY CAN HIT THAT MOVE AGAIN, ANYWHERE, ANY TIME.

WE'VE SEEN SKY ADOPT THIS STRATEGY BEFORE. HE'S NOT JUST TRYING TO SOFTEN HIS OPPONENTS PHYSICALLY BY TAKING THEM DOWN BEFORE A MATCH, HE'S ALSO GETTING INTO THEIR HEADS; TO THROW THEM OFF THEIR GAME.

OH, MY EARS! MAKE IT STOP!

YOU STOP. HERE COMES SKY'S OPPONENT, HIP HARRISON. THERE'S NO SHOWBOATING FOR THE CROWD FROM THE BEARDED BRUTE AS HE MARCHES TOWARDS THE RING WITH PURPOSE, EYES LOCKED ON THE MAN THAT BLINDSIDED HIM LAST WEEK.

MY NUMBER ONE WISH IS FOR THE BEARDED BUTTFACE TO BE GONE FROM THE GALACTIC WF. ALTHOUGH, AT THIS MOMENT, I'D SETTLE FOR SOME

BETTER ENTRANCE MUSIC. WITH SO MANY HITS TO CHOOSE BETWEEN, FROM BOTH EARTH'S CATALOGUE AND THE MUSIC PRODUCED HERE IN SIANARD, THERE'S NO EXCUSE FOR WALKING TO THE RING TO SOMETHING SO BLAND AND UNRECOGNISABLE.

THE MUSIC'S STOPPED. YOU CAN QUIT YOUR COMPLAINING NOW. THE REFEREE'S ABOUT TO RING THE BELL, AND WE'RE DOWN TO BUSINESS—

YES! FINALLY, SOME DECENT MUSIC.

ONE WAY OR ANOTHER, THE CHAMP IS HERE. HE'S BROUGHT A FOLDING CHAIR WITH HIM AND LOOKS TO BE SETTING UP ON THE STAGE.

THIS IS SMART. JUDAS KNOWS THAT, WHICHEVER WAY THIS BOUT GOES, HIS NEXT OPPONENT IS IN THE RING. BY GIVING HIMSELF A BIRD'S EYE VIEW AT THE TOP OF THE RAMP, HE ACCOMPLISHES TWO THINGS. FIRST: HE GETS TO SCOUT HIS NEXT OPPONENT. SECOND: MUCH LIKE WE JUST DISCUSSED REGARDING SNIPER SKY, THIS IS MIND GAMES AT ITS FINEST. THE DESTROYER IS GETTING IN THE HEADS OF BOTH FINALISTS BY LETTING THEM KNOW THAT HE'S WATCHING, WHILE ALSO REMINDING THEM THAT HE IS THE TOP DOG BY REMAINING ON THE STAGE. HE'S PHYSICALLY HIGHER THAN THEY ARE IN THE RING. IT'S A

METAPHOR THAT CREATES A VERY REAL PERCEPTION.

GREAT INSIGHT AS EVER, FARQUAD.

THANKS, GENE. I *WAS* ONE OF THE GREATEST TO EVER LACE UP A PAIR OF BOOTS. A MASTER OF PSYCHOLOGY.

AND HUMBLE, TOO.

SHUT UP AND CALL THE ACTION, GENE.

I APPEAR TO HAVE TOUCHED A NERVE AS THE HEAVYWEIGHT CHAMPION OF THE GALAXY TAKES A SEAT AND THE REFEREE CALLS FOR THE BELL.

HARRISON RUSHES SKY AND THEY GO RIGHT AT IT WITH A FLURRY OF RIGHT HOOKS.

THERE'S NO LOVE LOST BETWEEN THESE TWO AFTER THAT VICIOUS ASSAULT ON HARRISON FROM SKY LAST WEEK.

THEY'RE STILL HITTING EACH OTHER. NEITHER MAN IS BACKING DOWN.

I'VE SEEN NOTHING LIKE THIS AND NOR HAS THIS SOLD-OUT CROWD. NOT A SINGLE FAN IS IN THEIR SEAT AS THE BEARDED BRUTE AND SNIPER SKY CONTINUE PUMMELLING EACH OTHER.

THERE'S STILL ONE PERSON IN THEIR SEAT. THE CHAMP DOESN'T LOOK IMPRESSED. HE'S SMIRKING THOUGH.

THE MORE THESE TWO BEAT EACH OTHER DOWN, THE LESS OF A CHALLENGE JUDAS FACES. HE'S GOT TO BE ENJOYING THIS.

I'M ENJOYING IT TOO, ALTHOUGH SKY NEEDS TO TAKE THE UPPER HAND SOON AND… THAT'LL DO IT.

SNIPER SKY ENDS THE BACK-AND-FORTH RIGHT HANDS BY DELIVERING A SWIFT KICK TO THE MID-SECTION. HARRISON FALLS TO HIS KNEES, CLUTCHING HIS STOMACH, WHILE SKY TAKES A MOMENT TO SHAKE OFF THE COBWEBS. BOTH FIGHTERS HAVE ABSORBED SO MUCH PUNISHMENT, AND WE'RE MERE SECONDS INTO THIS MATCH.

IT'S RESEMBLED MORE OF A BRAWL THAN A WRESTLING MATCH.

I CAN'T ARGUE WITH THAT, FARQUAD. EMOTIONS ARE RUNNING HIGH AS HIP HARRISON MAKES IT BACK TO HIS FEET AND THE TWO COMBATANTS LOCK EYES ONCE MORE.

HERE THEY GO AGAIN!

THEY CHARGE TOWARDS THE CENTRE OF THE RING, ONLY THIS TIME, NO FISTS ARE FLYING. HARRISON AND SKY LOCK HORNS IN A COLLAR AND ELBOW TIE UP.

SOME ACTUAL GRAPPLING? TREMENDOUS STUFF. SKY'S ABOVE THIS BRAWLING CRAP ANYWAY. HIS STRENGTH LIES IN HIS ABILITY TO OUT-WRESTLE

HIS OPPONENTS. IF HE WANTS TO ENSURE VICTORY AND BECOME NUMBER ONE CONTENDER, HE NEEDS TO KEEP HIS COOL AND KEEP IT CLEAN.

THAT MIGHT BE EASIER SAID THAN DONE FOR SOMEONE OF SNIPER SKY'S DISPOSITION. HE'S NOT AS UNHINGED X-STATIC — ONE OF HIP HARRISON'S EARLIER OPPONENTS IN THIS TOURNAMENT. SKY CARRIES HIMSELF WITH A LEVEL OF COMPOSURE OUTSIDE THE RING THAT ONE WOULD EXPECT FROM A PROFESSIONAL. WHEREAS X-STATIC IS… A…

FRUITY PEBBLE?

I THINK YOU MEAN FRUIT LOOP AND YES, FOR LACK OF A BETTER TERM. THE PROBLEM SKY HAS IS THAT HE ALLOWS HIMSELF TO GROW FRUSTRATED WHEN THINGS AREN'T GOING HIS WAY, AND THAT LEADS HIM TO MAKE SOME QUESTIONABLE DECISIONS THAT OFTEN COST HIM A VICTORY.

I GUESS WE'LL SEE. FOR NOW, THESE TWO ARE TRYING TO OUT-GRAPPLE ONE ANOTHER AND IT LOOKS AS IF HIP TRASHINGTON MIGHT BE GAINING THE ADVANTAGE.

HARRISON PUSHES SKY BACK TOWARDS THE ROPES, ONE STEP AT A TIME. SKY MAY BE A TECHNICAL MARVEL BETWEEN THOSE ROPES, BUT HE'S GIVING UP A LOT OF SIZE AND MUSCLE MASS TO THE BEARDED BRUTE.

WHAT YOU'RE SAYING IS THAT TRASHINGTON HAS AN UNFAIR ADVANTAGE?

NOTHING OF THE SORT. PERHAPS SNIPER SKY NEEDS TO SPEND A LITTLE MORE TIME IN THE GYM.

NOW, HARRISON HAS SKY UP AGAINST THE ROPES. SNIPER STRUGGLES, BUT HARRISON CATCHES HIM IN A REVERSE HEADLOCK. SKY ATTEMPTS TO BREAK FREE WITH A FLURRY OF LEFT HOOKS TO THE ABDOMEN, BUT HE'S UNABLE TO HIT WITH ENOUGH FORCE FROM THAT ANGLE TO CAUSE AN IMPACT. HARRISON'S ABSORBING THOSE SHOTS LIKE THEY'RE NOTHING.

IS HE SMILING WHILE SNIPER STRUGGLES AGAINST HIM? THAT ARROGANT SON OF A POODWINK!

YOU'RE ONE TO TALK OF ARROGANCE, YOUR LORDSHIP. BUT YOU'RE RIGHT; IT LOOKS LIKE HARRISON IS LAUGHING. I THINK THOSE ATTEMPTED PUNCHES ARE TICKLING AS THEY BRUSH AGAINST HIP'S MID-SECTION.

WELL, IT'S A COUNTERATTACK. IT'S JUST A LITTLE UNORTHODOX.

IT APPEARS TO BE WORKING AS HARRISON LOSES HIS GRIP ON THAT HEADLOCK. HE BATTLES TO KEEP IT CINCHED IN BUT THE HOLD IS LOOSENING.

COME ON, SKY. JUST ONE BIG PUSH AND YOU'RE FREE.

ONE BIG SHOVE DOES IT. SNIPER SKY BREAKS FREE, SENDING HARRISON RUNNING ACROSS THE RING. HARRISON HITS THE ROPES, GAINING MOMENTUM AS HE HURTLES BACK TOWARDS SNIPER SKY.

LOOKOUT!

OH MY GOD! THE REFEREE IS DOWN. WHAT HAPPENED THERE?

THAT IDIOT, TRASHINGTON, JUST CLOBBERED AN INNOCENT MATCH OFFICIAL. THAT'S WHAT HAPPENED.

IT LOOKED TO ME LIKE HARRISON WAS AIMING TO HIT ONE OF HIS TRADEMARK CLOTHESLINES ON SNIPER SKY, ONLY FOR SKY TO PULL THE REFEREE BETWEEN THEM AT THE LAST SECOND.

DON'T BE SILLY, GENE. THERE'S NO WAY SNIPER SKY WOULD DO SOMETHING LIKE THAT.

I'M LOOKING AT THE INSTANT REPLAY ON MY MONITOR.

MY MONITOR'S GONE BLANK.

IT CLEARLY SHOWS SNIPER SKY GRABBING THE ARM OF JUDGE DREAD AND PULLING HIM INTO HARM'S WAY. WHAT A COWARD!

A LITTLE LESS BIAS, IF YOU WILL, GENE.

PAH! IT'S AS CLEAR AS DAY THAT THE EARLY ADVANTAGE GAINED BY HARRISON HAS SHAKEN SKY. THERE'S SO MUCH AT STAKE IN THIS MATCH AND SKY

MAY BE CRUMBLING ALREADY BENEATH THE PRESSURE.

HE'S JUST PLAYING THE SMART GAME. CASE IN POINT: AS HARRISON WASTES TIME CHECKING ON THE REFEREE, SKY ROLLS BENEATH THE ROPES TO TAKE A BREATHER OUTSIDE THE RING. SMART.

SKY DROPS TO THE FLOOR AND OUT OF SIGHT. SOMETHING FISHY IS TRANSPIRING IF YOU ASK ME. MEANWHILE, HARRISON REALISES THE MATCH OFFICIAL IS OUT COLD AND LOOKS AROUND FOR SOME MEDICAL AID. OUR REFEREES, JUST LIKE THOSE OF YOU WATCHING FROM THE SAFETY OF YOUR OWN HOMES, ARE NOT TRAINED TO TAKE A HIT LIKE THAT. OUR WRESTLING SUPERSTARS ARE FULLY TRAINED PROFESSIONALS, AND WE'D LIKE TO REMIND YOU TO NOT TRY THIS AT HOME.

IT AIN'T BALLET, FOLKS!

WITH NO HELP ON THE WAY, HARRISON CLAPS HIS HANDS TO HIS HEAD. HE KNOWS HE'S JUST LET SNIPER SKY OUT OF HIS SIGHT AND THAT, WITH NO REFEREE TO ENFORCE THE RULES, ANYTHING GOES.

HARRISON'S NOT THE ONLY ONE REALISING THE RING IS CURRENTLY RIPE FOR SHENANIGANS. JUDAS COULD BE ABOUT TO STORM THE RING.

THE CHAMP IS OUT OF HIS SEAT AND HAS TAKEN A COUPLE OF STEPS DOWN THE RAMP, THE GALACTIC

WF TITLE BELT DRAGGING ALONG BEHIND HIM. WHAT HAS JUDAS GOT IN MIND?

HE'S WEIGHING UP WHETHER HARRISON OR SKY WILL MAKE FOR AN EASIER TITLE DEFENCE. I KNOW I'D WANT TO FACE THE WEAKER OPPONENT.

THE DESTROYER'S HESITANCY MAY ALSO HAVE SOMETHING TO DO WITH THE FACT THAT HIP HARRISON HAS CLOCKED HIM. THE BEARDED BRUTE STANDS HIS GROUND IN THE CENTRE OF THE RING, STARING DOWN THE CHAMPION. I THINK JUDAS SEES HARRISON AS SOMEWHAT OF A THREAT TO HIS HISTORIC CHAMPIONSHIP REIGN.

DON'T BE SO STUPID. IT'S OBVIOUS THAT JUDAS SIMPLY WON'T LOWER HIMSELF TO GETTING INVOLVED WITH THIS PAIR OF GLORIFIED MID-CARDERS. WHY WASTE THE ENERGY WHEN THEY'VE DONE SUCH A GOOD JOB OF TORTURING EACH OTHER?

WHATEVER THE REASON, JUDAS WAVES HARRISON OFF, TURNS HIS BACK TO THE RING AND TAKES HIS SEAT AT THE TOP OF THE RAMP.

FORGET FINDING A REPLACEMENT AND SOME MEDICAL HELP FOR THE HOPELESS ZEBRA CARCASS IN THE RING. CAN SOMEBODY TRACK DOWN A MORE APPROPRIATE CHAIR FOR OUR CHAMPION? A THRONE, PERHAPS.

HARRISON HASN'T TAKEN HIS EYES AWAY FROM JUDAS AND HE DOESN'T SEE SNIPER SKY SLITHER INTO THE RING BEHIND HIM, LIKE A VIPER. SKY RISES LIKE A COBRA AND… WHAT'S THAT IN HIS HAND?

IT'S A DAMN PIZZA CUTTER, GENE. HE'S GOING TO SLICE TRASHINGTON UP LIKE PEPPERONI. THIS IS GOING TO BE GREAT!

THERE'S HIGH DRAMA IN OUR MAIN EVENT BUT I'M AFRAID WE MUST TAKE OUR FINAL COMMERCIAL BREAK OF THE EVENING. STICK WITH US AS WE'LL BE BACK IN JUST NINETY SECONDS WITH THE CONCLUSION OF THIS TOURNAMENT FINAL. DON'T GO ANYWHERE, FOLKS!

HOLY SHIDA! THAT SICKO JUST REACHED AROUND AND SLICED HARRISON RIGHT ACROSS THE FOREHEAD. I NEVER THOUGHT HE'D ACTUALLY… LOOK AT THE BLOOD AS IT POURS… AND NOW HE'S BITING—

***

Got the munchies? Dicey Pizza has you covered!

Grab a slice made with our signature, fleshy dough — it's crisp on the outside and oh-so chewy in the middle. This is pizza bread that offers the ultimate physical satisfaction for your pearly white gnashers, as well as a taste sensation that'll have your tongue salivating. We've got your whole mouth covered!

Just be sure to let your Dicey Pizza cool first. Our deliverynauts are the fastest in the galaxy, meaning your pie is almost fresh out of the oven when it reaches your door. Our cheeze is the creamiest, richest and gooiest you'll find anywhere in Sianard. We allow it to bubble in our pizza ovens until it's molten, and our deliverynauts will fly it to you within ten minutes of leaving the flames. Feeling ravenous? Oh, you know we've got you covered!

While the base is the best in the business and our cheeze will make you weak at the kneeze, our red sauce truly makes our pizza pie the greatest of all time. Combining vegetables from across the galaxy, mixed with secret herbs and spices, our sauce fully captures the crimson colour and coagulated consistency witnessed in commercials for our fellow pizza restaurants on Planet Earth. We guarantee the flavour will burst and flow unlike anything you've ever experienced. No imitations. No cheap pops!

So, what are you waiting for? If you've got a hankering for something incredible, call your local Dicey Pizza today.

Dicey Pizza. Slice it and dice it... We've got you covered!

***

I CAN'T BELIEVE IT. THE TOURNAMENT HAS ENDED WITH THE WORST POSSIBLE OUTCOME.

WE'RE BACK, LADIES AND GENTLEMEN. AS MY BROADCAST COLLEAGUE, LORD FARQUAD, HAS JUST MENTIONED, THE TOURNAMENT TO NAME A NEW NUMBER ONE CONTENDER TO THE GALACTIC WF CHAMPIONSHIP HAS INDEED CONCLUDED. OUR WINNER,

AS YOU SEE STANDING IN THE CENTRE OF THE RING WITH HIS HANDS RAISED, IS THE BEARDED BRUTE, HIP HARRISON.

IT HAPPENED SO FAST. I'VE SEEN NOTHING LIKE IT.

NOR HAVE I. THE CROWD HERE AT THE ROCK ARENA IS COLLECTIVELY ON ITS FEET; THE SOUND IS DEAFENING. THE MATCH, AND THE TOURNAMENT, FINISHED IN SUCH DRAMATIC FASHION. I'M SORRY TO SAY THAT THOSE OF YOU WATCHING AT HOME HAVE MISSED OUT ON SOMETHING SPECIAL.

A TRAVESTY IS WHAT THEY'VE MISSED OUT ON. AT LEAST YOU CAN HARDLY SEE THE SMUG EXPRESSION ON TRASHINGTON'S FACE BEHIND ALL THAT BLOOD.

IT PAINTS QUITE A PICTURE, DON'T IT? LET'S TAKE A LOOK BACK AT THE HIGHLIGHTS.

DO WE HAVE TO?

SNIPER SKY INTRODUCED THAT PIZZA CUTTER INTO THE MATCH EARLY ON, SLICING THE FOREHEAD OF HIP HARRISON LIKE A CHEEZE FEAST. AS WE CUT TO THE COMMERCIAL BREAK, SKY BIT THE BEARDED BRUTE'S FOREHEAD, WIDENING THE WOUNDS.

MAYBE SNIPER SKY MISTOOK TRASHINGTON'S FACE FOR A CHEEZE FEAST AFTER ALL?

DOUBTFUL. BUT HIS FOOD BIT BACK. OR SHOULD I SAY, KICKED! WHILE SKY WAS OUT OF HARRISON'S REACH, APPLYING AN UNORTHODOX HOLD FROM BEHIND, THE BEARDED BRUTE CONNECTED WITH A MUEL KICK BETWEEN SKY'S LEGS. WITH THE REFEREE STILL OUT OF COMMISSION, THE MATCH CONTINUED AND HARRISON WASN'T DISQUALIFIED.

A LOW MOVE.

NOTHING COMPARED TO THE BARBARIC VIOLENCE INFLICTED UPON HARRISON BY SKY.

WITH SKY REELING ON THE CANVAS, HARRISON WIPED SOME OF THE BLOOD FROM HIS EYES AND WAS ABLE TO REGROUP. THEN, SKY ROLLED OUT OF THE RING, PROMPTING HARRISON TO GIVE CHASE.

THIS WAS SUCH A SMART MOVE BY SNIPER SKY AND I CAN'T BELIEVE TRASHINGTON ACTUALLY FELL FOR IT. FORCING THE BEARDED IDIOT TO RUN CAUSED HIS BLOOD TO FLOW FASTER, THEREFORE INTENSIFYING HIS BLOOD LOSS. NOT ONLY DOES THIS MAKE HARRISON WEAKER, BUT DUE TO THE LOCATION OF THE WOUND, IT CONTINUES TO RENDER HIM BLIND.

YOU'RE RIGHT, FARQUAD. BUT IT WASN'T ENOUGH TO STOP HARRISON FROM ULTIMATELY SCORING THE VICTORY.

UGH!

HAVING COMPLETED A LAP OF THE RING, SKY SLID BACK INSIDE AND RAN ACROSS THE MAT. HARRISON CLIMBED IN AFTER HIS ADVERSARY BUT, BY THE TIME HE WAS IN THE CENTRE OF THE SQUARED CIRCLE, SKY HAD CLIMBED THROUGH THE ROPES ON THE OTHER SIDE OF THE RING, AND SPRINGBOARDED HIMSELF FROM THE TOP ROPE, HURTLING TOWARDS THE BEARDED BRUTE WITH A FLYING FOREARM.

BUT HARRISON SAW IT COMING AND HIS LIGHTNING-QUICK REFLEXES, WHICH WE'VE SEEN COME INTO PLAY SEVERAL TIMES THROUGHOUT THIS TOURNAMENT, KICKED IN. RATHER THAN ATTEMPT TO DODGE SKY'S AERIAL ADVANCE, THE BEARDED BRUTE COUNTERED, SPINNING ON HIS HEEL, JUMPING UP, AND MEETING SKY IN MID-AIR. HE WRAPPED HIS ARMS AROUND SNIPER'S NECK AND PULLED HIS OPPONENT ALL THE WAY DOWN TO THE CANVAS. NOT ONLY WAS IT THE MOST DEVASTATING CUTTER I'VE EVER SEEN, BUT HE HIT IT OUT OF NOWHERE!

STEALING AN OPPONENT'S MOVE INFRINGES ON THEIR BRAND. IT BREAKS ALL KINDS OF UNWRITTEN RULES. THE WRESTLER'S CODE IS SACRED AND—

WITH SNIPER SKY OUT COLD, HARRISON WENT FOR THE PIN IMMEDIATELY, BUT THE REFEREE, JUDGE DREAD, WAS ONLY JUST BEGINNING TO STIR AND NOT IN POSITION TO COUNT. DETERMINED TO ENSURE VICTORY,

HARRISON FLIPPED THE UNCONSCIOUS SNIPER SKY ONTO HIS FRONT AND APPLIED THE BRUTE LOCK. SKY REGAINED CONSCIOUSNESS IMMEDIATELY UNDER THE EXCRUCIATING PAIN BUT, WITH HIS LEFT ARM HELD IN PLACE BY HARRISON'S LEGS AND HIS HEAD WRENCHED BACK, ALL HE COULD DO, OTHER THAN SCREAM, WAS TO USE HIS FREE HAND TO TAP OUT JUST IN TIME FOR THE REFEREE TO TAKE NOTICE AND RING THE BELL. HIP HARRISON'S FACE WAS COVERED IN SO MUCH BLOOD THAT HE WAS UNAWARE THE MATCH HAD ENDED UNTIL JUDGE DREAD INTERVENED AND PULLED THE HOLD FREE. IT MADE FOR QUITE THE VISUAL AS THE TOURNAMENT REACHED ITS CLIMAX.

WHAT YOU FAILED TO MENTION WAS THAT OUR CHAMPION, JUDAS, WAS ON HIS FEET DURING THE FINAL MOMENTS OF THE MATCH. HIP HARRISON'S PRIZE IS A DATE WITH THE DESTROYER. MARK MY WORDS, THE WRECKING BALL OF THE RING *WILL* RETAIN HIS TITLE AT BATTLESTAR GALACTICA.

THAT'S A BOLD PREDICTION, ESPECIALLY GIVEN THE MOMENTUM HARRISON HAS BUILT THROUGHOUT THIS TOURNAMENT. I'M NOT SO SURE WHERE MY MONEY WOULD LIE.

IT'S NOT A PREDICTION. IT'S A SPOILER. I'LL GIVE IT TO TRASHINGTON, HE'S BEEN ON A HELLUVA

RUN, BUT HIS WINNING STREAK ENDS AT THE HANDS OF JUDAS.

SPEAKING OF THE CHAMPION, HE'S HOLDING A MICROPHONE.

***

'I might as well be the first to offer congratulations to you, Hip Harrison. You had the deck stacked against you and — to loan you a catchphrase — one way or another, you survived.

'But don't be mistaken. Survive is all you've done. In fact, I rather think you've been lucky to have made it past the first round. Just look back over your victories — all of them cheap. You beat Fatboy Slime because of his own ineptitude. X-Static fried and served himself up to you on a plate. Big Bale charged through a table all by himself and slept through the rest of the so-called match. And, as we've just seen, Sniper Sky's overzealousness allowed him to get caught. Each of your opponents defeated themselves. Your being there to pick up the recorded victory was incidental.

'So, enjoy this evening. You're a big winner! I hope that, after I've said my piece, the production crew have some confetti ready to rain down on you — perhaps they've even lined up a pyrotechnic display in celebration of your achievement — because once tonight ends, reality will come raining down instead.

'I am your future. I'm not overzealous, I'm certainly not inept, and I damn sure won't go stumbling into any tables or electric cables. I am the real deal inside that squared circle — the

best to ever lace up a pair of wrestling boots — and I will kick your head off at Battlestar Galactica.

'Luck is for losers, as you'll soon discover when you face a champion in that ring, but let's not allow some hard truths to ruin the biggest night of your pathetic career. I really hope you enjoy this moment, one way… or another.'

***

SOME HEAVYWEIGHT WORDS FROM OUR HEAVYWEIGHT CHAMPION. THERE'S STILL MORE THAN FOUR WEEKS TO GO UNTIL HIP HARRISON MEETS JUDAS WITH THE GALACTIC WF TITLE ON THE LINE AT BATTLESTAR GALACTICA BUT IT APPEARS THAT THE MIND GAMES HAVE ALREADY BEGUN.

WHEN JUDAS SAYS HE'S GONNA BEAT YOU ONE WAY OR ANOTHER, IT MEANS HE'S GOING TO DESTROY ANY SHRED OF SELF-CONFIDENCE YOU MIGHT HAVE HAD. IT'S HOW HE CAME TO ADOPT THE NICKNAME, THE DESTROYER, IN THE FIRST PLACE. WHEN THE BELL RINGS, WE ALL KNOW HE'S GOING TO WIN BY KICKING TRASHINGTON'S HEAD INTO THE CROWD, TEN ROWS BACK.

I WOULDN'T TAKE HIP HARRISON LIGHTLY. ONE THING HE PROVED THROUGHOUT THIS TOURNAMENT IS THAT HE IS MORE THAN CAPABLE OF FINDING *ONE WAY* TO WIN WHEN THE ODDS ARE AGAINST HIM, *OR ANOTHER.*

THAT'S BLASPHEMY, GENE!

WELL, I THINK IT'S APPROPRIATE AND, AS CONFETTI DOES INDEED RAIN DOWN OVER THE BEARDED BRUTE — OUR TOURNAMENT WINNER AND NEW NUMBER ONE CONTENDER — ALL THAT REMAINS IS FOR ME TO REMIND YOU TO ORDER BATTLESTAR GALACTICA ON PAY-PER-VIEW RIGHT NOW. YOU'RE NOT GOING TO WANT TO MISS WHAT I'M ANTICIPATING WILL BE THE HEAVYWEIGHT CLASH OF THE CYCLE. GOODNIGHT, EVERYBODY.

***

Hip Harrison celebrated amongst the confetti, doing his best to ignore the champion's words. Meanwhile, an enraged Judas stormed backstage to find that, rather uncharacteristically, Mr Montgomery had abandoned his usual post directly behind the curtain. The Destroyer grabbed multiple members of the production staff by the scruffs of their collars, demanding to know where the boss was, but nobody could provide an answer. It seemed that, for the first time in Galactic WF history, its founder was not the last person to leave the building on fight night.

As Hip Harrison exited the ring and walked up the ramp, he was surprised to hear a growing amount of cheers and applause mixed in with the usual chorus of abuse that the crowds typically showered him with. After all, through no fault of his own, the Galactic WF presented him as a 'heel' — a bad guy that audiences wanted to see get beat by the conquering heroes, such as Judas. An ever-larger part of the audience was seeing through the façade. They saw Hip Harrison as an unlikely underdog and, perhaps bored with The Judas Show, wanted to see someone new in the top spot.

Harrison considered what Judas had just said as he approached the top of the ramp. It had already crossed his mind that he'd perhaps fluked his way to victory in one or two of his matches. Would he really stand a chance against someone as polished between the ropes as Judas? But then he remembered that this is what Judas had done countless times before to hold on to his championship belt; he was a sadistic bastard in the ring, and a cerebral assassin outside of it. The champ had already defeated most of his opponents before the bell even rang to start their match via the mind games he played in the lead up. And Judas had started playing tonight, sitting at the top of the ramp, looking down on his future opponent, and sowing those first seeds of doubt inside Hip Harrison's head.

'I just need to brush it off,' Harrison said to himself as he pulled back the curtain. 'He's more scared of you than you are of him. You've won this tournament by outsmarting your opponents every step of the way, and you can damn sure outsmart a prick like Judas.'

Hearing his thoughts spoken aloud helped to reassure Hip Harrison, but it didn't stop a scruffed-up sound engineer from giving him a wide berth as he passed by. The sound engineer worked out long ago that all wrestlers were crazy in their own way, and the last couple of minutes had reaffirmed that fact.

WEEK FIVE

WELCOME BACK ON WHAT HAS BEEN ANOTHER RAUCOUS NIGHT FOR THE GALACTIC WRESTLING FEDERATION. WE'VE WITNESSED PLENTY OF ACTION HERE AT THE ROCK THIS EVENING, BUT NOW IT'S TIME TO HEAR FROM THE NEW NUMBER ONE CONTENDER TO THE HEAVYWEIGHT CHAMPIONSHIP, THE COMPETITOR THAT WILL FACE JUDAS IN THE MAIN EVENT AT BATTLESTAR GALACTICA: HIP HARRISON.

I THOUGHT WE USUALLY SAVED THE *BEST* FOR LAST…

WELL, I FOR ONE AM KEEN TO HEAR WHAT THE BEARDED BRUTE HAS TO SAY. OUR BROADCAST COLLEAGUE, MISS ELIZABETH BANKS, IS STANDING BY INSIDE THE RING. TAKE IT AWAY, LIZ!

***

Hip Harrison had spent all evening waiting to make his appearance. He was informed soon after winning the tournament final that he would not be competing in any other matches before the championship bout at Battlestar Galactica, as the promotion couldn't risk one half of the main event at the biggest show of the cycle suffering an injury.

However, Harrison was required at every television taping leading up to the pay-per-view extravaganza to promote his title fight with Judas. That was fine with Hip. He needed the time to recover from such a gruelling tournament, and promoting his match meant time in front of the crowds and television cameras with a live microphone in his hand — something the Galactic WF honchos had been reluctant to give him, even before he had almost revealed Mr Montgomery's true identity and the galaxy-wide cover-up the chairman was involved in.

Now wasn't the time for big reveals, though. The Fed might well advertise him as one half of the biggest match of the cycle, but Hip knew that he was ultimately disposable. If Harrison were to risk speaking out of turn now, not only would the production team cut the feed to his mic, but the Galactic WF would pull him immediately from all upcoming events and put out a short press release, falsely claiming that it had no choice but to remove him from the roster as a disciplinary precaution. Perhaps it would claim that he had failed a drug test. Maybe that he had abused members of the female division. Nothing was beneath the powers that be at the Galactic WF when it came to forming their own narrative. Mr Montgomery, control freak extraordinaire, rewrote history frequently to suit his needs. If a former star made a derogatory comment about the boss in some drunken radiocast interview heard by no more than fifty die-hard fans, you could be assured that a new Galactic WF commissioned documentary would be released within the cycle that retroactively cast a once champion as someone who only achieved any success due to sheer luck, while highlighting any poor life decisions they may have made. The Galactic WF-produced *Rise and Fall* docuseries sold well on Visiondisc. On the flip side, lower card acts who could never get enough wins under their figurative belts to capture a literal belt throughout their careers had been promoted to the status of 'legend', so long as they remained within the company's good books.

The fact of the matter was that no wrestler would ever speak out, as it would kill their chances of ever working with the largest wrestling promotion in the galaxy again — not to mention your name would be smeared across the media, killing any shred of credibility you might have held in the court of public opinion. Some fans recognised when The Fed took control over its narrative, bemoaning the constant change of 'historical fact' within the promotion on SIN message boards. Nevertheless, those same fans continued to tune in to the shows and buy the latest official Galactic WF merchandise. What these fans didn't realise was that the best way to communicate their disapproval was by voting with their wallets.

Hip had also known active wrestlers to be unceremoniously cut from the roster and subject to a public smear campaign for a lot less than uncovering a government conspiracy connected to the Galactic WF's owner. Just half a cycle ago, a promising up-and-comer by the name of Austin Gemini had been in contention for the Interplanetary Championship before disappearing from the show entirely. He was never mentioned on Galactic WF television again. The reason? There were a few rumours — all equally ridiculous — but the prevailing theory was that Austin had coughed in the presence of Mr Montgomery. Ever the control freak, the Galactic WF chairman reportedly detests involuntary bodily functions. He views them as a sign of weakness and a lack of self-control. Word among the wrestlers was that Mr Montgomery, red-faced, launched into a tirade, dressing down the promising young grappler before firing him on the spot. There was no appeal and, no matter how good a wrestler Austin Gemini was, no matter how many members of the management team enjoyed his work, Mr Montgomery would never admit to wrongdoing or having made a mistake. The boss certainly never lost control over anything so stupid as a scratchy throat… or his emotions.

The weeks leading up to Battlestar Galactica were therefore going to be a metaphorical tightrope walk for Hip Harrison. He needed to find the right balance and tread carefully to keep his spot and stand a chance of becoming the heavyweight champion. Harrison wasn't stupid and knew that Judas, for all his character flaws, was as good as they came between the ropes. The Destroyer had maintained a firm grip on the title for a reason, so The Bearded Brute was determined to train hard and not underestimate the champ. The Galactic WF Heavyweight Championship was an integral piece of Harrison and Nemo's plan. The belt commanded respect and, with it around your waist, there was no chance of The Fed dropping you like the victim of a piledriver. As Heavyweight Champion of the Galaxy, Hip Harrison could do and say what he liked with little in the way of repercussions. And the crowds would listen to what he had to tell them.

***

Television speakers throughout Sianard chimed with the instantly forgettable riff of Hip Harrison's entrance music. It somewhat resembled a shopping mall rip-off of *Sweet Child of Mine*.

One television recreating the sounds currently heard within The Rock Arena was inside the building itself. The large frame of Judas filled more than his share of a three-seater sofa, positioned directly in front of the television monitor. To the champion's left, leaning against his cane, was Sovereign Noble.

'It's almost time,' said the Galactic WF commissioner. 'Are you sure you're ready? You remember everything that Mr Montgomery laid out for you earlier?'

Judas raised an eyebrow. 'You doubt me? Who do you think I am?'

'I didn't mean... I'm sorry, I—'

'It's funny,' Judas stood up, slinging the championship belt over his left shoulder, 'I seem to remember destroying your leg, but

I don't recall giving you permanent brain damage. You need to use that grey matter of yours to consider who in the hell you're talking to, before I destroy that, too.'

'I'm sorry, Judas. Truly. I was just double checking. Mr Montgomery gave you a lot to remember for when you go out there. I know you're more than capable of—'

'Exactly. I'm more than capable. Do I remember everything the boss told us earlier? Of course not. That stuff's for him and his associates to concern themselves with. I've got my bullet points jotted down right here.' Judas tapped his forefinger on his temple. 'So, I know all the talking points I need to hit. And, of course, *who* I need to hit.'

'Good. I knew you'd have a handle on things.'

'You're damn right I have a handle on things. I've had a handle on this whole freaking organisation for cycles now. Never doubt me again or — I mean it — I'll end you.'

'I understand that. It's just that I know Mr Montgomery's researchers worked tirelessly to get the scoop on Harrison — everything you need to get into his head. That's why it's important to make sure you stick to the script, otherwise it'll be me who has to answer to the boss. Not to mention that it's imperative you strike the right person out there. We can't have you injure an innocent fan. Such an incident would be a catastrophe and ruin us all.'

'You don't know when to shut up, do you?' Even without a pre-match warm-up, Judas was lightning quick. He thrust out his left leg, kicking the cane from Sovereign Noble's hand. As the commissioner stumbled, the champ met him with an open palm to the jaw. The slap, coupled with the loss of balance, caused Noble to sprawl across the floor. His face hurt, but his pride had suffered the worst from the quick beating.

'You really think I wouldn't recognise that pencil-necked geek in the crowd? Ha!' Judas vacated the room, leaving Sovereign struggling to reach his cane.

On the television, Hip Harrison was about to speak. It was almost time for the champ to make an appearance.

***

'Hip Harrison, the world has watched as you've overcome some of the toughest competition that the Galactic Wrestling Federation has to offer. How does it feel to have emerged as number one contender?' Miss Elizabeth Banks thrust the microphone towards Hip's face.

'It feels pretty damn good to have got this far. But, make no mistake, I'm fully aware that the biggest challenge is yet to come.'

Miss Elizabeth swiftly pulled the microphone away. 'Many would agree with you. Judas is the most dominant force in Galactic Wrestling Federation history. His championship reign is unparalleled, and he truly is a once-in-a-lifetime athlete. What is your game plan for defeating The Destroyer?'

With speed and precision, Miss Elizabeth once again propelled the mic towards Hip Harrison's jawline. He couldn't help but to be impressed with how effortlessly Banks conducted her job. To speak as clearly as she did without ever stumbling over a word, presenting a relatable vibe that put the wrestlers she was interviewing at ease, while drawing in the audience, was something that not too many people could pull off. Some wrestlers belittled Liz, claiming she was overpaid for talking into a stick and looking pretty. In reality, she was always well prepared and knew how to steer an interview if it was going off track — which happened frequently as wrestlers got heated while discussing their latest rivals.

Liz was not only a razor-sharp interviewer but could also take direction better than anyone. Her official job title was 'Broadcaster'. Besides carrying out the role of a journalist, she pushed whatever narrative The Fed wanted to feed the audience with each feud. If the fans viewed the wrestlers as good guys and bad, they became more invested in what they were watching. The battle between babyfaces and heels, as they were so called behind the scenes, would often translate into higher television ratings, a boost in ticket sales, and more merchandise sold — by the babyfaces at least. Heels could expect to earn much less in royalties.

Galactic WF management had instructed Miss Elizabeth to reinforce Hip Harrison's standing as a heel. She was told to quash The Bearded Brute's growing fan support before it got out of hand. In the last moon orbit, Hip had sold more t-shirts than Judas, which was a bad sign. The Fed couldn't allow Harrison to walk into the most important event on its calendar to more cheers than Judas, who'd been the biggest fan draw for over two cycles. Judas was the hero. Hip Harrison was nothing but trouble — a wrongdoer who was out to take the Galactic Wrestling Federation down along with everyone who was a part of it. Management informed Liz that her job was on the line and that she needed to help save the company. As well as asking questions in such a way as to lead Harrison towards giving unpopular answers, to rile up the crowd, Liz was tasked with tricking The Bearded Brute into giving away his strategy for the championship fight, enabling Judas to better prepare.

'My game plan?' Harrison said, careful not to step into the trap. He had seen other wrestlers fall for it.

'That's right,' said Liz. 'How do you plan to defeat Judas? *Can* you beat Judas?'

The key was to remain confident. Let 'em sweat — Judas, Mr Montgomery, Sovereign Noble, all of them. 'Of course I can defeat Judas.' Harrison spoke clearly and methodically. 'What is it I hear them say on commentary? "Anything can happen in the Galactic Wrestling Federation"? I've just defeated four of the toughest, strongest, quickest, and most blood-thirsty, sadistic brutes that the Galactic WF has. But I took them all down in back-to-back weeks. You know how?'

Miss Elizabeth shook her head.

'Because I'm a brute too. And not just any brute. I'm The *Bearded* Brute. I won that tournament, became number one contender and, when Battlestar Galactica rolls around, I'm going to win the Galactic WF Championship... by any means necessary.'

The crowd cheered. This was not going well. Harrison had given nothing away about his strategy and, worse, had seemingly just coined catchphrase. If you had a strong catchphrase, you could do no wrong in the eyes of the fans. They would latch onto it like leeches, screaming it in unison each time you repeated it. Instead of booing you, they would listen intently to every word you said, ready to join in on cue.

By any means necessary. It even had a confidence to it that *One way or another* lacked, Liz thought.

Miss Elizabeth retained her calm, happy-go-lucky demeanour. She didn't easily become flustered — or, at least, she didn't let it show. This was live television; things went wrong, and the show must go on. But standing beside her, Harrison could tell she was rattled.

'An interesting choice of words,' Liz continued. 'What exactly do you mean by that?'

'It means I'll find a way, Miss Elizabeth. If you want to know just how I intend to defeat Judas and take his title, you'll have to watch along with everyone else.'

Harrison was clearly not going to divulge his strategy. The interview hadn't reached a complete dead end, though. As much as she quite liked Harrison (he was always polite, which was more than Liz could say for ninety percent of the male roster), she had her instructions from the office to turn the fans against him, and she was sure she could still pull this off. If what they had told her about Harrison was true, then maybe he wasn't such a nice guy after all.

'Any means necessary,' Liz said. 'I hate to put you on the spot like this, Hip, but are you implying that you're not above cheating to win?'

The Bearded Brute smiled as Miss Elizabeth directed the microphone towards him once again.

'Come on, Liz,' he said. 'I think that you, and these people,' — Harrison waved an arm around to signify the crowd circling the ring — 'know me better than that. I don't *need* to stoop to underhanded tactics. That's not to say I'm completely above performing a few dirty deeds if my opponent attempts something nefarious first.'

Liz smiled. Was this how Harrison intended to approach the title match? At the very least, it gave her employers some idea of what not to rule out.

'Now, Hip, I think what everybody here would really like to know is—'

One way or another... The pre-recorded voice of Judas echoed his catchphrase throughout the arena before the Blondie song of the same name kicked in.

The crowd collectively rose to its feet, cameras flashing from all angles, as the Heavyweight Champion pushed through the curtain and stepped onto the stage. Judas paused as he reached the top of the ramp, lifting his title belt up high for all to see, including Hip Harrison. He draped it over his enormous shoulder and continued marching towards the ring. He ascended the steps to the ring apron and climbed in between the top and middle ropes. As Judas rose to his full stature once inside the squared circle, his height advantage became apparent immediately. Hip Harrison was a big dude, but The Destroyer towered over The Bearded Brute by almost a foot.

Harrison showed no signs of intimidation. He didn't even flinch as Judas stepped up to him, butting heads in the first face-off between the new rivals. The roar of the crowd was thunderous as Sianard got its first preview of the biggest showdown in this cycle. Foreheads and noses touching, Judas smirked as he looked down at Harrison, but The Bearded Brute held his ground, staring defiantly up at the most dominant champion of all time. The mind games were in full swing.

Judas's smirk stretched into a wide grin as the champ took a step back, lifting his Heavyweight Championship belt high into the air once again, like an ancient conqueror holding aloft the head of a vanquished foe. The sound of Blondie's anthem died out, and Judas held his free hand out to the side. The nearest member of the production crew needed no further instruction, placing a microphone in The Destroyer's hand within seconds.

'How are you doing, Hip?' asked Judas. 'Tired from all that training you're doing, I imagine. After all, we're not far out from what will be the biggest match of your career. This will be the brightest the spotlight ever shines on you, so I hope you're doing your best to live in the moment and to drink it in, man!'

Harrison held his gaze and didn't respond.

Judas continued: 'Come on. This isn't the time to get star struck. For now, you and I are peers. Some might say that we are equals. Of course, that's a crock of shit — I'm the most dominant champion in the history of this sport, even tracing it back to its roots on Earth. But, for now, you're the next best thing.'

Still no response from Harrison.

'Splorg got your tongue? Look around you — these people watching have never been so invested in you, in your fight. Now is the time to let them know what you're all about. It bears repeating: this is the biggest moment of your career. Whereas, for me, you're just another chapter in the tome that is *The Era of Judas*.

'Scratch that — you'll be nothing more than a footnote.' Judas cackled, his deep tones resembling the rumblings of an earthquake.

Hip's face broke into a smile of its own, which immediately caused Judas to adopt a sterner look.

'What do you have to smile about? You're the one facing an uphill battle. And when you come within inches of reaching the summit, you're going to come face to face with The Destroyer. I'll start by crushing your fingers beneath my boots and ripping out that disgusting, overgrown mop on your face before sending you crashing back down all the way to base camp. You dig?'

By the time Judas had finished, Harrison was already laughing.

'You think this is funny? You won't have anything to laugh about when I'm finished with you.

'If I allow it, you'll have a nice little career for yourself in the mid-card, battling for the tag titles with some schmuck, or perhaps fighting for the Interplanetary Championship. You'll remain almost a household name through your brush with greatness, with me. But if you piss me off, you'll discover that The Destroyer is more than just a nickname used for marketing. I will destroy your body, your career, and your life. I will see that you have nothing left, Hunluka.'

A low murmur emanated from the live audience. Had Judas forgotten the name of his challenger? Hip Harrison, on the other hand, knew that Judas had got his name very much right. The Bearded Brute was no longer smiling.

'What's the matter, Hunluka?' Judas continued as the crown settled back down. 'Oh, whoops! Slip of the tongue. Ladies and gentlemen, Hunluka is the real name of our number one contender. Hip Harrison is nothing more than a flashy stage name.'

Harrison clenched his fists. He didn't like where this was going.

'I can see why you changed it. With a name like that, I would have done the same. I guess that's what you get when your parents come from different cultural backgrounds.'

There were some audible gasps from the crowd in response to the revelation that Harrison was mixed race. Although it was not quite the large reaction Judas had expected. The challenger would later reflect that Judas was perhaps falling a little behind the times regarding cultural and societal acceptance. The times, after all, were constantly changing. It could even have been that the vocal response from some members of the audience came as a negative reaction to the very fact that Judas had made a derogatory comment about Hunluka's race.

'What's the matter?' Judas said. 'Still at a loss for words? I would be too if I were you. Not only are you scheduled to get your head kicked off in a couple of moon orbits at Battlestar Galactica, but your mind is now racing. You're wondering, "if Judas knows my real name, what else does he know?" And you'd be right to think that. I've been at the top of this game for a long while and I know people in high places. Whereas your training focuses on how not to get your head kicked off — spoiler alert, there's no dodging it — my preparation for our championship clash involves finding out everything there is to know about Hunluka, the farm boy. With the knowledge I've already amassed, I'm confident that I've already got you beat. At Battlestar Galactica, your hopes and dreams go to die, just like your mothe—'

The Bearded Brute had heard more than enough, cutting Judas off with a ferocious headbutt. As the champion reeled, Harrison grabbed his soon-to-be opponent's wrist, dragging him towards the ground to apply the Brute Lock submission. But Judas, a true ring general, scrabbled for the ropes with his spare arm, and pulled himself loose from the hold before escaping to safety outside the ring.

Enraged, Harrison kicked the bottom rope, yelling for Judas to get back in the ring. The rest of the arena, meanwhile, fell into silence. Nobody had ever seen Hip Harrison lose his composure like this before.

Cradling his head, Judas retreated up the entrance ramp, walking backwards to ensure Harrison wasn't giving chase.

However, The Bearded Brute closed his eyes, took a deep breath, and backed away from the ropes. Occupying the centre of the ring once more, a shimmer of gold on the ground beside him caught Hip Harrison's attention. It was the Galactic Wrestling Federation Heavyweight Championship belt. In his haste to get out of harm's dodge, Judas had dropped his most prized possession. Harrison crouched down and took the strap in his hand. He slowly stood back up and held the belt, staring at it as a new parent looks upon their child for the first time.

'Give it back!' Judas cried, taking a few steps back towards the ring. As he drew closer, the champion stopped short of climbing back inside. Instead, he shouted: 'Get your hands off *my* title!'

Hip Harrison's demeanour returned to its default state. Snapping out of his trance, he reminded himself that what he held was the key to change — the token needed to expose those who currently held all the power. He looked down at Judas, a desperate champion whose reign was obsolete.

Holding the Heavyweight Championship of the Galaxy, a symbol of Sianard in its entirety, reminded Hunluka of his mission and highlighted the real possibility of pulling it off. The stunned crowd stirred, then roared its approval as Harrison raised the belt high above his head.

'You put that down!' Judas screamed. 'You have no right!'

Harrison held the belt aloft for a moment longer, before stepping forward and laying it beneath the bottom rope. Judas edged closer to the ring as Harrison stepped back. When he was certain that the coast was clear, Judas leapt forward, swiped the belt from the ring apron, and made a hasty retreat, clutching the title close to his chest.

Harrison was feeling it. The crowd was turning on Judas, their support shifting in favour of The Bearded Brute. Psychologically, it always helped to have the audience in your corner, cheering you on in the throes of a gruelling match. Judas would be out of his depth if he were to enter Battlestar Galactica to a chorus of boos.

The camera feed continued to cut between Harrison, standing tall in the ring, playing up to the crowd, and Judas, who was taking the less visible exit down the narrow gap between the entrance ramp and the crowd barricade. Harrison assumed Judas was embarrassed and looking to make a quick getaway from the arena, passing no other wrestlers or staff backstage. It might have been the adulation from the crowd, which was new to The Bearded Brute, that caused this lapse in judgement. After what was about to happen, Hip Harrison vowed to never underestimate The Destroyer again.

Carried away by the moment, Harrison turned his back on Judas and climbed to the second rope of the far turnbuckle, striking a pose for those in attendance with the benefit of flash photography.

Judas watched on the jumbotron at the top of the entranceway as Harrison lowered his guard. The Destroyer smiled. Everything had gone according to plan, and it was now time to strike.

In a display of his combined speed and strength, Judas grabbed a member of the audience by the head and catapulted him from his seat all the way up onto the entrance ramp. Those with tickets close to the victim shuffled away from the guardrail as far as they could get. There were screams as panic set in. The Heavyweight Champion of the Galaxy had just laid his hands on an innocent bystander. They weren't to know that this was a premeditated attack and that everyone else was safe.

Meanwhile, Hip Harrison soaked in the sounds of the crowd, mistaking the screams of terror for excitement. The camera flashes first alerted him to the fact that something was wrong. They almost entirely stopped. And where bright strobes had filled his vision, the people came into focus. Men, women and children from across the galaxy, all coming together to share in the experience of a live Galactic Wrestling Federation show. Not one face in the sea of Sianardianity was smiling. Shock and concern were the prevailing emotions.

Harrison hopped down from the ropes and spun around with fists up. He was expecting someone, possibly Judas, to be in the ring behind him, poised to attack. There was nobody there, but at the top of the entrance ramp he spied the bulky frame of The Destroyer, with somebody caught in a headlock as he dragged them onto the stage area against their will.

So, this is what the crowd was reacting to. Judas had flipped and was assaulting a civilian — a member of the crew, maybe. Surely not a fan.

Harrison's gaze raised to the jumbotron where a close-up shot of the activity taking place just below it was being projected. The Bearded Brute recognised Judas's victim immediately.

I should have known better, Harrison thought as he slid out of the ring as quick as a lightning bolt. After all, it was he who had arranged the complimentary ticket for his old friend Nemo.

Nemo wasn't going down without a fight. Assuming that he was safe as a member of the audience — not to mention that Judas couldn't possibly know who he was — the assault had completely blindsided Nemo. Now, his nose was throbbing and he couldn't breathe through it. His nostrils were either filled with blood or had completely caved in. Not that Nemo could specifically recall being hit in the face. Later, video footage of the incident would reveal that Nemo's face bounced off the floor or the entrance ramp when he landed.

As the shock dissipated, Nemo realised Judas must have something much worse in store for him. Fight for flight? There was nowhere to run with The Wrecking Ball's python-like biceps curled around his throat.

If I can just fight back long enough for Hip to reach me, Nemo thought, as he scratched and clawed at Judas's back. Surely The Bearded Brute had seen what was going on and would make the save before any further harm could come to his best friend...

Nemo registered a change in the crowd's tone. Shock and outrage gave way to thunderous cheers and applause.

Here he comes, Nemo told himself. *Judas only wanted me as bait. The real fight is with Hip.*

Nemo dug his heels into the ground to slow Judas down, although it had little effect, if any. Still, Nemo held onto the hope that Hip would break Judas's hold at any moment. But it was gone in an instant, as a mushroom cloud of sheer pain erupted from his cranium, engulfing his head before shooting down his spinal cord like a bullet. Sick of getting his back clawed by paper-thin fingernails, Judas had raised his left arm, balled up his hand into an almighty fist, and sent it hurtling down towards the top of Nemo's head. Nemo's body immediately fell limp as Judas continued to drag him stage left.

Hip Harrison had never run so fast in all his life. All his cardio training, which was so often ignored by larger wrestlers in favour of lifting yet another weight, came in handy. Yet, the ramp had never felt so long. He'd had dreams like this — where he'd needed to get somewhere, urgently, but his legs couldn't seem to get him there. The reality of it was that Hip's legs were working fine. Fans in attendance were stunned by the speed at which The Bearded Brute ascended the entrance ramp; television didn't do justice to his lightning speed. What ultimately caused him to slow down was an unforeseen roadblock.

X-Static came through the curtain first and positioned himself at the top of the ramp as Harrison made it three-quarters of the way up. Harrison slowed a little, registering the threat and instantly deciding the best course of action was to run right through

The Electrifying Psychopath with a shoulder tackle. The objective remained to save Nemo before it was too late.

But X-Static hadn't come alone. Before Harrison could reach him, Fatboy Slime and Big Bale flanked The Electrifying Psychopath. There was no way out. The Bearded Brute applied the brakes; he needed to fight his way past the two giants and twitchy psychopath.

Weighing up his options, Harrison determined that going for Big Bale first was the best course of action. To anyone watching, the enormous Bale would surely pose the biggest threat (no pun intended) out of the three combatants serving as a shield for Judas. But having recently shared a ring with each of them, Harrison knew Bale would be the last one they'd expect him to target first. His plan was simple and relied on his adversaries reacting accordingly, but it was Hip Harrison's only hope of reaching Nemo in time.

***

I CAN'T BELIEVE WHAT WE'RE WITNESSING. WE NOW APPEAR TO HAVE REACHED A STAND OFF.

WAIT A MINUTE, HARRISON'S MAKING A MOVE! HE MUST HAVE A DEATH WISH — HE'S CHARGING AT BIG BALE!

THE BEARDED BRUTE OPTS TO TAKE DOWN THE BIGGEST THREAT FIRST. BALE LUMBERS FORWARD TO GREET HARRISON WITH A RIGHT HOOK, BUT HARRISON DUCKS BENEATH IT.

WHAT'S HARRISON DOING?

HE'S DROPPED TO ALL FOURS RIGHT BEHIND BALE AND… OH WAIT— HARRISON HAS CLEARLY SEEN SOMETHING WE'VE MISSED. FATBOY SLIME, KNOWN FOR HIS OVERZEALOUSNESS IN THE RING, IS RUNNING, FULL STEAM AHEAD, TOWARDS HARRISON AND BALE.

HE'S OVERZEALOUS ALRIGHT. AN OVERZEALOUS JACKASS! HE WAS RUNNING GUNG HO FOR TRASHINGTON, WHO'S NOW DUCKED BEHIND BALE — LIKE A TOTAL COWARD, I MIGHT ADD — AND HE'S BUILT UP WAY TOO MUCH MOMENTUM TO STOP IN TIME.

THE IRRESISTIBLE FORCE IS ABOUT TO MEET THE IMMOVABLE OBJECT! SLIME TRIES TO STOP, BUT ALL HE CAN DO IS COVER HIS FACE WITH MEATY PALMS AS COLLISION IS INEVITABLE. BALE SCREAMS, HIS CHINS JIGGLE LIKE JELLY!

LOOK OUT!

SLIME CRASHES INTO BALE. BALE'S KNEES BUCKLE OVER THE CROUCHING HIP HARRISON, LYING IN WAIT LIKE A TIGER. BALE AND SLIME WRAP THEIR ARMS AROUND ONE ANOTHER, EACH GIANT ATTEMPTING TO USE THE OTHER TO KEEP THEIR BALANCE. BUT IT'S NO USE AS BOTH BEHEMOTHS FIND THEMSELVES ON A DOWNWARD TRAJECTORY.

THEY'RE GOING OVER THE EDGE OF THE RAMP. THAT MUST BE MORE THAN A FIFTEEN-FOOT DROP!

THE CROWD HAS COME TO ITS FEET AND THOSE AT THE FOOT OF THE RAMP HAVE FLED AS BALE AND SLIME PLUMMET TOWARDS THE GROUND. THEIR SCREAMS TELL ALL YOU NEED TO KNOW.

OH BRADSHAW! THEY'VE FLATTENED THOSE SEATS! I SWEAR I FELT THE GROUND TREMOR!

I HAVE NEVER SEEN SUCH DESTRUCTION, SUCH CALAMITY! I'VE BEEN CALLING THE ACTION AS A PROFESSIONAL WRESTLING COMMENTATOR FOR MORE CYCLES THAN I CARE TO COUNT AND I DON'T RECALL EVER SEEING SO MUCH FLESH AND BONE TAKE A FALL QUITE LIKE THAT.

WE'RE GOING TO NEED TO REINFORCE THAT FORKLIFT TO GET THOSE TWO OUT OF HERE AND TO A HOSPITAL.

AMID THE CARNAGE, WE MUSTN'T FORGET THE DRAMA THAT'S STILL UNFOLDING HERE, LADIES AND GENTLEMEN. JUDAS HAS THAT MAN — AN INNOCENT MEMBER OF OUR AUDIENCE — IN A VICE-LIKE GRIP. HARRISON MAY NOT HAVE SAVED THIS APPARENT FAN OF HIS YET BUT, BY TAKING THE BIG MEN OUT IN SUCH BREATHTAKING FASHION, HE SEEMS TO HAVE BOUGHT SOME TIME.

JUDAS CAN'T BELIEVE WHAT HE'S JUST WITNESSED. NEITHER CAN ANY OF US.

AS GIANTS FALL, LEGENDS RISE. HIP HARRISON RETURNS TO HIS FEET TO FACE THE STUNNED X-STATIC, WHO STANDS ACROSS THE RAMP. THE ELECTRIFYING PSYCHOPATH MIGHT BE SECOND GUESSING HIS COURSE OF ACTION IN STANDING AGAINST HIP HARRISON AS JUDAS BARKS ORDERS FROM THE STAGE.

THAT ELECTRIC PSYCHOTWIT HAS FROZEN ON THE SPOT. COME ON, LISTEN TO THE CHAMP. STOP THAT BEARDED BASTARD!

YOU SURELY DON'T SUPPORT THE CHAMPION'S CURRENT ACTIONS, FARQUAD?

…I DON'T KNOW. I STILL DON'T LIKE TRASHINGTON, THOUGH.

WHATEVER YOUR FEELINGS TOWARDS HARRISON, JUDAS'S ACTIONS ARE PLAIN WRONG. GALACTIC WRESTLING FEDERATION FANS SHOULD BE ABLE TO ATTEND A SHOW WITH NO FEAR OF ASSAULT. HEAVYWEIGHT CHAMPION OR NOT, JUDAS HAS CROSSED A LINE THIS EVENING.

YEAH, WELL, AS YOU OFTEN SAY, ANYTHING CAN HAPPEN IN THE GALACTIC WF.

HARRISON MAKES HIS WAY TOWARDS X-STATIC. THE ELECTRIFYING PSYCHOPATH IS EITHER STANDING HIS GROUND OR FROZEN IN FEAR. THE BEARDED BRUTE RAISES HIS FISTS. HE CAN ONLY BE TEN STEPS FROM

X-STATIC… NINE… EIGHT… SEVEN… WAIT A MINUTE! WHERE IN THE BLUE HELL DID HE COME FROM?

WHAT A CUTTER!

SEEMINGLY FROM OUT OF NOWHERE, SNIPER SKY TAKES OUT HIP HARRISON ON THE LIP OF THE STAGE ONCE AGAIN WITH A FIERCE CUTTER.

TRASHINGTON NEVER SAW IT COMING! BUT HE SURE SAW THE GROUND RAPIDLY APPROACHING THAT HAIRY FACE OF HIS!

X-STATIC IS GRINNING LIKE A CHESHIRE SPLORG! HE WASN'T FROZEN IN FEAR. THIS WAS ALL PART OF SOME SICK PLAN THAT IS STILL UNFOLDING BEFORE US.

PURE BRILLIANCE! SOMEBODY CALL THE ACADEMY AND ALERT THEM TO THAT ELECTRIFYING PERFORMANCE.

SNIPER SKY, THAT SON OF A— HE'S STARING INTO THE EYES OF X-STATIC AND HE'S SMILING. THEY'RE LAUGHING, FOR BRADSHAW'S SAKE, WHILE JUDAS, WHO'S HOLDING THE LIMP CARCASS OF HIS HOSTAGE BY THE SCRUFF OF THE NECK, IS GIVING OUT ORDERS.

I HAVE NO IDEA WHAT IS GOING ON, BUT THIS IS BRILLIANT.

FARQUAD, YOU REALLY THINK THIS IS ACCEPTABLE? OUR CHAMPION IS ASSAULTING A FAN. OUR PAYING CUSTOMERS ULTIMATELY PAY YOUR SALARY. ARE YOU SAYING THAT THE FANS SHOULD

EXPECT THIS KIND OF TREATMENT? BECAUSE IF YOU ARE, BUSINESS WILL SOON DRY UP.

COOL IT, GENE. I WAS TALKING ABOUT HOW THEY'VE TAKEN THAT PRETENTIOUS PIECE OF TRASH DOWN A PEG. AND BESIDES, IF YOU LOOK AROUND, IT DOESN'T LOOK AS IF THE OTHER FIFTY THOUSAND FANS IN ATTENDANCE HAVE BEEN SCARED AWAY BY WHATEVER JUDAS IS UP TO. THE CROWD IS ON ITS FEET AND NOBODY'S GOING ANYWHERE. WHY WOULD ANYONE WANT TO MISS THIS?

CALL IT MORBID CURIOSITY, FARQUAD.

AND WOULD YA' LOOK AT WHAT'S HAPPENING NOW. SNIPER SKY AND X-STATIC DRAG THE LIFELESS BODY OF HIP HARRISON ACROSS THE STAGE, TOWARDS THE DESTROYER AND HIS VICTIM.

GOOD TO SEE THAT THEY'RE PICKING UP THEIR LITTER AND TAKING IT WITH THEM. CAN'T LEAVE TRASH JUST LYING AROUND LIKE THAT.

HILARIOUS.

SARCASM. THE LOWEST FORM OF WIT.

THEY DROP HARRISON'S ARMS, HAVING PULLED HIM TO WITHIN TEN FEET OF JUDAS AND HIS MYSTERY VICTIM. SKY SQUATS OVER HARRISON'S BACK, EXTENDS HIS ARMS AROUND THE BEARDED BRUTE'S JAW AND PULLS BACK.

WE IN THE BIZ CALL THAT A CAMEL CLUTCH. ONE OF THE WORST SUBMISSION HOLDS YOU CAN FIND YOURSELF CAUGHT IN.

HARRISON, HIS NECK BENT AT AN UNBRADSHAWLIKE ANGLE, HIS TORSO PINNED TO THE GROUND WHILE HIS FACE IS HELD TOWARDS JUDAS, HAS REGAINED CONSCIOUSNESS. THAT SADISTIC X-STATIC HAS MADE SURE OF IT. THE ELECTRIFYING PSYCHOPATH IS CROUCHING DOWN AND SLAPPING THE DEFENCELESS NUMBER ONE CONTENDER ACROSS THE FACE, HARD AND REPEATEDLY. THESE GUYS, WHO ARE APPARENTLY IN ALIGNMENT WITH JUDAS, ARE MAKING SURE THAT HARRISON HAS A FRONT ROW SEAT TO WITNESS WHATEVER IS ABOUT TO HAPPEN.

TRASHINGTON'S EYES ARE OPEN WIDE. HE MUST REALLY WANT TO SEE THIS.

HIS LIPS SAY DIFFERENT. HE'S TELLING THEM TO STOP. HE'S BEGGING. BUT SKY AND X-STATIC HAVE HIM TRAPPED. THIS IS UNCOMFORTABLE TO WATCH.

JUDAS IS HAPPY WITH THE WORK OF HIS NEW FRIENDS. WE'RE ABOUT TO FIND OUT WHAT HE HAS IN STORE FOR THE MARK HE'S PLUCKED FROM THE CROWD.

JUDAS WRAPS HIS ARMS AROUND THE FAN'S WAIST AND HOISTS HIM ALL THE WAY UP SO THAT THE MYSTERY MAN SITS ON THE CHAMPION'S SHOULDERS.

HE FLIPPED THE GUY HEAD OVER HEELS LIKE HE WEIGHED NOTHING MORE THAN A PILE OF RAGS.

THE GUY'S CLEARLY NOT A WRESTLER. HE MUST WEIGH NO MORE THAN A HUNDRED POUNDS SOAKING WET. HE'S NOT TRAINED TO TAKE THIS KIND OF PUNISHMENT EITHER. HE WON'T HAVE LEARNED HOW TO TAKE A BUMP.

WHAT BETTER WAY TO LEARN THAN AT THE HANDS OF THE BEST IN THE BUSINESS?

JUDAS NOW WALKS WITH THE FAN UP ON HIS SHOULDERS, SWAYING. HE MIGHT BE COMING TO, ALTHOUGH HE'S STILL IN A DAZE. EITHER WAY, I DON'T THINK HE KNOWS WHERE HE IS.

THE LIGHTS ARE ON BUT NOBODY'S HOME!

HARRISON FIGHTS AGAINST THE CAMEL CLUTCH BUT SNIPER SKY WRENCHES AT HIS HEAD AND NECK. HARRISON CONTINUES TO STRUGGLE, TO FIGHT AND PLEAD WITH THIS… THIS GANG OF THUGS, TO STOP WHAT THEY'RE DOING.

IS HE CRYING? I THINK HE IS. WHAT A BABY!

WOULD YOU HAVE A HEART, FARQUAD? THIS IS NOT RIGHT.

WHAT DO YOU WANT ME TO DO? I'M JUST HERE TO CALL THE ACTION; IT'S NOT MY PLACE TO GET INVOLVED.

I HATE TO SAY IT, BUT I'D FEAR FOR MY SAFETY IF I WERE TO INTERVENE.

YOU'D ALSO LOSE YOUR JOB FOR ABANDONING YOUR POST.

OH BRADSHAW! JUDAS IS AT THE LIP OF THE STAGE, HIS TOES PROTRUDING OVER THE EDGE. THIS SITUATION HAS BECOME INCREDIBLY PRECARIOUS. NOT ONLY IS THAT FAN IN EXTREME DANGER, BUT THE CHAMPION IS ALSO AT RISK OF FALLING FROM THE STAGE IF HE'S NOT CAREFUL.

JUDAS IS A WORLD-CLASS ATHLETE. HE KNOWS HOW TO BALANCE. AND IT LOOKS AS IF HE'S ABOUT TO THROW THAT GUY OFF THE STAGE.

FOR THE LOVE OF BRADSHAW, DON'T DO THIS! THAT'S AT LEAST A TWENTY-FOOT DROP. THAT POOR, INNOCENT FAN MAY NOT SURVIVE.

WAIT A MINUTE. LOOK AT HARRISON!

YES! HIP HARRISON! THERE'S STILL FIGHT LEFT IN HIM. THE NEXT CHALLENGER FOR THE HEAVYWEIGHT CHAMPIONSHIP IS FIGHTING WITH ALL HE'S GOT TO BREAK FREE FROM SNIPER SKY'S CAMEL CLUTCH.

HE'S PUSHED HIMSELF UP TO HIS KNEES, FORCING SKY TO HIS FEET. WHERE IS THIS ENERGY COMING FROM?

IT'S GOT TO BE PURE ADRENALINE. GO ON, KID! YOU CAN DO IT!

X-STATIC IS HAVING NONE OF IT. HE'S SLAPPING THE TASTE RIGHT OUT OF THAT BEARDED BUFFOON'S MOUTH.

THOSE SLAPS DON'T APPEAR TO BE HAVING THE DESIRED EFFECT. THEY'RE ONLY ENRAGING HARRISON FURTHER.

HARRISON'S UP TO HIS FEET. HE'S BROKEN THE HOLD! EVEN I'VE GOT TO ADMIT, THIS IS INCREDIBLE.

HIP HARRISON HAS BROKEN FREE FROM THE CAMEL CLUTCH — A FEAT WE'VE RARELY, IF EVER, SEEN. NOW HE GOES TOE-TO-TOE WITH SKY AND X-STATIC, THROWING WILD PUNCHES LEFT AND RIGHT TO KEEP THEM BOTH AT BAY.

JUDAS HAS TURNED TO SEE WHAT THE COMMOTION IS ALL ABOUT. BUT HE'S STRUGGLING TO SEE WITH THAT FAN STILL ON HIS SHOULDERS, OBSCURING HIS VIEW.

THE DESTROYER WOULD NOT LIKE WHAT HE'D SEE RIGHT ABOUT NOW. WHATEVER THIS PLAN WAS, IT'S BACKFIRING BEFORE OUR EYES.

I CAN'T BELIEVE IT: HARRISON HAS THE UPPER HAND IN THIS TWO-ON-ONE FIGHT AGAINST SKY AND X-STATIC.

BOTH ARE TOP-TIER CONTENDERS WHO WERE, OF COURSE, COMPETING WITH HARRISON FOR THE RIGHT TO BE NUMBER ONE CONTENDER OVER THE PAST FEW

WEEKS. BUT WHILE HARRISON IS KEEPING BOTH OF HIS FOES AT BAY, HE'S NOT ABLE TO STUN EITHER OF THEM FOR LONG ENOUGH TO FOCUS ON TAKING THE OTHER OUT ENTIRELY. HARRISON'S NOT GETTING ANY CLOSER TO HELPING THAT FAN. HE'S STUCK IN LIMBO, YOU COULD SAY.

I THINK HE'S FOUND A WAY OUT. HE JUST ROCKED SKY WITH A MEAN RIGHT HOOK.

SKY REELS FROM THAT THUNDEROUS BLOW AND HARRISON TURNS HIS ATTENTION TO X-STATIC. THE ELECTRIFYING PSYCHOPATH BACKS AWAY SLOWLY. IT SEEMS HE NO LONGER WANTS A PIECE OF THE BEARDED BRUTE NOW THAT THE ODDS HAVE EVENED. LIKE ALL BULLIES, X-STATIC IS NOTHING MORE THAN A WEASEL-FACED COWAR—

WHOA! WHERE IN THE HECK DID JUDAS COME FROM?

DAMNIT STRAIGHT TO HELL. THAT SORRY EXCUSE FOR A CHAMPION, JUDAS, CAME STEAMING THROUGH LIKE A FREIGHT CRAFT, TAKING HARRISON DOWN SIDEWAYS WITH A HELLACIOUS SHOULDER TACKLE.

AS THE ANCIENT PROVERB GOES, IF YOU NEED SOMETHING DONE RIGHT, TAKE THEM OUT YOURSELF. I'D BE SURPRISED IF TRASHINGTON HASN'T DISLOCATED A SHOULDER.

WE'RE SEEING SLOW-MOTION REPLAYS THAT SHOW JUDAS DUMPED HIS HOSTAGE FOR THE MOMENT, PRESUMABLY FIGURING HE WASN'T GOING ANYWHERE, AND WHILE HARRISON WAS DISTRACTED BY THE RETREATING X-STATIC, THE CHAMPION POUNCED FROM JUST OUTSIDE OF THE BEARDED BRUTE'S PERIPHERAL VISION. IF THE FORCE OF THE HEAVYWEIGHT CHAMP COMING IN AT SUCH SPEED DIDN'T TAKE HARRISON OUT OF COMMISSION, THEN THAT LANDING ON THE STAGE MAY HAVE DONE.

BACK TO THE LIVE BROADCAST, GENE, AND JUDAS IS REPRIMANDING X-STATIC AND SLAPPING SOME SENSE INTO SNIPER SKY.

SKY IS STILL ROCKED FROM THAT RIGHT HOOK. THE CHAMP POINTS AT THE DOWNED HIP HARRISON AND TURNS HIS ATTENTION BACK TO THIS FAN, THIS MEMBER OF OUR AUDIENCE THAT HAS BECOME A VICTIM — SEEMINGLY UNPROVOKED — AT THE HANDS OF THE DESTROYER.

WE MAY NOT KNOW WHY JUDAS HAS ATTACKED THIS MYSTERY MAN, BUT ONE THING'S FOR SURE: WE HAVE CONFIRMATION THAT X-STATIC AND SNIPER SKY ARE FOLLOWING THE CHAMPION'S ORDERS. YOU'VE GOT TO IMAGINE THAT BALE AND SLIME WERE ALSO WORKING FOR THE DESTROYER.

BUT WHY? THAT'S WHAT I WANT TO KNOW. WHAT'S IN IT FOR THOSE GUYS?

IT'S GAINING THEM SOME EXPOSURE ON GALAXY-WIDE TELEVISION. THAT'S SOMETHING.

WHATEVER THE MOTIVATION, I JUST HOPE IT'S WORTH IT. THERE HAVE GOT TO BE RAMIFICATIONS FOR WHAT WE ARE WITNESSING. SERIOUS SANCTIONS. MAYBE EVEN PROSECUTION.

WE'LL HAVE TO WAIT AND SEE. FOR THE TIME BEING, JUDAS CONTINUES WITH WHATEVER HE HAD PLANNED. HE'S HOISTING THAT FAN, THAT MEMBER OF THE SIANARD GALAXY, UP ONTO HIS SHOULDERS ONCE AGAIN.

MEANWHILE, HARRISON REMAINS CONSCIOUS BUT THE GRIMACE ON HIS FACE BETRAYS HIS AGONY. SNIPER SKY HOLDS HARRISON'S LEFT ARM, WHILE THE ELECTRIFYING *SICKO* TAKES HIS RIGHT ARM AND SHOULDER. THE BEARDED BRUTE SCREAMS IN PAIN AS HE'S FORCED TO WATCH WHATEVER IS ABOUT TO TRANSPIRE.

ELECTRIFYING SICKO? WATCH IT WITH THE NAME-CALLING, GENE.

I'M NOT SURE WHETHER HARRISON IS SUFFERING MORE FROM THE PAIN OR FROM CONCERN FOR THE FAN ON THE CHAMP'S SHOULDERS. SNIPER SKY USES HIS FREE HAND TO APPLY A VICE-LIKE GRIP TO HARRISON'S

JAW, ENSURING THE BEARDED BRUTE WATCHES WHAT HAPPENS NEXT.

JUDAS IS DANGLING THAT GUY OVER THE EDGE OF THE STAGE AGAIN. IF HE LETS GO, THAT FELLA IS GOING TO PLUMMET BACKWARDS TWENTY FEET, PLUS HOWEVER HIGH JUDAS'S SHOULDERS ARE. IF MY MATH IS CORRECT, THAT'S TWENTY-SEVEN FEET!

HARRISON SCREAMS AT JUDAS NOT TO DO THIS. THE DESTROYER TURNS HIS HEAD BACK SLIGHTLY AND REVEALS A SMILE. THAT SICK SON OF A— AND HE— NO!

HE ACTUALLY DID IT!

FOR THE LOVE OF BRADSHAW! JUDAS THROWS THE FAN FROM THE TOP OF THE STAGE! HE'S FALLEN STRAIGHT TO HELL — WHICH IS WHERE JUDAS BELONGS AFTER THAT HEINOUS ACT!

IS OUR MYSTERY MAN STILL ALIVE?

WE NEED TO GET A CAMERA IN POSITION DOWN THERE TO FIND OUT. WHILE WE AWAIT AN UPDATE ON THE DESTROYER'S VICTIM, THE DRAMA CONTINUES ON THE STAGE, AS HARRISON RECEIVES A SURGE OF ADRENALINE. PAIN BE DAMNED — THE BEARDED BRUTE STILL FIGHTS AGAINST HIS RESTRAINTS. BUT JUDAS, THE BASTARD, IS SMILING.

WATCH IT, GENE. I'M NOT SURE I AGREE WITH WHAT WE JUST WITNESSED, BUT REMEMBER WHO YOU'RE TALKING ABOUT HERE.

DAMN IT ALL, FARQUAD! SKY AND X-STATIC HAVE ADJUSTED THEIR GRIPS AND IT DOESN'T LOOK GOOD FOR HIP HARRISON. JUDAS APPROACHES, SLOWLY, AND COMES FACE-TO-FACE, ONCE AGAIN, WITH HIS NEXT CHALLENGER, THAT SICK SMILE STILL ON THE CHAMPION'S FACE.

HE'S SAYING SOMETHING, GENE.

"THE WORST IS YET TO COME," — WHAT DOES THAT MEAN?

JUDAS IS BACKING UP. I THINK WE'RE ABOUT TO FIND OUT WHAT THE WORST IS.

COME ON. HAVEN'T YOU DONE ENOUGH, DESTROYER? HARRISON IS HELPLESS!

HERE IT COMES: THAT PATENTED DESTROYER KICK.

***

Hip Harrison remained calm as the sole of Judas's boot fast approached his face. Time slowed to a crawl. The Bearded Brute had never felt such anger. Nemo didn't deserve any of what had just happened to him. All he was guilty of was discovering something that inconvenienced the wrong people.

For those with all the power, the only thing that mattered was holding onto it at all costs. Even if it resulted in the end of the galaxy. How was it possible to be so greedy? So selfish? Harrison couldn't fathom it. Didn't they realise that the end of all life also applied to them?

Judas was likely ignorant of his puppet master's secrets. The champion had often exhibited psychotic tendencies in the ring, but never anything like this before. This, Harrison realised while Sniper Sky and X-Static held him in the path of Judas's oncoming foot, was an orchestrated assault, with Mr Montgomery serving as the conductor.

Hip Harrison, as number one contender, clearly threatened Judas. The Destroyer had made that clear by running his mouth a little more than usual in the week since the tournament final. Judas, for possibly the first time in his career, was nervous. So, when given the idea of taking out Harrison's best friend as the ultimate mind game, Judas had pounced on it like a splorg on a ball of string. Given Mr Montgomery's position in society, there would be no fear of legal repercussion. What Judas may not know was that he was killing another bird by injuring — perhaps even maiming — Nemo because, in powerbombing Harrison's best friend from the stage, the champ was also ensuring the silence of the world-ending whistle-blower.

In the still, between seconds, Harrison pondered all of this and prayed to Bradshaw that his best friend had survived being dropped from such a height, sustaining no life-changing (or ending) injuries. Praying to the wrestling gods was all The Bearded Brute could do for now. The still, which Harrison had thought about in depth, was something he experienced regularly in the ring. It's what enabled him to counter or dodge high-speed attacks. And whenever his shoulders were pinned to the mat by an opponent, time would subjectively slow right down as the referee slapped his or her hand to the mat, counting the one-two-three. More often than not, the still provided Hip with clarity and allowed him to regain his bearings if he had taken a beating — enough to kick out. There was no kicking out of this situation, though; Harrison had assessed his current predicament and accepted that he was about to eat a stiff boot to the face.

Time resumed its default pace and the last thing Hip Harrison registered was the beehive pattern that filled the bottom of Judas's footwear before the bright lights faded to black.

WEEK SIX

A broken nose, a fractured hand, and bruised ribs were, thankfully, the only injuries Nemo sustained. The attending doctor declared it a bigger miracle than Santino himself.

'Although it looked bad, they're saying that the table broke my fall and saved me from more perilous injuries,' Nemo explained from his hospital bed. In the room with him were Hip Harrison and Ivy Jane. A nurse had just undertaken a series of checks and left.

'I can believe it,' said Ivy. 'You wanna talk about stage fright? Television doesn't do justice to just how high up you are on that thing. Just imagine if you'd cracked your head on the concrete floor, falling from that height.'

When the camera crew manoeuvred into position to capture a shot of Nemo following his plunge from the stage, the image was devastating. Viewers from across Sianard called the Galactic WF hotline to express their concern and outrage that the federation could subject an innocent fan to such brutality. They were met with a pre-recorded message from Judas, reminding callers to stay in school, say no to drugs, and dream big, before the voice of Sovereign Noble took over the line to list upcoming event information and ticket details.

A folding table was set up against the wall of the stage for members of the production team and pyrotechnicians to tinker with their equipment. Nemo fell through the table at high velocity, shattering the timber on impact while the tools and equipment on its surface scattered on and around him. The image that was ultimately presented to television viewers depicted an unconscious Nemo lying on his back, spreadeagled amid the debris. Lucky for him, it looked worse than it was.

'It looked as if I'd been making snow angels in all that plunder,' said Nemo. He chuckled for a moment, but stopped abruptly.

'Take it easy, pal,' said Harrison. 'Bruised ribs might be preferable to broken ribs, but they're still no *laughing* matter.' Now it was The Bearded Brute's turn to laugh at his own joke.

Ivy rolled her eyes. 'You two are so lame.'

'Hey, I'm not lame,' said Nemo. 'I'm technically a professional wrestler now, right?'

'No,' Hip and Ivy both said in unison.

'You mean to say that I survived a beating from the Heavyweight Champion of the Galaxy, live on interplanetary television, and I'm still not deemed tough enough to be a pro wrestler?'

'Mm, you proved you can take a bump,' said Ivy, 'but if you want to earn your stripes as a pro, I wanna see you complete one of my training sessions without puking.'

'Even I struggle to keep up with her,' added Hip. 'She's a beast! You, on the other hand, are what we in the business call a spot monkey.'

'A spot monkey?' Nemo looked from Harrison to Ivy.

Ivy nodded. 'Someone who hasn't brushed up on the basics, the essential grappling holds that should form the foundation of your wrestling technique,' she explained. 'Many start out in their backyards, jumping onto their buddies from the roof of their parents' garage. Some gain a cult following, which gets them noticed by promoters that will exploit them for their daredevil antics. When I was on the indies, I saw guys dive from ballroom balconies more than forty feet in the air, just to get a pop out of the crowd. They damn sure weren't risking their lives for the pay. What they lacked in cash, they made up for in broken bones. If only those cheering, blood-thirsty fans could see what some of these guys were like after the show, when the adrenaline had worn off. I swear this shit is like a drug to some.

'These guys — *and* girls — think all they need to do to make a name for themselves is to leap from taller structures, to complete ever-crazier stunts. These cosplay wrestlers never win a thing outside the occasional fluke victory because they've never stopped to learn the two fundamentals: basic, tried-and-true wrestling holds — your armbars, arm drags, hip tosses, and sleepers — and ring psychology. The latter is essential if you ever want to make it to the top of this game. A good wrestler approaches a match like a game of chess, always trying to stay two steps ahead of their opponent and weighing up the risks of every move they attempt. By all means, use your surrounding environment to your advantage, but don't jump from a balcony through a flaming table just for the hell of it.

'In a nutshell, a spot monkey is nothing more than an amateur stunt performer who only knows how to go from one "high spot" to another.'

'Great promo there, Ivy,' said Harrison. 'I'm ready to see you school some spot monkeys at the pay-per-view now.'

Ivy kicked Harrison playfully in the shin. Harrison sold it like he'd been shot, crumbling to the floor and clutching his leg in mock agony.

'I hate to say it,' said Ivy, rolling her eyes again and turning her attention back to the bed-ridden Nemo, 'but your best friend Doink has just illustrated part of my argument about ring psychology. Sometimes, you want to make an opponent believe they have you hurting more than you really are. By playing possum, you can bait your opponent into letting their guard down and then strike with an offensive manoeuvre of your own. There will also be times when a particular body part will take a hard bump, in which case you'll be doing the opposite — pretending you're not as hurt as you really are to avoid your opponent targeting your vulnerability. This is the type of stuff that spot monkeys never pick up on.'

'Yeah, spot monkey.' Harrison interjected. 'Maybe stop and think next time you let yourself get thrown off a stage.'

'Didn't you jump from a forklift a few weeks ago?' Nemo asked.

'That was a means to an end, my friend. Desperate times and all that.'

'Back to business,' said Ivy, 'I know your injuries are minor considering what they could have been — not that a broken nose or fractured hand is anything to walk off — but have you looked into filing any legal proceedings? I mean, the bruised rib alone should see Judas sent down for aggravated assault, right? There's plenty of video evidence in addition to your injuries, and several thousand witnesses at the scene. Not to mention the millions and millions watching at home. It's an open-and-closed case.'

'Judas won't be prosecuted,' Nemo replied. 'I won't be pressing charges — not that I would be able to. As they wheeled me through the hospital, some stooge in a suit more or less informed me that it wouldn't be worth wasting police time. It was all, apparently, part of the show and I have no way to prove otherwise. He then attempted to buy my silence, dropping a thick envelope on my lap. I picked it up with my good hand and dropped it over the gurney. The goon bent down to pick it up, then told me I should have taken the money.'

'Montgomery will put the kibosh to any criminal charges, anyway. Given his political position, it's safe to say he's got the police in his pocket,' said Harrison.

'I figured,' said Nemo. 'The money was just extra insurance to keep me quiet. Besides, even if it was worth pursuing criminal charges, doing so would likely derail our plans. It's not worth it when we're so close. When *you're* so close, Hip. Closer to the prize at the end of the rope.'

Harrison nodded. 'You're right. If anything were to happen to Judas now, that's it: no title shot. And if I can't capture that championship, I won't have the platform necessary to make my voice truly heard. If I'm anything less than Heavyweight Champion of the Galaxy, I'll never be taken seriously if I try to expose Montgomery and his council cronies. Especially by those who might actually be able to save Sianard.'

'The weight of the world rests on your shoulders, eh?' said Ivy. 'Must feel like, what, ten pounds of gold?'

'It will do when I beat Judas. I'm not sure what's going to give me more satisfaction at this point — draping that championship belt over my shoulder, or exacting a measure of revenge for what that son of a poodwink did to Nemo.'

'I'll live,' said Nemo. 'Just don't let him get into your head, Hip. Stay focused.'

***

PREPARE FOR FIREWORKS TO FLY AS WE HAVE WHAT PROMISES TO BE ONE OF THE MOST EXPLOSIVE SHOWS IN GALACTIC WRESTLING FEDERATION HISTORY IN STORE. I'M GENE KELLY, JOINED AS ALWAYS BY MY BROADCAST PARTNER, LORD FARQUAD.

THAT'S RIGHT, GENE. AFTER THE SHOCKING EVENTS THAT CLOSED OUT LAST WEEK'S BROADCAST, HIP HARRISON AND GALACTIC WF CHAMPION JUDAS WILL MEET IN THE RING TONIGHT TO SIGN ON THE DOTTED LINE AND MAKE THEIR MATCH AT THE UPCOMING BATTLESTAR GALACTICA PAY-PER-VIEW OFFICIAL. WE HAVE OURSELVES A GOOD OLD-FASHIONED CONTRACT SIGNING!

REGULAR VIEWERS WILL KNOW THAT CONTRACT SIGNINGS HERE IN THE GALACTIC WF ARE ALWAYS BRIMMING WITH HIGH DRAMA. IF YOU'RE TUNING IN FOR THE FIRST TIME TONIGHT, I GUARANTEE YOU'RE NOT GONNA WANNA MISS THIS!

BEFORE WE GET TO THE ACTION, WE ALSO WANTED TO SAY A FEW WORDS TO PUT YOU, OUR LOYAL GALACTIC WF FANS, AT EASE. WE UNDERSTAND JUDAS'S ACTIONS LAST WEEK SPARKED SOME CONCERN.

THE GALACTIC WRESTLING FEDERATION HOLDS THE SAFETY AND WELLBEING OF ITS FANS IN THE HIGHEST REGARD.

THE GENTLEMAN YOU SAW ASSAULTED BY JUDAS WAS A PLANT. THE MAN IN QUESTION MAY HAVE APPEARED INCONSPICUOUS, BUT WE HAVE IT UNDER GREAT AUTHORITY THAT HE IS EXTREMELY DANGEROUS, AND THAT HIS TICKET WAS PROVIDED BY HIP HARRISON. THIS UNNAMED ASSAILANT WAS TARGETING JUDAS AS PART OF A PRE-ORDAINED ATTACK TO WEAKEN THE CHAMPION AHEAD OF HARRISON'S TITLE OPPORTUNITY.

WE ARE TOLD THAT JUDAS DETECTED THE THREAT AND BLOCKED HIS ATTACKER'S FIRST PUNCH. RATHER THAN ALLOW HIS AGGRESSOR THE CHANCE TO STRIKE AGAIN, JUDAS DECIDED, ON INSTINCT, TO NEUTRALISE THE THREAT.

IT MAY HAVE COME ACROSS ON-SCREEN AS OVER-THE-TOP, BUT LAW ENFORCEMENT AND LEGAL OFFICIALS HAVE RULED THAT JUDAS ACTED IN SELF-DEFENCE. JUDAS WAS SIMPLY ENSURING THAT HE WAS NO LONGER AT RISK.

WITH THAT CLARIFIED AND JUDAS'S NAME CLEARED IN THE COURT OF PUBLIC OPINION, THE GALACTIC WRESTLING FEDERATION WOULD LIKE TO ASSURE EVERY FAN WATCHING THAT ATTENDING ONE OF OUR SHOWS IS A PERFECTLY SAFE EXPERIENCE. BETTER THAN THAT: WITNESSING GALACTIC WF ACTION LIVE AND IN PERSON OFFERS MORE BANG FOR YOUR

BUCK THAN ANY OTHER FORM OF ENTERTAINMENT ACROSS THE FIVE PLANETS. THERE IS ABSOLUTELY NO REASON TO BE SCARED OR NERVOUS WHEN ATTENDING GALACTIC WF LIVE.

I TELL YOU WHAT, GENE, IT SURE DOESN'T SEEM LIKE THE GREAT GALACTIC WF FANS ARE NERVOUS OR SCARED. SINCE LAST WEEK, WE'VE SEEN TICKET SALES GO THROUGH THE ROOF. IN FACT, EVERY SINGLE GALACTIC WF SHOW FOR THE NEXT HALF-CYCLE HAS SOLD OUT — INCLUDING TONIGHT.

THE ROCK ARENA IS *ROCKING* THIS EVENING. THE ATMOSPHERE IS ELECTRIC AS THE FANS IN ATTENDANCE HAVE BEEN MAKING NOISE SINCE BEFORE THE DOORS EVEN OPENED.

THERE'S NOT AN EMPTY SEAT IN THE HOUSE AS WE KICK THINGS OFF WITH OUR OPENING CONTEST.

***

Hip Harrison found out about the contract signing scheduled for the main event slot of that week's Galactic WF television show when the public did. He read the announcement on The Fed's SIN message boards; Ivy saw it first and showed it to him.

When Hip and Ivy arrived at The Rock a few hours before showtime, the arena's head of security, Gilberg, informed The Bearded Brute that a special trailer had been provided for him.

'They've told me they want their number one contender to get changed in luxury,' Gilberg explained.

'More like they're limiting my time in the building, in case I cause any trouble,' Harrison replied.

'Still,' said Ivy, 'can't say no to our own personal trailer.'

'It's just round the corner there,' added Gilberg. 'I can tell you, they've spared no expense.'

Gilberg was right on the expense part. Although it wasn't exactly a trailer. Instead, what Hip and Ivy found as they turned the corner was a tour craft that even a band of degenerates could get down with. The vehicle was huge, featuring a bathroom, a bedroom with enough space for a double bed, and a kitchen. In the living space was a corner sofa that faced an enormous television screen, which filled the wall separating the area from the driver's cabin.

On the coffee table was a note stating that, as number one contender, the bus was Harrison's new private dressing room. No longer was he expected to join the general population in one of the communal locker-rooms — at least until Battlestar Galactica. If he were to become champion — and, in turn, The Fed's most precious asset — the bus would remain his to use.

Another note was found on the kitchen counter, this one letting Harrison know that a nutritiously balanced, yet delicious, dinner for two was waiting for them in the refrigerator. All they needed to do was pop their meals in the oven.

'This is nice and all, but I can't help but wonder what the catch is,' said Ivy.

'The catch is we're banned from the building,' said Harrison. 'Well, I am, at least. I'm sure they'd let you in if you asked.'

'How can they ban you from the arena, though? You make up one half of The Fed's biggest match of the year. I mean, they've even got you scheduled on tonight's show to promote the pay-per-view. Aren't they advertising the fact that you and Judas will both be in the ring together to sign the contract for the match? How's that going to work?'

'I imagine that, when the time comes, we'll receive a knock at that door,' — Harrison pointed towards the bus's exit — 'from Gilberg and his team. They'll walk me straight out to the ring and, once business is taken care of, they'll bring me right back out here.'

Sure enough, when it was time for Harrison's appearance on that evening's show, good ol' Gilberg came knocking on the door to the tour craft, accompanied by a dozen security personnel. Until that point, Harrison and Ivy sat back and watched the show on the big screen.

'What law enforcement have they been speaking to?' Ivy said quizzically, as they listened to Gene Kelly and Lord Farquad's statement at the start of the show.

'Either they've been speaking with the authorities to ensure they are in Montgomery's pocket, or they've not spoken to them at all,' said Harrison.

'They're trying to paint Nemo as a villain and you as the puppet master.'

'I'm not surprised, but I think this might backfire. Just listen to their delivery. Farquad is trying to sound as hyped up as he normally is, but he's a little more monotonous than usual. And Gene sounds as if they're force-feeding him a shit sandwich. You know they're being fed their lines through their headsets and neither of them is buying it — and neither will anyone watching. Wrestling fans aren't stupid. They know the difference between what's real and when somebody's faking it.'

As the show progressed, a female over-the-top-rope battle royale began with little fanfare and no prior promotion. The winner would challenge Sasha Stratosphere for the Galactic WF Female Championship at Battlestar Galactica.

'I guess I wasn't on the invite list,' said Ivy, letting out an almighty sigh and slumping back onto the sofa.

The final three entrants in the battle royale were Dirty Diana, Mad Donna, and Nessie. Although she had been on a major losing streak and had shown little improvement since being picked for the female roster when she was still extremely green, Mad Donna won the match, becoming next in line for a title shot when Nessie and Diana both spilled over the top rope and fell to the floor, eliminating themselves while still throwing strikes at each other.

'In the name of Bradshaw,' said Ivy Jane, slapping a palm on her forehead. 'At least if one of the others won it wouldn't have been a complete embarrassment to the female division.'

'Wasn't Diana ranked at the top of the division?' asked Harrison, sounding just as perplexed as Ivy.

'She was. I'm not sure why they didn't just announce her as Sasha's next challenger and felt the need to run with this ridiculous battle royale, but there we go. That sums up the state of things for the girls in this company.'

At some point, Ivy asked Hip whether he was planning on getting changed.

'Why?' Hip asked in response. 'It's not like I'm wrestling or anything tonight. All I've got to do is go out there and sign a piece of paper. What's wrong with what I'm wearing?'

Ivy shrugged. Hip was wearing a flannel shirt and jeans. Standard attire on the farm he grew up on, and all The Bearded Brute ever wore besides wrestling trunks.

And so it was that Hip Harrison wore his trademark checked flannel shirt (this one varying shades of blue) when Gilberg and the security team escorted the number one contender into the arena. The security personnel formed a circle around Hip, blocking his view almost entirely as they all marched towards the main arena entrance. They were all built from rock-solid muscle and Harrison wouldn't have been surprised to discover that they were all wannabe wrestlers.

Although Harrison couldn't see past his enforced detail, he could sense others — fellow wrestlers, production crew, etcetera — watching. A large group of large men, walking in sync — it wasn't exactly subtle.

The entourage guided Harrison left of the main entrance ramp, presumably to avoid a potential encounter with Mr Montgomery. They parked behind the towering black curtain that hid the backstage area from the view of fans in the arena. Gilberg threw up a hand and the entire security detail halted on the spot. Harrison then heard the booming voice of Costa Fortune echoing through The Rock Arena's public address system.

'Llllllaaaaaadddddiiiieeeesss and Gentlemeeeeennnnn, please welcome the number ONE contender for the Galactic WF Heavyweight Chammmmpionnnnship: THE BEARDED BRUTE, Hip Harrrrrrriiisssssonnnn!'

As the ring announcer concluded his introduction, his voice was replaced on the sound system by the monotonous beat of Hip Harrison's entrance music. The burly bouncers in front of Harrison stepped aside.

'We're under instruction to allow you to step through the curtain first,' said Gilberg. 'My men will remain two steps behind you and two of them are to accompany you inside the ring. The rest will be stationed at ringside.'

Harrison nodded and stepped between the curtains.

As he wasn't entering from centre stage, the audience didn't react right away when Harrison first appeared in the arena. He entered from the right of the stage — stage left — and wasn't visible from more than half of The Rock's seats, the stage itself blocking him from view. But as he walked around the stage, towards the front, a trickle of fans with seats beside the ramp spotted him — and cheered. Harrison considered that some cheers could have been derived simply from the excitement of a soon-to-be main eventer passing within a closer-than-expected proximity. But that idea lost ground as the whoops and hollas drew the attention of fans seated further back. As more and more fans glimpsed The Bearded Brute making his way to the ring, the cheering grew, rippling throughout the arena. By the time Harrison stood at the bottom of the main entrance ramp, in front of the ring, and in full view of every single member of the capacity crowd, the place was going banana! His theory that a few fans had been excited to be within spitting distance had completely evaporated — they were even cheering for him, and chanting his name, up in the nosebleeds. A Road Warrior pop if ever there was one, Hip Harrison received a hero's welcome.

Entering the ring, Harrison noted the table set up in the centre. A standard wooden affair the likes of which the production crew use when setting up for the show. The likes of which Big Bale had run into. The likes of which Nemo had crash-landed through a week before. A black sheet was draped over this table in an effort to dress it up for television.

Out of the corner of his eye, Hip saw somebody climbing the steel steps up to the ring apron. It was Sovereign Noble. In the commissioner's right hand was a clipboard, clutching several sheets of paper and a pen. His left hand was reserved for his cane. Harrison stepped forward, intending to hold the ropes apart as the commissioner stepped into the ring. Noble had struggled with climbing between the ropes since his career-ending injury, and his cane always seemed to get in the way, no matter how he positioned himself. But Hip only managed one step towards Noble when two members of the security detail grasped The Bearded Brute's shoulders and held him back. This took Harrison by surprise —

partly because he hadn't noticed the burly enforcers follow him into the ring, although he recalled Gilberg informing him of the plan just minutes earlier, and also because he had underestimated how much of a threat Montgomery and the Galactic WF brass viewed him as. Did they really think he was going to attack the commissioner? What would that have accomplished? After all, everybody knew Sovereign Noble was nothing more than a pawn — a visual figurehead and part-time scapegoat.

Hip Harrison backed off and nodded towards the commissioner when he finally got inside the ring.

'Evening, Hip,' said the once Crafty Kingsman. 'Let's hope this goes smoothly.'

'Good evening to you, Commissioner,' said Hip. 'I'd rather not repeat the level of drama we experienced last week. But all this pomp and circumstance over a contract signing is just asking for trouble. And I don't like the look of that table.'

'None of this is my idea,' said Noble. 'But needs must and all that.'

One way, or another. Judas's voice echoed throughout the arena.

'Well,' Noble muttered, 'here we go.'

The crowd continued to make plenty of noise. However, it wasn't exactly the reaction Judas was hoping to elicit. Cheers erupted as the opening chords of Blondie's smash hit played over the public address system, but that could well have been because the audience had been conditioned to root for the champ over the course of his dominant reign. The Destroyer was the franchise, the poster boy for the Galactic WF. His in-ring supremacy had seen Judas become the face employed in all promotional materials. In short, The Fed pushed Judas to the stars as its own top one. And crowds naturally cheered for the biggest and brightest star.

But now, after the events of last week, the fans grew uncomfortable as Judas appeared on the entrance stage. The initial pop subsided, and the sound of twenty thousand hushed conversations with a spattering of boos replaced the cheers.

'That won't be good for the ego,' said Noble.

Harrison smiled, while a visibly irate Galactic WF Heavyweight Champion marched down the ramp, and Costa Fortune announced Judas with as much gusto as he could muster.

'Please welcome the Galactic Wrestling Federation Heaaaaavvvyweight CHAAAAMMMMMPPPIIOOON! This is THE DESTROOOOOOYYYYYEEERRR! This is JUUUUUUUUUUDDDDAAAASSSSS!'

The spattering of boos swelled at the end of the announcement.

When Judas climbed into the ring, he slammed the championship belt down on the table and stood opposite Harrison and Noble, arms crossed. The two security personnel that had accompanied Harrison into the ring positioned themselves at either end of the table. The Bearded Brute pondered the gaping hole in their strategy; what if he simply lunged across the table to attack Judas? He'd get a good few punches in before *Jamie and Joey* (so he had named the security guards in his head) could do anything to stop him. Still, as the Kingsman to his left might have said, this was a time to show some decorum. Once the contract was signed, Hip Harrison was one step closer to the biggest prize in professional wrestling and to revealing the sinister truth to the people of Sianard.

The music faded out, which amplified the ambient noise without Blondie to mask it. Harrison realised, once again, that he was in a big spot — and standing face-to-face with the man in the biggest spot of all. Only, this week, he would not allow the audience adulation to go to his head. From this moment until the referee declared the end of their match at Battlestar Galactica, Hip Harrison was determined to remain completely focused on the task at hand. There'd be time for celebration when he held that big, gold belt in his hands, having won it fair and square.

Sovereign Noble placed the pen and clipboard on the table and took a microphone from Costa Fortune. 'All right, gentlemen,' the commissioner began, 'you both know why we're gathered here tonight. It's time to make your encounter at Battlestar Galactica official.

'I understand you have both read the terms of the contract and have agreed in principle to what it sets out. However, I must inform you that we have added one further stipulation. Now, this new term has been relayed to both of your attorneys, who have each responded that they are happy with this new condition, so long as you two competitors also agree. If you turn to page four of the agreement, you will find the new term under clause three, section sixteen. This term is non-negotiable as the Galactic Wrestling Federation board of directors has deemed it necessary following last week's shenanigans. The clause states that, from the moment you have both finished signing the contract, there is to be no physical contact between the two of you until the bell rings to start your main event match at the pay-per-view. Members of the board were a little nervous that you two wouldn't be able to stop yourselves from harming one another between now and Battlestar Galactica, which could, of course, jeopardise the biggest match of the year. You could say that they have insisted upon this clause to protect their own investment as it is your faces, Judas and Hip Harrison, that are front and centre on all marketing material.'

Judas demanded his own microphone from Costa, who promptly obliged. 'That's nice and all, Limp, but what are they going to do if we break the rules?'

'I'm glad you asked, Judas. Should your challenger, Hip Harrison, ignore this clause, then he will find himself immediately stripped of his status as number one contender. He will also receive a fine to cover any damages and losses incurred by the Galactic Wrestling Federation, and he will be suspended without pay while his continued position on the roster is debated by the board.'

Judas smirked.

'There's more,' Noble continued. 'There will, of course, be ramifications if you, Judas, were to initiate a physical assault on Mr Harrison.'

The smirk faltered momentarily. 'Ramifications, *please*. What ramifications?'

'Well, for one, the Galactic WF Championship will be vacated. You will no longer be champion.'

Judas's jaw dropped. Meanwhile, Harrison had adopted a smirk of his own.

Noble added, 'Of course, you would also be subject to fines and your own place here would come under scrutiny. So, if I were either of you two, I'd sign the contract and keep out of trouble.

'Now, Mr Harrison, are you happy with the conditions put forward?'

Hip Harrison nodded.

'Terrific. With that being the case, all we need is your autograph, if you would kindly squiggle it on the dotted line above your printed name.'

The commissioner handed Harrison the contract and the pen. The Bearded Brute glanced over the page on top, which was the final page of the contract he had already read. Noble had placed it at the front for the sake of ease in signing the agreement on television. Harrison flicked through the sheets beneath it to ensure it was the same as the copy he and his assigned lawyer had already seen. It appeared to be identical, with the addition of a final paragraph outlining the condition Sovereign Noble had just described. The clause was listed as an 'Aggression Disbarment' agreement, stating that if either party were to inflict physical harm upon the other, the contract for the match was void and that the offending party would be liable for damages and subject to disciplinary action.

Harrison let out a sigh and signed the contract.

'Thank you, Mr Harrison,' said Sovereign Noble as Harrison handed him back the clipboard. 'You're officially heading to the main event of Battlestar Galactica.

'Now, if I could ask our Galactic Heavyweight Champion, Judas, to sign on the dotted line beneath where his name is printed. Here you are, Sir.' Noble walked around the table, sidestepping past Joey the security guard to hand the contract to Judas, who snatched the clipboard from the commissioner's hands without taking his eyes off of Harrison.

After a few seconds, Judas finally turned to the commissioner. 'Gimme the damn pen!' The Destroyer barked.

The once Crafty Kingsman complied, receiving no thanks.

Judas feigned interest in the contract before putting pen to paper. He knew everything was in order. Montgomery always had his back, and that weasel Noble was too spineless to try anything. The cursory glance was for the benefit of the audience and the television cameras. Part of the show.

'Excellent,' said Sovereign Noble. The commissioner held out a hand for the contract, but Judas, once again, wasn't paying much attention to the man he'd permanently injured. Instead, the champion thrust the clipboard into Noble's chest, momentarily knocking the wind out of the Galactic WF commissioner. Noble quickly regained his composure and checked that the two signatures were present. 'Ladies and gentlemen, it is official! Your main event for Battlestar Galactica will pit the challenger, Hip Harrison, versus the Galactic WF Champion, Judas, with the Heavyweight Championship on the line.'

The crowd erupted with excitement. Cheers ultimately giving way to applause.

Judas smiled. He still held his microphone.

'May I shake the challenger's hand?' said The Destroyer. 'I wish to show my opponent — my fellow ring warrior — the respect he deserves. And I hope Harrison will reciprocate that respect. I only ask as I don't wish to break this Aggression Disbarment agreement over something so stupid.'

'I believe that will be fine, so long as no act of physical harm is enacted,' Noble said.

'Don't you worry,' said Judas. 'I won't squeeze too hard.' The champion smiled and held out a hand across the table.

Harrison considered the outstretched hand before him. In normal circumstances, there was not a chance in hell that he would have shaken the champion's hand; not after what Judas had done to Nemo. But this was another mind game — as well as a potential opportunity for Judas to flip a portion of the audience back onto his side. The idea of 'respect' was a very real and fickle thing. Sure, Judas had clearly overstepped a boundary, but that was *last week*. If Harrison were to reject a handshake now, that's the thing that some fans would remember. With heelish behaviour, proportionality is easily overridden by what's more recent.

Why did Harrison — and Judas, for that matter — care about audience response so much? A figurative 'home-field advantage' was a very real thing in the throes of combat. A crowd chanting your name not only gave you a boost in confidence but, when it was time to dig deep late into a match, when every fibre of your being felt battered and bruised, it also provided the adrenaline needed to carry on and overcome. If the audience was rooting against you, the opposite was true — your self-worth took a hit.

There were exceptions to the rule: those who thrived on a negative reaction and liked to prove the audience wrong by burying their favourites. However, Judas was not one of those wrestlers — he drank in the adulation. Relished it. His huge ego was like an over-inflated balloon — slowly deflating if the fans ever cooled on him and, if it came under too much pressure, fit to burst.

Harrison considered this, looking around the arena, studying the faces in the front row and peering all the way up to the nosebleed seats. He was winning them over and wanted to keep them on his side. Judas could play all the games he wanted.

The Bearded Brute raised his arm, hesitated, allowing the audience to take in the moment, then plunged his hand into that of his nemesis. The crowd reacted favourably and Harrison felt a shiver run down his spine in the emotional juxtaposition of it all. He was playing the game as well as he could, and was making great strides towards the top of the mountain, yet here he was, shaking hands with a scumbag like Judas.

Payback for Nemo will come when I beat this son of a poodwink and take his most prized possession, Harrison told himself. *And then, it'll be time for the rest of them to cough up.*

The handshake felt uncomfortably long. Judas muttered something, but Harrison wasn't listening. Cameras flashed all around the arena and, at some point, those photo flashes morphed into photopsia. Harrison was seeing stars and reeling from a blow to the temple.

***

OH, COME ON! WHAT THE HELL IS THIS?

I DON'T KNOW, GENE. I'M ALL FOR PUNCHING HIP HARRISON IN THE FACE, BUT JUDAS MAY HAVE JUST COST HIMSELF THE GALACTIC HEAVYWEIGHT CHAMPIONSHIP. WHAT IS HE THINKING?

I HAVE NO CLUE. HE SIGNED THAT CONTRACT JUST MOMENTS AGO, STIPULATING THAT HE AND HARRISON WERE NOT TO GET INTO ANY PHYSICAL ALTERCATIONS BETWEEN NOW AND THEIR ENCOUNTER AT BATTLESTAR GALACTICA. SOVEREIGN NOBLE EVEN WARNED HIM OF THE CONSEQUENCES, YET JUDAS, WHO SEEMS TO BE SPIRALLING OUT OF CONTROL IN RECENT WEEKS, HAS LOST IT COMPLETELY.

WATCH WHAT YOU'RE SAYING, GENE.

WITH THAT SAID, SOVEREIGN NOBLE'S FACE SAYS IT ALL: WHAT IS JUDAS THINKING?

LADIES AND GENTLEMEN WATCHING AT HOME, IF YOU MISSED IT, JUDAS AND HIP HARRISON WERE SHAKING HANDS TO CONCLUDE THE CONTRACT SIGNING, MAKING THEIR UPCOMING CHAMPIONSHIP CLASH AT BATTLESTAR GALACTICA OFFICIAL, WHEN JUDAS SUDDENLY PULLED HARRISON TOWARDS HIM, ACROSS THE TABLE, AND CLOCKED THE CHALLENGER WITH A HELLUVA RIGHT HOOK TO THE SIDE OF THE HEAD.

WITH HARRISON STUNNED, JUDAS GRABBED HIS HEAD AND BASHED IT REPEATEDLY INTO THE TABLE UNTIL THE BEARDED BRUTE LOST CONSCIOUSNESS AND FELL TO THE GROUND. NORMALLY, I'D BE ALL FOR THIS, BUT GIVEN THE RULES LAID OUT IN THAT CONTRACT, JUDAS HAS JUST FORFEITED THE TITLE WITH HIS ACTIONS. HE MAY EVEN BE SUSPENDED OR, WORSE, RELEASED FROM THE GALACTIC WF.

JUDAS NOW MAKES HIS WAY AROUND THE TABLE AS HARRISON LOOKS TO BE GETTING BACK UP. THE BEARDED BRUTE IS ON HIS HANDS AND KNEES AND — NO! — JUDAS LANDS A FIFTY-YARD PUNT TO THE ABDOMEN OF HIP HARRISON.

THAT CERTAINLY WOKE HIM UP.

NOW'S NOT THE TIME FOR SARCASM, FARQUAD. HIP HARRISON, STILL DAZED FROM THE REPEATED BLOWS HE JUST ENDURED TO THE HEAD, HAS NOW HAD

THE WIND KNOCKED COMPLETELY OUT OF HIM. HE'S WRITHING IN PAIN.

AND JUDAS IS SMILING. HE'S GOTTA BE UP TO SOMETHING.

I'M NOT SURE WHAT HIS GAME PLAN COULD BE. HE'S JUST KILLED HIS CAREER AND JEOPARDISED THE BIGGEST SHOW OF THE YEAR. AND FOR WHAT? TO GET A FEW CHEAP SHOTS IN ON HARRISON?

JUDAS IS SMARTER THAN THAT. LET'S NOT FORGET, HE'S THE MASTER OF THE MAT: ONE OF THE MOST CALCULATING COMPETITORS WE'VE EVER SEEN.

THAT MAY BE, BUT HIP HARRISON DOES SEEM TO HAVE GOTTEN INSIDE THE CHAMPION'S HEAD, UNLIKE ANY PREVIOUS CHALLENGER JUDAS HAS HAD BEFORE.

THE COMMISSIONER IS AS SHOCKED AS I AM. AS MANY OF THESE FANS IN ATTENDANCE ARE. SOVEREIGN NOBLE HAS PUT HIMSELF BETWEEN JUDAS AND THE DOWNED HIP HARRISON. I'VE NEVER SEEN THE KINGSMAN LOOK SO ENRAGED; HE'S SCREAMING AT JUDAS, ASKING, 'WHAT HAVE YOU DONE?'
I KNOW I WANT ANSWERS.

JUDAS IS STILL SMILING. THERE'S GOT TO BE MORE TO THIS THAN— WHOA!

JUDAS SHOVES THE COMMISSIONER ASIDE. SOVEREIGN NOBLE IS DOWN. HE MAY HAVE BEEN ONE

OF THE TOUGHEST WRESTLERS TO EVER STEP BETWEEN THE ROPES BUT, AS WE KNOW, NOBLE NOW REQUIRES THAT CANE TO MAKE HIS WAY AROUND, EVER SINCE HIS LEG WAS MASHED LIKE A DAMN POTATO BY JUDAS OF ALL PEOPLE.

THEY DO HAVE A HISTORY. YOU'D HAVE THOUGHT THAT SOVEREIGN NOBLE WOULD HAVE BEEN SMART ENOUGH TO KEEP OUT OF THE CHAMPION'S WAY.

THIS ISN'T RIGHT. BUT WITH NOBLE EASILY DESPATCHED, JUDAS SETS HIS SIGHTS ONCE AGAIN ON HARRISON. THE BEARDED BRUTE IS DEFENCELESS AND, FOR SOME REASON, THE SECURITY PERSONNEL SURROUNDING THE RING ARE DOING NOTHING TO STOP THIS HEINOUS ASSAULT. HELL — A COUPLE OF THOSE GUYS ARE ACTUALLY IN THE RING! WHAT THE HELL IS THIS?

CALM DOWN, GENE. REMEMBER, THE ADDED SECURITY IS THERE TO PROTECT JUDAS FROM ATTACK. THEY CLEARLY WEREN'T INSTRUCTED TO STOP JUDAS FROM CARRYING OUT AN ATTACK OF HIS OWN.

THIS WHOLE THING STINKS. HARRISON IS STRUGGLING BACK TO HIS HANDS AND KNEES, BUT JUDAS LIFTS A BOOT AND STAMPS DOWN ONTO HARRISON'S BACK.

WITH THE BEARDED BRUTE SPRAWLED ACROSS THE MAT, THE DESTROYER REACHES DOWN, CLASPS HIS ARMS AROUND HARRISON'S TORSO AND GUTWRENCHES HIM FROM THE CANVAS.

AN INCREDIBLE SHOW OF STRENGTH FROM THE DESTROYER. HARRISON IS DEAD WEIGHT.

JUDAS SWINGS THE LIFELESS BODY OF HIP HARRISON, BUILDING MOMENTUM, AND HOISTS THE BEARDED BRUTE UP SO THAT HE'S PERCHED ON THE DESTROYER'S SHOULDERS, CASTING TERRIFYING SHADES OF LAST WEEK.

AT LEAST THEY'RE NOT ON THE STAGE. HARRISON CAN COUNT HIS BLESSINGS.

NO, BUT THERE IS A—

TABLE!

FOR THE LOVE OF BRADSHAW! JUDAS DRIVES HIP HARRISON THROUGH THE TABLE WITH A THUNDEROUS ONE-WAY POWERBOMB. THE VERY TABLE ON WHICH THEY BOTH JUST SIGNED THE CONTRACT FOR THEIR UPCOMING CHAMPIONSHIP MATCH. THE VERY CONTRACT THAT STIPULATED NO ACTS OF VIOLENCE BETWEEN NOW AND THEN.

EVEN IF THE CHAMPIONSHIP MATCH AT BATTLESTAR GALACTICA COULD GO AHEAD, I DOUBT HIP HARRISON WOULD BE IN ANY CONDITION TO COMPETE AFTER THIS. JUST LOOK AT HOW THAT

TABLE HAS BROKEN IN HALF — THAT'S SURELY GOTTA EQUATE TO A BROKEN RIB OR TWO. AFTER ALL, FOR EVERY ACTION, THERE IS AN EQUAL AND OPPOSITE REACTION. IT'S BASIC PHYSICS, GENE!

THANKS FOR THE SCIENCE LESSON, EINSTEIN!

I THINK YOU'LL FIND IT WAS NEWTON WHO—

SORRY TO INTERRUPT, FARQUAD, BUT THINGS ARE GETTING HEATED BETWEEN JUDAS AND SOVEREIGN NOBLE. THE COMMISSIONER IS BACK ON HIS FEET AND HE'S NOT HAPPY.

THAT CRAFTY KINGSMAN HAD BETTER WATCH IT, WAVING THAT CANE IN THE DESTROYER'S FACE LIKE THAT. JUDAS MIGHT DESTROY NOBLE'S OTHER LEG IF HE GETS MAD ENOUGH.

NORMALLY I'D ARGUE THAT JUDAS HAS MORE SENSE THAN TO ATTACK AN AUTHORITY FIGURE LIKE THAT. BUT, CLEARLY, OUR HEAVYWEIGHT CHAMPION HAS LOST HIS DAMN MIND. JUDAS HAS ALREADY FORFEITED THE TITLE AND IS LIKELY OUT OF THE GALACTIC WRESTLING FEDERATION BECAUSE OF HIS ACTIONS. WHAT ELSE HAS HE GOT TO LOSE BY TAKING OUT ANY REMAINING FRUSTRATIONS ON THE COMMISSIONER?

NOBLE CONTINUES TO SCOLD JUDAS LIKE A DOG; HE WANTS TO KNOW JUST WHAT IN THE HELL JUDAS WAS THINKING AND, TRUTH BE TOLD, SO DO I.

I WOULDN'T MIND KNOWING WHAT'S GOING ON EITHER, BUT YOU KNOW THERE'S MORE TO THIS STORY. JUST LOOK AT THE EXPRESSION ON THE CHAMPION'S FACE.

FOR THE LOVE OF… HE'S LAUGHING. THAT SON OF A— HE'S JUST JEOPARDISED HIS OWN CAREER, AS WELL AS HIP HARRISON'S HEALTH, AND THE ENTIRE GALACTIC WRESTLING FEDERATION. AND HE'S LAUGHING!

HOLD ON, GENE. HE'S SAYING SOMETHING TO NOBLE. THE COMMISSIONER LOOKS SOMEWHAT CONFUSED — NOT THAT THAT'S AN UNUSUAL SIGHT.

JUDAS IS TELLING NOBLE TO CHECK THE CONTRACT. I'D SAY THE COMMISSIONER LOOKS MORE PERPLEXED THAN ANYTHING AS HE STRUGGLES TO BEND DOWN, SEARCHING FOR THE CLIPBOARD.

THERE IT IS. AMONGST THE RUBBLE!

THIS ENTIRE SCENE IS RIDICULOUS. NOBLE, WHO STRUGGLES TO WALK EVEN WITH THE AID OF A CANE, LET ALONE CROUCH DOWN, IS HAVING TO LIFT THE LIFELESS LEFT LEG OF HIP HARRISON TO RETRIEVE THE CLIPBOARD HOLDING THE CONTRACT. JUST WHAT IS JUDAS UP TO?

THIS SOLD-OUT CROWD HAS GONE EERILY QUIET. YOU CAN JUST HEAR THE ODD MURMUR QUIETLY RUMBLING BETWEEN FANS. LOOK AT THEM:

THEY LOOK LIKE MEERSPLORGS, POKING THEIR HEADS UP TO SEE WHAT'S GOING ON.

NOBLE IS BACK TO A VERTICAL BASE—

HE'S STANDING UP, LADIES AND GENTLEMEN.

—CONTRACT IN HAND, AND HE EXAMINES IT, AS INSTRUCTED BY JUDAS. THE DESTROYER CONTINUES TO GRIN.

THE LOOK ON SOVEREIGN NOBLE'S FACE SAYS ALL YOU NEED TO KNOW. HE'S BLUSHING. JUDAS MUST HAVE PULLED ONE OVER ON HIM. ON EVERYONE, FOR THAT MATTER.

THE COMMISSIONER SHAKES HIS HEAD, APPEARS DEFLATED. I THINK EVERYONE IN THIS DAMNED ARENA WANTS TO KNOW WHAT'S GOING ON AND WE WON'T HAVE TO WAIT LONG AS NOBLE'S CALLING FOR A MICROPHONE.

***

'You think you're clever, do you?' Sovereign Noble asked Judas when the ring announcer handed him a mic. 'You may still be champion, for now, and there may be no repercussions stemming from what you've just pulled, but if Hip Harrison cannot compete at Battlestar Galactica, I'll make bloody well sure that you face some sort of ramification, Sunshine!'

Judas chuckled before resuming his smarky smirk.

'Now,' Noble continued, 'finish signing the bloody contract.'

***

HA HA! THAT'S GENIUS!

I SHOULDN'T BE SURPRISED, NOT AFTER THE CRAP WE'VE SEEN JUDAS PULL OVER THE PAST COUPLE OF WEEKS. BUT THIS IS DOWNRIGHT PATHETIC. AS YOU CAN SEE, LADIES AND GENTLEMEN, AS OUR INCREDIBLY HARD-WORKING GALACTIC WF CAMERA CREW GET IN POSITION TO GIVE YOU THE FULL PICTURE, JUDAS ONLY SIGNED PART OF HIS NAME. WITHOUT A COMPLETE SIGNATURE, THE AGGRESSION DISBARMENT AGREEMENT WAS NOT YET IN EFFECT.

THAT IDIOT, TRASHINGTON, WOULDN'T HAVE KNOWN WHAT HIT HIM. AND ALL BECAUSE JUDAS WAS MISSING THE 'S' FROM THE END OF HIS JOHN HANCOCK.

SURELY THERE'S SOMETHING THE COMMISSIONER CAN DO ABOUT THIS?

LIKE WHAT? HE LAID DOWN THE TERMS OF THE AGREEMENT, PLAIN FOR ALL TO SEE AND HEAR. TRASHINGTON SHOULD HAVE BEEN PAYING CLOSER ATTENTION TO THE PROCEEDINGS.

NOW LOOK AT THIS: THAT POOR EXCUSE FOR A CHAMPION HOLDS UP THE CONTRACT AND PEN AS IF HE'S JUST WON ANOTHER GALACTIC TITLE.

BRAINS MAKE THE CHAMPION AS MUCH AS THE BRAWN. THE PEN IS MIGHTIER THAN THE SWORD, AFTER ALL.

I'D NORMALLY AGREE WITH YOU ON THAT, BUT THIS IS OUTRAGEOUS. AND OUR LIVE AUDIENCE APPEARS TO BE WITH ME ON THAT, AS THIS CAPACITY CROWD SHOWERS THE DESTROYER IN A CHORUS OF BOOS.

DISRESPECTFUL PEONS.

REMEMBER WHO ULTIMATELY PAYS OUR WAGES, FARQUAD. OUR LOYAL AND ENTHUSIASTIC GALACTIC WRESTLING FEDERATION FANS.

WHATEVER. JUDAS HAS SCRIBBLED AN 'S' ON THE DOTTED LINE. THE MAIN EVENT FOR BATTLESTAR GALACTICA IS SET. ARE YOU HAPPY NOW, GENE?

NOT IN THE LEAST. I HOPE THE BEARDED BRUTE IS HEALTHY ENOUGH TO GET THERE AND KICK JUDAS'S ASS ACROSS THE GALAXY.

WHILE MY BROADCAST PARTNER LOSES ANY REMAINING SHRED OF PROFESSIONALISM HE MAY HAVE BEEN HOLDING ONTO, ALLOW ME TO BID YOU ADIEU, LADIES AND GENTLEMEN, BOYS AND GIRLS. I CAN THINK OF NO BETTER VISUAL TO END THIS PROGRAMME ON THAN THE SIGHT OF HIP HARRISON'S POTENTIALLY BROKEN CARCUS LYING DECIMATED AMONGST THE DEBRIS AND

SPLINTERS OF WHAT ONCE WAS A FAIRLY SOLID TABLE. GOODNIGHT!

WEEK SEVEN

'What the bloody hell were you playing at last week?' Sovereign Noble was livid. He'd been trying to contact Judas all week, to get some answers out of the champion — and perhaps, as unlikely as it may be, an apology for the minor assault The Destroyer had committed against the commissioner. Judas, however, had ghosted Noble. And, even more concerning for The Crafty Kingsman, his line of communication with Mr Montgomery had seemingly been severed. With an entire week having passed, and no sense made of what went down during the previous show's contract signing, Sovereign Noble was fuming as he barged into Judas's private dressing room.

Judas sat on the sofa, smirking. 'Good, wasn't it? Everything went exactly as planned and nobody saw it coming. Especially that poor man's excuse for a challenger.'

'Not only did you make me look a right bloody fool out there, but you could have bloody well jeopardised the main event for Battlestar Galactica. What the bloody hell were you thinking?

'In fact, I think I'll answer that for you. You bloody well weren't thinking! You're just lucky that Hip Harrison sustained nothing more than a bruised rib. Call yourself a champion? You're a bloody hooligan!'

Judas remained silent, allowing Noble's rant to fizzle out. 'Are you done?' he eventually said.

Noble nodded.

'Good. I'll allow our boss to fill you in.'

'Boss?'

'Yes, *the* boss.' The rattlesnake-like voice of Mr Montgomery croaked from behind Noble. The commissioner's eyes closed as his mouth dropped open. He hadn't seen the Galactic WF chairman sitting in the room's corner behind him.

'I understand why you might be upset over what happened during last week's contract signing,' Mr Montgomery continued. 'Judas and I concocted the plan to give our fine champion a psychological edge, as well as the obvious physical advantage, over his upcoming opponent. I'm deeply sorry that we couldn't let you in on our scheme before it played out, but we needed to be sure that you could play your part as the impartial authority figure with conviction. As it goes, you played in perfectly and nobody suspects that this thing goes any deeper than Judas playing mind games with an opponent.'

'I don't… sorry, I… yes, Mr Montgomery. But, Sir, what I don't understand is why this elaborate plan to mess with Harrison? Do we not have confidence in Judas to beat him in a fair fight?'

'Watch your tongue, Commish!' said Judas. 'You wouldn't want to run that mouth of yours so fast that it gets away from you and your crippled legs again.'

Noble stood his ground, doing his best to conceal the shiver that trickled down his spine. If his pinky finger so much as twitched an inch, Mr Montgomery would never forgive what he perceived as a sign of weakness.

'Now, now, boys,' interrupted the chairman. 'Let's not have any squabbling. The simple fact of the matter, Sovereign, is that we need to protect my investment — that being the Galactic Wrestling Federation. We know that Judas as champion sells. Just look at him: his face and that body on a poster — he's like a real-life superhero. Easy marketing. Someone like Harrison is an unproven draw with the audience and we can't take that risk. Besides, since Judas has been out there, toying with Harrison like a splorg with a mouse, ratings have gone through the roof. Everyone wants to see what the supposedly unhinged Galactic WF Champion is going to do next.'

The television ratings and proven business model may have formed part of the reason for sabotaging Harrison, but Noble knew he wasn't getting the full story from his boss. Not by a long shot.

'Okay, Sir,' Noble said, relaxing his shoulders, but keeping his eyes on Judas. 'What did you have in mind for this evening? Perhaps Judas might like to take part in an exhibition match with some up-and-coming rookie. You know, to keep in ring-shape before the big title fight.'

Judas laughed. 'Oh, we've got a plan for tonight, alright.'

'Yes,' added Mr Montgomery. 'And this week, Sovereign, we need you in the know. Our champion is heading out on a field trip.'

***

'Just stay on the bus,' Ivy Jane pleaded. 'Nobody expects you to make an appearance tonight after what you've been through the last couple of weeks. You need to take it easy and heal up. There's no need to risk further injury with only two weeks to go until your title shot.'

'I get it, but I can't stay cooped up in here,' said Harrison. 'I need to be there at ringside to make sure you're safe. After Judas's actions — and management's inaction — I don't trust anyone. They know they can get to me through you, and I won't let it happen. I won't let them hurt you.'

'I can take care of myself, you know.'

'Oh, I know. But it's just… what if Judas were to attack you?'

'Don't be ridiculous.'

'I wouldn't put anything past him at this point.'

'Well, even if he did, it's not like you could do anything to help without losing your title match and getting fired. That contract of theirs has seen to that.'

'At the very least, my being out there gives me a chance to pull you to safety. I could even position myself between you and Judas if he were to do anything stupid. Remember, he can't touch me either. Not without getting himself stripped of the championship immediately.'

'Fair enough,' said Ivy. 'Just try not to go looking for trouble. Besides, there's a part of me that wants to know how I'd measure up in the ring against the heavyweight champ.' The Man Eater winked and kissed Harrison on the nose.

The Bearded Brute leaned back to look Ivy in the eyes. 'Have they even told you who your opponent is tonight?'

'All they've said is that it's an exhibition meant to showcase my talents and rebuild my standing with the audience. Apparently, it's with some rookie who's still in wrestling school and only has a couple of matches under her belt. Should be a total squash.'

One of the Galactic WF's tried and tested methods for building up a wrestler's profile in the eyes of the fans was to book them in what competitors dubbed 'squash matches'. A 'squash' was a match against an inexperienced opponent that typically wouldn't last more than a minute, with the idea being that the featured fighter would appear all the more dominant.

'Hmm,' said Harrison, pulling Ivy in close.

***

WE HAVE A SURPRISE GUEST, LADIES AND GENTLEMEN. HIP HARRISON, NUMBER ONE CONTENDER TO THE

GALACTIC HEAVYWEIGHT CHAMPIONSHIP, IS ACCOMPANYING IVY JANE TO THE RING FOR HER MATCH TONIGHT.

WHAT IN THE BLUE HELL IS HE DOING HERE, GENE? SHOULDN'T HE BE RESTING UP AFTER JUDAS EMBARRASSED HIM LAST WEEK?

HE'S SHOWING JUDAS AND THE WORLD THAT YOU CAN'T KEEP HIM DOWN THAT EASY. TABLES BE DAMNED!

IF YOU ASK ME, ALL HE'S SHOWING US IS THAT HE'S AN EVEN BIGGER MORON THAN I'D GIVEN HIM CREDIT FOR. HIS CHAMPIONSHIP BOUT — THE *BIGGEST* MATCH OF HIS CAREER BY *FAR* — IS LESS THAN A MOON ORBIT AWAY. NOT ONLY SHOULD HE BE HOME, LICKING HIS WOUNDS, BUT HE SHOULD KEEP HIS MIND ON THE TASK AT HAND INSTEAD OF DISTRACTING HIMSELF WITH WHATEVER HIS GIRLFRIEND IS UP TO THIS WEEK. MAN, I TELL YOU, BACK IN MY DAY—

YES, YES, FARQUAD. WE'VE ALL HEARD YOUR 'BACK-IN-MY-DAY' STORIES. NO NEED FOR ONE NOW WHEN WE'VE GOT ACTION TO CALL.

FOR ONCE, GENE, I THINK YOU'RE RIGHT. TRASHINGTON DOESN'T DESERVE MY CAREER ADVICE — AND NEITHER DO THE NEANDERBRAINS CHEERING HIM ON AT HOME.

I APOLOGISE FOR MY COLLEAGUE'S LACK OF PROFESSIONALISM, LADIES AND GENTLEMEN, AND I'D LIKE TO REMIND YOU THAT WE AT THE GALACTIC WRESTLING FEDERATION TRULY VALUE AND APPRECIATE EVERY SINGLE ONE OF OUR FANS. WITHOUT YOU, THERE IS NO GALACTIC WF.

***

As Ivy Jane's entrance music, *Mz. Hyde* by Halestorm, faded out, the noise from the crowd grew louder. The Man Eater faced the entrance ramp, awaiting her opponent while Hip Harrison stood behind her left shoulder.

'You know all this cheering is for you,' Ivy called back to Hip. 'Judas's best-laid plans aren't going so well. The fans are firmly on your side.'

'Thanks, but don't go thinking they're *all* cheering for me. You have plenty of fans of your own.'

'Aww, you're sweet. But don't insult my intelligence.'

'Okay, take a quick look over to your right, third row. What do you see?'

Ivy scanned the third row to her right and saw what Hip was referring to: a pair of young girls wearing "Man Eater, World Beater" t-shirts. They both stared excitedly back at Ivy.

'And four or five rows back, right next to the entrance ramp, on the left,' Harrison continued.

Ivy didn't need to look. She'd already clocked the fan with the neon sign that read, "Ivy Jane brings the pain!"

Ivy had brought a somewhat niche fanbase with her when she first joined The Fed. That fanbase grew when Ivy arrived in the Galactic WF because of the exposure that comes with being on television, but her constant low placement on the card — if she was even on the card — kept her fan following to those who were labelled by management as 'alternative'; a subsection of the audience that kept watching the product to root for their favourites, who they perceived as underdogs against the 'mainstream' talents and 'the machine'. To an extent, these fans were correct in their perceptions, as the likes of Ivy Jane often faced an uphill battle just to receive a televised match.

But now, since aligning herself on-camera with one half of the next big main event a few weeks back, Ivy had seen her popularity — and merchandise sales — soar. She would not let it go to her head though, as she knew that those who had hopped aboard her bandwagon could just as easily jump off again when somebody new took their fancy. Hell, the same fans would probably abandon their support for Hip should he lose against Judas. Wrestling fans could be extremely fickle.

'Okay,' said Ivy. 'But don't you go thinking the audience would be as interested in my match if you weren't here with me. You're the focal point of the entire promotion at the moment.'

Harrison shrugged. He knew it was true and to say anything else would be patronising. Maybe he should have stayed away after all.

'Come on,' Ivy said a few seconds later. 'Where's this opponent of mine?'

'Hello, Hip!' A familiar voice echoed throughout the arena's sound system. After a few moments, Judas appeared on the big screen above the entrance curtain. 'I see you're showing support for your girlfriend. That's nice and all but watch yourself. I hear Ivy likes to eat men. I'm not sure whether that's in the cannibalistic sense or more of a carnal manner, but then again, I'm sure you'd have a good idea by now.'

Harrison, incensed by the remark, leant over the top rope, calling for a member of the production crew to give him a microphone. There were apparently none available.

Ivy, who'd heard every sexist insult in the book, told Hip to calm down. The champion was trying to mess with his head yet again, and was succeeding.

'I wouldn't mind getting to know Ivy a little better myself,' Judas continued. 'One way or another. But for now, Hip, I thought I'd turn to somebody else you're close with. After all, if you're next in line for an opportunity at the gold,' The Destroyer paused, to pat the championship belt that lay across his shoulder, 'then I needed to know that you were of worthy stock. And what better way to find out what kind of man you are than by visiting the one who raised you? Ladies and gentlemen, allow me to introduce Hip Harrison's father, Franklo.'

The camera zoomed out. Until then, all that could be seen on the jumbotron was Judas's head and shoulders, along with the title belt, barely lit. The background was too dark to make out. As the frame widened, a bloody and battered Franklo was revealed, sitting in a chair next to where Judas stood. In the ring at The Rock Arena, Hip Harrison kicked the bottom rope and pulled his hands through his hair. He recognised where Judas was: the champ was in his father's workshop.

'Ol' Franklo and I had a good talk, didn't we?' Judas said jovially.

Franklo looked up, hitting Judas with a hard stare, and spat in the champion's face.
Judas smiled, then slapped Franklo across the jaw before wiping the gob from his cheek.

'Come on now, Frankie. I told you, I only wanted to talk. Why do you keep provoking me?'

'Go to hell, you worthless waste of space! My son's going to teach you a lesson next moon orbit. Give you the spanking your daddy should've given ya'!'

Still watching from the ring, Hip Harrison silently pleaded with his dad to stop talking and for Judas to leave the old man alone.

On the screen, Judas continued: 'You just don't learn, do you? Well, I'll just have to give you a taste of what's in store for your son at Battlestar Galactica.

'To bring those of you watching up to speed, when I arrived here at Franklo's compound, about an hour ago, I found him messing around with this strange device. Would you like to tell the people what this is, Frankie?'

Franklo sighed. Mumbled.

'A little clearer, if you will.'

'It's a motor I've been working on.'

'It's more than that,' said Judas. 'When I walked in here, you were handling this thing with great care; treating it almost as if it were your child.'

'Don't—'

'So, what better way to demonstrate how it's going to feel when I destroy your only son in the middle of the ring than by destroying this motor of yours?'

'Please, you don't understand. I've almost perfected it. Once I've got it working, it'll be the answer to all of Sianard's energy problems.'

'Looks more like a hunk of junk to me.'

'It's a theory I developed years ago, after an old craft of mine had a leaky battery.' Franklo spoke hurriedly. 'What if all you needed to power an engine — or anything, for that matter — was just an initial injection of fuel?'

Judas shook his head and shrugged.

'With this motor, in theory, you feed it fuel to begin with — even cooking oil will do — and then the motor uses that to power itself up. Are you with me so far?'

'Sounds like any other motor, old man.' Judas chuckled.

In the ring, it alarmed Harrison to see that his father had forgotten about the danger he faced, speaking to Judas as if The Destroyer gave a damn.

'See, that's where it's different,' Franklo enthused. 'What the motor does is take that fuel and through what I've called the cyclone system, it never actually burns said fuel away, apart from a tiny amount we lose with ignition the first time you switch it on. Rather, it pushes the oil around the system, over and over, building momentum. It only needs the oil in the first place to self-lubricate so that friction is no longer much of a factor. Then, the motor, powered by the kinetic energy from the oil cycling around, keeps pushing that same oil around faster and faster, which creates an ever-larger excess of power that can drive other things. Do you see?'

'So, what you're saying is that this thing creates power and the longer it runs, the more it produces?' Judas scratched his chin in mock intrigue.

'That's precisely it!' Franklo was excited now. 'I've just got a couple more kinks to iron out and then I think this thing can make a real difference in saving our galaxy.'

'That's what you think, huh?' Judas held the motor up with one hand, studying it in the light. 'Well, you wanna know what I think?'

The excitement drained out of Franklo's face. He'd got carried away with talking about his motor — an obsession of which he had never spoken of, going back at least twenty cycles. Despite the circumstances, it had felt good to tell someone — or the entire galaxy, in fact — about his work. But, although he had dedicated such a large amount of time to tinkering away in his garage, Franklo could still read people. He picked up on social cues. And now, he realised Judas was playing with him.

'I think you're full of crap, just like that worthless son of yours. I think crap is all you can produce. Let's look at the evidence: we have your boy, Hunluka — a piece of trash who's in way over his head; and then we have this piece of garbage, which even you admit doesn't even work properly yet.'

'I've almost got it working. I just need to—'

The sound of his motor crashing to the floor interrupted Franklo.

'No, please don't... I can still fix—'

'SHUT UP!' The verbal venom with which Judas barked those words made even Hip Harrison wince while watching on the jumbotron. Franklo cowered back in his chair, against his worktop.

Judas turned to face directly into the camera. 'Hip, I hope you realise just how much danger you're in. But just in case you haven't quite received the message yet, I'll leave it again, this time care of Daddy!'

The Destroyer, living up to his moniker, raised his left boot and brought it down hard on the motor, smashing the device to smithereens.

'No!' Franklo cried. Not only had Judas destroyed a potential solution to the galaxy's energy and environmental crises, but he'd also robbed Franklo of the past twenty cycles of his life's work.

'Quit your whining, old man,' said Judas, still looking into the camera. 'This is nothing compared to what I'm about to do to you. Ready for round two?

'And, Hip, I'll see you soon. One way or another.'

The screen abruptly cut to black.

Inside the ring, Hip Harrison paced frantically back and forth, both hands on his head, pulling at his hair. Ivy tried in vain to calm him down.

'I've got to go. I've got to go right now. I need to make sure Dad's alright. I've got to get over there.'

'Okay,' said Ivy, 'but I'm coming with you.'

Hip Harrison hopped between the middle and top ropes and dropped down to the floor. Ivy followed. As they marched up the ramp, chants of 'Hip! Hip! Hip!' serenaded them. Every fan in attendance wanted to see Judas get his comeuppance — and they didn't want to wait a week and a half until Battlestar Galactica. They wanted to see Hip Harrison gain some measure of revenge tonight.

As they reached the stage, they were met by Sovereign Noble. The commissioner hobbled through the curtain with a microphone in hand.

'Hip, I'm sorry about what just happened to your father. Truly I am. And I understand you need to leave immediately and that's fine, as we don't have a match scheduled for you tonight. You go now, take care of your father and get your head in the right space for your upcoming title match.

'As for you, Ivy Jane, I'm afraid you *do* have a match tonight, so I'm going to need you to stay right here.'

'Please, can't I go with him?'

Sovereign gave his reply away from the microphone. 'I'm afraid not. We have your opponent waiting in the wings and, well, to give up this television time wouldn't do you any favours with the booking committee.'

'Don't worry about me,' said Hip. 'I'll take care of my dad. You have your match and then you can catch up with me.' Harrison made his way through the curtain where a camera crew was waiting to follow him through the backstage area.

Ivy watched on the big screen, along with the sold-out crowd at The Rock Arena and the millions watching at home, as Hip ran past a couple of members of the production crew, who were standing around, eating sandwiches and swigging from Snoda bottles. The camera remained five or six steps behind The Bearded Brute as he pushed open a fire exit door and picked up the pace to a full sprint, passing an assortment of crafts and vehicles, including the Galactic WF production juggernaut, on which was emblazoned a 20-foot tall image of Judas's snarling face.

Harrison eventually reached his maroon Lite-Craft 7S, jumped into the driver's seat and caused the pursuing camera crew to dive out of harm's way when he reversed out of the parking space as if he were practising a handbrake turn. The camera operator steadied himself and re-established the shot just as Harrison's craft accelerated up and out into the stars.

Sovereign Noble turned to Ivy Jane and spoke into the microphone. 'You can stay out here. Your match is still up next.'

The crowd noise swelled. There were gasps and murmurings and more than a few boos.

'In fact,' Sovereign continued. 'Your opponent is here.'

The camera fixed on Ivy Jane and Sovereign Noble from halfway up the entrance ramp spun around to focus on the source of the commotion: Ivy Jane's opponent, who was standing in the ring.

***

WHAT THE HELL IS THE MEANING OF THIS?

I DON'T KNOW, I DIDN'T THINK HE WAS IN THE BUILDING.

I'M STILL REELING FROM WHAT WE JUST WITNESSED, WITH JUDAS ASSAULTING HIP HARRISON'S FATHER, FOR BRADSHAW'S SAKE! NOT TO MENTION THE BREAKING AND ENTERING, AND PROPERTY DAMAGE CHARGES. I'M CERTAIN EVERYBODY WATCHING, HERE AT THE ROCK ARENA AND AT HOME, FEELS AS SICKENED AS I DO TO KNOW THAT NOT ONLY HAVE WE SAT HERE AND ENDURED THOSE HEINOUS ACTS AT THE HANDS OF THE MAN WE CALL A CHAMPION, BUT THAT WE'VE ALSO BEEN DUPED BY THE SAME SICK SON OF A—

AS A FORMER COMPETITOR, GENE, I GET IT TO SOME EXTENT. I USED TO PLAY MIND GAMES WITH THE BEST OF THEM AND, MORE OFTEN THAN NOT, I'D

HAVE MY OPPONENT BEAT BEFORE WE'D EVEN STEPPED FOOT BETWEEN THE ROPES. BUT EVEN I'M UNCOMFORTABLE WITH WHAT WE'RE SEEING HERE. I ASSUME THE FOOTAGE WE SAW ON THE TRON WASN'T A LIVE FEED AFTER ALL.

TAPE DELAY! THIS WHOLE THING HAS BEEN ORCHESTRATED DOWN TO THE FINEST OF DETAILS. THAT CRAFTY KINGSMAN'S GOT TO BE IN ON THIS. LOOK AT HIM NOW, TELLING IVY JANE THAT SHE'S GOT TO GO DOWN TO THAT RING AND FACE THE HEAVYWEIGHT CHAMPION. THAT'S NOT A FAIR FIGHT; JUDAS IS TWICE HER SIZE.

IF THERE'S ANY GLIMMER OF HOPE, GENE, IT'S THAT IVY JANE HAS EXPERIENCE COMPETING WITH MALE WRESTLERS. SHE IS THE MAN-EATER AFTER ALL.

THAT MAY BE SO, FARQUAD, AND NOT TO TAKE ANYTHING AWAY FROM IVY JANE, WHO'S A HELLUVA COMPETITOR, BUT SHE'S NEVER FACED A MALE SUPERSTAR ON JUDAS'S LEVEL. IVY MAY BE THE BEST WRESTLER ON THE WOMEN'S ROSTER, AND THE SKILLS SHE'S SHOWN IN THE RING COULD WELL MATCH THAT OF THE DESTROYER — BUT THERE'S NO GETTING AWAY FROM THE SIZE AND POWER ADVANTAGE JUDAS HOLDS.

IVY'S ASKING SOVEREIGN NOBLE IF HE'S SERIOUS. SHE'S LOOKING AT THE COMMISSIONER AS IF HE'S LOST HIS MIND.

THAT HE DAMN WELL HAS! JUDAS, MEANWHILE, STANDS IN THE RING, BECKONING IVY JANE TO JUST BRING IT WITH AN OUTSTRETCHED PALM THAT'S GOT TO BE BIGGER THAN IVY'S HEAD. WE'RE NOT SURE HOW HE EVEN GOT THERE, BUT ONE WOULD ASSUME HE CAME IN THROUGH THE CROWD. WHAT I WANT TO KNOW IS: HOW LONG AGO DID HE COMMIT THAT ASSAULT ON HIP HARRISON'S FATHER, AND WHO ELSE IS IN ON THIS DESPICABLE PLOT?

I'M NOT SURE WHAT THE COMMISSIONER SAID TO IVY, BUT HE JUST POINTED TOWARDS THE RING.

ONE WOULD IMAGINE THE CHOICE WAS TO COMPETE OR LOSE HER SPOT ON THE ROSTER. DON'T DO IT, IVY! IT'S NOT WORTH THE COST TO YOUR HEALTH!

EVEN IF SHE COULD HEAR YOU, GENE, I DON'T THINK IVY JANE WOULD PAY ANY ATTENTION. LOOK: SHE SHRUGS IN THE FACE OF AUTHORITY AND RUNS DOWN THE RAMP.

BY BRADSHAW! THE GUTS AND DETERMINATION THIS YOUNG LADY EXUDES ARE NOT TO BE UNDERESTIMATED. SHE CHARGES STRAIGHT INTO THE FIRING LINE WITHOUT A SHIMMER OF FEAR OR HESITATION.

SHE SLIDES INTO THE RING. HERE WE GO!

THE SADISTIC JUDAS SMILES AS THE TIMEKEEPER RINGS THE BELL. AND IVY JANE IS BRINGING THE FIGHT, CHARGING TOWARD THE GALACTIC WF CHAMPION.

JUDAS IS COMING BACK AT HER WITH A CLOTHESLINE.

BUT IVY DUCKS IT. JUDAS STAGGERS. IVY PERFORMS A HANDSTAND, HER LEGS SPRINGBOARD OFF THE ROPES AND SHE CATAPULTS HERSELF BACK TOWARDS JUDAS AS HE TURNS AROUND.

OOMPH! SHE NAILED HIM RIGHT ON THE NOSE WITH A VICIOUS AND PERFECTLY TARGETED ELBOW.

SHE'S LIKE AN ASSASSIN WITH THAT MOVE. FEW COULD CONNECT ACCURATELY WITH A BACK ELBOW AT ANY SPEED, LET ALONE HEAD OVER HEELS AND AT THE HIGH VELOCITY IVY JUST CAME IN AT.

UH OH! I DON'T THINK THAT WAS SUCH A WISE MOVE. JUDAS IS STILL STANDING.

THE CHAMPION — THE *MALE* CHAMPION, THAT IS — IS ROCKED AND CLUTCHING HIS NOSE, BUT HE'S MAINTAINED A VERTICAL BASE.

JANE'S NOT WAITING AROUND. SHE'S GOING FOR SOMETHING ELSE.

IF SHE HAS ANY CHANCE OF TAKING THE DESTROYER OFF HIS FEET, SHE'S GOT TO USE HER SPEED AND KEEP UP THE ATTACK.

JUST LIKE THAT. A LOW DROP KICK TO THE RIGHT KNEE OF JUDAS TAKES HIM DOWN TO JUST THE LEFT KNEE.

SOVEREIGN NOBLE WATCHES ON FROM THE STAGE. HE LOOKS MORE THAN A LITTLE CONCERNED. PERHAPS THIS ISN'T PLAYING OUT AS PLANNED. YOU'VE GOT TO BELIEVE HE'S IN ON THIS… THIS… PLOT WITH JUDAS.

JUDAS DOESN'T LOOK SO CONCERNED. HE MAY BE DOWN ON ONE KNEE, BUT HE'S STILL SMILING. IF YOU DIDN'T KNOW ANY BETTER, YOU'D THINK HE WAS ABOUT TO PROPOSE TO THE MAN EATER.

I'M NOT SURE WHAT HE'S SMILING ABOUT BECAUSE IVY'S NOT STOPPING. SHE DARTS BEHIND THE CHAMPION, BOUNCES OFF THE ROPES ONCE AGAIN AND FLIES THROUGH THE AIR, CONNECTING WITH A SHINING WIZARD, AND JUDAS IS DOWN!

I GUESS THAT WAS A NO ON THE PROPOSAL. PROBABLY FOR THE BEST AS WEDDINGS ARE EXPENSIVE. I SHOULD KNOW; I'VE HAD FIVE OF THEM. AND THE DIVORCES COST EVEN MORE!

THANKS FOR THE LIFE LESSON, FARQUAD. NOW, LET'S GET BACK TO CALLING THE ACTION. IVY JANE IS SURPRISING US ALL.

I'LL GIVE IT TO HER. I'VE NEVER SEEN A SHINING WIZARD LOOK QUITE SO CRISP. CHECK OUT

THIS REPLAY — SHE EXTENDS HER KNEE AT THE EXACT MOMENT IT MAKES CONTACT WITH THE BACK OF JUDAS'S HEAD.

THE CROWD IS GOING WILD. THE BUILDING IS SHAKING. WE COULD BE ABOUT TO WITNESS THE GREATEST UPSET IN THE HISTORY OF THIS SPORT.

NOT SO FAST, GENE. JUDAS MAY BE OUT COLD, BUT HE'S FACE-DOWN. IVY'S STILL GOTTA ROLL HIM OVER IF SHE'S GOING TO SCORE THE PIN.

THAT APPEARS TO HAVE CROSSED THE MAN EATER'S MIND. SHE SURVEYS HER SURROUNDINGS, WEIGHING UP HER OPTIONS.

DECISION MADE — IF IN DOUBT, CLIMB TO THE TOP ROPE AND JUMP ON 'EM!

IVY JANE STEPS BETWEEN THE ROPES AND MAKES HER WAY ACROSS THE RING APRON TO THE CORNER TURNBUCKLE. SHE ASCENDS THE ROPES AS IF THEY'RE THE STURDY RUNGS OF A LADDER. SHE PLANTS HER FEET ON THE TOP ROPE, ONE EITHER SIDE OF THE TURNBUCKLE, AND RISES LIKE A PHOENIX. SHE TAKES AIM—

LOOK WHO ELSE IS RISING. JUDAS JUST SPRUNG TO HIS FEET. HE'S STILL GOT THAT GRIN ON HIS FACE.

IT'S SAFE TO ASSUME JUDAS WAS PLAYING POSSUM, THAT HE WAS TOYING WITH HIS OPPONENT. BUT IVY JANE DOESN'T LOOK DETERRED.

SHE LOOKS CALM AND COLLECTED. JUDAS HASN'T FAZED HER — LOOK AT THIS! CONFIDENCE IF I EVER SAW IT.

IVY JANE HONOURS JUDAS WITH A ONE-FINGER SALUTE. AND SHE TAKES FLIGHT.

JUDAS HAS BEEN CAUGHT OFF GUARD. HE FLINCHED.

AND IVY JANE TAKES ADVANTAGE. SHE PUSHES OUT HER FEET IN MID-AIR, WRAPS HER LEGS AROUND THE NECK OF JUDAS AND TWISTS HER UPPER BODY IN A DOWNWARD SPIRAL.

HURRICANRANA!

NOT SO FAST. JUDAS HOLDS ON. NORMALLY, THE PULL CREATED BY IVY JANE'S TORSO, ALLOWING GRAVITY TO DO ITS WORK, WOULD WRENCH HER OPPONENT FORWARD, HEAD OVER HEELS. BUT JUDAS'S FEET REMAIN PLANTED TO THE SPOT.

HE DIDN'T EVEN BUDGE. IVY'S HANGING THERE, UPSIDE-DOWN AND DEFENCELESS.

IVY RELINQUISHES HER GRIP, BUT JUDAS HAS A HOLD OF HER WAIST. SHE'S STUCK WITH NO WAY OUT. AND NOW JUDAS LAUGHS AS HE TAKES A STROLL

AROUND THE RING, IVY'S HAIR SWEEPING THE CANVAS. THIS IS HUMILIATING.

I AGREE WITH YOU, GENE. I'VE BEEN A BIG FAN OF JUDAS FOR A LONG TIME, BUT WHILE I COULD DEFEND HIS ACTIONS OVER THE PAST COUPLE OF WEEKS, EVEN I THINK THIS TAKES THINGS TOO FAR. THIS GOES BEYOND MIND GAMES.

THE CROWD CONCURS; I'VE NEVER HEARD SUCH LOUD, IMPASSIONED DISDAIN FROM OUR AUDIENCE.

JUDAS PARADES IVY JANE AROUND THE RING AND NOW, LOOK AT THIS. FOR LACK OF BETTER TERMINOLOGY, HE'S THRUSTING HER FACE INTO THE BOTTOM ROPE.

CAN'T THE REFEREE STOP THIS? WHY IS OUR COMMISSIONER ALLOWING THIS VILE BEHAVIOUR TO CARRY ON? AND TO THINK, HE'S THE ONE WHO MADE THIS SO-CALLED MATCH IN THE FIRST DAMN PLACE.

TECHNICALLY IT IS A ROPE BREAK. THE REF'S COUNTING: ONE, TWO, THREE, FOU—

JUDAS STEPS AWAY FROM THE ROPES BEFORE THE REFEREE REACHES FIVE, WHICH WOULD HAVE RESULTED IN A DISQUALIFICATION. IVY'S STILL TRYING TO BREAK FREE AS JUDAS WALKS THEM INTO THE CENTRE OF THE RING. JUDAS WRENCHES IVY UP TO HIS SHOULDERS ONCE MORE. HE'S GOT TO BE LOOKING TO HIT THAT ONE-WAY POWERBOMB OF HIS.

BUT IVY'S RESISTING IT, SWINGING AWAY, TRYING TO GET A HIT IN.

YOU'VE GOT TO ADMIRE THE HEART AND DETERMINATION THAT THIS YOUNG WOMAN DISPLAYS.

WHOA-HO-HO! WHAT A BLOW!

IVY JANE NAILS JUDAS WITH A HELLUVA RIGHT HAND TO THE CRANIUM. SHE BROUGHT HER FIST DOWN LIKE A HAMMER.

IT WORKED… SORTA. IVY'S ONCE AGAIN DANGLING UPSIDE-DOWN IN JUDAS'S GRIP. SHE NEEDS TO FIND A WAY OUT OF THIS.

LOOKING AT THIS THROUGH ANALYTICAL EYES, THE CHAMPION WOULD BE WISE TO RELEASE HIS OPPONENT FROM THIS HOLD. HOWEVER, EMOTIONS APPEAR TO HAVE GOT THE BEST OF THE DESTROYER, WHO LOOKS INTENT UPON CAUSING SERIOUS HARM TO IVY JANE, WHO— OH MY BRADSHAW!

SHE'S BITING HIM!

IVY JANE, FIGURING THERE WAS NO WAY TO WRESTLE HER WAY OUT OF THIS HOLD, HAS EMPLOYED WHAT SOME MIGHT CALL A DIRTY TACTIC. WHILE STILL UPSIDE-DOWN, THE BLOOD RUSHING TO HER HEAD, SHE TAKES HOLD OF JUDAS'S LEFT LEG WITH BOTH HANDS AND SINKS HER TEETH INTO HIS CALF LIKE IT'S A BARBECUE STEAK!

IT MAY BE DIRTY BUT THE CROWD IS CHEERING. BESIDES, IT WORKED. JUDAS IS CRYING OUT IN PAIN AND RELINQUISHES HIS GRIP ON IVY'S MID-SECTION.

IVY JANE BOUNDS TO HER FEET AND THROWS ANOTHER FIST AT JUDAS'S HEAD. SHE CONNECTS WITH HIS CHIN. JUDAS HOLDS HIS JAW AND… GRINS.

I THINK ALL THAT PUNCH DID WAS MAKE JUDAS FORGET ABOUT THE HAMMER-BLOW TO THE BRAIN AND CHUNK TAKEN OUT OF HIS LOWER LEG. WE'VE SEEN THAT LOOK ON THE DESTROYER'S FACE BEFORE; IVY'S JUST AWOKEN THE BEAST.

IVY THROWS A RIGHT HOOK, BUT JUDAS CATCHES HER HAND IN HIS OWN. I THINK YOU'RE RIGHT, PARTNER. JUDAS IS TAKING THIS MATCH MUCH MORE SERIOUSLY NOW, AND I'M CONCERNED FOR THE HEALTH AND WELLBEING OF IVY JANE.

HE'S NOT LETTING GO. HE'S TRYING TO CRUSH HER HAND. IVY'S STRUGGLING TO GET AWAY.

JUDAS WAGS A FINGER IN IVY'S FACE, AS IF TO SAY, 'NO, NO, NO!' AND THE MAN EATER RESPONDS BY SPITTING IN *HIS* FACE.

WHAT A LOOGIE!

JUDAS LETS GO OF JANE'S HAND AND WIPES THE SALIVA FROM HIS CHEEK. JANE THROWS ANOTHER HOOK — A LEFT THIS TIME — AND HITS THE CHAMP

SQUARE IN THE CHIN. BUT JUDAS RETALIATES IMMEDIATELY WITH A STIFF KNEE TO JANE'S STOMACH. SHE DOUBLES OVER, DROPPING TO THE CANVAS.

WE MIGHT NEED A DOCTOR, GENE. THAT WAS AS HARD AS I'VE EVER SEEN A KNEE CONNECT WITH AN OPPONENT IN MORE THAN THIRTY CYCLES IN THIS BUSINESS, AND JUDAS IS MORE THAN DOUBLE JANE'S WEIGHT.

THE REFEREE NEEDS TO STOP THE DAMN MATCH.

JUDGE DREAD IS CHECKING WITH IVY, AND HE ALLOWS THE MATCH TO CONTINUE.

SOMEONE WITH THE HEART AND PASSION OF IVY JANE WILL NEVER QUIT. THE REFEREE NEEDS TO MAKE THAT DECISION HIMSELF. AND WOULD YOU LOOK AT THIS: JUDAS PULLS IVY, BY THE HAIR, UP TO HER FEET. COME ON, REF!

I DON'T THINK I CAN WATCH MUCH MORE OF— WHOA! DID YOU SEE THAT? IVY JANE STRUCK JUDAS WITH AN ALMIGHTY SLAP.

WAS THAT THE LAST STAND FROM A DEFIANT IVY JANE? JUDAS ONCE AGAIN WITH A KNEE TO THE MID-SECTION – WHILE STILL GRASPING HER HAIR IN A BUNCH – AND HE REACHES AROUND IVY'S WAIST TO WRENCH HER UP FOR THE ONE-WAY POWERBOMB.

UP ON JUDAS'S SHOULDERS, IVY LOOKS AS IF SHE'S RUN OUT OF FIGHT. AND YOU KNOW WHY

JUDAS CALLS HIS POWERBOMB 'ONE-WAY'; IT'S BECAUSE THE ONLY WAY TO GO IS DOWN.

JUDAS PUSHES IVY JANE UP AS HIGH AS HE CAN — THERE'S REALLY NO NEED BUT THE SON OF A POODWINK IS DOING IT ANYWAY — AND HE SLAMS HER TO THE MAT AS HARD AS HE CAN. THE SOUND OF IVY JANE'S BODY HITTING THE RING IS THUNDEROUS, ECHOING THROUGHOUT THE ARENA AS THIS CROWD HAS GONE DEATHLY SILENT.

JANE'S NOT MOVING. AT LEAST IT'S GOT TO BE OVER NOW. SMALL MERCY AND ALL.

YOU'RE RIGHT, FARQUAD. AS SOON AS JUDAS SCORES THE PIN, HE CAN STEP ASIDE AND ALLOW THE MEDICAL PROFESSIONALS AT RINGSIDE TO LOOK AT HER.

WAIT — HE'S NOT GOING FOR THE COVER. WHAT'S HE DOING?

IF HE DOESN'T MAKE THE PIN, THE REFEREE SHOULD END THE MATCH REGARDLESS. IVY IS OUT AND THERE'S NO WAY SHE CAN CONTINUE.

HE'S PICKING HER UP!

THAT TOTAL SON OF A— JUDAS GUT-WRENCHES IVY JANE UP ONTO HIS SHOULDERS AGAIN. WHAT IS THE MEANING OF THIS? WHAT HAS JUDAS GOT TO PROVE BY RISKING FURTHER INJURY TO THIS DEFENCELESS YOUNG COMPETITOR?

IT'S MAKING *MY* GUT WRENCH JUST TO WATCH IT.

AT LEAST EVERYONE NOW SEES THE CHAMPION FOR WHAT HE IS: A WORTHLESS PIECE OF—

HE'S LIFTING HER UP AS HIGH INTO THE AIR AS HE CAN. HIGHER THAN LAST TIME. SHE'S NOT CONSCIOUS. SHE CAN'T PROTECT HERSELF!

NO! IVY JANE ONCE AGAIN CRASHES TO THE MAT WITH BRUTAL FORCE. ALL THAT'S BELOW THAT CANVAS IS A THIN LAYER OF FELT COVERING UNFORGIVING WOODEN PANELS. THE SOUND OF IVY JANE LANDING IS THE ONLY SOUND TO BE HEARD IN THE ROCK ARENA OTHER THAN THE VOICES OF MY BROADCAST PARTNER AND MYSELF. LOOKING AT THE FACES IN THE AUDIENCE, MANY HERE ARE SICKENED BY WHAT THEY'RE SEEING.

I JUST HOPE THEY END IT NOW, ONE WAY OR ANOTHER... SORRY, I DIDN'T MEAN TO QUOTE THAT CATCHPHRASE.

THE REFEREE, JUDGE DREAD, IS HAVING SOME SORT OF DISCUSSION WITH JUDAS. HE'S TELLING THE CHAMPION THAT ENOUGH IS ENOUGH, THAT IT'S TIME TO END THIS. BUT JUDAS SHOVES THE REFEREE ASIDE, TURNS IVY JANE OVER AND WRAPS HIS ARMS AROUND HER YET AGAIN!

HE JUST GUT-WRENCHED HER UP TO HIS SHOULDERS FROM THE CANVAS.

JUDGE DREAD IS STILL CALLING FOR JUDAS TO STOP WHILE THE UNCONSCIOUS IVY JANE RESTS ON THE CHAMPION'S SHOULDERS. THE REF TURNS TO FACE THE TIMEKEEPER OUTSIDE THE RING AND CALLS IT.

THANK BRADSHAW FOR THAT. THE BELL RINGS, THE MATCH IS OVER DUE TO A RARE TKO STOPPAGE, AND JUDAS IS DECLARED THE WINNER. NOW, PUT HER DOWN!

COSTA FORTUNE MAKES THE ANNOUNCEMENT. THE WINNER OF THIS MATCH IS INDEED JUDAS VIA TECHNICAL KNOCKOUT. JUDGE DREAD INSTRUCTS JUDAS TO LOWER IVY JANE DOWN TO THE MAT GENTLY AS DOCTORS CONGREGATE OUTSIDE THE RING.

JUDAS IS COMPLYING. THAT'S A RELIEF.

THE DAMAGE IS DONE. NO NEED TO ADD ANY FURTHER RISK OF INJURY TO SUCH A PROMISING TALENT. SURELY JUDAS EVEN UNDERSTA— NO, I STAND CORRECTED. JUDAS FLINGS IVY JANE HIGH INTO THE AIR AND WHIPS HER STRAIGHT BACK DOWN TO THE MAT IN WHAT I CAN ONLY DESCRIBE AS A WHIPLASH-INDUCING POWERBOMB! ANOTHER DEVASTATING BLOW TO AN ALREADY DOWNED IVY JANE!

THE REFEREE IS BESIDE HIMSELF. HE'S ASKING WHAT EVERYONE WATCHING WANTS TO KNOW: WHY IN THE BLUE HELL DID JUDAS DO THAT?

JUDAS GIVES NO ANSWER. INSTEAD, HE SMIRKS AT THE REFEREE AS HE LEAVES THE RING. MEDICAL STAFF NOW ENTER TO ATTEND TO IVY JANE AS JUDGE DREAD APPEARS TO BE HAVING ANOTHER CONVERSATION WITH RING ANNOUNCER COSTA FORTUNE.

THIS SHOULD BE GOOD.

***

'Ladies and gentlemen, the referee has informed me that because Judas ignored his instruction and put the safety of another competitor at risk, he is reversing his decision. Therefore, the winner of this match, as a result of a disqualification, is Ivy Jane!'

***

THERE IS ALMOST UNIVERSAL EUPHORIA HERE AT THE ROCK ARENA FOLLOWING THAT ANNOUNCEMENT. THE LIVE AUDIENCE ARE ON THEIR FEET, CHEERING AND CLAPPING FOR IVY JANE, AS WELL AS, ONE WOULD ASSUME, THE REFEREE FOR WHAT I WOULD AGREE IS THE RIGHT CALL IN THESE CIRCUMSTANCES. I SAY THE FEELING IS *ALMOST* UNIVERSAL AS JUDAS HAS COME TO A HALT NEAR THE TOP OF THE RAMP, HIS HEAD TURNED DOWN. WE CAN'T GET A READ ON HIS FACE, BUT YOU

HAVE TO KNOW HE WON'T BE HAPPY WITH THIS NEWEST DEVELOPMENT.

IF I WERE JUDGE DREAD, I'D EXIT SWIFTLY THROUGH THE CROWD. WITH THE RAMPAGE JUDAS HAS BEEN ON LATELY, I DOUBT HE'S ABOVE ROUGHING UP A REFEREE HE FEELS HAS CROSSED HIM.

I'M MORE CONCERNED FOR IVY JANE, WHO'S STILL LIFELESS IN THE RING, AS WELL AS THE MEDICAL TEAM WORKING ON HER. THEY'RE SITTING DUCKS IF JUDAS MAKES AN ABOUT-TURN AND TAKES HIS ANGER AND FRUSTRATION OUT IN THE RING.

THIS IS A TENSE SITUATION IF I EVER SAW ONE. SOVEREIGN NOBLE IS STILL UP HERE ON THE STAGE, LOOKING EITHER ANGRY OR SCARED — POSSIBLY BOTH. IF HE FACILITATED THIS ENTIRE THING FOR JUDAS TONIGHT, HE MUST BE LIVID AT THE REFEREE FOR SCUPPERING THEIR BEST-LAID PLANS. BUT NOW, IF I WERE THE COMMISSIONER, I'D BE TERRIFIED THAT A VEXED DESTROYER MIGHT TAKE IT OUT ON ME. AT THE VERY LEAST, THE CRAFTY KINGSMAN NEEDS TO LIVE UP TO THAT MONIKER AND GET AS FAR AWAY FROM THE CHAMPION AS HE CAN ON THAT CANE. THE WORST THING YOU COULD BE RIGHT NOW IS THE PERSON PHYSICALLY CLOSEST TO JUDAS.

TOO LATE. JUDAS RAISES HIS HEAD AND, LADIES AND GENTLEMEN, THERE IS NO NEED TO ADJUST THE COLOUR SETTINGS ON YOUR TELEVISION MONITORS, AS THE DESTROYER'S FACE REALLY HAS TURNED A DARK SHADE OF PURPLE.

SOVEREIGN NEEDS TO RUN. NOW! BEFORE THAT BLOOD VESSEL ON THE CHAMP'S FOREHEAD BURSTS.

IT'S TOO LATE, FARQUAD.

WHAT? DID THAT THING ACTUALLY POP?

NO, BUT IT LOOKS LIKE THE CHAMPION IS CONSIDERING TAKING OUT HIS FRUSTRATIONS ON THE COMMISSIONER. JUDAS SLOWLY STEPS TOWARDS SOVEREIGN NOBLE. THERE ARE EVIL INTENTIONS IN THOSE EYES.

ON SECOND THOUGHT, I'M GLAD NOBLE DIDN'T LEAVE. OTHERWISE, WE'D HAVE BEEN THE NEAREST LIVING BEINGS TO JUDAS, AND I DON'T FANCY TAKING MY MEALS THROUGH A STRAW FOR THE REST OF MY LIFE.

THAT COULD BE THE FATE OF OUR COMMISSIONER. JUDAS GRABS HIM BY THE COLLAR. THE DESTROYER PRESSES HIS FOREHEAD AGAINST NOBLE'S IN A DISPLAY OF INTIMIDATION.

I CAN JUST ABOUT MAKE OUT WHAT HE'S SAYING. HE'S TELLING NOBLE THAT IF HE DOESN'T GET HIS REFEREES IN LINE, IF SOMETHING LIKE THIS

WERE TO HAPPEN AGAIN, IT WILL BE NOBLE'S *NECK* WEDGED BETWEEN THE CHAIR THIS TIME.

JUDAS IS REFERRING TO THE TIME HE PLACED SOVEREIGN NOBLE'S LEG IN BETWEEN THE TWO HALVES OF A FOLDING, STEEL CHAIR AND JUMPED ON IT FROM THE TOP ROPE, DESTROYING NOBLE'S LEG. THAT SAW AN END TO NOBLE'S IN-RING CAREER AND IS THE REASON HE WALKS WITH A CANE. AND NOW HE HAS THE GALL TO THREATEN TO DO IT AGAIN, ONLY THIS TIME BREAKING THE MAN'S NECK?

THAT MIGHT DECAPITATE HIM. IF IT DIDN'T KILL NOBLE, IT WOULD PARALYSE HIM.

NOBLE MUST REALISE THAT TOO. I'VE NEVER SEEN ANYONE LOOK SO SCARED. JUDAS STILL HAS HIM BY THE COLLAR, THE INTIMIDATION CONTINUING AND— WAIT A MINUTE!

JUDAS JUST KICKED THE CANE FROM SOVEREIGN NOBLE'S HAND. THE COMMISSIONER STRUGGLES TO BALANCE ON ONE LEG AS THE DESTROYER, STILL WITH A GRIP ON THE SCRUFF OF HIS NECK, SHAKES HIM LIKE A RAG DOLL!

YOUR TELEVISION SETS DON'T PROVIDE THE FULL EXTENT OF THE ATMOSPHERE HERE. ONCE AGAIN, THIS EVENING, OUR LIVE AUDIENCE AT THE ROCK ARENA INHALES A COLLECTIVE GASP BEFORE FALLING INTO

DEATHLY SILENCE. IT IS UNCOMFORTABLE TO SAY THE LEAST.

CAN'T ANYONE STOP THIS?

WHO'S GOING TO STOP THIS, FARQUAD? NORMALLY, THE COMMISSIONER WOULD SEND REINFORCEMENTS OUT HERE TO PREVENT THINGS FROM ESCALATING ANY FURTHER. WHY DON'T YOU DO SOMETHING ABOUT IT? YOU WERE A WRESTLER. YOU'VE BEEN ON GOOD TERMS WITH THE CHAMPION IN THE PAST.

I DON'T THINK HE'S IN THE MOOD TO LISTEN TO REASON.

YOU WERE ONE OF THE NASTIEST PLAYERS IN THE GAME, FARQUAD. IF ANYONE CAN STAND UP TO AN ENRAGED DESTROYER, IT'S YOU.

WHAT'S HE DOING NOW? HE'S DRAGGING SOVEREIGN NOBLE THIS WAY.

THE CHAMPION LOOKS PAST US, TOWARDS THE EDGE OF THE STAGE. YOU DON'T THINK HE'S PLANNING TO THROW THE COMMISSIONER OVER THE EDGE, DO YOU?

OH, HELL!

…

MY BROADCAST COLLEAGUE HAS DITCHED HIS HEADSET. NOT A MEMBER OF THE AUDIENCE HERE IS STILL IN THEIR SEAT AS CHEERS RING OUT FOR LORD

FARQUAD, WHO AS SOME OF OUR OLDER VIEWERS MAY REMEMBER WAS ONCE KNOWN AS THE MOST CUNNING COMPETITOR TO LACE A PAIR OF BOOTS.

LORD FARQUAD LEAPS IN FRONT OF THE DESTROYER. YOU COULD SAY HE'S OBSTRUCTING THE PATH OF DESTRUCTION. JUDAS STOPS AS SOVEREIGN NOBLE, WITH HIS ONE GOOD LEG, TRIES TO REGAIN SOME BALANCE WHILE THE CHAMPION HAS HIM HELD TIGHT IN A HEADLOCK.

THE ACTION IS TAKING PLACE JUST A FEW FEET IN FRONT OF ME. THIS IS A PRECARIOUS SITUATION. I CAN HEAR FARQUAD EXPLAIN TO JUDAS THAT WHATEVER HE HAS IN MIND FOR NOBLE, IT'S NOT WORTH IT. HE'S TELLING THE CHAMPION THAT HE'S DONE MORE THAN ENOUGH TO MESS WITH THE MIND OF HIP HARRISON. FARQUAD POINTS OUT THAT WHAT JUDAS DID TO IVY JANE TOOK PLACE DURING A SANCTIONED WRESTLING MATCH, WHILE ANYTHING HE DOES TO SOVEREIGN NOBLE COULD LEAD TO MORE SERIOUS REPERCUSSIONS. HE ALSO REMINDS THE CHAMP THAT HARRISON LIKELY DOESN'T CARE MUCH FOR THE COMMISSIONER, SO WHY TAKE THE RISK? JUDAS NEEDS TO CALM DOWN AND GET HIS HEAD BACK IN THE GAME FOR BATTLESTAR GALACTICA.

JUDAS MULLS FARQUAD'S WORDS OVER. COOLER HEADS MIGHT ACTUALLY PREVAIL.

I SPOKE TOO SOON. JUDAS PUSHES PAST LORD FARQUAD AND CONTINUES TO DRAG SOVEREIGN NOBLE TOWARDS THE LIP OF THE STAGE. LORD FARQUAD, NEVER ONE TO GIVE UP EASILY, GRABS JUDAS BY THE ARM AND PULLS THE CHAMPION BACK TO FACE HIM.

FARQUAD ASKS JUDAS WHAT HE'S DOING, POINTING OUT THAT HE — JUDAS — ALREADY INJURED NOBLE, ENDING HIS — NOBLE'S — WRESTLING CAREER. HE MIGHT KILL HIM IF HE GOES ANY FURTHER.

JUDAS NODS. LIKE MOST OF TODAY'S COMPETITORS, HE GREW UP WATCHING LORD FARQUAD WRESTLE. FARQUAD COMMANDS A LEVEL OF RESPECT THAT NON-ATHLETES, SUCH AS MYSELF, DO NOT AROUND HERE.

THE CHAMPION LOOSENS HIS GRIP AROUND SOVEREIGN NOBLE'S NECK AND THE CRAFTY KINGSMAN SCURRIES FREE, HOPPING OVER TO THE ANNOUNCE DESK TO HOLD ON FOR BALANCE. ARE YOU OKAY, SOVEREIGN?

THE COMMISSIONER TELLS ME HE WILL BE FINE. JUDAS IS HAVING WORDS WITH LORD FARQUAD. MEANWHILE, THE MEDICAL TEAM IN THE RING LIFTS IVY JANE ONTO A STRETCHER. IF FARQUAD CAN KEEP JUDAS'S ATTENTION, THEY CAN GET HER OUT OF HERE AND TO SAFETY.

AS SOME SEMBLANCE OF DECORUM RESUMES, MY THOUGHTS TURN BACK TO HIP HARRISON AND HIS FATHER, WHO ONE ASSUMES WAS ASSAULTED HOURS AGO AND MAY NEED URGENT MEDICAL ATTENTION.

MY THOUGHTS ARE ALSO WITH IVY JANE, WHO WE ALL HOPE WILL BE—

WHAT THE HELL? WHAT ARE YOU DOING, YOU DERANGED PSYCHOPATH?

I APOLOGISE FOR MY OUTBURST, BUT IN CASE YOU WEREN'T FACING YOUR TELEVISION MONITOR, JUDAS STRUCK LORD FARQUAD WITH AN UPPERCUT THAT MIGHT'VE TAKEN THE HEAD OFF A REGULAR BEING. FARQUAD WENT DOWN, BUT HE DIDN'T STAY THERE FOR LONG. MY BROADCAST PARTNER REALLY WAS ONE OF THE TOUGHEST TO EVER DON A PAIR OF WRESTLING TRUNKS. HE NOW STAGGERS BACK TO HIS FEET AND TRIES TO SHAKE OFF THE COBWEBS WHILE THAT SICK SON OF A POODWINK JUDAS GRINS FROM EAR TO EAR.

FARQUAD RAISES HIS ARMS TO THE GUARD POSITION AND LOOKS AS IF HE WANTS TO FIGHT. BUT HE WOBBLES. HE'S GOTTA BE SEEING STARS RIGHT NOW.

JUDAS GRABS ONE OF FARQUAD'S FISTS AND STRIKES WITH A VILE KNEE TO THE STOMACH — SHADES OF WHAT THE CHAMPION DID TO IVY JANE MOMENTS AGO. FARQUAD HAS NO TIME TO REEL FROM

THE BLOW, AS JUDAS SETS HIM UP FOR THE ONE-WAY POWERBOMB.

FOR THE LOVE OF BRADSHAW, JUDAS, IF YOU CAN HEAR ME, PLEASE DON'T DO THIS! JUDAS! FOR BRADSHAW'S SAKE, DON'T— NO!

…

I DON'T KNOW WHAT TO SAY. JUDAS THREW LORD FARQUAD, A RESPECTED LEGEND AND SOMEONE I CALL A FRIEND OFF THE SIDE OF THE STAGE. I'LL DO MY BEST TO MAINTAIN MY PROFESSIONAL COMPOSURE BUT, QUITE FRANKLY, I'M DISGUSTED BY EVERYTHING WE HAVE SEEN FROM OUR SO-CALLED CHAMPION TONIGHT. IVY JANE HAS, THANKFULLY, BEEN REMOVED FROM THE ARENA. I HOPE SHE MAKES A SPEEDY RECOVERY AND THAT WE'LL SEE HER BACK IN ACTION SOONER RATHER THAN LATER.

FARQUAD, ON THE OTHER HAND, PLUMMETED THE TWENTY FEET OR SO OFF THE SIDE OF THE STAGE. HIS FALL WAS BROKEN BY A TABLE USED BY OUR PRODUCTION TEAM, WHICH BROKE UPON IMPACT. AS GNARLY AS IT LOOKS WITH BROKEN SHARDS OF WOOD SURROUNDING MY COLLEAGUE, THE TABLE MAY HAVE PREVENTED FARQUAD FROM SUFFERING A WORSE FATE HAD IT BEEN A STRAIGHT DROP TO THE ARENA FLOOR.

NOW, IF YOU'LL EXCUSE ME, LADIES AND GENTLEMEN, OUR TIME IS ALMOST UP FOR THIS EDITION

OF GALACTIC WF TELEVISION. I THANK YOU FOR JOINING US, APOLOGISE FOR THE DISTRESSING SCENES WE'VE ALL WITNESSED, AND BID YOU FAREWELL UNTIL NEXT WEEK. I'VE GOT TO GO CHECK ON MY FRIEND…

…

…

DID EVERYONE ENJOY THE SHOW? I CERTAINLY DID.

FOR THOSE OF YOU AT HOME WHO HAVE TUNED IN FOR THE FIRST TIME AND ARE WONDERING WHAT IN SIANARD IS GOING ON HERE, LET ME FILL YOU IN. MY NAME IS JUDAS AND I AM THE GALACTIC WF HEAVYWEIGHT CHAMPION. I RUN THIS SHOW! I AM THE SHOW! IF ANYBODY SAYS OTHERWISE, I'LL SEE THAT THEY MEET A SIMILAR FATE TO LORD FARQUAD OVER THERE, OR IVY JANE, OR HIP HARRISON'S DEAR OL' DADDY.

THERE'S MORE TO COME. WHAT I'VE DONE TONIGHT IS NOTHING COMPARED TO WHAT I'M GOING TO PUT HIP HARRISON THROUGH IN LESS THAN ONE MOON ORBIT AT BATTLESTAR GALACTICA. I WILL REMAIN CHAMPION UNTIL THE GALAXY MEETS ITS END — YOU MARK MY WORDS.

NOW, GET THIS HEADSET OFF. DAMN THING REEKS OF OLD MAN SLOBBER.

WEEK EIGHT

GOOD EVENING AND WELCOME TO WHAT IS SURE TO BE A NOTEWORTHY EDITION OF GALACTIC WF TELEVISION. I'M GENE KELLY AND, TONIGHT, I'M CALLING THE ACTION SOLO AS MY TAG TEAM PARTNER BEHIND THE COMMENTARY BOOTH, LORD FARQUAD, IS RESTING AT HOME AFTER OUR DESPICABLE EXCUSE FOR A GALACTIC HEAVYWEIGHT CHAMPION, JUDAS, POWERBOMBED HIM OFF THE SIDE OF THE STAGE LAST WEEK. WE'LL RECAP THE SHOCKING EVENTS FROM LAST WEEK LATER ON DURING THIS BROADCAST.

AS THIS IS THE FINAL STOP ON THE INTERGALACTIC HIGHWAY TO BATTLESTAR GALACTICA, WE'LL BE HEARING FROM BOTH PARTICIPANTS IN THE MAIN EVENT AT THIS WEEKEND'S

EXTRAVAGANZA: NUMBER ONE CONTENDER HIP
HARRISON; AND GALACTIC WF CHAMPION JUDAS.

***

Later in the evening, Hip Harrison made his way to the ring. He appeared to be in a trance, almost as if he were sleepwalking. He didn't register the noise of the crowd (they were loud for him these days; all cheers, no jeers) nor the stock music assigned to him as an entrance theme when he'd first signed with The Fed.

Harrison's gaze remained fixed on the ground just a few feet ahead of him. He didn't make eye contact with the fans or the cameras. A member of the production crew had left a microphone for him at the top of the ring steps, which The Bearded Brute took as he made his ascent to the ring apron. He climbed through the ropes and took his position in the centre of the ring, still facing down — now towards the canvas. The house lights dimmed, and a spotlight found its mark. Those in attendance paused their cheering to listen to what Hip Harrison had to say, both following the events of the previous weeks and with his shot at the championship just days away, as well as a chance at revenge.

'*You've sunk even lower than I could have possibly imagined. I knew you could stoop to some nasty depths, but who knew that anyone could be capable of some of the things you've done in the past couple of moon orbits? Sianard sees you for what you truly are, and those closest to me have endured it.*

'*Maybe I underestimated you — or overestimated you, depending on your perspective. You may have gone lower than I'd expected, but don't you go thinking you've ducked me entirely. Your mistake was not going low enough. You left us all with our hearts still beating, our lungs still breathing, and blood pumping through our veins.*

'What you might not know — and I'm happy to provide you a spoiler here — is that I can go low, too. We all can. You've given us no choice but to sink to your putrid level. There is no ducking us now. We're coming for you, for the championship, and for the truth. By any means necessary.

'I'll go low right now and steal a terrible catchphrase: One way... or another, I will win at Battlestar Galactica and become the Heavyweight Champion of the Galaxy.'

***

WE HEARD SOME HAUNTING WORDS FROM THE MOUTH OF HIP HARRISON EARLIER THIS EVENING. THE NUMBER ONE CONTENDER DIDN'T DISPLAY HIS USUAL LEVEL OF ENERGY. INSTEAD, HE LOOKED LASER-FOCUSED ON THE TASK AHEAD OF HIM THIS WEEKEND. ALTHOUGH HE DID NOT PROVIDE A MEDICAL UPDATE ON EITHER HIS FATHER OR IVY JANE, IT APPEARS HE IS USING THE INJURIES THEY HAVE SUSTAINED AT THE HANDS OF THE DESTROYER AS MOTIVATION. THE BEARDED BRUTE IS NOW DRIVEN BY DARKNESS AND, IF I WERE JUDAS, I WOULD WORRY THAT MY MASTER PLAN MIGHT JUST HAVE BACKFIRED.

SPEAKING OF THE CHAMPION, HE'S MAKING HIS WAY TO THE RING TO DELIVER HIS OWN CLOSING REMARKS BEFORE THIS WEEKEND'S MAIN EVENT. OUR LIVE AUDIENCE PROVIDES THE CHAMPION WITH A FROSTY RECEPTION.

***

The lights dimmed as Judas took his mark in the centre of the ring. The spotlight found its way to the champion and its reflection shone from the big gold belt around his waist as he raised a microphone up to his lips. Like that, he stood, not saying a word as the crowd gathered at The Rock Arena continued to jeer in waves. Every so often, the booing would taper off, only for someone in the tiers to bellow their displeasure at the champion with renewed vigour, starting the chorus of derision all over again.

Judas, still with the microphone held an inch away from his mouth, smiled. As the wave of taunts from the audience rose again, the grin resembled that of The Joker from Earth's old *Batman* movies. The sickening smile was projected on the jumbotron and, as each member of the crowd saw that maddening face, they fell silent, one by one, until all that could be heard was the faint sound of someone coughing way up in the bleachers.

Judas still didn't speak. Instead, he began chuckling to himself. His mouth opened wider, and the chuckle grew until it was a fully fledged laugh. The laughter became frenzied and tears streamed down Judas's face. The crowd maintained its stunned silence as the Galactic WF Champion succumbed to hysterics. This state of affairs lasted for several minutes until Judas finally snapped out of it and regained some composure.

He sighed, his massive shoulders sagging, and he dropped the mic. The Destroyer turned to leave the ring and immediately halted. At the top of the entrance ramp stood Hip Harrison. Unlike his future opponent, The Bearded Brute wasn't smiling.

Harrison remained still, not even blinking. He glared at Judas, staring daggers through him, as the old Earth saying went. What more could he do? He wanted to rip the champion to shreds, but the contract stipulation — what had it been called? The aggression disbarment agreement — meant Harrison could not legally lay a hand on Judas until the bell rang for the start of their match at Battlestar Galactica. There was, therefore, nothing else for Hip Harrison to do but to wait patiently and to let Judas know just how much anger he was bringing to the pay-per-view. Not that The Destroyer seemed to care.

After all that Judas had done to Hip Harrison's friends and family — hell, even The Bearded Brute's detractors weren't safe. Just ask Lord Farquad — The Destroyer's Day of Reckoning was almost upon him. Harrison had already suffered more pain and agony in the last few weeks than he could ever experience in the ring. Judas wouldn't understand that kind of pain, though. He would, however, understand the pain of The Brute Lock when it was applied. Harrison would gain some small measure of payback. Of that, he was sure.

Let's not forget that Judas was merely a puppet. The true villain in all of this would also pay at Battlestar Galactica. Mr Montgomery, the string master. Every despicable act Judas had committed against Hip Harrison and his nearest and dearest had been nothing more than the desperate acts of a terrified chairman. And what could someone so rich and powerful have to fear? Exposure, of course. The Bearded Brute couldn't wait to remove the proverbial mask and reveal the Galactic WF chairman to be a prominent member of the Galactic Council of Sianard, along with the crucial data that he was helping to conceal for the sake of the status quo. Only those with the power have something to fear from the destruction of the present state of things, or so it seems.

In the ring, Judas wiped a tear from his eye as his laughter subsided. As he settled into a smirk, his eyes met Hip Harrison's from across the arena. The Galactic WF copyright graphic appeared in the bottom corner of viewers' television monitors as the final broadcast before the ultimate showdown at Battlestar Galactica came to a close.

BATTLESTAR GALACTICA

WELCOME, ONE AND ALL, TO THE GALACTIC WF'S BIGGEST EVENT OF THE CYCLE — THIS IS BATTLESTAR GALACTICA. I'M GENE KELLY, AND I'M PLEASED TO REVEAL THAT I'M NOT HERE ALONE. SEATED TO MY LEFT IS MY BROADCAST PARTNER, LORD FARQUAD.

FARQUAD, IT'S GREAT TO SEE YOU BACK SO SOON.

THANKS, GENE. I WOULDN'T HAVE MISSED TONIGHT FOR THE GALAXY. I MAY BE IN A WHEELCHAIR, THE DOCTORS MAY HAVE TOLD ME I NEED TO KEEP THIS NECKBRACE ON DAY AND NIGHT, AND IT MAY HURT EVERY TIME I SPEAK, BUT NOTHING WAS GOING TO STOP ME FROM BEING HERE

TO CALL THIS EVENING'S MAIN EVENT. I WANTED TO BE HERE IN PERSON TO WITNESS HIP HARRISON TAKE THE FIGHT TO JUDAS. I'D LOVE NOTHING MORE THAN TO SEE HIS SORRY ASS TAPPING OUT TO THE BRUTE LOCK.

I'M SURE THE MAJORITY OF FANS WATCHING ACROSS SIANARD TONIGHT WILL BE IN HIP HARRISON'S CORNER. WE KNEW JUDAS COULD EXHIBIT RUTHLESS AGGRESSION BUT, IN RECENT WEEKS, THE GALACTIC WF CHAMPION HAS REVEALED HIMSELF TO BE TOTALLY PSYCHOTIC.

OF THAT, I'M CERTAIN. BUT THERE'S SOMETHING I'M NOT SO SURE OF, GENE.

WHAT'S THAT, FARQUAD?

I'M NOT SURE I CAN WAIT UNTIL THE MAIN EVENT. BUT I'LL HAVE TO.

LUCKY FOR YOU, WE HAVE A HELLUVA CARD TO KEEP YOU OCCUPIED UNTIL THE BEARDED BRUTE FACES THE DESTROYER. IN FACT, OUR OPENING CONTEST IS ABOUT TO GET UNDER WAY, AS THE INTERPLANETARY CHAMPIONSHIP IS ON THE LINE…

***

'This is it. Tonight's the night.' Hip Harrison paced back and forth, from one end of his trailer to the other, and back again.

'Calm down.'

'How can I? This is it: everything I've been working towards. Most wrestlers never even make it to the Galactic Wrestling Federation, let alone a shot at the championship. It's a big deal on its own. I'd bet every other previous challenger has felt nervous before the bell rings. Becoming the Heavyweight Champion is what we all get into this business for. Every wrestler should aspire to be the best in the galaxy and to wear the belt that proves it. If not, then what's the point of sacrificing your body, your mind, your family life?'

'Of course, it's normal to feel nerves, but you're burning energy with all that walking around. Try to rest a little.'

Hip Harrison stopped. Then, started pacing again as his thoughts resumed. 'On top of the pressure that comes with achieving personal success and gaining the immortality that comes with having your name engraved on the big, gold belt, I have the fate of the entire galaxy resting on my shoulders. Tonight is about more than a title, more than Hip Harrison the wrestler. It's about exposing the truth and saving Sianard. Talk about pressure. Do you think Judas even has a clue about what he's fighting for? He's not just defending the gold; he's defending the GCS and Mr Montgomery and their deadly secrets. Do you think he knows?'

'I don't know.'

'What if I fail? That's what I keep wondering. What happens then?'

'None of us know.'

'I mean, if I don't become champion, who cares, right? It's not the end of the galaxy. Sure, I'd be a little disappointed, having dreamed of winning the big one since I was a kid, but I could dust myself off and work my way back up the rankings. But what happens to Sianard? There's no way I could expose Mr Montgomery and his cronies, and what they've hidden. They would shut my voice out like all the others. And then what? The galaxy continues to spiral until it comes to an abrupt end, until we meet the same fate as those people on Earth? I don't think I could take that. I need to win tonight. I need it more than anything you could ever imagine.'

'That I know. You've done the work. You're primed and in the best shape of your life. And, although he would never admit it, you are clearly occupying space in Judas's head. You're right that a lot of the things he's done in recent weeks have been part of a script, orchestrated by the man in charge, but he's also gone off-script too. Laying his hands on Sovereign Noble and throwing Lord Farquad off that stage. Those things wouldn't have been in Mr Montgomery's master plan. No, those were the acts of someone so scared and desperate to cling onto their prize that they've lost control over their actions. If any wrestler can take advantage of that, it's you, Hip.'

'Thanks. I'm glad to have you here tonight. Especially after what happened.'

***

'Ladies and gentlemen, it's TIIIIMMMME for the MAAAIN EVENT! The following contest, scheduled for one fall, is for the GALACTIC

WRESTLING FEDERATION CHAMPIONSHIP and… in this contest, there will be NO DISQUALIFICATIONS!'

***

WHAT? NO DISQUALIFICATIONS! WHEN WAS THAT ADDED?

I DON'T KNOW, GENE. THE WAY OUR RING ANNOUNCER, COSTA FORTUNE, TACKED THAT SMALL DETAIL ONTO THE END THERE MAKES ME WONDER WHETHER HE RECEIVED A LAST-MINUTE INSTRUCTION THROUGH HIS EARPIECE.

WELL, I DON'T LIKE IT. SMELLS TO ME LIKE SOMETHING FISHY'S GOING ON.

YOU KNOW IT HAS TO BE. BUT LET'S NOT FORGET THAT WITH NO DISQUALIFICATIONS, IT GOES BOTH WAYS. JUDAS CAN USE ALL THE WEAPONS HE WANTS, AND I'M SURE THERE IS SOME OUTSIDE INTERFERENCE PLANNED, BUT HIP HARRISON HAS ACCESS TO ALL OF THE SAME LUXURIES. GIVEN HOW PISSED OFF HIP HARRISON MUST BE WITH JUDAS RIGHT NOW, I WOULDN'T WANT TO BE THE CHAMP FACING OFF AGAINST THE BEARDED BRUTE WHEN THERE ARE NO RULES TO FOLLOW.

THAT'S RIGHT, FARQUAD. IT'S ANYTHING GOES — NO HOLDS BARRED! THE ONLY WAY TO WIN IS VIA PIN OR SUBMISSION.

WHAT'S THAT SOUND, GENE? THAT'S NOT HIP HARRISON'S MUSIC. IT'S AN ELECTRIC GUITAR THAT SOUNDS LIKE A PULSE. IT'S ELECTRIFYING!

IT APPEARS HIP HARRISON HAS INVESTED IN SOME NEW ENTRANCE MUSIC, FARQUAD. LOOK AT THE BIG SCREEN ON THE TRON. WE'RE SEEING FOOTAGE FROM THE BEARDED BRUTE'S VICTORIES EN ROUTE TO THIS CHAMPIONSHIP BOUT.

THE GREAT GOLIATH: DONE! FATBOY SLIME: DONE! X-STATIC: DONE! BIG BALE: DONE! SNIPER SKY: DONE! AND NOW HE MOVES ON TO JUDAS.

I UNDERSTAND THE SONG IS *ALL MY LIFE* BY AN OLD EARTH BAND KNOWN AS THE FOO FIGHTERS — AN APT NAME AS THE BEARDED BRUTE IS IN FOR THE FIGHT OF HIS LIFE. THE MUSIC HITS A CRESCENDO AS THE HIGHLIGHT REEL ON THE JUMBOTRON ALLOWS OUR AUDIENCE TO RELIVE THE INCREDIBLE MOMENT HIP HARRISON LEAPT FROM UP HIGH ON THAT FORKLIFT TRUCK TO DRIVE BIG BALE THROUGH OUR COMMENTARY DESK.

AND THERE HE IS! THE MAN HIMSELF, HIP HARRISON.

THE CROWD GOES BANANA! YOU COULD EVEN SAY THE PLACE HAS COME UNGLUED AS THE ROCK ARENA SEEMS TO BE SHAKING. I'VE BEEN IN THIS GAME A LONG TIME, AND I DON'T THINK I'VE EVER

EXPERIENCED AN ATMOSPHERE QUITE LIKE THIS, FOLKS.

ME NEITHER. THE FANS WERE ALWAYS EXCITED TO SEE LORD FARQUAD IN ACTION, BUT THIS RESPONSE IS ON ANOTHER LEVEL.

THE LOOK ON HIP HARRISON'S FACE SAYS IT ALL. HE MARCHES DOWN THE ENTRANCE RAMP WITH PURPOSE, AS IF HE CARRIES THE WEIGHT OF THE GALAXY. THAT'S WHAT THE GALACTIC WF CHAMPIONSHIP MEANS TO HIM. IT TRULY IS THE RICHEST PRIZE IN OUR BUSINESS.

I'M NOT DISPUTING THE IMPORTANCE OF THE TITLE, GENE, BUT THIS MATCH HAS GOT TO MEAN MUCH MORE TO HARRISON. THIS IS AN OPPORTUNITY FOR VENGEANCE. JUDAS HAS MADE THIS MORE THAN PERSONAL AND HIP HARRISON MUST HAVE RETRIBUTION IN MIND. THE CHAMPIONSHIP WILL ALMOST COME AS A BONUS FOR WINNING THIS CONTEST.

YOU MIGHT BE RIGHT, FARQUAD. HARRISON ENTERS THE RING AND THERE'S NONE OF THE USUAL INTERACTION WITH THE CROWD. THE SHOWBOATING HAS BEEN DOCKED. IT'S ALL HANDS ON DECK TONIGHT.

ENOUGH OF THE NAUTICAL NONSENSE, BURCHILL!

AS THE SCREAMS OF DAVE GROHL ECHO OUT, THE NOISE FROM THIS CROWD GROWS EVEN LOUDER. THIS IS AS CLOSE TO A HOMEFIELD ADVANTAGE AS YOU COULD EVER GET IN THIS SPORT, IN THIS ARENA.

NO MATTER WHO JUDAS HAS BEHIND HIM, THEY'RE SURELY NO MATCH FOR FIFTY-THOUSAND-PLUS HIPSTERS.

I HOPE HIP HARRISON IS TAKING THIS MOMENT IN. NO MATTER WHAT HAPPENS THIS EVENING, HE'S MORE THAN EARNED THE RESPECT OF EVERYONE HERE AND HE DESERVES TO BASK IN THEIR ADULATION.

HE CAN SOAK IT IN AFTER THE MATCH. NOW'S NOT THE TIME FOR DISTRACTIONS, GENE.

AND HERE IT IS, LADIES AND GENTLEMEN: THE ULTIMATE MOOD-KILLER. THE ARROGANT TONE OF JUDAS'S VOICE ECHOES AROUND THE ARENA, BRINGING WITH IT THAT ALL-TOO-FAMILIAR CATCHPHRASE — ONE WAY OR ANOTHER — BEFORE THE ICONIC GUITAR RIFF OF BLONDIE'S HIT SONG KICKS IN.

IT'S STILL A TREMENDOUS TUNE. IT'S JUST A SHAME THAT IT'S ASSOCIATED WITH THAT PIECE OF SIANARDIAN SCUM, JUDAS.

I WOULDN'T WORRY ABOUT IT, FARQUAD. YOU CAN BARELY HEAR THE SONG OVER THE CHORUS OF BOOS THAT THIS CAPACITY CROWD IS RAINING DOWN UPON THE CHAMPION. AS THE DESTROYER MAKES HIS

WAY THROUGH THE CURTAIN, THE JEERING INTENSIFIES. IN THE SPACE OF JUST A FEW WEEKS, JUDAS HAS GONE FROM BEING ONE OF THE MOST MUST-SEE PERFORMERS OF ALL TIME TO A REVILED PSYCHOPATH.

AS SOMEONE WHO WAS SINGING JUDAS'S PRAISES UNTIL RECENTLY, MY THEORY IS THAT HE WAS ALWAYS PSYCHOTIC, HIDING IN PLAIN SIGHT. ALL IT TOOK WAS FOR A CHALLENGER WHO ACTUALLY STOOD A CHANCE AGAINST HIM TO RISE THROUGH THE RANKS, LIKE HIP HARRISON, AND THE MASK SLIPPED.

JUST LOOK AT JUDAS'S FACE AS HE WALKS, SLOWLY AND METHODICALLY, DOWN THE ENTRANCE RAMP. WE TALKED ABOUT HOW HIP HARRISON HAS HIS GAME FACE ON. WELL, IT APPEARS JUDAS IS FEELING MORE THAN A LITTLE CONFIDENT GOING INTO THIS FIGHT. HELL, I'D CALL HIM COCKY AND OVERCONFIDENT. HIS EYES ARE TRAINED ON HIS OPPONENT IN THE RING BEFORE HIM, AND HIS LIPS ARE UPTURNED IN SOMETHING BETWEEN A SMILE AND A SMIRK. HE'S REVELLING IN OUR AUDIENCE'S CONDEMNATION.

HE CAN PLAY THE VILLAIN ALL HE WANTS, BUT IF HE'S NOT TAKING THIS MATCH WITH HIP

HARRISON SERIOUSLY, THEN HIS TITLE REIGN IS IN SERIOUS JEOPARDY.

WE'LL NEVER KNOW WHAT GOES ON INSIDE THE TWISTED MIND OF THE DESTROYER AS HE STEPS BETWEEN THE ROPES. JUDAS TURNS HIS GAZE AWAY FROM THE BEARDED BRUTE AND MAKES HIS WAY ACROSS THE RING TO THE FAR CORNER, CLIMBING TO THE SECOND ROPE AND HOLDING THE CHAMPIONSHIP BELT ALOFT FOR ALL TO SEE. THE GOLD REFLECTS THE BRIGHT LIGHTS THAT SHINE DOWN UPON THE CHAMPION, GLORIFYING THE MONSTER.

YOU HOPED HARRISON WAS SOAKING IT ALL IN A FEW MOMENTS AGO, GENE. WELL, JUDAS CERTAINLY SEEMS TO BE. HIS EYES ARE CLOSED, HIS SMIRK IS STILL PRESENT. HE'S WATERLOGGED!

THE CHAMPION OPENS HIS EYES — WHAT EVIL LIES BEHIND THEM? – AND THE SMILE WIDENS. HE CLIMBS DOWN TO THE CANVAS, TURNS AROUND AND—

***

WHOA! HARRISON CLOCKED HIM WITH A THUNDEROUS RIGHT HOOK!

THE REFEREE CALLS FOR THE BELL AND THIS MATCH IS UNDER WAY. THE ATMOSPHERE IS ELECTRIC HERE!

HARRISON'S UNLOADING WEEKS OF ANGER AND FRUSTRATION ON JUDAS. EACH OF THOSE RIGHTS

MUST BE LIKE A BULL HAMMER TO THE CHAMPION'S HEAD.

JUDAS REELS AS JUDGE DREAD SCOOPS UP THE GALACTIC WF CHAMPIONSHIP BELT, WHICH THE DESTROYER DROPPED TO THE MAT AS THIS BRAWL BEGAN. THAT GOES TO SHOW WHAT THIS MATCH IS ALL ABOUT. IT'S ABOUT MORE THAN TITLES. THIS IS PERSONAL. THIS IS HIP HARRISON'S VENGEANCE DAY.

I BET JUDAS NEVER EXPECTED THIS. HE'S ALREADY BACKED INTO A CORNER JUST SECONDS INTO THE MATCH. THIS PLACE IS GOING WILD!

IT'S GOT TO BE ONE OF THE BIGGEST POPS FROM A CROWD I'VE EVER HEARD. AND THE NOISE LEVELS REMAIN WITH EVERY FIST HARRISON LANDS ON JUDAS'S SKULL.

JUDGE DREAD STEPS UP TO HARRISON, TELLING THE BEARDED BRUTE TO BACK OFF WHILE JUDAS IS ON THE ROPES. BUT HARRISON KEEPS SENDING HAYMAKERS FLYING AT THE CHAMPION.

HE'S GOING TO GET HIMSELF DISQUALIFIED IF HE'S NOT CAREFUL. I'M SURPRISED THAT THE REF HASN'T STARTED A FIVE COUNT ALREADY.

NORMALLY, HE WOULD HAVE. BUT THIS IS NO LONGER A TRADITIONAL CHAMPIONSHIP MATCH. IT'S NO DISQUALIFICATION. ANYTHING GOES AND, WHILE THE OFFICIAL CAN ADVISE THE COMBATANTS TO

FOLLOW THE TYPICAL RULES, THERE ARE NO CONSEQUENCES FOR IGNORING THEM. JUDGE DREAD'S SOLE PURPOSE IN THIS CONTEST IS TO COUNT A PINFALL OR TO CALL A SUBMISSION VICTORY.

I'M NOT ENTIRELY SURE HOW THE NO-DISQUALIFICATION STIPULATION CAME ABOUT, ALTHOUGH I HAVE A GOOD IDEA, AND I'M CERTAIN THIS ISN'T HOW THE MATCH WAS SUPPOSED TO GO. DESPITE THE REFEREE'S BEST EFFORTS, HARRISON IS STILL HAMMERING JUDAS IN THE HEAD. IF ANYTHING, HE'S SPEEDING UP!

JUDAS SINKS IN THE CORNER, HIS BACK SLIDING DOWN THE TURNBUCKLE AS THE BEARDED BRUTE AIMS HIS BARRAGE AT THE TOP OF THE CHAMPION'S CRANIUM. THE SPEED OF HARRISON'S PUNCHES IS LIKE LIGHTNING.

WE'VE SEEN THE CHALLENGER FLOAT LIKE A BUTTERFLY AS HE COMES OFF THE TOP ROPE IN THE PAST, AND NOW IT SEEMS HE CAN STING LIKE A BEE.

THE CROWD REACHES A FEVER PITCH HERE AT THE ROCK ARENA AS THIS BEARDED BARRAGE COMES TO A CRESCENDO AND, FINALLY, HIP HARRISON, RELENTS, TURNING AWAY FROM HIS DOWNED OPPONENT TO CATCH HIS BREATH AND, MOST LIKELY, TO GIVE HIS ARM TIME TO REST.

THE REACTION FROM OUR AUDIENCE IS UNLIKE ANYTHING I'VE EVER HEARD. HARRISON'S FEELING IT TOO! A SHARED SENSE OF CATHARSIS.

HIP HARRISON IS FULLY IMMERSED IN THE MOMENT. HE LETS LOOSE WITH A PRIMAL SCREAM THAT CAN BE HEARD EVEN OVER THE FIFTY-THOUSAND IN ATTENDANCE. HOW GOOD MUST IT FEEL TO HAVE FINALLY BEEN ABLE TO GET HIS HANDS ON THE DASTARDLY DESTROYER, THE VILE JUDAS?

HIP NEEDS TO BE CAREFUL. THE JOB ISN'T DONE YET.

AS IF HEARING MY COLLEAGUE'S WORDS, HARRISON TURNS HIS ATTENTION BACK TOWARDS JUDAS. THE CHAMPION, MEANWHILE, USES THE TURNBUCKLE TO PULL HIMSELF BACK TO A VERTICAL BASE. HARRISON APPROACHES, GOES IN FOR THE GRAPPLE, BUT JUDAS STRIKES WITH THAT STIFF KNEE OF HIS, STRAIGHT TO THE BEARDED BRUTE'S STOMACH.

THAT'S WHAT I WAS TALKING ABOUT. YOU SHOULD NEVER TURN YOUR BACK ON THE CHAMPION. NEVER LET UP ON THE ATTACK. OTHERWISE, YOU'LL SOON FIND YOURSELF ON THE DEFENSIVE.

HIP HARRISON HAS LEARNT THAT LESSON THE HARD WAY. JUDAS, STILL TRYING TO DUST OFF THE

PROVERBIAL COBWEBS, PUTS HARRISON IN A HEADLOCK.

THE CHAMP IS IN A DAZE, BUT HE'S SO REFINED IN HIS WORK INSIDE THE RING THAT HE OPERATES INSTINCTIVELY. IN OTHER WORDS: HE'S RUNNING ON AUTOPILOT.

JUDAS SQUEEZES, APPLYING PRESSURE TO THE HEAD AND NECK OF THE CHALLENGER. BUT HARRISON FIGHTS BACK WITH JABS TO THE MIDSECTION AND JUDAS STRUGGLES TO MAINTAIN HIS GRIP. CHANGING TACK, THE CHAMPION LOOSENS HIS GRIP AND SENDS HARRISON RUNNING TOWARDS THE ROPES WITH AN IRISH WHIP. HARRISON HOLDS ON, AND COUNTERS WITH AN IRISH WHIP OF HIS OWN.

JUDAS IS HEADING TOWARDS THE ROPES LIKE A RUNAWAY FREIGHT SHIP. THE JUDAS EXPRESS REBOUNDS OFF THE ROPES AND FINDS ITSELF ON A COLLISION COURSE WITH THE BEARDED BRUTE.

JUDAS RAISES AN ARM TO TAKE HARRISON DOWN WITH A CLOTHESLINE, BUT HARRISON DUCKS IT. THE CHAMPION REACHES THE OPPOSITE SIDE OF THE SQUARED CIRCLE, REBOUNDING ONCE AGAIN. THE DESTROYER GAINS MOMENTUM AS THE BEARDED BRUTE STEPS TOWARD THE ONCOMING IMPACT.

HARRISON SIDE-STEPS THE CHAMP LIKE THIS IS A GAME OF CHICKEN.

JUDAS, HAVING EXPECTED TO COLLIDE WITH HARRISON AT THAT JUNCTION, STUMBLES BUT AVOIDS LOSING HIS FOOTING COMPLETELY. HE MAKES IT TO THE ROPES AND STEADIES HIMSELF. HE TURNS TO FACE THE CENTRE OF THE RING — AND HIS OPPONENT — BUT HERE COMES HARRISON!

FORGET THE JUDAS EXPRESS. THE BEARDED EXPRESS STEAMROLLS THE CHAMPION!

FOR THOSE WATCHING WHO BLINKED AND MISSED IT, HARRISON CHARGED ACROSS THE RING IN PURSUIT OF THE DESTROYER, REACHING A HIGH VELOCITY BEFORE POUNCING. HARRISON'S BODY CONTORTED IN MID-AIR SO THAT BY THE TIME HE MADE CONTACT WITH THE CHAMPION, HE WAS FLYING HORIZONTALLY AND CONNECTED WITH A HIGH CROSS-BODY TO JUDAS'S CHEST. BOTH COMPETITORS TUMBLED OVER THE TOP ROPE, WITH JUDAS FALLING HEAD OVER HEELS, BOUNCING OFF THE RING APRON AND, ULTIMATELY, LANDING ON THE FLOOR BELOW.

HARRISON KNEW EXACTLY WHAT HE WAS DOING THERE. WHILE JUDAS NEVER SAW IT COMING, HARRISON HELD THE TOP ROPE AS THEY WENT OVER. SO, WHILE JUDAS CAME CRASHING DOWN AND LIKELY HURTS INSIDE AND OUT, THE BEARDED BRUTE SWUNG FROM THE ROPE, LIKE TARZAN ON A VINE, AND LANDED ON HIS FEET, ON THE RING APRON.

WHILE WE WERE RECAPPING, THE BEARDED BRUTE TOOK A MOMENT TO SURVEY THE SCENE. HE SAW JUDAS STIRRING AND CLIMBED THROUGH THE ROPES TO STAND HIS GROUND IN THE RING.

BIG MISTAKE! THERE ARE NO COUNTOUTS AND NO DISQUALIFICATIONS IN THIS MATCH. I WOULD HAVE HOPPED DOWN TO THE FLOOR AND CONTINUED TO TAKE THE FIGHT TO A DOWNED DESTROYER.

DON'T COUNT HIP HARRISON OUT JUST YET, FARQUAD. I'M SURE HE HAS SOMETHING UP HIS SLEEVE. IN FACT, HE'S KEEPING A CLOSE EYE ON HIS OPPONENT.

THE CHAMPION HAS ALREADY MADE IT TO HIS HANDS AND KNEES. HE'LL BE UP IN NO TIME AND HARRISON HAS ALLOWED IT TO HAPPEN.

DON'T SPEAK TOO SOON, FARQUAD. THE BEARDED EXPRESS, AS YOU SO NAMED IT, IS ON THE MOVE ONCE AGAIN. HARRISON RUNS *AWAY* FROM WHERE HIS DOWNED OPPONENT TRIES TO GET BACK TO HIS FEET, COMES OFF THE ROPES WITH EXTRA MOMENTUM, AND NOW HEADS TOWARDS THE CHAMPION.

JUDAS GETS TO HIS FEET, TURNS TOWARD THE RING AND IS MET WITH A FLYING BRUTE, AS HIP HARRISON LEAPS, HEADFIRST, BETWEEN THE MIDDLE AND TOP ROPES, TACKLING THE DESTROYER ON THE WAY TO THE FLOOR.

A PICTURE-PERFECT TOPE SUICIDA IF I EVER SAW ONE.

HARRISON SPRINGS BACK TO HIS FEET AND THE DESTROYER IS ONCE AGAIN DOWN ON THE OUTSIDE. ALTHOUGH THE BEARDED BRUTE HAS THE UPPER HAND, HE CANNOT WIN THE CHAMPIONSHIP OUTSIDE THE RING. DECISIONS CAN ONLY BE CALLED BY THE REFEREE BETWEEN THE ROPES.

AT LEAST THERE ARE NO COUNTOUTS IN THIS NO-DISQUALIFICATION AFFAIR. IF THIS WERE A TYPICAL MATCH, HARRISON WOULD SOMEHOW NEED TO GET JUDAS BACK INSIDE THE RING BEFORE THE REF'S COUNT OF TEN. THE TITLE CAN'T CHANGE HANDS ON A COUNTOUT OR DISQUALIFICATION — NOT THAT IT MATTERS MUCH HERE.

HARRISON SLIDES IN BENEATH THE BOTTOM ROPE. HE STANDS TALL, ONCE AGAIN, ALONE INSIDE THE RING, PLOTTING HIS NEXT MOVE.

THERE ARE REALLY ONLY TWO OPTIONS, GENE. HE CAN EITHER TAKE A BREATHER AND WAIT FOR JUDAS TO MAKE HIS OWN WAY BACK INTO THE RING — AT WHICH POINT, HARRISON CAN POUNCE ON THE CHAMPION AS HE ENTERS, EASILY RETAINING THE UPPER HAND WHILE JUDAS IS CAUGHT BETWEEN THE ROPES. OR, HE CAN TRY TO BRING JUDAS BACK INTO THE RING BEFORE THE CHAMP RECOVERS.

HARRISON HAS IDEAS OF HIS OWN. HE'S GOING TO THE WELL ONCE AGAIN. HE'S GOING FOR ANOTHER SUICIDE DIVE. IT'S A GREAT STRATEGY, AS THE SPEED AT WHICH YOU TACKLE AN OPPONENT WHEN YOU'VE HAD THE ENTIRE LENGTH OF THE RING TO ACCELERATE, COMBINED WITH THE ASSISTANCE OF GRAVITY, CANNOT BE REPLICATED BETWEEN THE ROPES. EACH TIME HE BLASTS JUDAS WITH A TOPE SUICIDA, IT WEAKENS THE CHAMPION SIGNIFICANTLY.

THAT IS EXACTLY RIGHT, GENE. THE REWARD IS HUGE. HOWEVER, THE RISK IS ALSO HIGH. IF JUDAS WERE TO COUNTER OR TO SIDE-STEP THE ONCOMING BEARDED TORPEDO, HARRISON WOULD CRASH AND BURN. HE'D BE EASY PICKINGS FOR THE DESTROYER AFTER A FALL LIKE THAT. NOT TO MENTION THE FACT THAT HARRISON EVEN RISKS INJURING HIMSELF IF HE CONNECTS WITH JUDAS. WE SOMETIMES FORGET, BUT IT'S A LONG WAY DOWN FROM THE ROPES TO THE FLOOR BELOW. A GOOD NINE OR TEN FEET AT LEAST. AND WHILE THAT THIN LAYER OF MATTING IS THERE TO PREVENT SCRAPES ON THE CONCRETE BELOW, IT DOESN'T DO MUCH TO BREAK YOUR FALL.

JUDAS MAKES HIS WAY BACK TO A VERTICAL BASE AND THERE GOES HARRISON. THE BEARDED BRUTE REBOUNDS OFF THE FAR SIDE OF THE RING AND

GAINS SPEED. BUT HE GRABS ONTO THE ROPES AND GRINDS TO A HALT RATHER THAN FLY THROUGH THEM. WHAT MADE HIM STOP?

WHAT ARE *THEY* DOING HERE?

IT'S X-STATIC AND SNIPER SKY, WHO EARLIER THIS EVENING BECAME THE GALACTIC WF TAG TEAM CHAMPIONS WHEN THEY DEFEATED THE GHOSTBUSTERS IN NEFARIOUS FASHION. THEY'RE HELPING JUDAS TO HIS FEET AND PROTECTING THE CHAMPION FROM FURTHER ONSLAUGHT. THIS MUST BE THE REASON FOR THE NO-DISQUALIFICATION STIPULATION — SO JUDAS CAN HAVE HIS CRONIES COME AND RUN INTERFERENCE.

I'M CERTAIN THE ONLY REASON THOSE TWO FOUND THEMSELVES IN CONTENTION FOR THE TAG TITLES THIS EVENING WAS AS A RETURN FAVOUR FOR HAVING JUDAS'S BACK A FEW WEEKS AGO.

YOU'RE ONTO SOMETHING THERE, PARTNER. THESE TWO WEREN'T EVEN A TEAM THREE WEEKS AGO. THEN, THEY ASSIST JUDAS IN BEATING DOWN HARRISON THE NIGHT THE DESTROYER POWERBOMBED THE BEARDED BRUTE'S FRIEND OFF THE STAGE, AND SUDDENLY THEY'RE THE NUMBER ONE RANKED TAG TEAM IN THE GALACTIC WRESTLING FEDERATION WITH A GUARANTEED SPOT ON THE BIGGEST SHOW OF THE YEAR. IT'S ALL TOO CONVENIENT.

IT'S CONVENIENT FOR JUDAS TOO. THE RELATIONSHIP, WHETHER IT'S STRICTLY BUSINESS OR OTHERWISE, APPEARS TO BE A CONTINUAL ARRANGEMENT.

JUDAS IS BACK UP TO HIS FEET. SNIPER SKY KEEPS A WATCHFUL EYE ON HIP HARRISON, WHO CLUTCHES THE TOP ROPE FROM HIS POSITION INSIDE THE RING.

THREE AGAINST ONE. I DON'T LIKE THOSE ODDS, GENE.

I DON'T EITHER, BUT HARRISON LOOKS AS IF HE MIGHT. HE'S SMILING LIKE HE KNOWS SOMETHING SKY 'N' STATIC DON'T. SNIPER SKY TURNS TO WHISPER SOMETHING TO THE DESTROYER — BUT THAT MAY HAVE COST HIM! QUICK AS A VIPER, HARRISON PULLED BACK ON THE TOP ROPE AS HARD AS HE COULD AND CATAPULTED HIMSELF OVER, SOMERSAULTING THROUGH THE AIR AND LANDING ON THE TAG CHAMPS.

SKY TURNED HIS BACK ON THE BEARDED BRUTE FOR JUST ONE MOMENT AND THAT WAS ALL IT TOOK.

HARRISON WAS QUICK, BUT SKY CAN ALSO THINK FAST. SPOTTING THE FLYING BRUTE SOARING TOWARDS THEM, SNIPER SKY PUSHED JUDAS OUT OF HARM'S WAY BEFORE BEING TAKEN OUT ALONG WITH X-STATIC.

THEY MUST HAVE SOME MORE PERKS COMING FOR STAYING ON JUDAS'S GOOD SIDE. WHY ELSE

WOULD THEY SACRIFICE THEMSELVES FOR A WORTHLESS SKIDMARK LIKE JUDAS?

ONE WOULD IMAGINE THE PLAN IS FOR THEM TO HOLD ONTO TAG TEAM GOLD FOR QUITE SOME TIME, FARQUAD. THEY'VE SERVED THEIR PURPOSE FOR NOW, AS JUDAS MAKES HIS WAY AROUND THE SIDE OF THE RING AND SLIDES IN BENEATH THE BOTTOM ROPE. AT LEAST HARRISON HAS NEUTRALISED THE THREAT FROM SKY 'N' STATIC, EVEN IF TEMPORARILY.

HARRISON'S NOT WASTING ANY TIME, NOT NOW THAT THE SCALES ARE UNBALANCED. HE'S GUNNING FOR THE CHAMPION. HARRISON WANTS TO — *NEEDS* TO — FINISH THIS THING QUICKLY.

OH NO! HARRISON RUNS STRAIGHT INTO THE SOLE OF THE CHAMPION'S BOOT AS JUDAS CONNECTS WITH A VICIOUS DESTROYER KICK.

IT'S OVER, GENE. JUDAS HAS TWO FINISHING MOVES — MANOEUVRES THAT NOBODY KICKS OUT OF — THE ONE-WAY POWERBOMB, AND THE DESTROYER KICK.

JUDAS COVERS FOR THE FIRST PINFALL ATTEMPT OF THE MATCH. THE REFEREE COUNTS: ONE, TWO, THR— NO! I DON'T BELIEVE IT. HIP HARRISON KICKS OUT!

NOBODY KICKS OUT OF THE DESTROYER KICK!

NOBODY UNTIL NOW. THE FIGURATIVE ROOF HAS ONCE AGAIN COME OFF THIS PLACE. THE FANS

THOUGHT IT WAS OVER TOO. JUBILATION FILLS THE ENTIRE ROCK ARENA.

NOT EVERYONE IS SO PLEASED, GENE. LOOK AT JUDAS. WE'VE ALL SEEN HIM ANGRY BEFORE, BUT NEVER LIKE THIS. HE'S ARGUING WITH THE REFEREE WHEN THE SMART MONEY SAYS TO KEEP TAKING THE FIGHT TO HARRISON. FINISH HIM WHILE HE'S ALREADY DOWN.

ALL THIS COMPLAINING TO THE OFFICIAL IS GETTING JUDAS NOWHERE. A TWO-COUNT IS A TWO-COUNT. YOU'LL NEVER CHANGE A REFEREE'S MIND ON THAT. JUDGE DREAD IS THE BEST IN THE GAME — HE IS PERFECTLY CONSISTENT WITH HIS CADENCE.

THE JUDGE REMINDS JUDAS OF JUST THAT. AND LOOK: HARRISON'S GETTING UP. THE DESTROYER HAS GIVEN THE CHALLENGER TIME TO RECOVER FROM THAT DESTROYER KICK.

JUDAS TURNS HIS ATTENTION BACK TO HARRISON BUT WALKS INTO AN UPPERCUT. JUDAS RETALIATES WITH A PUNCH OF HIS OWN AND WE HAVE OURSELVES A GOOD OL' FASHIONED SLUGFEST, FOLKS!

JUDAS AND HARRISON ARE TRADING RIGHTS BACK AND FORTH. THE FANS ARE GETTING INVOLVED, TOO, CHEERING EVERY PUNCH HARRISON THROWS WHILE BOOING EVERY SHOT THAT JUDAS

FIRES. WE'VE SAID IT ALREADY AND I'LL SAY IT AGAIN: THE ATMOSPHERE HERE IS ELECTRIC.

NEITHER COMPETITOR IS BACKING DOWN… FINALLY, HARRISON DUCKS A PUNCH FROM JUDAS AND GRABS THE CHAMPION FROM BEHIND IN A WAIST LOCK. HARRISON ATTEMPTS TO LIFT JUDAS FOR A GERMAN SUPLEX, BUT THE CHAMPION ADJUSTS HIS CENTRE OF GRAVITY AND GETS HIS FEET BACK DOWN TO THE GROUND. THE BEARDED BRUTE MAINTAINS THE WAIST LOCK; HE MAY BE GOING FOR THAT SUPLEX ONCE MORE. JUDAS BLINDLY THROWS ELBOWS BEHIND HIM. ONE OR TWO OF THEM HIT HARRISON IN THE HEAD AND THE BEARDED BRUTE HAS NO CHOICE BUT TO RELINQUISH THE HOLD AS HE FEELS THE FULL FORCE OF THE JUDAS EFFECT.

JUDAS MEANS BUSINESS NOW. HE'S REALISED THE URGENCY WITH WHICH HE MUST FIGHT TO DEFEAT HIP HARRISON. I THINK THE CHAMPION UNDERESTIMATED THE CHALLENGER GOING INTO THIS MATCH. HE MAY HAVE THOUGHT ALL THE MIND GAMES HE PLAYED OVER THE LAST FEW WEEKS HAD KNOCKED HARRISON OFF HIS GAME. BUT, IF ANYTHING, IT'S MADE HARRISON FIGHT EVEN HARDER.

AS HARRISON REELS FROM THE ELBOW SHOTS, JUDAS TURNS, GRABS THE NUMBER ONE CONTENDER BY

THE WRIST, AND WHIPS HIM INTO THE ROPES. THE DESTROYER IMMEDIATELY LAUNCHES HIMSELF IN THE OPPOSITE DIRECTION, MEANING A COLLISION IS IMMINENT. BOTH COMBATANTS REBOUND OFF THE ROPES ACROSS FROM EACH OTHER. JUDAS FLICKS HIS LEG UP, GOING FOR ANOTHER DESTROYER KICK, BUT HARRISON DUCKS UNDERNEATH. THEY'RE STILL RUNNING BUT HAVE SWITCHED SIDES AS THEY COME OFF THE ROPES AGAIN. THIS TIME IT'S HIP HARRISON THROWING OUT AN ARM, ATTEMPTING A CLOTHESLINE, BUT JUDAS SIDE-STEPS IT.

IT'S LIKE WATCHING A JOUST, GENE! WHO'S GOING TO FALL FROM THEIR FIGURATIVE HORSE FIRST?

JUDAS AND HARRISON HIT THE ROPES ONCE MORE AND SLING THEMSELVES BACK TOWARDS EACH OTHER. THEY BOTH APPEAR TO BE ON THE OFFENSIVE — HARRISON JUMPS, LOOKING TO LAND A CROSS BODY, AND JUDAS DOES THE SAME. GOOD BRADSHAW, ALMIGHTY! WHAT IMPACT!

THE FANS HERE AT THE ROCK COLLECTIVELY GASPED. IT WAS AS IF THE WIND WAS KNOCKED OUT OF EVERYONE IN HERE, JUST AS IT WOULD HAVE BEEN FOR JUDAS AND HIP HARRISON. IF WE LOOK AT THE SLOW-MOTION REPLAY, YOU CAN SEE THAT BOTH COMPETITORS TILTED TO THEIR RESPECTIVE

RIGHTS AS THEY JUMPED, LOOKING TO HIT THE OTHER WITH A CROSS BODY PRESS. WHAT HAPPENED, AS A RESULT, IS THAT THEY MET EACH OTHER MID-AIR, FORMING AN X AS THEIR MID-SECTIONS SLAMMED INTO ONE ANOTHER. THEY THEN FELL TO THE CANVAS IN A HEAP, BOTH STRUGGLING FOR BREATH.

CHAMPION AND CHALLENGER ARE DOWN IN OUR MAIN EVENT HERE AT BATTLESTAR GALACTICA. WHO CAN CATCH THEIR BREATH FIRST AND CAPITALISE ON THE SITUATION?

WAIT A MINUTE, GENE. SOMEONE JUST WALKED PAST US ON THE STAGE. THEY'RE HEADING DOWN THE RAMP TOWARDS THE RING. IS THAT… IS THAT WHO I THINK IT IS? CAN WE GET A CAMERA ON THEM?

I DON'T BELIEVE IT. LADIES AND GENTLEMEN, THAT IS THE OWNER AND CHAIRMAN OF THE GALACTIC WRESTLING FEDERATION, MR MONTGOMERY.

HE NEVER SHOWS HIS FACE ON CAMERA! WHAT'S HE DOING OUT HERE NOW, DURING THE BIGGEST MATCH OF THE CYCLE? PERHAPS EVEN THE BIGGEST MATCH IN GALACTIC WF HISTORY?

IT REMAINS TO BE SEEN BUT, GIVEN EVENTS IN RECENT WEEKS, I HAVE AN IDEA HE'S OUT HERE TO THROW HIS SUPPORT BEHIND THE CHAMPION. WE

ASKED HOW JUDAS COULD HAVE PULLED OFF A STUNT LIKE HE DID WHEN HE FOOLED US ALL INTO THINKING HE WAS AT THE HOME OF HIP HARRISON'S FATHER, ONLY TO SHOW UP HERE AT THE ROCK TO BATTLE IVY JANE AS SOON AS THE BEARDED BRUTE HAD LEFT. WELL, WITH THE MOST POWERFUL SIANARDIAN IN NOT JUST THIS PROMOTION, BUT THE INDUSTRY AS A WHOLE, BACKING YOU… I THINK I NEED SAY NO MORE.

I WAS ABOUT TO TELL YOU TO WATCH YOUR WORDS, GENE. THAT YOU CAN'T GO AROUND MAKING SUCH ACCUSATIONS WITHOUT EVIDENCE — ESPECIALLY AGAINST OUR BOSS. BUT I THINK YOU'RE RIGHT. LOOK AT WHAT HE'S DOING NOW. HE'S PRODDING SKY 'N' STATIC WITH HIS FEET AND YELLING AT THEM TO GET UP. HE'S TRYING TO GET THEM INTO THE RING. I THINK THE FIX IS IN.

THE AUDIENCE SENSES WHAT'S GOING ON AND THEY DON'T LIKE IT. AS I THINK BACK, IT'S ALL COMING TOGETHER. DURING THE NUMBER ONE CONTENDER'S TOURNAMENT, WHEN HIP HARRISON HAD JUST DEFEATED FATBOY SLIME IN THE SECOND ROUND, HE MENTIONED MR MONTGOMERY BY NAME. IN FACT, IF I REMEMBER CORRECTLY, HARRISON REVEALED MR MONTGOMERY'S POSITION AS OWNER OF THE GALACTIC WF AND SAID THAT HE HAD SOMETHING ELSE TO SHARE WITH THE WORLD ABOUT THE CHAIRMAN BEFORE HIS

MICROPHONE CUT OUT. THIS HAS GOT TO HAVE SOMETHING TO DO WITH THAT. THERE'S BEEN A CONSPIRACY UNFOLDING BEFORE OUR VERY EYES TO PREVENT HIP HARRISON FROM BECOMING CHAMPION. THE BEARDED BRUTE CLEARLY KNOWS SOMETHING THAT MONTGOMERY DOES NOT WANT TO GET OUT — AND THE BOSS IS TAKING MATTERS INTO HIS OWN HANDS TO ENSURE HARRISON REMAINS VOICELESS.

THE OLD MAN IS MAN-HANDLING X-STATIC AND SNIPER SKY. HE ROLLS THEM, ONE AT A TIME, INTO THE RING, TELLING THEM TO 'FINISH THE JOB'. THIS IS RIDICULOUS BUT IT'S A NO-DISQUALIFICATION MATCH. IF IT BECOMES THREE-ON-ONE, THE REFEREE IS POWERLESS TO STOP IT.

SKY USES THE ROPES FOR BALANCE AND FINDS HIS WAY TO HIS FEET FIRST. HE HELPS X-STATIC UP AND NOW THE TAG TEAM CHAMPIONS STOMP A MUDHOLE, SO TO SPEAK, INTO HIP HARRISON. THIS IS ATROCIOUS.

THOSE ARE SOME STIFF KICKS TO A DOWNED HIP HARRISON. THIS IS UNCOMFORTABLE TO WATCH.

WHO'S THIS NOW? SOMEBODY ELSE HAS JUST PASSED US UP HERE ON THE STAGE.

IT'S SOVEREIGN NOBLE! WHAT'S THE COMMISSIONER GOING TO DO? CANE HARRISON?

YOUR GUESS IS AS GOOD AS MINE. A MOON ORBIT AGO, WE WITNESSED THE CRAFTY KINGSMAN ASSIST

JUDAS WITH HIS NEFARIOUS SCHEMES. AND WHY WOULDN'T HE? AFTER ALL, SOVEREIGN NOBLE REPORTS DIRECTLY TO THE BOSS, TO MR MONTGOMERY. IT'S HIS JOB TO DO THE CHAIRMAN'S BIDDING.

THE COMMISSIONER HOBBLES DOWN THE RAMP AND LIMPS AROUND THE RING TOWARDS MR MONTGOMERY. HE — NOBLE — LOOKS ANGRY.

PERHAPS THE COMMISSIONER HAS GROWN A BACKBONE AFTER JUDAS LOOKED SET TO THROW HIM OFF THE STAGE A COUPLE OF WEEKS BACK. OF COURSE, HE HAS YOU TO THANK FOR TAKING THE FALL FOR HIM, FARQUAD.

THE THANK YOU NOTE MUST BE IN THE MAIL.

I THINK HE ACTUALLY MIGHT HAVE — GROWN A BACKBONE, THAT IS. HE'S QUESTIONING MR MONTGOMERY, ASKING HIM WHY HE'S OUT HERE AND WHY SKY 'N' STATIC ARE GETTING INVOLVED IN THIS CHAMPIONSHIP MATCH.

SOVEREIGN NOBLE WAS ONCE AN IN-RING COMPETITOR, DON'T FORGET. MORE THAN ANYONE, THOSE OF US WHO ONCE LACED UP A PAIR OF BOOTS AND STEPPED INSIDE THE SQUARED CIRCLE TO COMPETE HATE TO SEE ANY MATCH RUINED LIKE THIS, LET ALONE ONE FOR THE HEAVYWEIGHT TITLE ON THE GRANDEST STAGE THERE IS. IT MAKES A MOCKERY OF THE SPORT.

MR MONTGOMERY HAS GONE PURPLE IN THE FACE. I CAN TELL YOU, LADIES AND GENTLEMEN, THAT HE DOES NOT TAKE KINDLY TO HAVING HIS ACTIONS OR DECISIONS CALLED INTO QUESTION. WHAT HE SAYS GOES AND, IF YOU DON'T LIKE IT, YOU'LL FIND YOURSELF IN THE UNEMPLOYMENT LINE.

THE BOSS HAS LAUNCHED A VERBAL TIRADE AT SOVEREIGN NOBLE. HOWEVER, THE COMMISSIONER LOOKS TO HAVE GROWN IMMUNE TO THE CHAIRMAN'S YELLING. NOBLE'S LETTING IT WASH COMPLETELY OVER HIM.

SOVEREIGN NOBLE'S LACK OF REACTION IS CAUSING MR MONTGOMERY TO GROW EVEN MADDER. THE CHAIRMAN LIKES TO BE IN CONTROL AND HE DOESN'T SEEM ABLE TO EXERT ANY OVER THE COMMISSIONER IN THIS MOMENT.

YOU GET SHOWERED IN CRAP LONG ENOUGH, YOU LEARN TO BRING AN UMBRELLA.

MR MONTGOMERY HAS REACHED A LOSS FOR WORDS. NOBLE STARES HIM DOWN WITHOUT SPEAKING. INSIDE THE RING, THE TAG TEAM CHAMPIONS LIFT HIP HARRISON TO HIS FEET. SKY HAS THE BEARDED BRUTE HELD WITH HIS ARMS RESTRAINED AND X-STATIC LAYS IN PUNCHES.

NOBLE'S GETTING IN THE RING! AND THE CROWD IS... THEY'RE ACTUALLY CHEERING.

SOVEREIGN NOBLE SLIDES HIS CANE INTO THE RING, THEN AWKWARDLY CLIMBS IN AFTER IT AS SKY 'N' STATIC CONTINUE TO PUMMEL HIP HARRISON. THE COMMISSIONER USES THE ROPES FOR ASSISTANCE AS HE GETS TO HIS FEET AND PICKS UP THE CANE. HE HEADS TOWARD THE TAG CHAMPIONS WITH A FACE LIKE THUNDER.

SAY WHAT YOU WILL ABOUT THE CRAFTY KINGSMAN BUT, BACK IN HIS FIGHTING DAYS, HE NEVER BACKED DOWN FROM A CONFRONTATION.

NOBLE GRABS SNIPER SKY BY THE SHOULDER AND YELLS FOR HIM TO LET HARRISON GO. SKY, STILL HOLDING HARRISON IN A FULL NELSON, LOOKS AT SOVEREIGN NOBLE LIKE THE CRAFTY KINGSMAN IS SOMETHING HE STEPPED IN.

DID YOU HEAR THAT? THE MICS JUST ABOUT PICKED IT UP. X-STATIC LEANED IN AND TOLD SOVEREIGN NOBLE THAT HE'S NOT THE BOSS OF THEM. AND HE FOLLOWED IT UP BY SPITTING IN THE COMMISSIONER'S FACE.

WHAT UTTER DISRESPECT SHOWN BY THE NEW TAG TEAM CHAMPIONS. THEY'RE EVERY BIT AS DESPICABLE AS THE HEAVYWEIGHT CHAMPION.

NOBLE'S FACIAL EXPRESSION! LOOK AT THAT.

HE LOOKS DOWNRIGHT DISGUSTED — AND RIGHTFULLY SO.

I HAVEN'T SEEN THAT LOOK ON HIS FACE SINCE HE WAS FORCED TO RETIRE FROM IN-RING ACTION. THAT WAS THE LOOK HE USED TO GIVE HIS OPPONENTS BEFORE BEATING THEM INTO A BLOODY MESS.

SNIPER SKY AND X-STATIC HAVEN'T NOTICED. THEY'VE GONE BACK TO WAGING THEIR ASSAULT ON HIP HARRISON. NOBLE PULLS A HANDKERCHIEF FROM HIS POCKET AND WIPES THE SALIVA FROM HIS CHEEK. HIS LIP CURLS UP.

MR MONTGOMERY HAS NOTICED. THE CHAIRMAN CLIMBS TO THE RING APRON AND COMMANDS NOBLE TO GET OUT OF THE RING.

BUT THE COMMISSIONER HAS ENTERED A TRANCE, THE LIKES OF WHICH WE HAVEN'T SEEN SINCE HE WAS RIDING HIGH AS THE INTERPLANETARY CHAMPION. HIS EYES FIXED ON THE BACK OF SNIPER SKY'S HEAD, SOVEREIGN NOBLE RAISES THE CANE AND — IN TURN — THE CROWD, AS EVERYONE WATCHING COMES TO THEIR FEET.

HE'S GOING TO BASH SKY OVER THE HEAD WITH THAT THING. IT'LL KNOCK HIM OUT COLD!

THE CANE IS HIGH ABOVE NOBLE'S HEAD. HE'S GOING TO SWING— NO, WAIT! MR MONTGOMERY STOPS IT! THE OWNER OF THE GALACTIC WRESTLING FEDERATION HAS CLIMBED INTO THE RING AND

ATTEMPTS TO WRENCH THE CANE FROM SOVEREIGN NOBLE'S HANDS.

LISTENING TO THE NOISE FROM OUR AUDIENCE, MR MONTGOMERY ISN'T PROVING VERY POPULAR DURING HIS TELEVISED DEBUT.

NOBLE TURNS ON HIS GOOD LEG TO SEE JUST WHY HIS CANE IS STUCK IN MIDAIR, THAT TRADEMARK SNARL OF HIS NOW DIRECTED AT MR MONTGOMERY. THE CRAFTY KINGSMAN TRIES TO PULL THE CANE FROM THE BOSS'S HANDS, BUT MR MONTGOMERY AIN'T LETTING GO.

AS THE COMMISSIONER PUTS ONE FOOT FORWARD, HE HAD BETTER WATCH HIS STEP, FIGURATIVELY SPEAKING. NOT ONLY DOES MR MONTGOMERY HAVE THE JURISDICTION TO FIRE YOU ON THE SPOT, BUT HE ALSO HAS THE POWER TO MAKE YOUR LIFE A LIVING HELL.

NOBLE DOESN'T APPEAR TO CARE ABOUT ANY OF THAT RIGHT NOW. HE TAKES ANOTHER LIMP TOWARDS THE CHAIRMAN, WHO LOWERS HIS END OF THE CANE, USING THE WALKING AID AS A ROD TO KEEP SOME DISTANCE BETWEEN HIMSELF AND THE CRAFTY KINGSMAN.

IF NOBLE IS CAPABLE OF HALF THE LEVEL OF VIOLENCE THAT WE USED TO SEE FROM HIM IN THAT

RING, THEN MR MONTGOMERY IS A DEADMAN WALKING.

SOVEREIGN NOBLE USES THE LOWERED CANE TO HIS ADVANTAGE, PULLING IT — AND THE CHAIRMAN — TOWARDS HIM LIKE THEY'RE PLAYING TUG OF WAR.

WHO'S THE PUPPET MASTER NOW?

MR MONTGOMERY HANGS ON TO THAT CANE FOR DEAR LIFE. HOWEVER, SOVEREIGN NOBLE IS THE STRONGER OF THE TWO, EVEN ON ONE GOOD LEG. YOU COULD SAY THE CHAIRMAN IS CAUGHT BETWEEN A ROCK AND A HARD PLACE AS, IF HE CONTINUES TO PULL ON THE CANE, UNSUCCESSFULLY AS HE IS, THE COMMISSIONER WILL SOON BE IN REACHING DISTANCE. BUT, IF HE RELINQUISHES HIS HOLD ON THE STICK, NOBLE WILL HAVE FREE REIN TO CLOBBER WHOMEVER HE LIKES.

MONTGOMERY'S SQUIRMING. NOBLE'S A FINGERTIP AWAY FROM BEING ABLE TO REACH HIM—

OH, COME ON! JUDAS HITS SOVEREIGN NOBLE WITH A DEVASTATING DESTROYER KICK TO THE BACK OF THE HEAD. THE COMMISSIONER IS DOWN AND LOOKS TO BE OUT COLD AS THE CHAMPION AND THE CHAIRMAN SHARE A LAUGH.

THEY'RE SHAKING HANDS! I DON'T BELIEVE THIS. THEY COULDN'T BE ANY MORE BRAZEN.

THEY'RE NOT EVEN HIDING THE FACT THAT THE OWNER OF THIS PROMOTION IS BACKING THE CHAMPION. BIAS SHOULD PLAY NO PART IN THIS GREAT SPORT, LET ALONE AT THIS ELITE, CHAMPIONSHIP LEVEL. DO YOU THINK THE PROMOTERS ON EARTH WOULD HAVE EVER HAND-PICKED THEIR CHAMPIONS? OF COURSE NOT! THIS IS AN INSULT TO PROFESSIONAL WRESTLING IN ITS ENTIRETY — PAST, PRESENT, AND FUTURE.

IT'S SICKENING IS WHAT IT IS. MEANWHILE, X-STATIC LANDS ONE FINAL PUNCH TO THE GUT OF HARRISON AND DIRECTS SNIPER SKY'S ATTENTION TO THE CHAMPION AND THE CHAIRMAN. SKY TURNS WITH HARRISON STILL HELD IN THAT FULL NELSON AND SHOVES THE NUMBER ONE CONTENDER DOWN TO THE MAT BESIDE JUDAS. MR MONTGOMERY, STILL WITH THAT EVIL SMILE ETCHED ACROSS HIS FACE, RAISES BOTH ARMS, GESTURING TOWARDS HIP HARRISON'S LIFELESS BODY. IT'S AS IF HE IS PRESENTING THE CHAMPION WITH A VICTORY.

FOR THE SAKE OF BRADSHAW AND ALL THAT IS SHIDA. THIS COMPLETELY DIMINISHES THE PRESTIGE AND VALUE OF THE GALACTIC HEAVYWEIGHT CHAMPIONSHIP. IF JUDAS WINS IN THIS WAY, THE TITLE IS MEANINGLESS.

MR MONTGOMERY EXITS THE RING AND CALLS FOR SKY 'N' STATIC TO DO THE SAME. JUDAS ROLLS HARRISON OVER ONTO HIS BACK…

HE'S REALLY GOING TO TAKE THE EASY WIN, SERVED UP ON A SILVER PLATTER. I DON'T THINK I CAN WATCH.

…AND GOES FOR THE COVER, HOOKING THE BEARDED BRUTE'S LEG FOR ADDITIONAL LEVERAGE THAT IS LIKELY NOT NEEDED.

WHY DON'T I HEAR A COUNT?

JUDGE DREAD STANDS IN THE CENTRE OF THE RING LOOKING JUST AS ANGERED AND PERPLEXED AS THE REST OF US, FARQUAD. HE APPEARS TO BE QUESTIONING THE CHAIRMAN. JUDAS, FROM HIS PINNING POSITION, LOOKS UP AND SCREAMS AT THE REFEREE WHILE MR MONTGOMERY SHAKES HIS FINGER AT CHAMPION AND CHALLENGER, REMINDING JUDGE DREAD THAT THIS IS A NO-DISQUALIFICATION MATCH AND TELLING HIM TO DO HIS ONLY JOB IN COUNTING THE PINFALL.

WHAT IF DREAD REFUSES?

HIS ONLY OTHER OPTION IS SURELY TO RUN. OTHERWISE, YOU'VE GOT TO THINK THAT MONTGOMERY WILL SIC JUDAS AND THE TAG CHAMPIONS ON HIM.

LET ME SEE… HE'S LOWERING HIMSELF TO THE MAT TO MAKE THE COUNT. I CAN'T SAY I BLAME HIM AFTER WHAT HAPPENED TO ME A MOON ORBIT AGO, BUT I DON'T LIKE IT ONE BIT.

ONE — THE JUDGE SLAPS HIS HAND TO THE MAT. MR MONTGOMERY AND JUDAS BOTH DEMAND THAT DREAD COUNT FASTER AS HIS CADENCE IS SLOWER THAN USUAL. THE REFEREE IS A SIANARDIAN OF TRUE INTEGRITY AND THIS SITS ABOUT AS WELL WITH HIM AS A FIVE-DAY-OLD BARBECUE BURRITO.

TWO.

JUDGE DREAD SHAKES HIS HEAD AS HIS ARM LIFTS FOR A FINAL TIME BEFORE CALLING AN END TO THIS FARCE OF A CHAMPIONSHIP MATCH. HIS HAND APPROACHES THE MAT AND THAT'S ALL—

HE KICKED OUT! I DON'T BELIEVE IT!

NEITHER DO I. THAT WAS A TWO-POINT-NINE COUNT IF EVER THERE WAS ONE. HIP HARRISON GETS HIS RIGHT SHOULDER UP AND I CAN TELL YOU THAT YOUR TELEVISION SETS WILL NOT DO JUSTICE TO TWO THINGS: HOW LOUD THIS PLACE SUDDENLY BECAME AFTER OUR LIVE AUDIENCE HAD FALLEN INTO A SUBDUED, SICKENED SILENCE; AND JUST HOW DEEP A SHADE OF PURPLE MR MONTGOMERY'S FACE HAS BECOME.

I'VE NEVER SEEN HIM SO ANGRY, AND HE'S GENERALLY OF AN ENRAGED DISPOSITION.

INSIDE THE RING, JUDAS IS UP AND BACKS JUDGE DREAD INTO A CORNER. HE'S SLAPPING HIS HANDS TOGETHER TO INDICATE THE SPEED AT WHICH HE WOULD PREFER THE REFEREE TO COUNT. I'M SURE JUDGE DREAD WOULD RATHER CALL A FAIR FIGHT THOUGH.

MR MONTGOMERY IS UP ON THE APRON AGAIN. HE'S TELLING JUDAS TO LEAVE THE REFEREE ALONE AND TO FINISH THE JOB. THE BOSS IS DESPERATE TO KEEP THE GALACTIC WF CHAMPIONSHIP BELT AWAY FROM THE WAIST OF HIP HARRISON.

THAT HE IS, FARQUAD. FOR SOMEONE WHO HAS DONE EVERYTHING WITHIN THEIR POWER TO REMAIN FIRMLY BACKSTAGE AND OUT OF THE SPOTLIGHT, IT'S UNSETTLING FOR THOSE OF US WHO HAVE WORKED FOR MR MONTGOMERY TO SEE HIM NOW, JUMPING UP AND DOWN IN FRONT OF THIS CAPACITY CROWD AND THE MILLIONS WATCHING ON TELEVISION ACROSS THE GALAXY.

I WONDER IF JUDAS KNOWS WHAT THE BOSS IS HIDING. DO YOU THINK HE'S IN ON IT?

MY GUT'S TELLING ME NO. GIVEN THE DESPERATION WE'RE SEEING FROM THE CHAIRMAN, HE OBVIOUSLY DOESN'T WANT ANYONE TO FIND OUT

WHATEVER HIP HARRISON HAS BECOME PRIVY TO. AND THAT WOULD INCLUDE JUDAS.

YOU'RE PROBABLY RIGHT, GENE. BESIDES, JUDAS IS NO DOUBT HAPPY TO GO BLINDLY ALONG WITH MR MONTGOMERY'S PLANS SO LONG AS HE GETS TO KEEP HIS STRANGLEHOLD ON THE BIGGEST PRIZE IN THIS SPORT: THE GALACTIC WF HEAVYWEIGHT CHAMPIONSHIP. IT'S NOT ALWAYS TALKED ABOUT, BUT THERE'S A LOT OF EXTRA BUCKS THAT COME WITH BEING THE CHAMPION — NOT ONLY FROM THE WINNERS' PURSES, BUT FROM ENDORSEMENT DEALS AND MEDIA APPEARANCES AND MERCHANDISING OPPORTUNITIES. THAT BIG, GOLD BELT PROVIDES JUDAS WITH EVERYTHING HE COULD EVER WANT.

BACK TO THE ACTION: JUDAS STEPS AWAY FROM JUDGE DREAD AND, TAKING MR MONTGOMERY'S ADVICE, LIFTS HARRISON UP TO HIS FEET. THE BEARDED BRUTE, HOWEVER, STRIKES WITH AN UPPER CUT THAT SENDS JUDAS REELING MOMENTARILY, BUT IT IS NOT ENOUGH TO CHANGE THE TIDE IN THIS MATCH. JUDAS RETALIATES WITH THAT STIFF KNEE OF HIS, STRAIGHT TO THE STOMACH OF HARRISON. THE SAME STOMACH THAT SKY 'N' STATIC JUST GOT DONE TENDERISING FOR HIM.

THIS PLACE CAME ALIVE AGAIN FOR A SPLIT SECOND WHEN HARRISON CLOCKED JUDAS IN THE CHIN. NOW, IT'S LIKE THE AIR HAS BEEN SUCKED OUT OF THE BUILDING, JUST AS HARRISON HAD THE WIND KNOCKED OUT OF HIM.

HIP HARRISON DOUBLES OVER AND JUDAS WRAPS THOSE PYTHON-LIKE ARMS AROUND THE BEARDED BRUTE'S WAIST. THE DESTROYER HOISTS HIS CHALLENGER UP AND OVER, ONTO HIS SHOULDERS. HE'S GOING TO END THIS WITH THE ONE-WAY POWERBOMB.

AT LEAST IT'LL BE OVER QUICKLY ONCE HE HITS THIS.

MEMBERS OF THE GALAXY IN ATTENDANCE ARE CALLING FOR HIP HARRISON TO WAKE UP, TO COUNTER THIS MOVE BEFORE IT'S TOO LATE. BUT THE BEARDED BRUTE IS OUT COLD UP THERE ON JUDAS'S SHOULDERS. THE CHAMPION PARADES HIM AROUND THE RING, SHOWING OFF HIS PREY TO THE CROWD BEFORE PUTTING HIM DOWN FOR GOOD.

AT LEAST THE AUDIENCE HERE AT THE ROCK ARENA CAN GET BACK INTO THE MATCH, EVEN IF IT'S NOT EXACTLY GOING THE WAY ANY OF US WOULD LIKE IT TO. WITHOUT THE BENEFIT OF BEING ABLE TO HEAR OUR COMMENTARY, THE VAST MAJORITY OF THE CROWD MUST HAVE NO IDEA WHO MR

MONTGOMERY IS, NOR WHY HE'S HERE AND WHAT HE'S DOING.

JUDAS COMPLETES HIS PRE-VICTORY LAP AND TURNS TOWARD THE CENTRE OF THE RING, WHERE HIP HARRISON IS ABOUT TO COME CRASHING DOWN.

WHAT'S GOING ON NOW? THERE'S SOME SORT OF COMMOTION GOING ON OUTSIDE THE RING. FANS ARE GOING WILD AND SECURITY PERSONNEL ARE RUNNING OVER. BUT SOMEONE'S JUMPED THE BARRICADE.

THE CHAMPION CAN'T SEE WHAT'S GOING ON WITH HIP HARRISON STILL PERCHED ON HIS SHOULDERS. BUT THE SUDDEN BURST OF NOISE, NOT TO MENTION THE FACT THE CHAIRMAN AND TAG TEAM CHAMPIONS ARE CALLING TO HIM FROM RINGSIDE, HAS CAUSED JUDAS TO HESITATE FOR JUST A MOMENT. AND THAT MOMENT'S ENOUGH TO PREVENT THE ONE-WAY POWERBOMB AS THE HOODED ASSAILANT — THE BARRICADE-JUMPING MEMBER OF THE GALACTIC WF FANBASE — SLIDES INTO THE RING AND TACKLES THE DESTROYER. JUDAS TAKES THE BRUNT OF THAT CATACLYSMIC CATASTROPHE, BREAKING HARRISON'S FALL.

THAT GUY WITH THE HOOD HAS GOT TO BE — WHAT? — THIRTY-THREE AND A THIRD PERCENT OF THE SIZE OF JUDAS, IF THAT? I WANT TO MAKE IT

CLEAR TO THOSE OF YOU WATCHING AND WONDERING HOW SOMEONE AS BIG AS JUDAS COULD BE TAKEN DOWN BY A SMALLER-THAN-AVERAGE SIANARDIAN, THAT JUDAS HAD HIS VIEW OBSTRUCTED AND, THEREFORE, NEVER SAW HIS ATTACKER COMING. ONCE HIS CENTRE OF GRAVITY WAS KNOCKED, AND WITH HARRISON UP ON HIS SHOULDERS, HE FELL LIKE TIMBER.

THANKS FOR THE PHYSICS LESSON, FARQUAD. IN SUMMARY, YOU'RE SAYING THAT WITH JUDAS'S VISION COMPROMISED, IT LEFT HIM OPEN TO THE ELEMENT OF SURPRISE AND THAT, WITH HARRISON'S WEIGHT TO SUPPORT, HE LOST HIS BALANCE.

TO PUT IT CONCISELY: YES.

MR MONTGOMERY DIRECTS SKY 'N' STATIC TO GET INTO THE RING AND TAKE THE INTRUDER OUT. I WOULD REMIND ALL OUR FANS THAT IT IS NEVER A GOOD IDEA TO CROSS THE BARRICADE WHEN ATTENDING A GALACTIC WF EVENT IN PERSON. THE BARRIER IS THERE FOR YOUR SAFETY, AS WELL AS THAT OF OUR WRESTLERS. WE IN NO WAY CONDONE THE ACTION OF THIS HOODED INTRUDER, EVEN IF HE'S ACTING WITH HONOURABLE INTENTIONS, TO PREVENT THIS MAIN EVENT FROM ENDING AS A COMPLETE FARCE.

THE INTRUDER SLIDES OUT BELOW THE BOTTOM ROPE, HEADING TOWARD THE ENTRANCE

RAMP. A WISE DECISION AS SNIPER SKY AND X-STATIC HAVE ENTERED THE RING. HE'S REMOVING THE HOOD! HE'S… I RECOGNISE THAT GUY. WHAT WAS HIS NAME AGAIN?

THAT'S NEMO — THE FRIEND OF HIP HARRISON THAT WAS POWERBOMBED OFF THE STAGE THE MOON ORBIT BEFORE YOU MET THE SAME FATE, FARQUAD.

ALWAYS NICE TO SHARE SOMETHING IN COMMON, I SUPPOSE.

NEMO, NOW REVEALING A CAST BENEATH THE SLEEVE ON HIS RIGHT HAND, JUST SAVED THE MATCH FOR HIP HARRISON AND GETS OUT OF DODGE. THE TAG TEAM CHAMPIONS ARE SEEMINGLY RELUCTANT TO GIVE CHASE, INSTEAD SHOUTING THREATS FROM INSIDE THE RING.

THEIR PRIORITY IS TO ENSURE HARRISON REMAINS NEUTRALISED FOR JUDAS TO PICK UP THE EASY WIN.

THEY'VE SO FAR FAILED ON THAT FRONT. WHILE SKY 'N' STATIC HAVE PUT ALL OF THEIR ATTENTION ON THAT NEMO KID, HIP HARRISON HAS RISEN TO HIS FEET.

THE TAG CHAMPS MAY NOT HAVE TURNED AROUND YET, BUT THEY CAN SENSE SOMETHING IS UP. AT THE VERY LEAST, THEY CAN HEAR THIS CROWD'S REACTION, WHICH, I CAN ASSURE YOU, WASN'T FOR NEMO'S GRAND REVEAL.

SNIPER SKY AND X-STATIC TURN AROUND, SLOWLY, TOWARDS THE CENTRE OF THE RING, TO FIND AN ANGRY BEARDED BRUTE CHARGING AT THEM. HIP HARRISON EXTENDS BOTH OF HIS ARMS OUT, LIKE THE WINGS OF AN AEROCRAFT, AND CLOTHESLINES THE TAG TEAM CHAMPIONS OVER THE TOP ROPE.

THEY BOTH TUMBLED TO THE FLOOR BELOW WITH SUCH FORCE THAT I WOULD BE SURPRISED IF THERE WEREN'T AN INJURY OR TWO SUSTAINED. AT LEAST, FOR HARRISON'S SAKE, THEY HAVE BEEN REMOVED FROM THE EQUATION FOR THE TIME BEING.

IT WAS AN INCREDIBLY STIFF SHOT BUT WHAT ELSE COULD HARRISON DO TO GET THIS THING BACK TO SOMETHING RESEMBLING A FAIR FIGHT?

IT LOOKS AS IF YOU'RE GOING TO GET WHAT YOU WANT, GENE. JUDAS IS BACK TO HIS FEET AND HARRISON LOCKS EYES WITH HIM. ASIDE FROM THE FACT THAT THE BEARDED BRUTE HAS ABSORBED A HELLUVA BEATING, WE'RE BACK TO SQUARE ONE WHERE IT'S ONE-ON-ONE.

HARRISON, AS YOU SAY, IS AT A HUGE HANDICAP GIVEN THE BEATDOWN HE SUSTAINED AT THE HANDS OF THE TAG TEAM CHAMPIONS. BUT IF WE'VE LEARNED ANYTHING ABOUT THE CHALLENGER OVER THE LAST FEW MOON ORBITS, IT'S THAT HE'S GOT GRIT AND

DETERMINATION, HE'S RESOURCEFUL AS HELL, AND HE WON'T GIVE UP WITHOUT A FIGHT.

IT'S NOT QUITE ONE-ON-ONE. MR MONTGOMERY IS STILL OUTSIDE THE RING, CALLING FOR JUDAS TO FINISH IT QUICKLY AND FLINGING INSULTS AT HARRISON. THAT'S GOTTA BE DISTRACTING.

LET THE OLD MAN RANT AND RAVE. HIS WILD WAILING CAN'T BE HEARD OVER THE SOUND OF THIS SOLD-OUT AUDIENCE CHANTING, 'HA-RRI-SON!' IN UNISON. THOSE CHEERS MUST BE GETTING RIGHT BENEATH THE DESTROYER'S SKIN.

JUDAS IS MAKING SOME NOISE OF HIS OWN. I WONDER WHAT HE'S SAYING TO HARRISON.

I'M NOT SURE, BUT HARRISON DOESN'T LOOK TOO IMPRESSED AS BOTH COMBATANTS CIRCLE THE RING, EACH WAITING FOR THE MOST OPPORTUNE TIME TO STRIKE.

I THINK WE HAVE ANOTHER SECURITY BREACH, GENE. LOOK — SOMEBODY'S CLIMBING OVER THE BARRICADE AT THE FAR SIDE NOW. RIGHT BEHIND MR MONTGOMERY.

I MUST REITERATE TO EVERYONE WATCHING THAT WE DO NOT CONDONE THIS KIND OF BEHAVIOUR. IT CAN BE EXTREMELY DANGEROUS TO ENTER THE

RINGSIDE AREA — AND YOU CAN FORGET ABOUT THE RING.

BY THE SAME TOKEN, THAT NEMO KID SURVIVED AND HELPED EVEN THE SCORE.

HE DID, BUT I'D ARGUE HE WAS LUCKY. WHERE IS SECURITY?

THEY MUST BE ESCORTING THAT NEMO GUY OUT OF THE BUILDING. THIS NEW INTRUDER IS A LITTLE LESS PENCIL-NECKED BUT A LOT SLOWER. HE MIGHT BE AN OLDER GENTLEMAN.

THE CAMERAS HAVE FOUND HIM AND IT'S ONCE AGAIN SOMEONE WE RECOGNISE. IT'S HIP HARRISON'S FATHER.

THE SAME ONE WE SAW TIED UP AT THE HANDS OF JUDAS?

YES INDEED. DON'T FORGET THAT JUDAS ALSO DESTROYED THAT CONTRAPTION HARRISON'S FATHER HAD BEEN WORKING ON.

HE JUST SHOULDER-BUMPED MR MONTGOMERY AS HE JOGGED PAST. THE CHAIRMAN ALMOST STUMBLED OVER AND HAD TO CATCH HIMSELF ON THE EDGE OF THE RING. THE BOSS HAS TURNED THE COLOUR OF A BEETROOT AGAIN AS HARRISON'S BIG, BAD, BOOTY DADDY CLIMBS THE STEPS TO THE RING APRON.

THE CHAMPION SPOTS HIS CHALLENGER'S FATHER — HIS NAME IS FRANKLO, IF I REMEMBER CORRECTLY — CLIMBING INTO THE RING. HARRISON ALSO SEES HIS OLD MAN, ENTERING THE WAR ZONE AND ASKS WHAT IN THE HELL HE, HIS FATHER, IS DOING THERE.

OL' FRANKLO IS SPORTING A PAIR OF BLACK EYES. I'D HAZARD A GUESS THAT HE'S SEEKING A MEASURE OF REVENGE, GENE.

HE'S NOT TRAINED AS A WRESTLER, AS FAR AS I KNOW, FARQUAD. AND EVEN IF HE WERE, HIS HEYDAY WOULD BE LONG BEHIND HIM. HE CERTAINLY WOULDN'T BE ANYWHERE CLOSE TO THE LEVEL OF THE MASTER OF THE MAT.

YOU'RE ABSOLUTELY RIGHT, GENE. HE DOESN'T STAND A CHANCE AGAINST JUDAS, BUT IT DOESN'T MEAN HE CAN'T AT LEAST TRY TO UNDERTAKE SOME COURSE OF VENGEANCE. IT'S A NO-DISQUALIFICATION MATCH AFTER ALL AND HIP COULD DO WITH SOME ADDITIONAL RECOVERY TIME.

FRANKLO TELLS HIS SON TO STAND BACK AND LET HIM HAVE AT THE CHAMPION. HIP HARRISON PLEADS WITH HIS FATHER TO VACATE THE RING. HOWEVER, THE SENIOR HARRISON WILL NOT BACK DOWN, USHERING THE BEARDED BRUTE INTO THE CORNER BEFORE TURNING TO FACE JUDAS, WHO LEANS AGAINST THE TURNBUCKLE ACROSS THE RING.

JUDAS IS LAUGHING AND BECKONING THE ELDER HARRISON TO HAVE AT IT.

FRANKLO HARRISON RAISES HIS FISTS TO FORM A GUARD AND ADOPTS A FIGHTING STANCE. HE MARCHES FORWARD.

THIS ISN'T BOXING! WHAT DOES HE THINK HE'S DOING?

HE'S PROVING THAT HE DOES, IN FACT, HAVE NO WRESTLING TRAINING UNDER HIS BELT. MEANWHILE, JUDAS STEPS FORWARD AND THE TWO COME FACE TO FACE IN THE CENTRE OF THE RING. THE DESTROYER LOWERS HIS HEAD AND OFFERS FRANKLO A FREE SHOT.

HARRISON — HIP, THAT IS — YELLS AT HIS DAD TO BACK DOWN, TO LEAVE THE RING.

THERE IS NO SHAME IN BACKING DOWN FROM A FIGHT WITH THE HEAVYWEIGHT CHAMPION OF THE GALAXY. BUT THIS IS A POINT OF PRIDE FOR FRANKLO. TO EXACT SOME REVENGE ON THE SCUMBAG WHO BROKE INTO HIS HOME, BEAT HIM UP, AND DESTROYED HIS LIFE'S WORK.

HE HIT HIM!

FRANKLO STRIKES JUDAS WITH A STRAIGHT PUNCH TO THE MOUTH, MUCH TO THE APPROVAL OF OUR AUDIENCE HERE AT THE ROCK. YET, JUDAS DIDN'T REACT AT ALL.

RUN, FRANKIE, RUN! IF YOU TAKE A FREE SHOT AND IT DOESN'T KNOCK THE OTHER GUY OUT, THEY'RE GOING TO HIT YOU BACK — AND A LOT HARDER.

UPPERCUT! JUDAS HITS WITH VIPER-LIKE SPEED AND PRECISION. FRANKLO GOES DOWN IMMEDIATELY. JUDAS LIFTS HIS HEAD, TURNING HIS ATTENTION BACK TO THE MORE JUNIOR HARRISON. BUT HE'S A SECOND TOO LATE, AS AN ENRAGED HIP TAKES THE DESTROYER DOWN WITH A WICKED SPEAR.

JUDAS MADE A HUGE MISTAKE IN TAKING DOWN HIP HARRISON'S FATHER. ALL IT'S DONE IS LIGHT A FIRE UNDER THE BEARDED BRUTE. IT'S AS IF THAT WERE THE BOLT OF LIGHTNING NEEDED TO BRING HIM BACK FROM THE DEAD.

HARRISON RAINS PUNCHES DOWN ON JUDAS, WHO TRIES TO COVER UP.

IT'S AMAZING WHAT A SHOT OF ADRENALINE CAN DO. ONE MOMENT, HIP'S LEANING AGAINST THE TURNBUCKLES, CLUTCHING THOSE INJURED RIBS, THE NEXT HE'S FIRING ON ALL CYLINDERS WITH JUDAS IN HIS SIGHTS. LET'S JUST HOPE HE HAS ENOUGH ADRENALINE COURSING THROUGH HIS VEINS TO LAST HIM THE REST OF THE MATCH.

THE MOMENTUM HAS INDEED SHIFTED, LADIES AND GENTLEMEN. JUDAS IS ON THE DEFENSIVE, WHICH

IS SOMETHING WE RARELY, IF EVER, SEE. HARRISON KEEPS THE CHAMPION GROUNDED, THROWING PUNCH AFTER PUNCH, LIKE A MAN POSSESSED HAMMERING A NAIL INTO A STUBBORN FLOORBOARD.

MR MONTGOMERY IS CLIMBING INTO THE RING AGAIN. I STILL CAN'T BELIEVE WHAT I'M SEEING. THE BOSS HAS ALWAYS BEEN SO PRIVATE AND NOW HERE HE IS, GETTING HIMSELF INVOLVED ONCE AGAIN WHEN THE ENTIRE GALAXY IS WATCHING.

IT WAS ONE THING TO ENTER THE SQUARED CIRCLE WHEN HIS APPARENT INNER CIRCLE WAS IN CONTROL, BUT NOW HE'S ENTERING A HOSTILE ENVIRONMENT WITH HARRISON IN THE DRIVER'S SEAT.

THE CHAIRMAN INSTRUCTS THE REFEREE TO PUT A STOP TO THIS. HE'S TELLING JUDGE DREAD TO DISQUALIFY HARRISON FOR EXCESSIVE AGGRESSION. THE JUDGE SHRUGS HIS SHOULDERS IN RESPONSE.

IT'S GREAT TO SEE JUDGE DREAD STANDING HIS GROUND AS WELL AS EVER. MR MONTGOMERY MUST BE THE ONE WHO MADE THIS A NO-DISQUALIFICATION MATCH IN THE FIRST PLACE. YOU REAP WHAT YOU SOW, BOSS.

HE'S GRABBED JUDGE DREAD BY THE COLLAR. HE'S THREATENING HIM, HE'S PLEADING WITH HIM — PRACTICALLY BEGGING. BUT THE JUDGE IS THE FAIREST AUTHORITY THERE IS.

MEANWHILE, JUDAS REACHES THE ROPES. NORMALLY, THIS WOULD RESULT IN A ROPE BREAK AND HARRISON WOULD HAVE UNTIL THE COUNT OF FIVE TO BACK AWAY FROM THE CHAMPION OR ELSE HE WOULD BE DISQUALIFIED AND LOSE THE MATCH. BUT, ONCE AGAIN, THERE IS NO DISQUALIFICATION IN THIS CONTEST. JUDGE DREAD SMILES AS HARRISON CONTINUES TO BEAT DOWN ON THE DESTROYER. ALL MR MONTGOMERY CAN DO IS LOOK ON.

DON'T SPEAK TOO SOON, GENE. THE BOSS HAS GIVEN UP ON TRYING TO APPEAL TO THE REFEREE. HE'S ROLLING UP HIS SLEEVES, LITERALLY, WHILE CROSSING THE RING TOWARDS CHAMPION AND CHALLENGER.

MR MONTGOMERY GRABS HARRISON FROM BEHIND BY BOTH SHOULDERS AND ATTEMPTS TO GET HIM AWAY FROM JUDAS. THE BEARDED BRUTE DOESN'T BUDGE BUT RELENTS ON DISHING OUT FURTHER PUNISHMENT TO JUDAS. HARRISON STANDS, TURNS TO FACE THE CHAIRMAN, AND MEETS AN OPEN-HANDED SLAP TO THE CHEEK.

THE WAY HARRISON SOLD THAT WAS AS IF A FLY JUST FLEW IN HIS FACE. A MINOR IRRITATION BUT NOTHING MORE. I THINK IT MIGHT BE MR MONTGOMERY'S TURN TO MAKE LIKE SOME HAY AND BAIL.

MR MONTGOMERY APPEARS TO HAVE REACHED THAT SAME CONCLUSION. HE TURNS AND BOLTS FROM THE RING. HIP HARRISON WISELY OPTS TO LET THE BOSS GO, INSTEAD KEEPING HIS ATTENTION ON HIS OPPONENT AND THE TASK AT HAND.

THE CHAIRMAN HAS ESCAPED HIP HARRISON, BUT HE'S BLINDLY RUN INTO THE COMMISSIONER OUTSIDE THE RING. I TOLD YOU SOVEREIGN NOBLE WAS AS TOUGH AS THEY CAME AND HERE'S PROOF: HE'S ALREADY BACK TO HIS FEET MERE MINUTES AFTER TAKING THAT DESTROYER KICK TO THE BACK OF THE HEAD.

MR MONTGOMERY LOOKS LIKE HE'S SEEN A GHOST. SOVEREIGN NOBLE SMILES BACK AT HIM AND THE CHAIRMAN'S FACE AND POSTURE RELAX A LITTLE.

WHY DO I HAVE A FEELING THAT THE CRAFTY KINGSMAN IS NOT, IN FACT, PLEASED TO SEE MR MONTGOMERY?

MAYBE BECAUSE HE'S DISPLAYING ANOTHER OF THOSE FACIAL EXPRESSIONS WE BECAME SO ACCUSTOMED TO SEEING WHEN NOBLE WAS A MEMBER OF THE ACTIVE ROSTER. HE'D FLASH THAT SAME GRIN AT HIS OPPONENTS, LULLING THEM INTO A FALSE SENSE OF SECURITY BEFORE STRIKING. MR MONTGOMERY HAS EITHER FORGOTTEN THAT OR WASN'T PAYING ENOUGH

ATTENTION TO THE FINER DETAILS DURING SOVEREIGN NOBLE'S MATCHES.

MR MONTGOMERY HAS BEEN WELL AND TRULY LULLED. HE'S EVEN PUT A HAND ON SOVEREIGN NOBLE'S SHOULDER, LIKE THEY'RE OLD BUDDIES MEETING AT A BAR.

THE CRAFTY KINGSMAN ALLOWS THE MASK TO SLIP. THE SMILE FADES, REPLACED BY A FROWN SO COLD IT'LL SEND SHIVERS DOWN YOUR SPINE. A LARGE CONTINGENT OF OUR LIVE CROWD REMEMBERS WHAT THAT LOOK MEANS. CATCHING A CLOSE-UP VIEW ON THE JUMBOTRON, THEY REACT POSITIVELY.

YOU CAN CALL MR MONTGOMERY THE RAINMAKER BECAUSE THE PENNY JUST DROPPED. HE'S STILL GOT THAT HAND ON SOVEREIGN NOBLE'S SHOULDER BUT HE SEES THE FROWN AND HE'S JUST LOST HIS SMILE.

SOVEREIGN NOBLE FEINTS A JAB AT MR MONTGOMERY WITH HIS CANE. IT'S ENOUGH TO SEND THE CHAIRMAN HIGH-TAILING IT UP THE ENTRANCE RAMP WHILE THE COMMISSIONER'S FACE CONTORTS ONCE AGAIN — THIS TIME, MORPHING INTO A SMIRK.

HARRISON GOES FOR HIS FIRST PINFALL ATTEMPT OF THE MATCH!

HIP HARRISON COVERS JUDAS. JUDGE DREAD SLIDES IN TO MAKE THE COUNT — ONE… TWO… AND JUDAS KICKS OUT.

HARRISON WAS RIGHT TO TRY FOR THE PIN AFTER ALL OF THAT GROUND AND POUND BUT, IN MY OPINION, YOU'LL NEED TO HIT SOMETHING BIGGER THAN A SERIES OF STRIKES TO KEEP THE CHAMPION DOWN.

I'M NOT DISPUTING YOU, FARQUAD, BUT I WILL SAY IT'S IMPRESSIVE THAT JUDAS KICKED OUT FROM THAT. EACH OF THOSE PUNCHES CAME DOWN ON THE HEAD OF THE CHAMPION LIKE A METEORITE FROM DEEP SPACE. THAT WOULD HAVE BEEN MORE THAN ENOUGH TO PUT ANYONE ELSE AWAY.

HARRISON'S GOTTA STAY ON HIM. DON'T GIVE JUDAS ANY TIME TO RECOVER. DON'T GET FRUSTRATED AND FOCUS ON FINISHING THE MATCH.

THE BEARDED BRUTE HAS A HIGH RING I.Q. HE MAY WELL BE THE SMARTEST COMPETITOR WE HAVE IN THE GALACTIC WF. NOT ONLY DOES HE KNOW HOW TO USE THE ENVIRONMENT AND, OFTEN, HIS OPPONENTS' WEAKNESSES AND MISTAKES TO HIS ADVANTAGE, BUT HE ALSO KNOWS NOT TO WASTE TIME ARGUING WITH A REFEREE'S COUNT.

I'M NOT SO SURE I WOULD BE DOING WHAT HE'S DOING THOUGH. HE'S CLIMBING TO THE TOP ROPE.

THEY SAY IT'S HIGH RISK, HIGH REWARD WHEN YOU JUMP FROM THE TOP TURNBUCKLE. HIP HARRISON HAS OBVIOUSLY TAKEN STOCK OF THE SITUATION AND DECIDED THAT, WITH JUDAS BARELY ABLE TO KICK OUT A MOMENT AGO, THERE'S LITTLE RISK OF THE DESTROYER DODGING AN AERIAL STRIKE.

I HOPE HE'S RIGHT. I DON'T WANNA SEE THE BEARDED BRUTE CRASH AND BURN.

HARRISON LEAPS INTO THE AIR AS THOUSANDS OF CAMERAS BLAST OUR RETINAS WITH THEIR FLASHES HERE AT THE ROCK ARENA.

THEY LOOK LIKE FIREFLIES.

THE FIREFLIES ARE BUZZING AT THE SIGHT OF HIP HARRISON AS HIS ARMS AND LEGS SPRING UP AND DOWN, BUILDING MOMENTUM BEFORE HE LANDS ON JUDAS'S MID-SECTION, CONNECTING WITH AN ALMIGHTY FROG SPLASH.

THAT WAS A PICTURE-PERFECT FROG SPLASH, AS I'M SURE THE THOUSANDS OF PHOTOS SNAPPED HERE WILL CONFIRM. HARRISON'S BODY HIT JUDAS WITH SUCH FORCE THAT THE BEARDED BRUTE BOUNCED BACK UP AND FLEW HALFWAY ACROSS THE RING. IT WILL HAVE TAKEN ALMOST AS MUCH OUT OF HARRISON AS IT HAS JUDAS, ESPECIALLY GIVEN THE BEATING HARRISON'S RIBS TOOK FROM SKY 'N' STATIC. THE MORE I THINK ABOUT IT, I WONDER WHY

HE DIDN'T GO FOR SOMETHING A LITTLE LESS TAXING, LIKE AN ELBOW DROP.

THIS MATCH IS FOR THE RICHEST PRIZE IN OUR SPORT. HIP HARRISON HAS PUT IT ALL ON THE LINE TO MAKE SURE HE CAN PUT JUDAS AWAY. AN ELBOW DROP MAY NOT HAVE CUT THE MUSTARD, SO HE'S HIT SOMETHING BIGGER. IT SEEMS TO HAVE WORKED, AS JUDAS'S BODY FOLDED IN HALF ON IMPACT, BEFORE SPLAYING BACK ON THE MAT.

AS HARRISON CRAWLS DESPERATELY TOWARDS THE COVER, I CAN ADMIT THERE WERE TIMES I'D BE IN THE RING AND ATTEMPT A MOVE IN THE HEAT OF THE MOMENT THAT, ON LATER REFLECTION, WASN'T THE BEST OF IDEAS. THERE'S AN OLD SAYING ABOUT COOLER HEADS PREVAILING, BUT IT'S DIFFICULT TO KEEP A COOL HEAD BETWEEN THOSE ROPES, AND YOU NEED TO ACT FAST.

HIP HARRISON DRAPES AN ARM ACROSS JUDAS'S CHEST. JUDGE DREAD SLIDES IN TO MAKE THE COUNT: ONE... TWO... THR— NO, I DON'T BELIEVE IT.

YOU MENTIONED HARRISON'S RING I.Q. A MOMENT AGO, GENE. WELL, LET'S ACKNOWLEDGE JUDAS AND HIS ELEVATED RING INTELLECT. WITH NO RESERVE OF POWER LEFT TO KICK OUT OF THAT PIN — OR PERHAPS HE'S SIMPLY PRESERVING ALL THE ENERGY HE HAS LEFT — JUDAS MADE USE OF HIS

SURROUNDINGS AND, WITH FULL AWARENESS OF HIS RING POSITIONING, RAISED HIS RIGHT LEG AND DROPPED IT ONTO THE NEARBY BOTTOM ROPE.

HE MUST HAVE KNOWN EXACTLY WHERE HE WAS INSIDE THE RING TO HAVE HAD THE CONFIDENCE TO GO FOR THE ROPE BREAK INSTEAD OF SUMMING UP THE ENERGY TO KICK OUT.

IT TAKES THOUSANDS OF HOURS OF TRAINING AND COMPETITION TO DEVELOP A RING AWARENESS LIKE THAT. SAY WHAT YOU WILL ABOUT OUR CHAMPION — AND BELIEVE ME, I HAVE A FEW COLOURFUL NAMES FOR HIM — BUT THAT IS THE MARK OF AN INCREDIBLE WRESTLER.

IT WAS SUCH A CLOSE CALL THAT ALMOST EVERYONE IN THIS ARENA THOUGHT IT WAS A THREE-COUNT. I DON'T THINK ANYONE IN THE BUILDING IS STILL IN THEIR SEAT FOLLOWING THE CHEERS THAT ERUPTED AS THE REFEREE'S ARM CAME DOWN FOR A THIRD SLAP OF THE MAT THAT NEVER WAS. AS REALISATION SETS IN, MASS CONFUSION FILLS THE ROCK.

I'M LOOKING AT MR MONTGOMERY, WHO'S STANDING ACROSS THE STAGE FROM US. HE LOOKS AS IF HE'S JUST UNDERGONE CARDIAC ARREST.

IN THE RING, HARRISON PULLS HIMSELF BACK TO HIS FEET, USING THE ROPES FOR LEVERAGE.

JUDAS IS GETTING BACK TO HIS FEET TOO. IT'S A RACE TO A VERTICAL BASE!

BUT WE HAVE COMPANY. THE TAG TEAM CHAMPIONS, SKY 'N' STATIC HAVE RECOVERED AND TOGETHER THEY SLIDE INTO THE RING. THEY STALK HARRISON LIKE A PAIR OF VULTURES. THE BEARDED BRUTE SENSES TROUBLE BEHIND HIM AND TURNS RIGHT INTO A CUTTER FROM SNIPER SKY. X-STATIC FOLLOWS UP WITH BOOTS TO THE RIBS.

HERE COMES HARRISON SENIOR! THERE'S FIGHT LEFT IN THE OLD DOG YET.

THERE'S ONLY SO MUCH PUNISHMENT A PARENT CAN WATCH THEIR CHILD ENDURE.

SKY'S SMILING AT THE OLD MAN.

THE ELDER HARRISON HAS HIS GUARD UP AGAIN, YET THE TAG CHAMPS DON'T SEEM TO CONSIDER HIM MUCH OF A THREAT. X-STATIC THROWS OUT A COUPLE OF HALF-HEARTED PUNCHES THAT FRANKLO DODGES, BUT THEY PROVE TO BE NOTHING MORE THAN A QUICK DISTRACTION AS SNIPER SKY HITS ANOTHER CUTTER — THIS TIME ON HIP HARRISON'S FATHER. FOR BRADSHAW'S SAKE, HE'S OLD ENOUGH TO BE A GRANDFATHER!

BOTH HARRISONS ARE DOWN. OLD FRANK MAY HAVE BEEN DISTRACTED BY X-STATIC'S FEINTING, BUT HE PROVIDED A DISTRACTION OF HIS OWN FOR

THE TAG TEAM CHAMPIONS. LOOK WHO'S ONCE AGAIN CLIMBED INTO THE RING WITH CANE IN TOW!

SOVEREIGN NOBLE — THE CRAFTY KINGSMAN — HAD SPOTTED AN OPENING. WHILE SKY 'N' STATIC WERE PAYING ALL OF THEIR ATTENTION TO A MAN WITH MORE CYCLES ON THE CLOCK THAN THE TWO OF THEM COMBINED, THE COMMISSIONER CREPT BACK INTO THE RING WITHOUT THE TAG CHAMPS NOTICING.

HE'S RIGHT BEHIND THEM!

AND HE CRACKS X-STATIC OVER THE HEAD WITH HIS CANE. THE FORCE OF THE BLOW SENDS THE ELECTRIFYING PSYCHOPATH DOWN TO THE MAT AND TUMBLING OUT OF THE RING, BENEATH THE BOTTOM ROPE. SNIPER SKY TAKES A MOMENT TO FIGURE OUT WHY HIS PARTNER IN CRIME HAS JUST DROPPED LIKE A HOT POTATO. DUMBFOUNDED, SKY TURNS TO RECEIVE A SHOT TO THE FOREHEAD FROM NOBLE'S CANE.

SKY IS OUT ON HIS FEET. BLOOD TRICKLES DOWN FROM HIS BROW.

WHAT'S THE EXPRESSION LUMBERJACKS HAVE FOR WHEN A TREE FALLS? YOU SAID IT EARLIER.

YOU MEAN, TIIIIMMMMBEEERRRRR!

THAT'S THE ONE, FARQUAD. JUST LIKE A TREE DURING LOGGING SEASON, SNIPER SKY FALLS. AS SOON AS HE HITS THE GROUND, NOBLE MAKES USE OF HIS

CANE ONCE MORE — THIS TIME TO PUSH THE UNCONSCIOUS SKY OUT OF THE RING.

WITH ALL THAT EXCITEMENT GOING ON, I HADN'T NOTICED MR MONTGOMERY MAKING HIS WAY BACK DOWN THE RAMP.

WHAT'S HE UP TO NOW? HE'S GOT ONE OF THOSE FOLDING, STEEL CHAIRS IN HIS HAND. HE PASSES IT UNDER THE ROPES TO JUDAS, WHO CONCEALS IT BENEATH HIS TORSO. SOVEREIGN NOBLE SPOTS THE CHAIRMAN AT RINGSIDE AND MAKES HIS WAY ACROSS THE RING, DEMANDING THAT MR MONTGOMERY LEAVE AT ONCE.

BUT NOBLE HAS NO IDEA THAT JUDAS IS EVEN CONSCIOUS. LET ALONE THAT HE HAS A WEAPON.

THE COMMISSIONER LEANS THROUGH THE ROPES TO ADMONISH MR MONTGOMERY AND JUDAS STRIKES, JAMMING THE END OF THAT STEEL CHAIR INTO SOVEREIGN NOBLE'S RIBS. AS THE CRAFTY KINGSMAN DROPS TO HIS KNEES, CLUTCHING THE RIGHT SIDE OF HIS STERNUM, JUDAS RISES TO HIS FEET AND SWINGS THE CHAIR DOWN. LIKE A THUNDERCLAP, IT CRACKS NOBLE ACROSS THE BACK.

NOBLE'S COMPLETELY LAID OUT, BUT I DON'T THINK JUDAS IS DONE WITH HIM JUST YET. WHAT HAS HE GOT IN MIND NOW?

JUDAS REPOSITIONS NOBLE'S LIFELESS BODY SO THAT HE'S FACE UP. THE DESTROYER PICKS UP THAT DAMN CHAIR AGAIN AND… OH NO. HE CAN'T DO THIS. SOMEBODY'S GOT TO STOP THIS!

I DON'T THINK I'VE EVER SEEN MR MONTGOMERY LOOK SO HAPPY AS HE IS RIGHT NOW. THE CHAIRMAN HAS LOST HIS MIND; HE'S CHEERING JUDAS ON.

JUDAS PLACES SOVEREIGN NOBLE'S RIGHT LEG — HIS *GOOD* LEG — BETWEEN THE SEAT AND THE BACKREST. THE CHAMPION IS GOING TO SHATTER IT JUST LIKE HE DID THE COMMISSIONER'S LEFT LEG ALL THOSE CYCLES AGO.

I DON'T THINK I CAN WATCH THIS.

I DON'T LIKE IT ONE BIT EITHER, BUT WE'VE GOT TO REMAIN PROFESSIONAL, FARQUAD. AS PROFESSIONAL AS WE CAN, AT LEAST. IMPARTIALITY IS OUT THE WINDOW, BUT WHO CAN BLAME US?

JUDAS CLIMBS TO THE TOP ROPE. IF HE LANDS ON THE LEG OF THAT CHAIR, NOBLE WON'T BE ABLE TO GET AROUND WITH THAT CANE ANYMORE. HE'S GOING TO NEED A WHEELCHAIR.

THE DESTROYER JUMPS AND— YES! THANK BRADSHAW FOR THAT! IN THE NICK OF TIME, HIP HARRISON RECOVERED, SAW WHAT WAS GOING ON AND INTERCEPTED JUDAS IN MIDAIR WITH ANOTHER SPEAR.

THAT SOUND YOU HEARD WAS EVERYONE IN THE BUILDING BREATHING A COLLECTIVE SIGH OF RELIEF. I'M SWEATING.

HAVING TACKLED JUDAS, HARRISON REMOVES THE CHAIR FROM AROUND SOVEREIGN NOBLE'S LEG. IT'S PROMISING TO SEE THAT THE CRAFTY KINGSMAN IS RESPONDING TO HARRISON, EVEN IF HE IS IN RATHER A LOT OF PAIN.

IT'S NICE AND ALL THAT HARRISON IS HELPING NOBLE EXIT THE RING TO GET OUT OF HARM'S WAY, BUT IF I WERE HIP, I'D BE FOCUSED ON JUDAS. ALTHOUGH THAT MID-AIR TACKLE PREVENTED THE CHAMPION FROM PULVERISING THE COMMISSIONER'S LEG, IT WON'T KEEP THE DESTROYER DOWN FOR LONG.

HARRISON HAS NOBLE UP TO HIS FEET — OR RATHER, TO HIS FOOT, AS THE COMMISSIONER HOPS TOWARDS THE ROPES WITH AN ARM AROUND THE BEARDED BRUTE'S SHOULDERS. HARRISON SITS ON THE BOTTOM ROPE, LOWERING IT SO THAT NOBLE CAN CLIMB OUT OF THE RING A LITTLE EASIER.

GOOD, NOW GO AND FINISH JUDAS WHILE THERE ARE NO MORE DISTRACTIONS AND INTERFERENCES.

DON'T SPEAK TOO SOON, FARQUAD. MR MONTGOMERY IS BACK UP ON THE APRON. HARRISON

LAUGHS OFF THE CHAIRMAN'S IDLE THREATS BUT MONTGOMERY SPITS IN THE BEARDED BRUTE'S FACE.

HE MUST HAVE BEEN WORKING ON THAT LOOGIE FOR QUITE SOME TIME.

HARRISON WIPES THE SALIVA AND SNOT FROM HIS CHEEK ONTO HIS WRISTBAND. HE'S PLAYING RIGHT INTO THE CHAIRMAN'S HANDS, TAKING A SWING AT MONTGOMERY, WHO DODGES THE PUNCH BY HOPPING DOWN OFF THE RING APRON.

TURN AROUND, HIP!

JUDAS CRAWLS UP BEHIND HARRISON AND HITS THE CHALLENGER WITH A LOW BLOW.

THAT SHOT HAS GIVEN ME SYMPATHY PAINS. THAT WAS A WILD SWING TO THE GONADS. AND HARRISON NEVER SAW IT COMING.

HARRISON DOUBLES OVER AND COLLAPSES TO THE CANVAS. IN AN ORDINARY MATCH, A LOW BLOW IN FRONT OF THE REFEREE WOULD HAVE RESULTED IN AN IMMEDIATE DISQUALIFICATION, BUT THERE ARE, OF COURSE, NO DISQUALIFICATIONS IN THIS CONTEST. JUDGE DREAD IS POWERLESS TO DO ANYTHING ABOUT JUDAS GAINING THE UNFAIR ADVANTAGE.

SHADES OF CLIFF HARDCASTLE AND BRUTUS MAXIMUS. THE END COULD BE IN SIGHT, GENE. I DON'T SEE HARRISON RECOVERING FROM THAT.

OUTSIDE THE RING, MR MONTGOMERY IS JUMPING UP AND DOWN LIKE A CHEERLEADER AT A PEP RALLY, IN SHEER CONTRAST TO THE PAYING AUDIENCE THAT SURROUNDS HIM. THE BOOS ARE DEAFENING.

I'M SURPRISED TO SEE JUDAS TAKING HIS TIME. THE CHAMPION IS SOAKING IN THE CONDEMNATION FROM THE FANS, AS IF HE ENJOYS IT.

YOU'RE RIGHT — A TYPICAL JUDAS MATCH WOULD SEE THE DESTROYER GOING IN FOR THE KILL RIGHT AWAY. BUT I THINK HARRISON — AND PERHAPS MR MONTGOMERY — HAS GOTTEN INTO HIS HEAD. HE'S BEEN OUT OF SORTS IN RECENT WEEKS, AS WE'VE SEEN AND YOU'VE EXPERIENCED FIRST-HAND, FARQUAD.

HE'S BEEN OFF HIS USUAL GAME TONIGHT. IT'S LIKE THE ADDED PRESSURE OF THIS MATCH HAS BEEN MESSING WITH HIS MIND. BUT NOW THAT HE'S FIRMLY IN CONTROL, HE'S TAKING A MOMENT TO REGAIN HIS COMPOSURE BEFORE ENDING HIP HARRISON'S TITLE ASPIRATIONS.

JUDAS, RELISHING THE DISAPPROVAL OF THE CROWD MORE THAN HE EVER SAVOURED THEIR PRAISE AND ADULATION, EXHALES AND SETS HIP HARRISON WITHIN HIS SIGHTS.

WAIT — THERE'S SOMEONE ON THE TOP TURNBUCKLE! WHO IS IT NOW?

IT'S IVY JANE! THE MAN EATER IS HERE AND THE ROCK ARENA, NOT FOR THE FIRST TIME TONIGHT, HAS ERUPTED. I DON'T THINK A SINGLE PERSON IN THIS ARENA IS IN THEIR SEAT, AND THAT INCLUDES LORD FARQUAD AND MYSELF.

JUDAS SPOTS HER. WHAT'S SHE GOING TO DO?

JUDAS STEPS TOWARDS THE CORNER IN WHICH IVY JANE STANDS POISED. SHE LEAPS FORWARD WITH SPLORG-LIKE PRECISION AT SUCH SPEED THAT JUDAS DOESN'T HAVE TIME TO REACT.

SHE'S FLYING LIKE A MISSILE.

JANE LANDS ON THE CHAMPION'S SHOULDERS AND HOOKS HER LEGS AROUND THE DESTROYER'S NECK.

JUDAS STAGGERS. HE'S LOST CONTROL.

AND IVY JANE THROWS THE FULL WEIGHT OF HER BODY BACKWARDS, PULLING JUDAS FORWARD WITH MORE MOMENTUM THAN THE CHAMPION CAN CURRENTLY HANDLE.

HURRICANRANA! IVY JANE HIT IT ON JUDAS.

THIS WAS ABOUT MORE THAN EVENING THE ODDS FOR HIP HARRISON — ALTHOUGH THAT WILL HAVE PROVIDED SOME INCENTIVE FOR THE MAN EATER — THIS WAS ALSO ABOUT RETRIBUTION FOR HOW JUDAS TREATED IVY JANE A MOON ORBIT AGO.

WHAT BETTER WAY TO SCORE A MEASURE OF REVENGE — AS WELL AS SOME VINDICATION — THAN BY PULLING OFF THE VERY MOVE JUDAS BLOCKED DURING THEIR MATCH?

THE HURRICANRANA SENDS JUDAS SLINGSHOTTING INTO THE ROPES. IVY JANE HAS TAKEN THE DESTROYER TO HIS KNEES AS HIS HEAD AND ARMS HANG OVER THE MIDDLE ROPE LIKE A DISGRACED NE'ER-DO-WELL CONFINED TO PILLORY.

HE'D BETTER WATCH OUT. IVY AIN'T FINISHED YET.

IVY JANE SETS OFF AT A SPRINT, REBOUNDS OFF THE ROPES AT THE OPPOSITE SIDE OF THE RING, AND BUILDS UP VELOCITY. THE CHAMPION DOESN'T SEE IT COMING.

SHE'S GOING TO LAND A KICK… SHE—

SHE USES JUDAS'S BACK AS A LAUNCH PAD. IVY JANE SPRINGS INTO THE AIR AND SOMERSAULTS OVER THE CHAMPION AND THE TOP ROPE, CRASH-LANDING ONTO MR MONTGOMERY. THE ROCK ARENA IS SHAKING FROM THE MAGNITUDE OF SOUNDWAVES GENERATED BY THE FANS IN ATTENDANCE.

I CAN'T SAY I'VE NOT BEEN SHOCKED TO SEE MR MONTGOMERY'S DIRECT INVOLVEMENT IN THIS MATCH. EVEN WHEN HARRISON AND HIS ALLIES TOOK OUT THE LIKES OF SNIPER SKY AND X-STATIC,

THE CHAIRMAN WAS ENOUGH OF A THORN IN THE BEARDED BRUTE'S SIDE TO CAUSE A DISTRACTION WHEN JUDAS NEEDED IT. BUT NOW, IVY JANE HAS TAKEN THE BOSS OUT OF THE EQUATION.

IVY JANE HAS ALWAYS SHOWN NO FEAR — CERO MIEDO, IF YOU WILL — WHETHER THAT'S FROM TAKING RISKS PHYSICALLY IN THE RING OR BY STANDING UP FOR WHAT IS RIGHT. THE MAN EATER FEARS NO MAN, AND THAT INCLUDES THE CHAIRMAN OF THE BOARD.

SHE CERTAINLY DOESN'T FEAR JUDAS, WHO'S GIVING IVY JANE A PIECE OF HIS MIND.

THE GALACTIC WF CHAMPION IS STILL ON HIS KNEES INSIDE THE RING BUT LEANING OUT BETWEEN THE MIDDLE AND TOP ROPES, SPITTING VERBAL BILE AT IVY JANE. THE MAN EATER, HOWEVER, IS UNPHASED BY THE DESTROYER'S RANTING AND RAVING.

IVY'S NOT NORMALLY ONE FOR SMILING, BUT SHE'S GRINNING NOW AS SHE COMES FACE TO FACE WITH JUDAS.

IT'S AS IF SHE KNOWS SOMETHING HE DOESN'T.

BAM! THAT'LL BE IT!

IVY WAS PROVIDING THE DISTRACTION FOR SOVEREIGN NOBLE. WITH THE FULL EXTENT OF JUDAS'S RAGE TRAINED ON IVY JANE, THE COMMISSIONER STRIKES FROM THE SIDE, HIS CANE CONNECTING WITH THE CHAMPION'S TEMPLE.

JUDAS IS REELING. HE'S BACK TO HIS FEET BUT HE'S STUMBLING BLINDLY BACKWARDS, HOLDING HIS HEAD.

HE DOESN'T SEE HARRISON, WHO'S RECOVERED AMID THE CHAOS. THE BEARDED BRUTE, ON ALL FOURS, POSITIONS HIMSELF BEHIND JUDAS IN THE CENTRE OF THE RING AND— WOW! THEY SAY TURNABOUT IS FAIR PLAY: HIP HARRISON STRIKES JUDAS WITH A LOW BLOW OF HIS OWN.

THE BEARDED BRUTE WARNED US HE WAS PREPARED TO GO LOW IF NEEDED. BY ANY MEANS NECESSARY.

HARRISON SWEEPS THE LEGS AND ROLLS JUDAS UP WITH THE CHAMPION'S SHOULDERS PINNED TO THE MAT. JUDGE DREAD LEAPS INTO POSITION AND THIS IS IT, WE MAY HAVE A NEW CHAMPION. ONE… TWO… THR— NO. JUDAS SOMEHOW MANAGES TO WRIGGLE OUT. BUT HARRISON IMMEDIATELY CINCHES IN THE BRUTE LOCK, TRAPPING JUDAS'S LEFT ARM BETWEEN HIS — HARRISON'S — LEGS AND WRENCHING BACK ON THE CHAMPION'S HEAD AND NECK WITH BOTH HANDS WRAPPED AROUND THE DESTROYER'S FOREHEAD.

THIS PLACE IS GOING ABSOLUTELY WILD. I'VE BEEN HERE FOR A LOT OF EXCITING MOMENTS OVER THE CYCLES, BUT I'VE EXPERIENCED NOTHING AS FRENZIED AS THIS.

JUDAS IS CAUGHT IN THAT EXCRUCIATING HOLD WITH NOWHERE TO GO. HE REACHES OUT WITH HIS FREE HAND BUT HE'S NOWHERE NEAR THE ROPES. THE CHAMPION TRIES TO SWAT AT HARRISON, BUT IT'S NO USE. THE BEARDED BRUTE PULLS BACK EVEN HARDER ON THE DESTROYER'S FOREHEAD. JUDAS'S NECK MUST BE REACHING ITS BREAKING POINT AS THE FANS CHANT, 'TAP! TAP! TAP!'

MR MONTGOMERY IS UP. HE'S TRYING TO GET INTO THE RING BUT IVY JANE IS HOLDING HIM BACK.

THE CHAIRMAN BARKS ORDERS AT THE CHAMPION, COMMANDING THE DESTROYER NOT TO TAP OUT. BUT JUDAS IS STRUGGLING TO HOLD ON. HE'S FADING AS HIP HARRISON MAINTAINS A TIGHT HOLD.

JUDAS IS AT RISK OF PASSING OUT FROM THE PAIN. NOT TO MENTION THE LONG-LASTING DAMAGE THAT COULD BE DONE TO THE DESTROYER'S BODY IF HE DOESN'T FIND A WAY OUT OF THAT BRUTE LOCK SOON. THERE'S NO SHAME IN TAPPING OUT.

THERE MAY BE NO SHAME, BUT THERE'S MORE AT STAKE HERE. MORE THAN EVEN THE HEAVYWEIGHT CHAMPIONSHIP, SEEMINGLY.

JUDGE DREAD IS ASKING JUDAS WHETHER HE GIVES UP.

JUDAS'S FREE ARM — HIS RIGHT HAND — LIFTS OFF THE MAT. HE MIGHT BE ABOUT TO TAP OUT. MR

MONTGOMERY IS DESPERATE IN HIS ATTEMPT TO GET THROUGH THE ROPES, TO BREAK THE HOLD, BUT SOVEREIGN NOBLE HAS JOINED IVY JANE IN HOLDING THE BOSS BACK.

AS MUCH AS I HATE THE GUY, IT SPEAKS TO THE INTESTINAL FORTITUDE OF JUDAS THAT HE'S STILL HANGING IN THERE.

THE GALACTIC WF CHAMPION'S HAND WAVERS. HE'S ABOUT TO PASS OUT, AS YOU INTIMATED, FARQUAD.

WHOA! HARRISON PULLS BACK EVEN FURTHER. SIANARDIAN HEADS ARE NOT MEANT TO BEND BACK THAT FAR. JUDAS MUST BE IN SERIOUS AGONY.

JUDAS FORMS A FIST WITH HIS RIGHT HAND. HE'S TRYING TO CHANNEL THE PAIN TO FIND SOME WILL, SOME WAY TO ESCAPE THIS PREDICAMENT. HIS ARM IS SHAKING, HE'S RALLYING HIMSELF, BUT IT'S AN IMPOSSIBLE SITUATION. IT'S THE MOST BRUTAL BRUTE LOCK WE'VE EVER SEEN. IT'S... IT'S...

IT'S A NEW CHAMPION! JUDAS IS TAPPING!

JUDAS TAPS OUT AND JUDGE DREAD CALLS FOR THE BELL. ONCE AGAIN, TONIGHT, WE MUST HAVE SET A NEW RECORD FOR THE NUMBER OF DECIBELS PRODUCED HERE AT THE ROCK ARENA. YOU CAN BARELY HEAR THE FOO FIGHTERS PLAYING THROUGH THE P.A. SYSTEM OVER THIS CROWD.

HIP HARRISON HAS DONE IT! LOOK AT MR MONTGOMERY! HE'S GONE FROM LOOKING DESPERATE AND DERANGED TO DEFEATED AND DEVASTATED.

HE ALSO LOOKS TERRIFIED, WHICH IS IRONIC CONSIDERING THE FEAR HE'S COMMANDED BACKSTAGE OVER THE CYCLES. WHATEVER SECRETS THE CHAIRMAN HAS BEEN HIDING COULD BE ABOUT TO COME OUT.

JUDGE DREAD HANDS THE CHAMPIONSHIP BELT TO HIP HARRISON. JUDAS HAS BEEN CHAMPION FOR SO LONG THAT IT SEEMS STRANGE TO SEE THE TITLE IN THE HANDS OF ANYBODY ELSE.

THE REFEREE RAISES HARRISON'S HAND AND COSTA FORTUNE IS ABOUT TO MAKE THE OFFICIAL ANNOUNCEMENT.

'*Here is your winner, and NEEEEWWWWWWW Galactic Wrestling Federation CHAMPIOOOON: Hip HAAAAAAAAARRRIIIISSONN!*'

IVY JANE IS THE FIRST TO ENTER THE RING. SHE TAKES THE TITLE BELT FROM HIP HARRISON, STEPS BEHIND THE NEW CHAMPION AND TIES IT AROUND HIS WAIST.

THE *FORMER* CHAMPION, JUDAS, HAVING WITNESSED THAT SCENE, HAS ROLLED OUT OF THE RING WITH HIS TAIL BETWEEN HIS LEGS. GOOD RIDDANCE.

THE DESTROYER HAS BECOME THE DESTROYED. HE'S IN A LOT OF PAIN AS HE MAKES A QUICK EXIT.

HE'S ATTEMPTING TO GET OUT OF HERE, BUT MR MONTGOMERY IS TRYING TO STOP HIM.

THE CHAIRMAN INSTRUCTS JUDAS TO GET BACK INTO THE RING, TO FINISH THE JOB AND TAKE OUT HIP HARRISON. SO, THIS WAS NEVER ABOUT THE CHAMPIONSHIP AT ALL.

MAYBE NOT FOR MR MONTGOMERY, BUT THAT TITLE MEANT MORE TO JUDAS THAN ANYTHING. HAVING LOST IT, HE'S DONE.

YOU'RE RIGHT, FARQUAD. THE GALACTIC WF CHAMPIONSHIP WAS AN OBSESSION FOR JUDAS. HE SHRUGS OFF THE CHAIRMAN'S COMMANDS AND MAKES HIS WAY OUT OF THE ARENA, DOWN BESIDE THE ENTRANCE RAMP.

MOST OF THE AUDIENCE ARE TOO BUSY SNAPPING PHOTOGRAPHS OF THE NEW CHAMPION TO NOTICE JUDAS LEAVING, BUT I'M HAPPY TO HEAR A SMALL CONTINGENT SERENADING HIM WITH A CHORUS OF *NA NA HEY HEY KISS HIM GOODBYE*.

MEANWHILE, COSTA FORTUNE HANDS IVY JANE A MICROPHONE. SHE PASSES IT TO HIP HARRISON. THIS SHOULD BE INTERESTING.

MR MONTGOMERY IS NOT GOING TO ALLOW THE BEARDED BRUTE TO SPEAK WITHOUT A FIGHT.

HE'S ROUSING SNIPER SKY AND X-STATIC, ORDERING THE TAG TEAM CHAMPIONS TO HIT THE RING.

X-STATIC SLIDES INTO THE RING BUT IVY JANE INTERCEPTS HIM BEFORE THE ELECTRIFYING PSYCHOPATH CAN CLUB HARRISON IN THE BACK OF THE HEAD.

KICK! WHAM! STUNNER! WOO-HOO!

IVY JANE, QUICK AS A LIGHTNING BOLT, CATCHES X-STATIC WITH A KICK TO THE MID-SECTION, SPINS AROUND WHILE GRIPPING HIM AROUND THE BACK OF THE HEAD AND NECK, AND LANDS IN WHAT TRAMPOLINISTS MIGHT CALL A SEAT DROP. X-STATIC'S HEAD REBOUNDS OFF HER SHOULDERS, SENDING HIM FLYING BACKWARDS AND TUMBLING OUT OF THE RING.

WHO'S THE ELECTRIFYING ONE NOW, HUH?

SNIPER SKY HAS CIRCLED THE RING. WITH HARRISON'S ATTENTION ON IVY JANE AND THE QUICKLY DESPATCHED X-STATIC, THEY DON'T SEE HIM COMING.

SOVEREIGN NOBLE DOES, THOUGH. HE'S STILL AT RINGSIDE, AND ALERTING HARRISON AND JANE TO THE IMMINENT THREAT.

HARRISON TURNS TOO LATE AND SKY GOES FOR THE CUTTER. BUT WAIT! HARRISON BLOCKS IT. HE SHOVES SNIPER SKY AWAY BUT THE TAG TEAM CHAMPION REBOUNDS OFF THE ROPES AND BUILDS

MOMENTUM AS HE CHARGES TOWARD THE BEARDED BRUTE. HOWEVER, HARRISON IS LYING IN WAIT AND CATCHES SKY WITH A CUTTER OF HIS OWN, TO THE DELIGHT OF THE FANS, WHO ARE ENJOYING SOMEWHAT OF AN ENCORE HERE AT BATTLESTAR GALACTICA.

IVY JANE ROLLS SNIPER SKY OUT OF THE RING BUT NOW MR MONTGOMERY IS CLIMBING ONTO THE APRON.

THE CHAIRMAN IS STAGING A LAST-DITCH EFFORT TO KEEP HIP HARRISON FROM SPEAKING. BUT SOVEREIGN NOBLE MEETS HIM ON THE RING APRON, CANE HELD ALOFT.

THE BOSS HAS FROZEN. HE DOESN'T KNOW WHETHER TO BACK DOWN OR RISK A SHOT FROM THAT CANE.

HE'S NOT BACKING DOWN JUST YET. WHATEVER DIRT HIP HARRISON'S GOT ON HIM HAS GOT TO BE BAD.

THAT KID IS BACK. NEMO! HE'S RUNNING DOWN THE RAMP.

AND HERE COMES THE TEAM OF SECURITY OFFICERS IN HOT PURSUIT. IT APPEARS NEMO HAS GREAT CARDIO CONDITIONING.

HE'S SLIDING INTO THE RING TO JOIN HARRISON AND IVY JANE.

THE SECURITY DETAIL HALTS OUTSIDE THE RING AT THE COMMAND OF SOVEREIGN NOBLE. MR

MONTGOMERY ORDERS THEM TO STORM THE RING, BUT NOBLE EXTENDS HIS CANE TOWARDS THEM AND— OH, THIS IS INCREDIBLE! SOVEREIGN NOBLE COMMANDS SECURITY TO REMOVE MR MONTGOMERY FROM THE RINGSIDE AREA.

HA! THE COMMISSIONER IS POINTING OUT THAT THE BOSS DOESN'T HAVE A LICENCE TO BE AT RINGSIDE. FOR THOSE AT HOME WHO DON'T KNOW WHAT I'M TALKING ABOUT, EVERY COMPETITOR, REFEREE, AND MANAGER THAT PERFORMS AT RINGSIDE MUST BE FORMALLY LICENSED BY THE GALACTIC WRESTLING FEDERATION. IT'S FOR INSURANCE PURPOSES AS MUCH AS ANYTHING. AS COMMISSIONER AND MATCH-MAKER, SOVEREIGN NOBLE HOLDS ONE, TOO. BUT MR MONTGOMERY HAS NEVER HAD THE NEED FOR ONE.

THE SECURITY TEAM STEPS TOWARDS THE BOSS, AND MR MONTGOMERY RUNS ACROSS THE APRON, DOWN THE STEPS, AND AROUND THE RING. TWO OF THE SECURITY OFFICERS GIVE CHASE.

WHERE DOES HE THINK HE'S RUNNING TO?

THE CHAIRMAN HAS CLEARLY NOT GIVEN THE DESTINATION MUCH THOUGHT. HE COMPLETES A NEAR-LAP OF THE SQUARED CIRCLE AND RUNS RIGHT INTO THE WAITING ARMS OF ANOTHER SECURITY OFFICER.

I CAN'T BELIEVE WHAT I'M SEEING. THEY'RE ESCORTING MR MONTGOMERY OUT OF HIS OWN SHOW. THEY'RE CARRYING HIM UP THE ENTRANCE RAMP. HOW HUMILIATING!

MR MONTGOMERY POINTS AT HIP HARRISON'S FRIEND NEMO, WHO ALSO DOES NOT POSSESS A RINGSIDE LICENCE. ONE OF THE SECURITY OFFICERS HEADS BACK TOWARDS THE RING, BUT SOVEREIGN NOBLE YET AGAIN HOLDS OUT HIS CANE. THE COMMISSIONER EXPLAINS THAT NEMO IS AN INVITED GUEST OF THE CHAMPION. NOT TO MENTION THE FACT THAT NEMO HAS COME BACK FROM A HELLUVA BEATING AT THE HANDS OF THE FORMER HEAVYWEIGHT CHAMPION AND CURRENT TAG CHAMPIONS.

HIP HARRISON'S FATHER IS ALSO JOINING THE GROUP GATHERED IN THE RING. I'M ASSUMING HE'S A GUEST TOO.

I WOULD THINK SO, FARQUAD. AND NOW, WITH MONTGOMERY TAKEN CARE OF, SOVEREIGN NOBLE CLIMBS THROUGH THE ROPES AND SPEAKS INTO ONE OF THE TELEVISION CAMERAS. HE INSTRUCTS THE PRODUCTION CREW TO SWITCH ON THE MICROPHONE IN HIP HARRISON'S HAND.

HERE WE GO! THAT LIVE MIC MAY AS WELL BE A PIPEBOMB!

***

'I'm tired. Physically exhausted and mentally drained. But, despite the struggles, we made it. We did it! I say, "we," and not, "I," because this victory wasn't all my doing.

'My best and oldest friend, Nemo, played a huge role in this. You all saw some of that first-hand tonight. This isn't the first time he and I have had to stand up to bullies. However, there's so much more that he's done, away from the cameras and out of the spotlight, that nobody yet knows about. And it's time we changed that.

'Then, there's my father, Franklo. Give them a wave, Dad! As the whole of Sianard saw a couple of weeks ago, Judas dragged Dad into this fight at the command of his master. The so-called Destroyer is nothing more than a lapdog. But what they didn't count on was that my old man is as tough as they come. We've been through worse than anything Judas could do, and we're quick to bounce back. Not only do I need to thank you, Dad, for your help in the ring tonight, but for everything: for doing your best to raise me when Mum died, and for instilling a sense of decency and determination within me. We made it through those hard times, and your lessons have led us here.

'I must confess, I had no idea this next person would feature in my victory speech. I had written him off as another one of the master's lapdogs. I'd forgotten he was — and still is — the craftiest player in the game. He was dastardly, ruthless and vicious, yet competed with a measure of integrity, intensity and intelligence that *was unrivalled. I looked up to him before I made it to the Galactic Wrestling Federation and, tonight, I have a renewed admiration for him. Sovereign Noble, I can't imagine what it has taken for you to go against the wishes of our boss and the repercussions you might face. But you've done the right thing this evening and, for that, I thank you wholeheartedly.*

'And I mustn't forget my favourite person in the whole wide galaxy. My partner in crime. My rock, who keeps me grounded while simultaneously encouraging me to soar. She is sweet and kind and tender and just the loveliest person you could hope to meet. That is, until she enters this ring, where she becomes the ultimate badass. Ivy Jane has been one of the absolute best wrestlers in all of Sianard for quite some time, but you would never know it given the lack of opportunity the Galactic WF has afforded her in front of the cameras. They call her The Man Eater because, before she signed her contract here, she was regularly beating guys on the independent wrestling circuit. In the last few weeks, you've seen her hold her own against Judas, and you've gotta believe me when I say that all you've had is a taster of what Ivy Jane is capable of. The tip of the comet.

'Ivy, I love you, and thank you for supporting me in getting through these last few moon orbits, as well as for getting physical tonight.

'My final thanks go to every single one of you: the fans — both here in person and watching from home on pay-per-view. Most of you were booing me when the number one contender tournament

began — and that's okay. It's how the Galactic WF presented me to you — as someone to be reviled. But, as the weeks went on, and I fought and overcame every obstacle they put in front of me, you all saw through the machine's bullshit and let us all know it. You began cheering for me and reacted accordingly to some of the heinous acts Judas committed. Knowing that I had most of Sianard behind me is what kept me going when I felt like I was at rock bottom. Your cheers were vindication, especially as I was doing this for the entire galaxy.

'Now, you may be wondering what I mean when I say I was doing this for all of Sianard, and why the Galactic WF has been trying to vilify me. Well, allow me to introduce you all to Mr Montgomery.

'He's the purple-faced gentleman being detained at the top of the ramp. Most of you won't have heard of him, as he likes to keep a low profile. However, Mr Montgomery is responsible for the show you're currently watching. He's responsible for this championship belt around my waist. He created the Galactic Wrestling Federation from the ground up, his iron will forging this promotion into the galaxy-wide juggernaut that it is today. It's given many of my fellow wrestlers the biggest stage imaginable to hone our craft on, moulding us into superstars. It's also provided you, the fans, with countless hours of entertainment and escapism when you need to forget your troubles. Watching the Galactic WF certainly helped a teenage Hip Harrison when he was grieving the death of his mother. So, for that, Mr Montgomery, I thank you, too.

'*But the gratitude ends there. While it's true that Mr Montgomery's vision has enabled dreams to come true, he has also given many of us nightmares. Behind the scenes, he can be a tyrant. If you're one of his hand-picked favourites — a chosen one, like Judas — then life in the Galactic Wrestling Federation can be tremendous. You get all the main events and championship opportunities needed to become a star. The fame and fortune follow. On the other hand, should you not quite look the part of a prototypical wrestling superstar, the way they appear in the chairman's demented mind, then your ride in the Galactic WF is going to be a rocky one. Ivy Jane can attest to that. I think we can all agree that she is incredibly beautiful. However, she doesn't conform to the same supermodel looks you see in a swimsuit magazine. She wears her hair how she likes it and is comfortable in her own skin. We should celebrate that, but Mr Montgomery buries Ivy down the card in favour of whichever shiny new toy he's picked out of a lingerie catalogue. Nothing against those girls, either — many of them work extremely hard and deserve plenty of praise, but not at the expense of someone who works even harder and possesses more talent than they can ever hope to achieve.*

'*You even saw it with me and the brackets assigned to me in the number one contender tournament. I faced the biggest, the meanest, and the toughest competition imaginable, each and every week. And let me tell you something, brothers and sisters: the brackets weren't random. It was all by design to ensure I didn't make it through. Unfortunately for the boss, he didn't count on my tenacity. The obstacles before me only motivated me to train harder. And look at me now!*

'You might think, as chairman, of course Mr Montgomery pulls all the strings around here. It's his company, and he has the right to run it as he sees fit. That's a fair point. I won't complain or argue against that. Yet, you'd also think that would be more than enough to keep anyone busy, right? Not for Mr Montgomery, though. He's the pre-eminent workaholic. For him, it wasn't enough to have created his own world — his own universe *— in which he got to play matchmaker. Once the Galactic WF was undeniably the pinnacle of professional sports and entertainment, he needed something else to sink his teeth into. You see, with people like Mr Montgomery, life is all about power and taking control. An initial measure of authority and influence gained by, say, running the premier wrestling federation in Sianard, breeds the opportunity to seize an even higher power.*

'When you're rich and powerful, you inevitably come into contact with other rich and powerful people. To cut a long story short, as we're rapidly running out of time on the broadcast, Mr Montgomery's brash attitude and unparalleled work ethic were championed in some all-elite circles. Those running the galaxy sponsored Montgomery to take a seat on the Galactic Council of Sianard — better known as the GCS. In more recent cycles, Mr Montgomery has become one of the council's more senior members and what he, along with a select few Sianardians of similar wealth, decides impacts everyone in the galaxy. They're clever about it, and

nothing obviously bad happens to the rest of us ordinary folk. But that doesn't mean they don't vote to sell us out. If there's a chance they can make themselves even more money than they already possess — which is a lot — they won't hesitate to sell all of Sianard down the intergalactic highway. And that is exactly what Mr Montgomery and his cronies have done. They've betrayed us worse than you could ever imagine, and if the council had its way, we wouldn't know about it until it was too late.

'My friend Nemo previously worked for the Sianard Scientific Council. He worked on a project that sought to collect images of Earth with a view to making contact with the humans. That project was successful in that images were obtained. Isn't that right, Nemo?'

Nemo nodded in confirmation as gasps arose from the audience.

'What Nemo and his colleagues discovered upon reviewing the images was that Earth is no more. The planet is nothing more than a charred husk. All life forms are extinct. A subsequent project, in which the Scientific Council team sent a satellite to retrieve all broadcast signals from Earth that hadn't yet reached us here in Sianard, revealed that Earth's climate soared at an accelerated rate. They referred to it as "climate change", and the humans' way of life is largely what caused it. Their vehicles, their manufacturing, their entire way of life — all centred on convenience.

'You might all be wondering why this hasn't been big news. You might also be wondering what Mr Montgomery and the GCS have got to do with this. Would you like to tell them yourself, Boss?'

At the top of the entrance ramp, Mr Montgomery struggled against the security personnel restraining him. 'You son of a…' he screamed, trailing off as the realisation that he had already been rumbled set in. He'd always been so careful to avoid succumbing to scandal — or so he had thought.

'Okay, I guess I'll continue,' said Hip Harrison.

'The findings of the project were classified. When Nemo questioned this, he was discredited and dismissed from the Sianard Scientific Council. He then alerted the GCS about what he had discovered, so that the high council could act now and spare Sianard from a fate similar to that of Earth. After all, we've adopted so much of Earth's culture that we're likely on the same path of destruction. But what Nemo found when he arrived at the GCS was betrayal. It turns out there's quite a bit of crossover between councils. The same few people run more of our lives than we know, hiding behind multiple organisations.

'In addition to some of his former colleagues from the Scientific Council, Nemo also met Mr Montgomery at the GCS. None of them were interested in doing anything to prevent Sianard from falling victim to what ultimately killed Earth. And why would they be when they make a lot of money with life in Sianard continuing as it is? So what if Sianard burns in the future if there's profit to be made today? Why mess with the status quo?

'I can see our ring announcer — ladies and gentlemen, please give it up for Costa Fortune! He's done an incredible job of introducing every wrestler that's performed tonight, and now he's gesturing that we're off the air in about a minute's time. So, I'll end things by asking security to get that stain on the underwear of life, Mr Montgomery, out of here, and by asking Sianard's law enforcement agencies to investigate the GCS immediately.

'Now, hit my music and let the celebrations resume!'

***

THEY SAY THAT IN THIS BUSINESS YOU SHOULD MAKE EVERY MOMENT OF TELEVISION TIME COUNT AND MAXIMISE YOUR MINUTES ON THE MIC, BUT THAT WAS A HECK'VE A LOT OF INFORMATION TO DIGEST IN JUST A COUPLE OF MINUTES. EARTH IS DEAD?

LADIES AND GENTLEMEN, WE WILL NEED TO VERIFY WHETHER WHAT HIP HARRISON HAS JUST SAID IS TRUE. I IMAGINE THAT COULD TAKE SOME TIME. FOR NOW, WE HAVE A NEW GALACTIC WRESTLING FEDERATION CHAMPION AND HIS NAME IS HIP HARRISON. BUT HAVE WE JUST LOST AN OWNER AND CHAIRMAN? WHO'S GOING TO STEER THE SHIP FROM HERE? HOW WILL JUDAS REACT TO NO LONGER HOLDING THE GOLD? AND WHO WILL TAKE AIM AT THE FRESHLY PAINTED TARGET ON THE BEARDED BRUTE'S BACK? TUNE IN TO THE GALACTIC WF THIS STARSUN

EVE AS WE HOPE TO PROVIDE YOU WITH SOME
ANSWERS.

**MR MONTGOMERY IS BEING ESCORTED OUT OF
THE ARENA. CONFETTI IS FALLING AND FIREWORKS
ARE GOING OFF. HIP HARRISON IS CELEBRATING
WITH THE CHAMPIONSHIP HELD HIGH ABOVE HIS
HEAD. A NEW ERA HAS BEGUN IN THE GALACTIC WF.**

FOR NOW, WE THANK YOU ALL ONCE AGAIN FOR
INVITING US INTO YOUR HOMES. GOODNIGHT,
EVERYBODY!

About the Author

J.A. Cooke – also known as James Cooke – is an author and editor. He spent several years working in a variety of jobs before finding a way into publishing via B2B trade magazines.

Having been published in various online publications, as well as in the bestselling book *DAD: Untold stories of Fatherhood, Love, Mental Health and Masculinity* from Music.Football.Fatherhood, James's hobby of writing fiction has become his latest career step with the release of *Galactic WF: Pro Wrestling in Space* – a concept that occurred to him in the small hours of the night when in the throes of life with a newborn during the Covid-19 pandemic.

He lives in the Garden of England with his wonderful wife, two awesome dudes, and a pair of frantic felines.

www.JACooke.com